Across a Field of Starlight

Across a Field of Starlight was outlined and thumbnailed in a notebook, then drawn, lettered, and colored digitally using a Wacom tablet and Clip Studio Paint.

Text, cover art, and interior illustrations copyright © 2022 by Blue Delliquanti

All rights reserved. Published in the United States by RH Graphic, an imprint of Random House Children's Books, a division of Penguin Random House LLC, New York.

RH Graphic with the book design is a trademark of Penguin Random House LLC.

Visit us on the web! RHKidsGraphic.com • @RHKidsGraphic

Educators and librarians, for a variety of teaching tools, visit us at RHTeachersLibrarians.com

Library of Congress Cataloging-in-Publication Data is available upon request.
ISBN 978-0-593-12414-7 (hardcover) — ISBN 978-0-593-12413-0 (pbk)
ISBN 978-0-593-12415-4 (ebk)

Designed by Patrick Crotty

MANUFACTURED IN CHINA
10 9 8 7 6 5 4 3 2 1
First Edition

A comic on every bookshelf.

Across a Field of Starlight

BLUE DELLIQUANTI

ALSO BY
BLUE DELLIQUANTI

Meal (with Soleil Ho)
O Human Star

To those who know a better world is possible.
In solidarity.

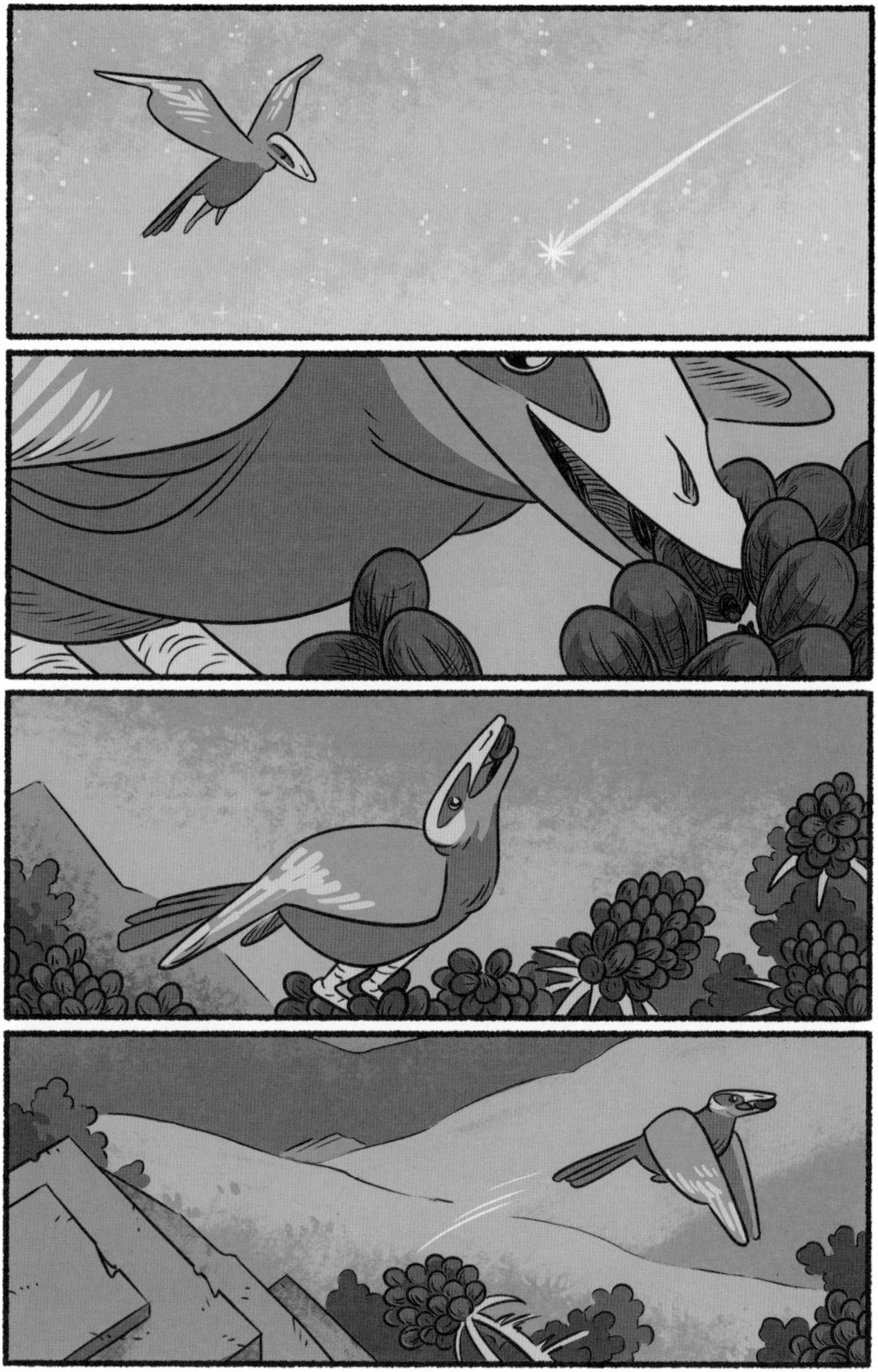

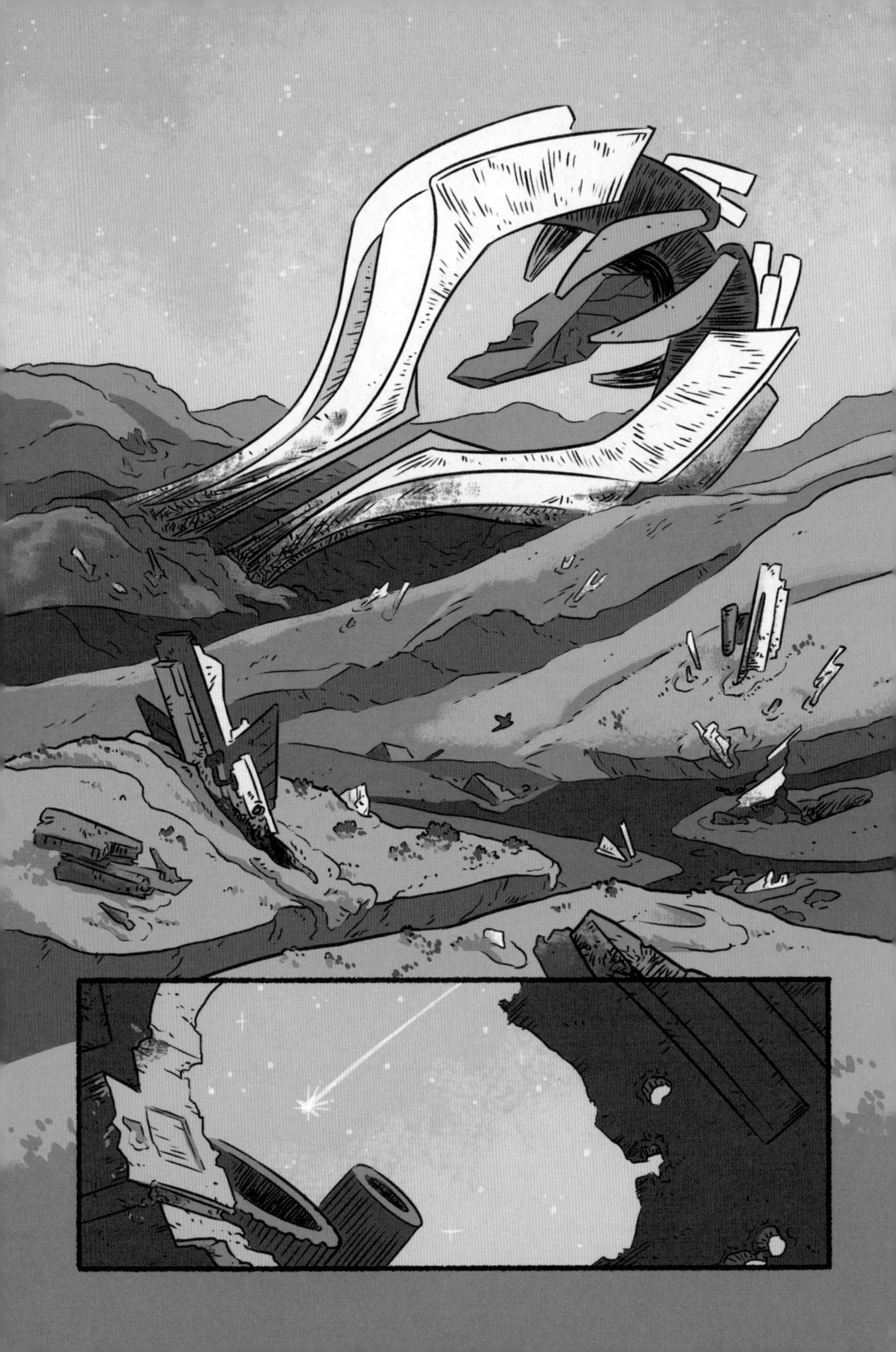

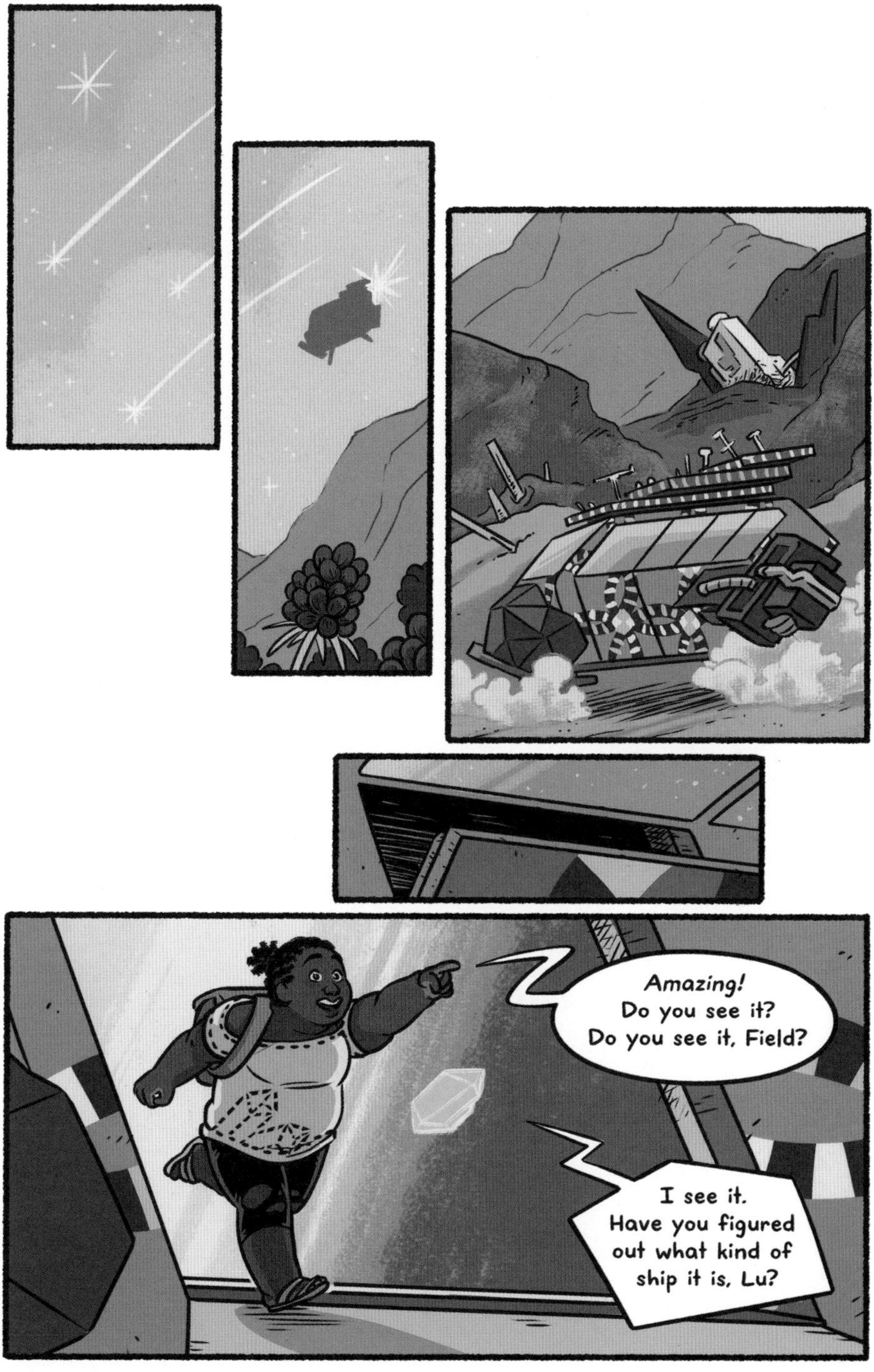
Amazing!
Do you see it?
Do you see it, Field?
I see it.
Have you figured
out what kind of
ship it is, Lu?

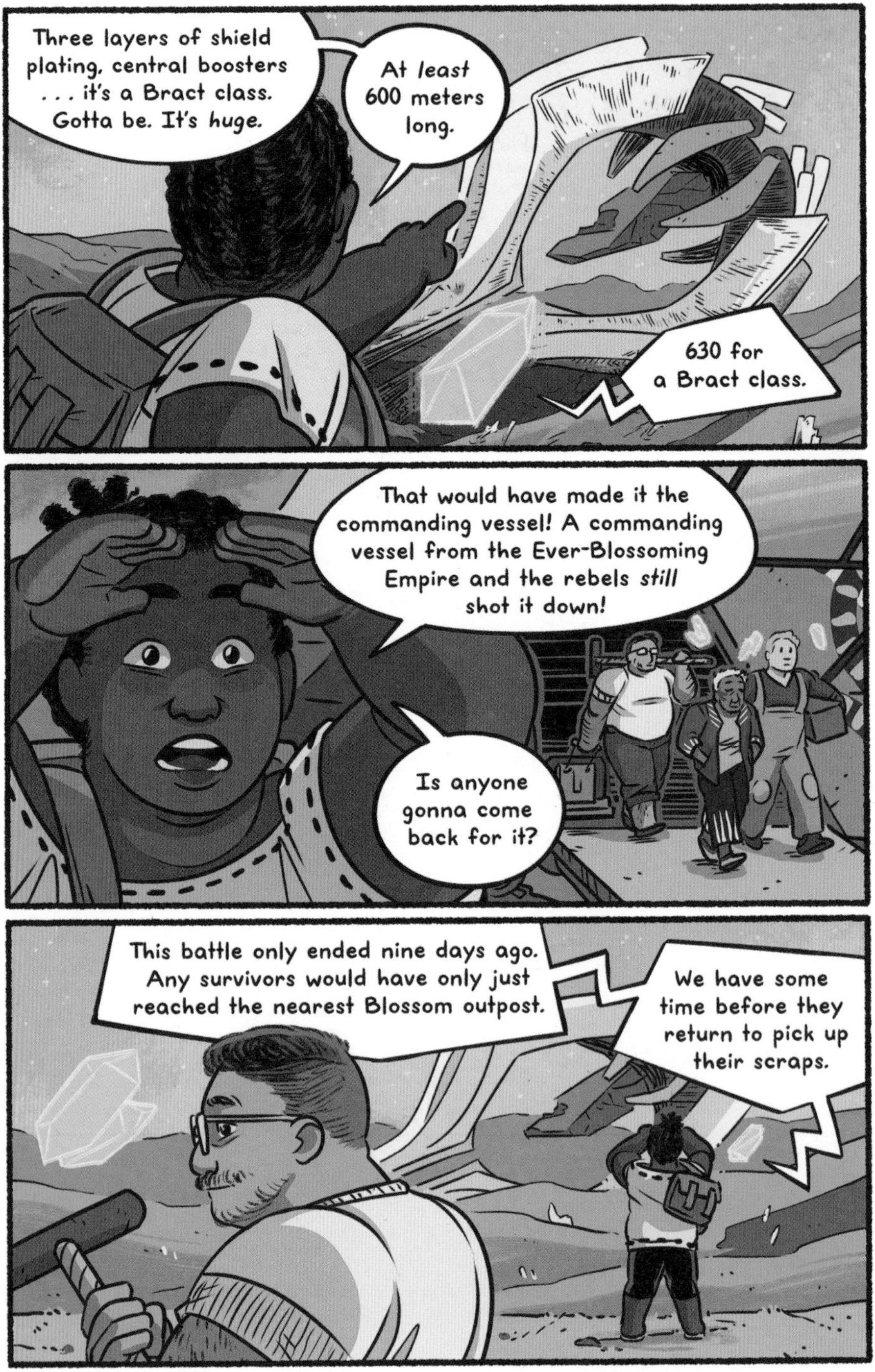

Three layers of shield plating, central boosters . . . it's a Bract class. Gotta be. It's *huge.*
At *least* 600 meters long.
630 for a Bract class.
That would have made it the commanding vessel! A commanding vessel from the Ever-Blossoming Empire and the rebels *still* shot it down!
Is anyone gonna come back for it?
This battle only ended nine days ago. Any survivors would have only just reached the nearest Blossom outpost.
We have some time before they return to pick up their scraps.

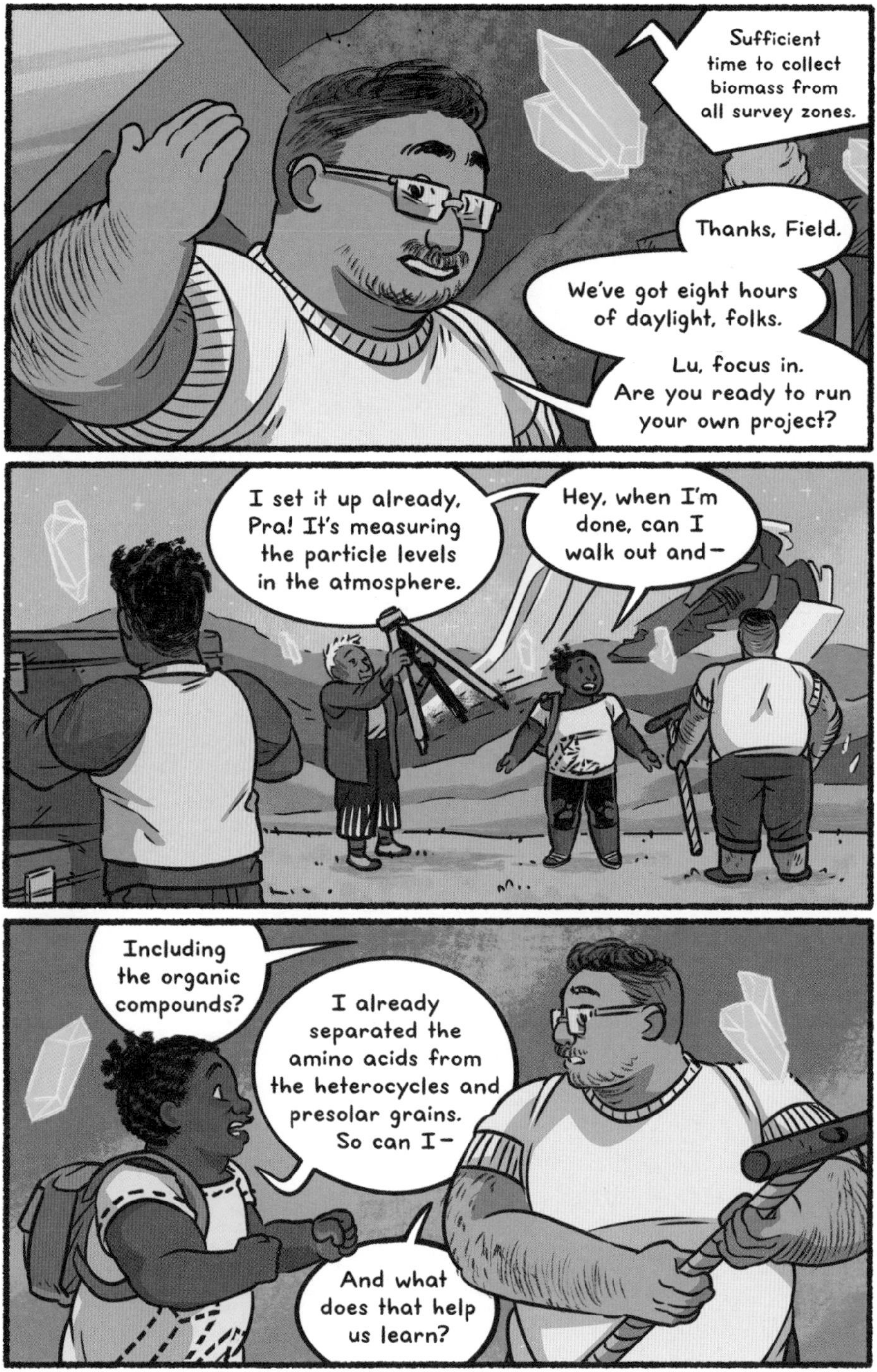
Sufficient time to collect biomass from all survey zones.
Thanks, Field.
We've got eight hours of daylight, folks.
Lu, focus in. Are you ready to run your own project?
I set it up already, Pra! It's measuring the particle levels in the atmosphere.
Hey, when I'm done, can I walk out and–
Including the organic compounds?
I already separated the amino acids from the heterocycles and presolar grains. So can I–
And what does that help us learn?

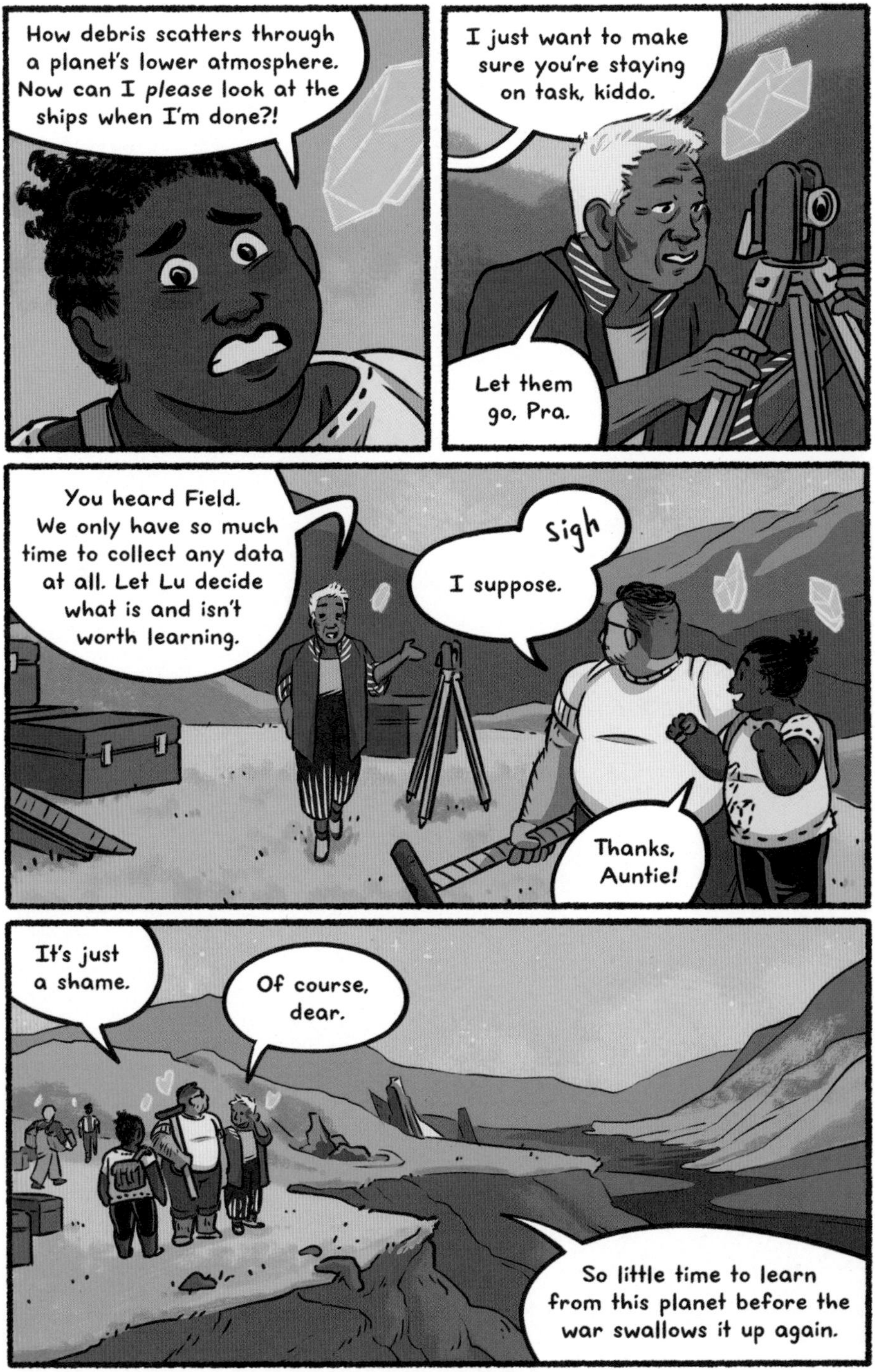
How debris scatters through a planet's lower atmosphere. Now can I *please* look at the ships when I'm done?!
I just want to make sure you're staying on task, kiddo.
Let them go, Pra.
You heard Field. We only have so much time to collect any data at all. Let Lu decide what is and isn't worth learning.
Sigh
I suppose.
Thanks, Auntie!
It's just a shame.
Of course, dear.
So little time to learn from this planet before the war swallows it up again.

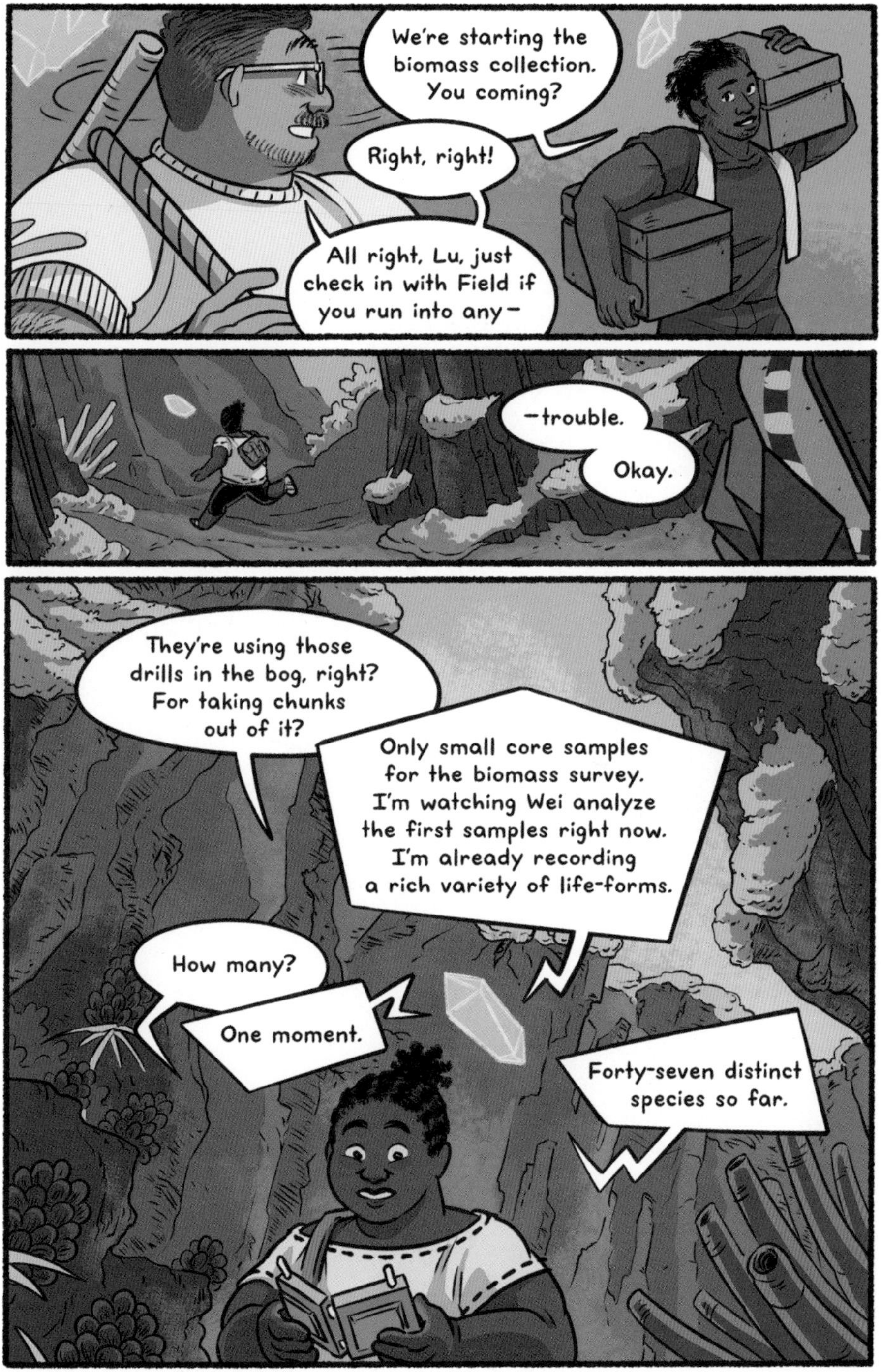
We're starting the biomass collection. You coming?
Right, right!
All right, Lu, just check in with Field if you run into any–
–trouble.
Okay.
They're using those drills in the bog, right? For taking chunks out of it?
Only small core samples for the biomass survey. I'm watching Wei analyze the first samples right now. I'm already recording a rich variety of life-forms.
How many?
One moment.
Forty-seven distinct species so far.

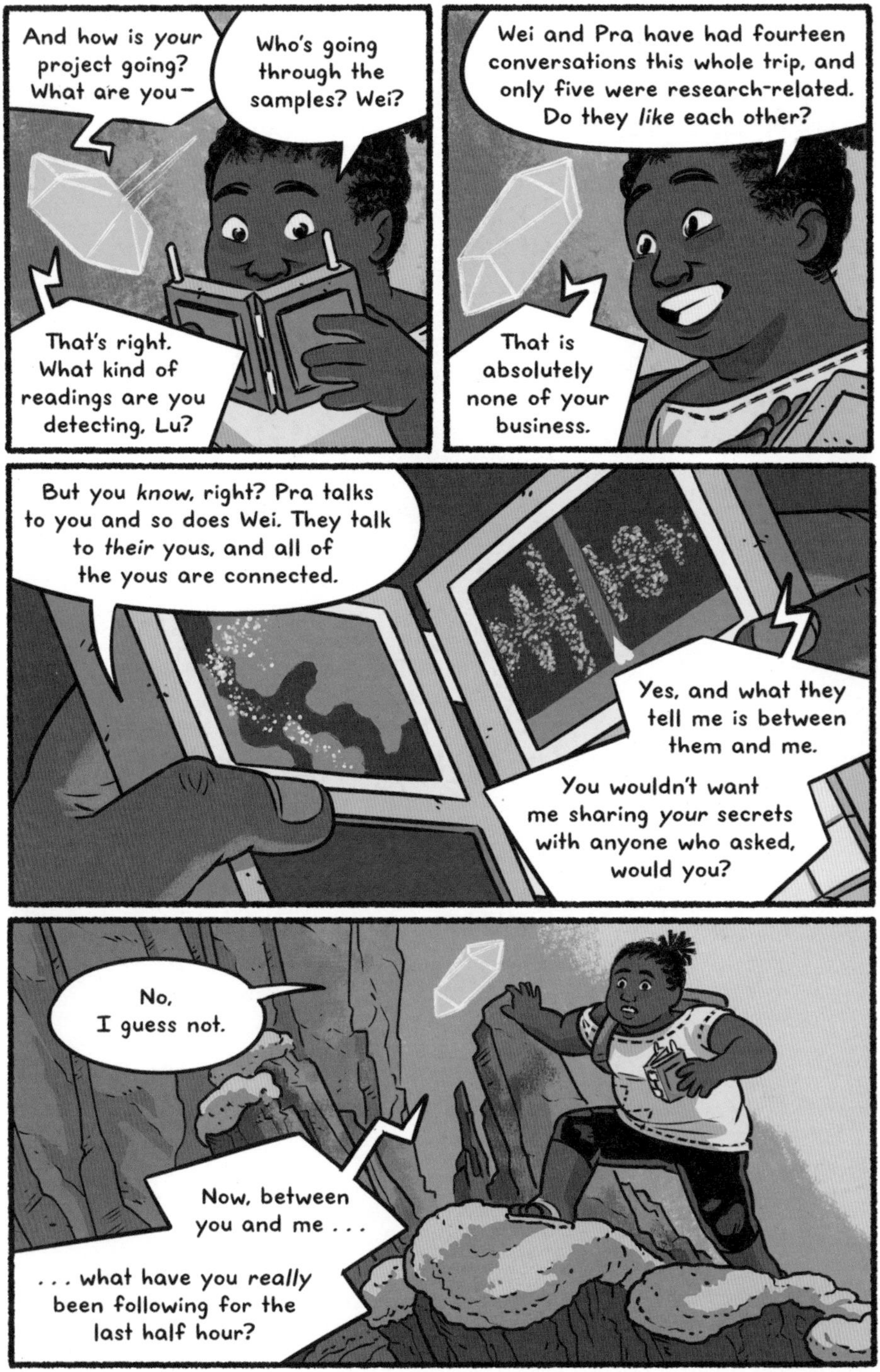
And how is *your* project going? What are you—
Who's going through the samples? Wei?
That's right. What kind of readings are you detecting, Lu?
Wei and Pra have had fourteen conversations this whole trip, and only five were research-related. Do they *like* each other?
That is absolutely none of your business.
But you *know*, right? Pra talks to you and so does Wei. They talk to *their* yous, and all of the yous are connected.
Yes, and what they tell me is between them and me.
You wouldn't want me sharing *your* secrets with anyone who asked, would you?
No, I guess not.
Now, between you and me . . .
. . . what have you *really* been following for the last half hour?

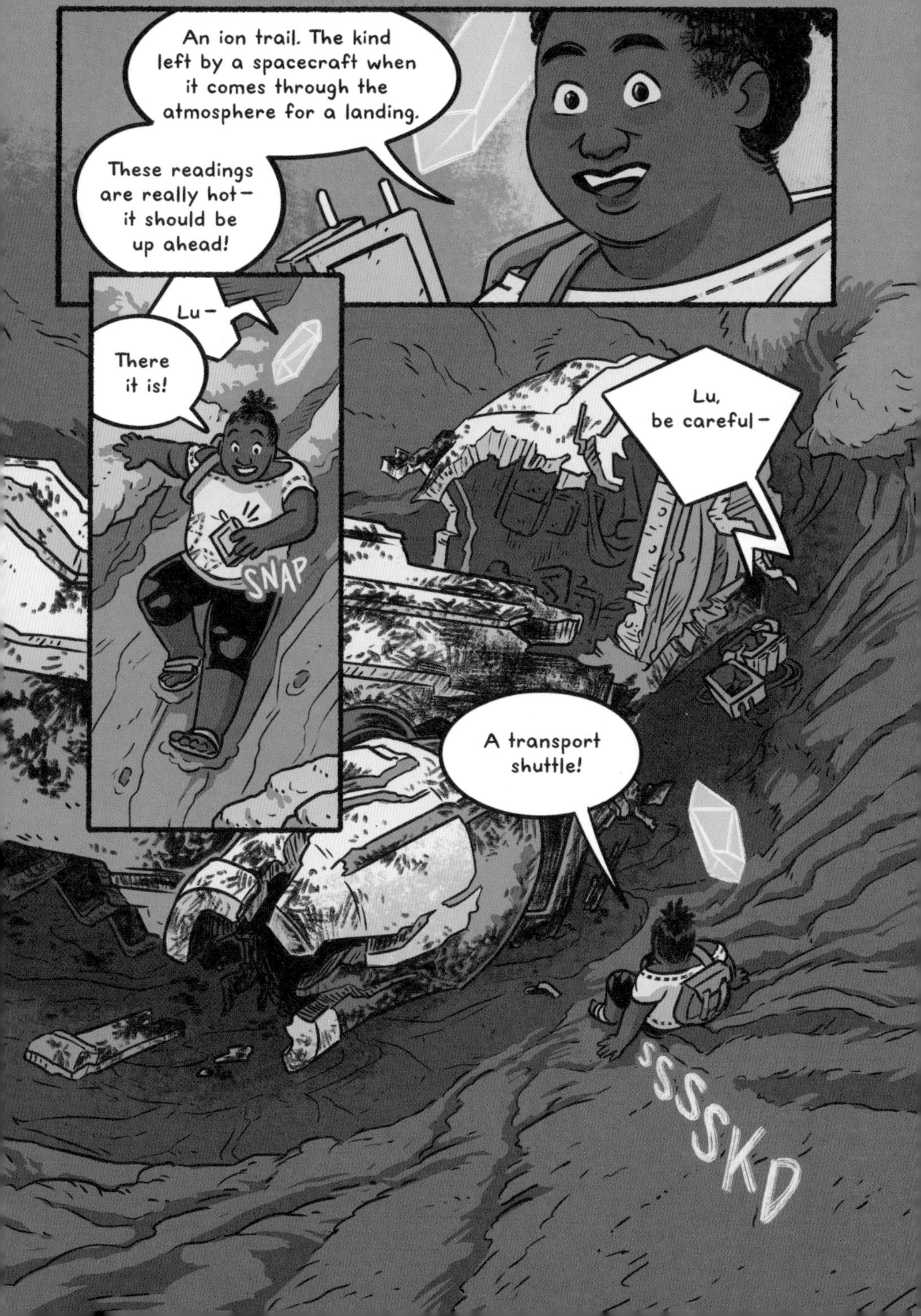
An ion trail. The kind left by a spacecraft when it comes through the atmosphere for a landing.
These readings are really hot—it should be up ahead!
Lu—
There it is!
SNAP
Lu, be careful—
A transport shuttle!
SSSSKD

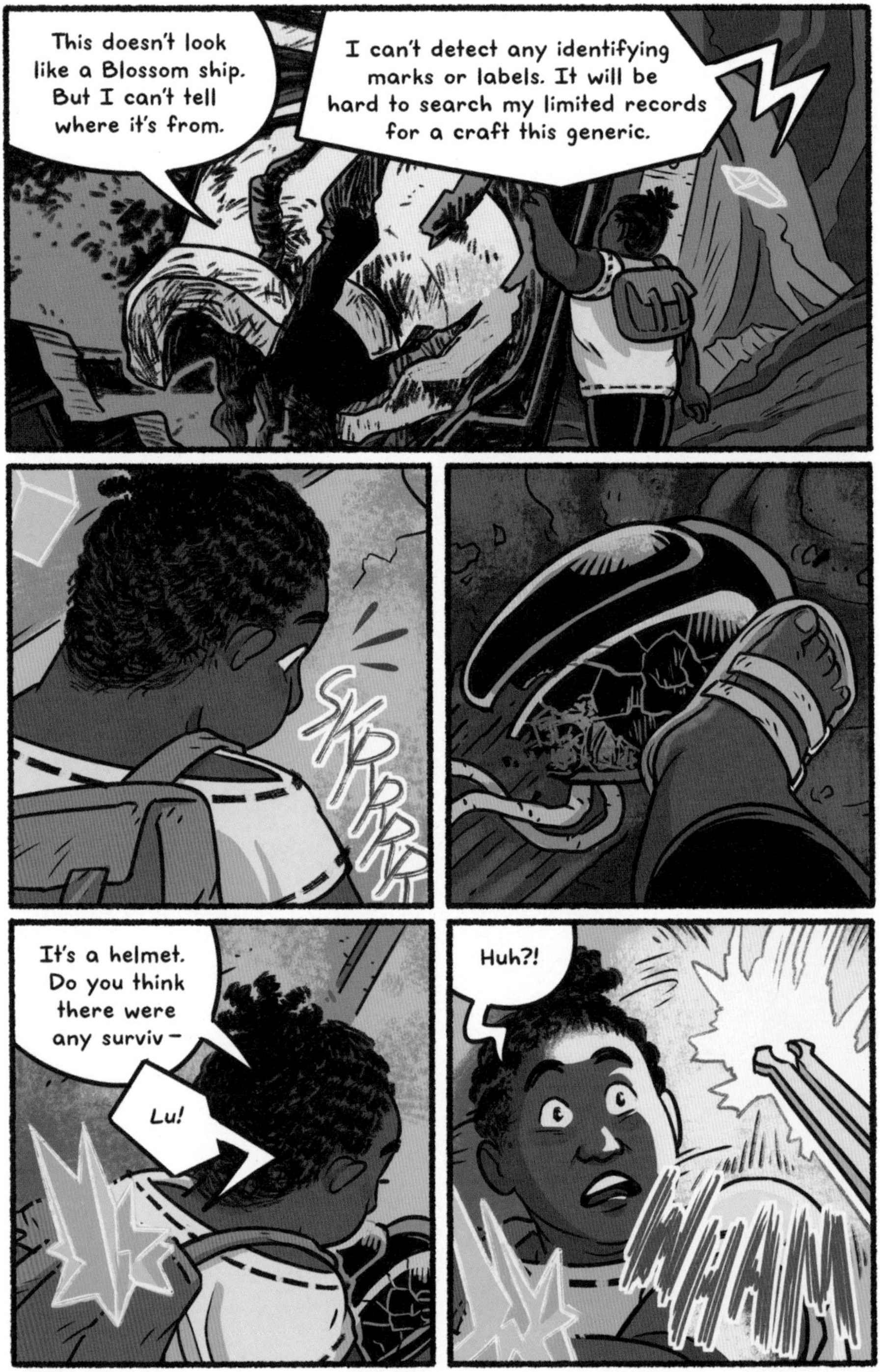
This doesn't look like a Blossom ship. But I can't tell where it's from.
I can't detect any identifying marks or labels. It will be hard to search my limited records for a craft this generic.
SKRRRRT
It's a helmet. Do you think there were any surviv—
Lu!
Huh?!
WHAM

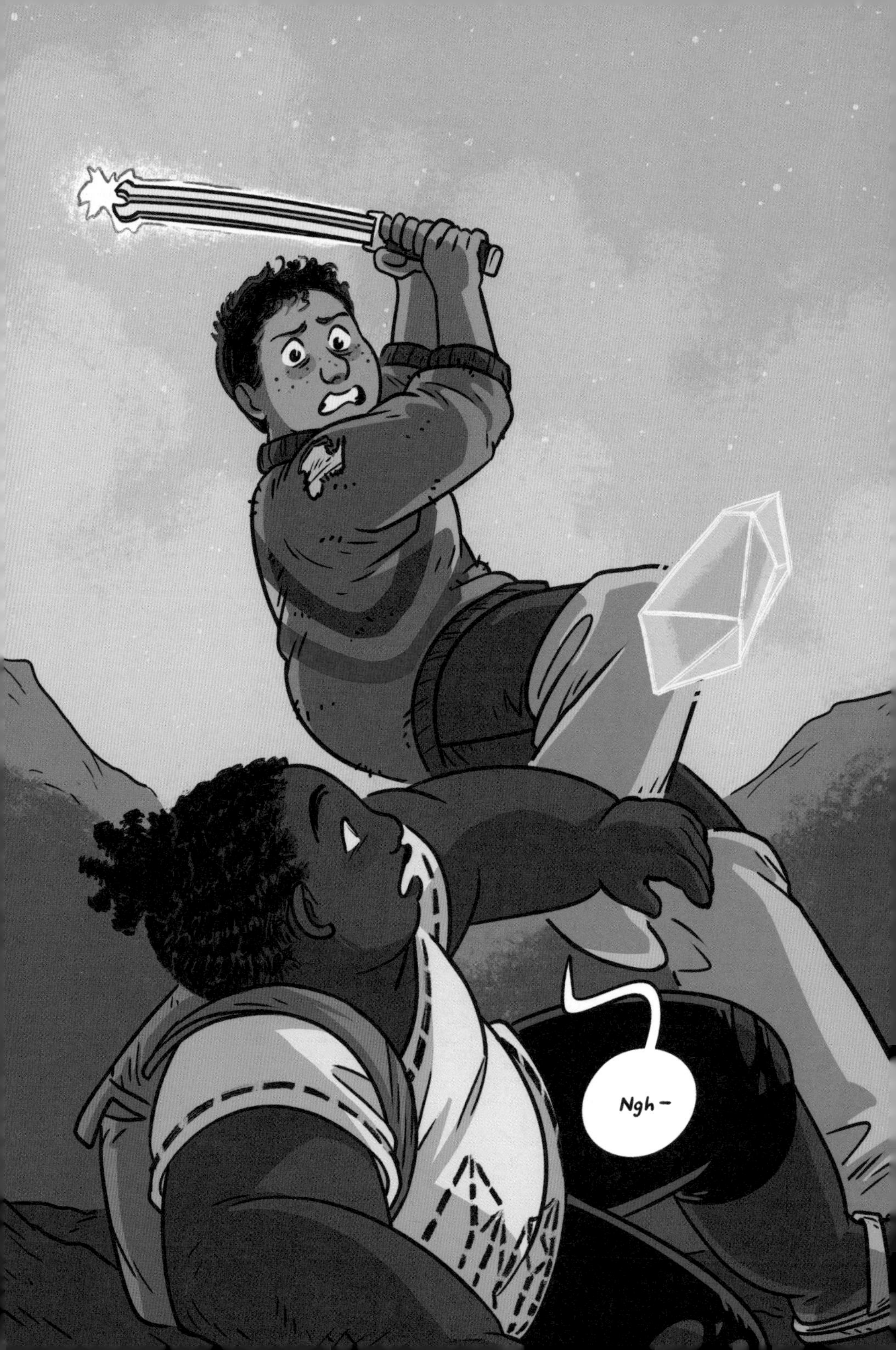
Ngh-

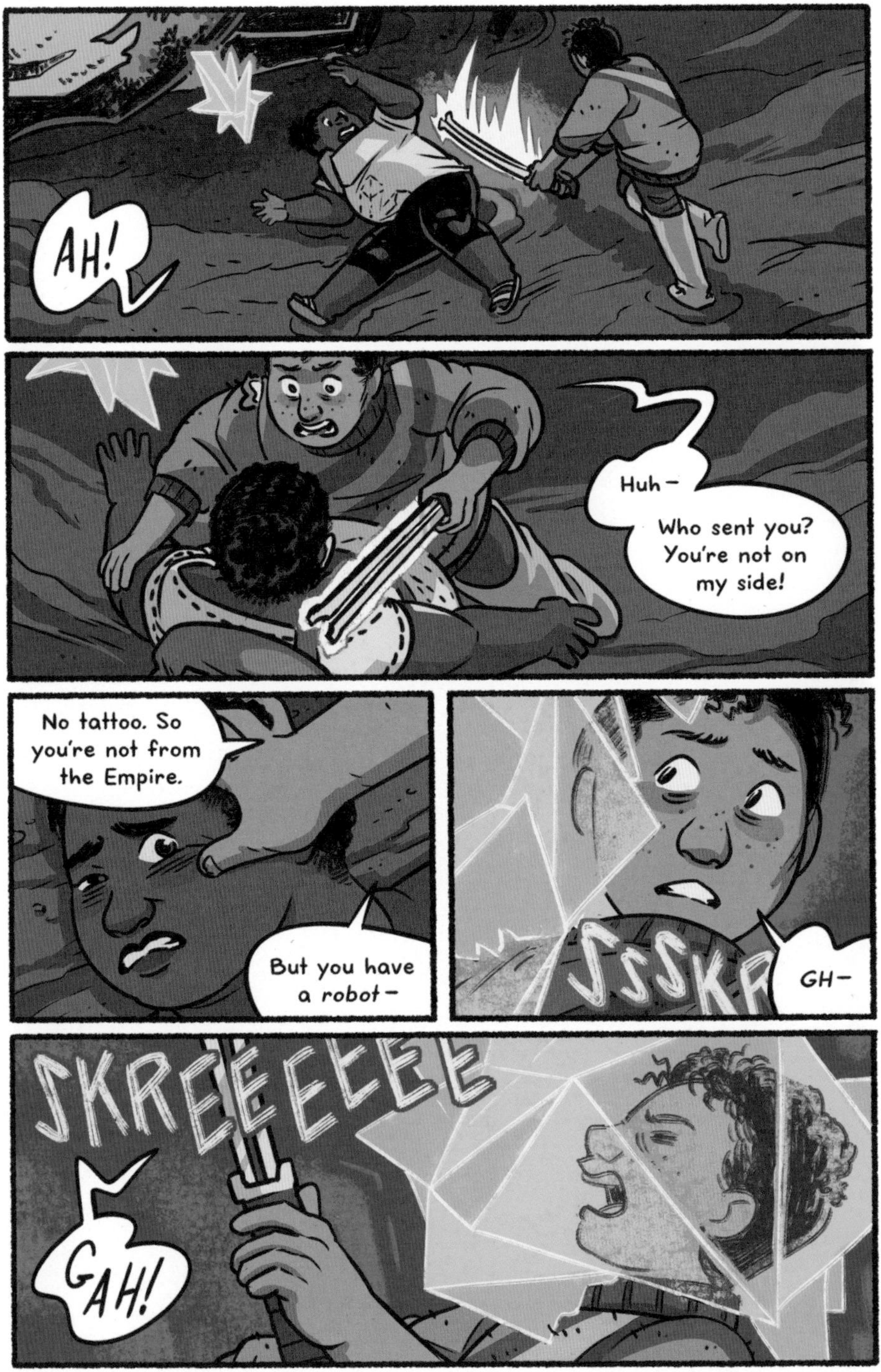
AH!
Huh—
Who sent you? You're not on my side!
No tattoo. So you're not from the Empire.
But you have a *robot*—
SSSKR
GH—
SKREEEEEEE
GAH!

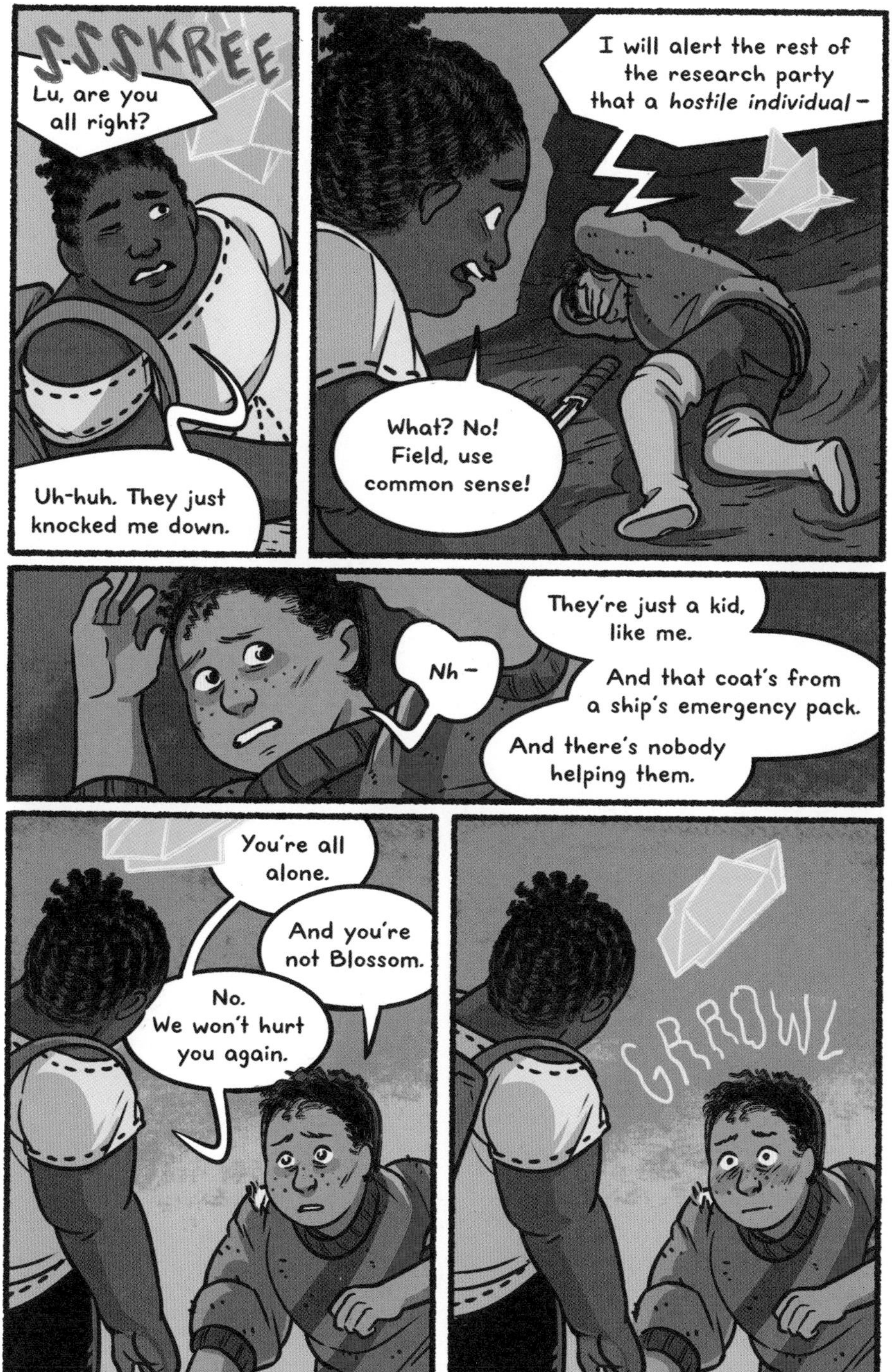
SSSKREE
Lu, are you all right?
Uh-huh. They just knocked me down.
I will alert the rest of the research party that a *hostile individual*–
What? No! Field, use common sense!
Nh–
They're just a kid, like me.
And that coat's from a ship's emergency pack.
And there's nobody helping them.
You're all alone.
And you're not Blossom.
No. We won't hurt you again.
GRROWL

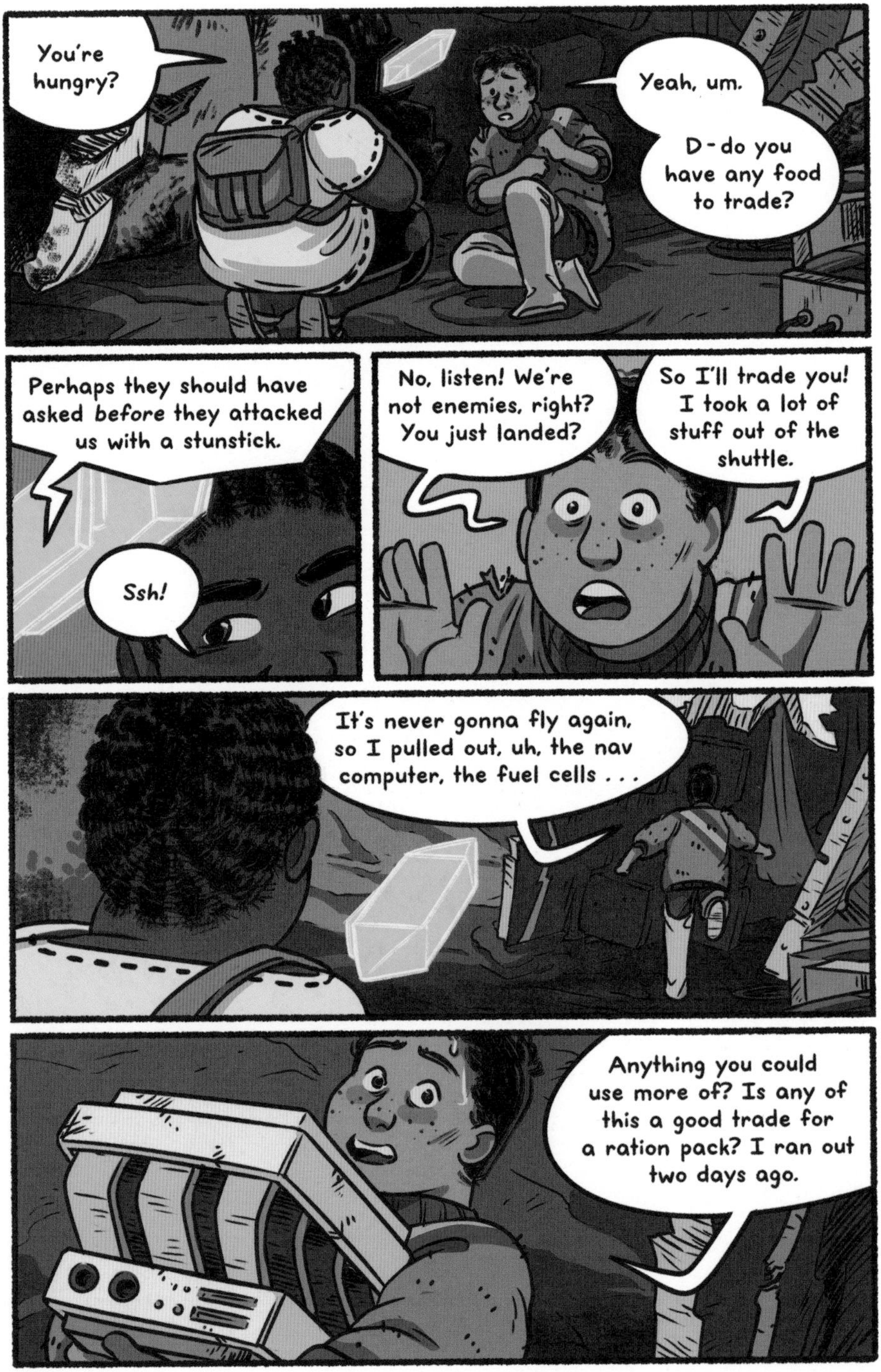
You're hungry?
Yeah, um.
D-do you have any food to trade?
Perhaps they should have asked *before* they attacked us with a stunstick.
Ssh!
No, listen! We're not enemies, right? You just landed?
So I'll trade you! I took a lot of stuff out of the shuttle.
It's never gonna fly again, so I pulled out, uh, the nav computer, the fuel cells . . .
Anything you could use more of? Is any of this a good trade for a ration pack? I ran out two days ago.

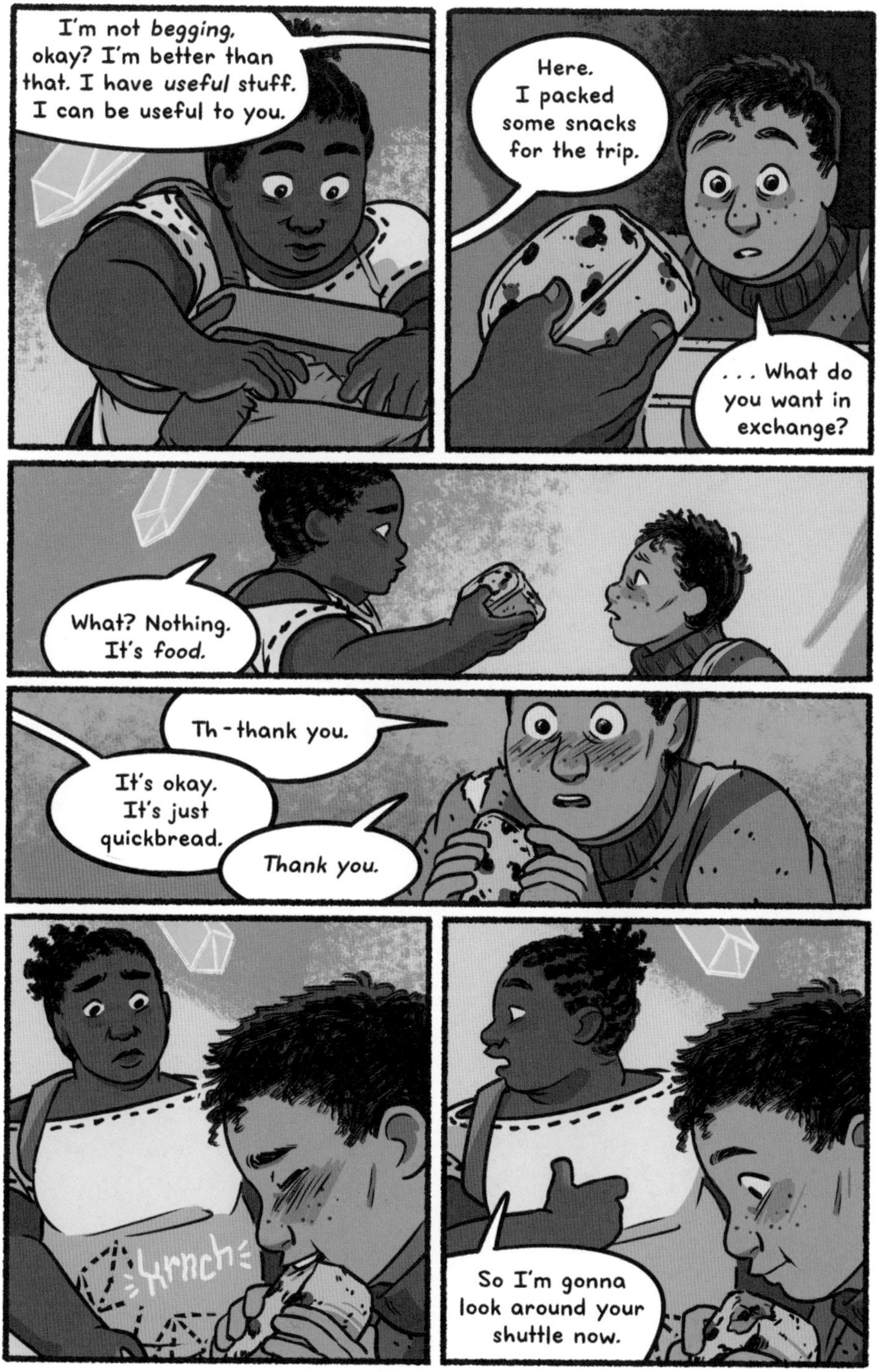
I'm not *begging*, okay? I'm better than that. I have *useful* stuff. I can be useful to you.
Here. I packed some snacks for the trip.
. . . What do you want in exchange?
What? Nothing. It's *food.*
Th-thank you.
It's okay. It's just quickbread.
Thank you.
krnch
So I'm gonna look around your shuttle now.

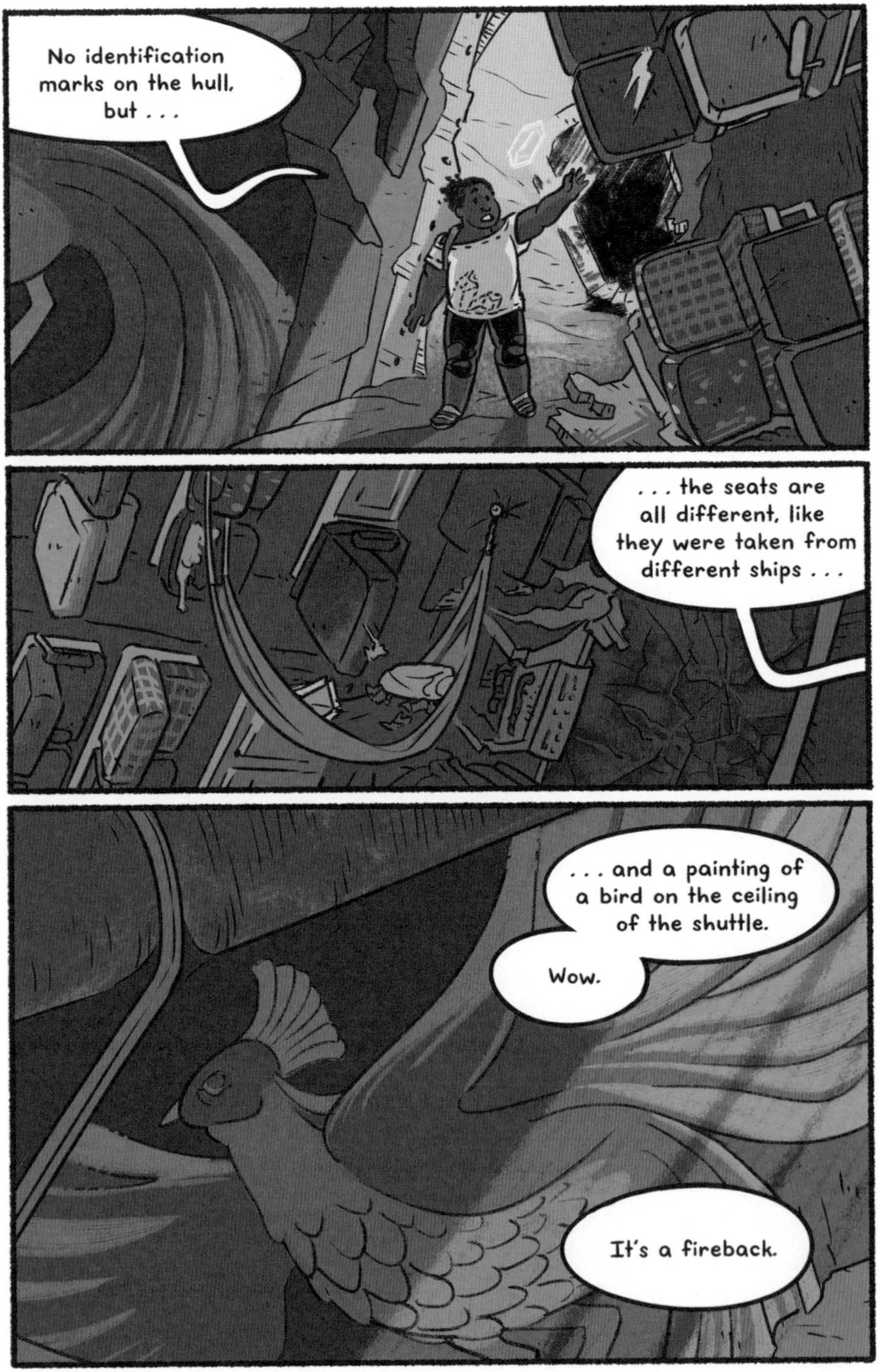
No identification marks on the hull, but . . .
. . . the seats are all different, like they were taken from different ships . . .
. . . and a painting of a bird on the ceiling of the shuttle.
Wow.
It's a fireback.

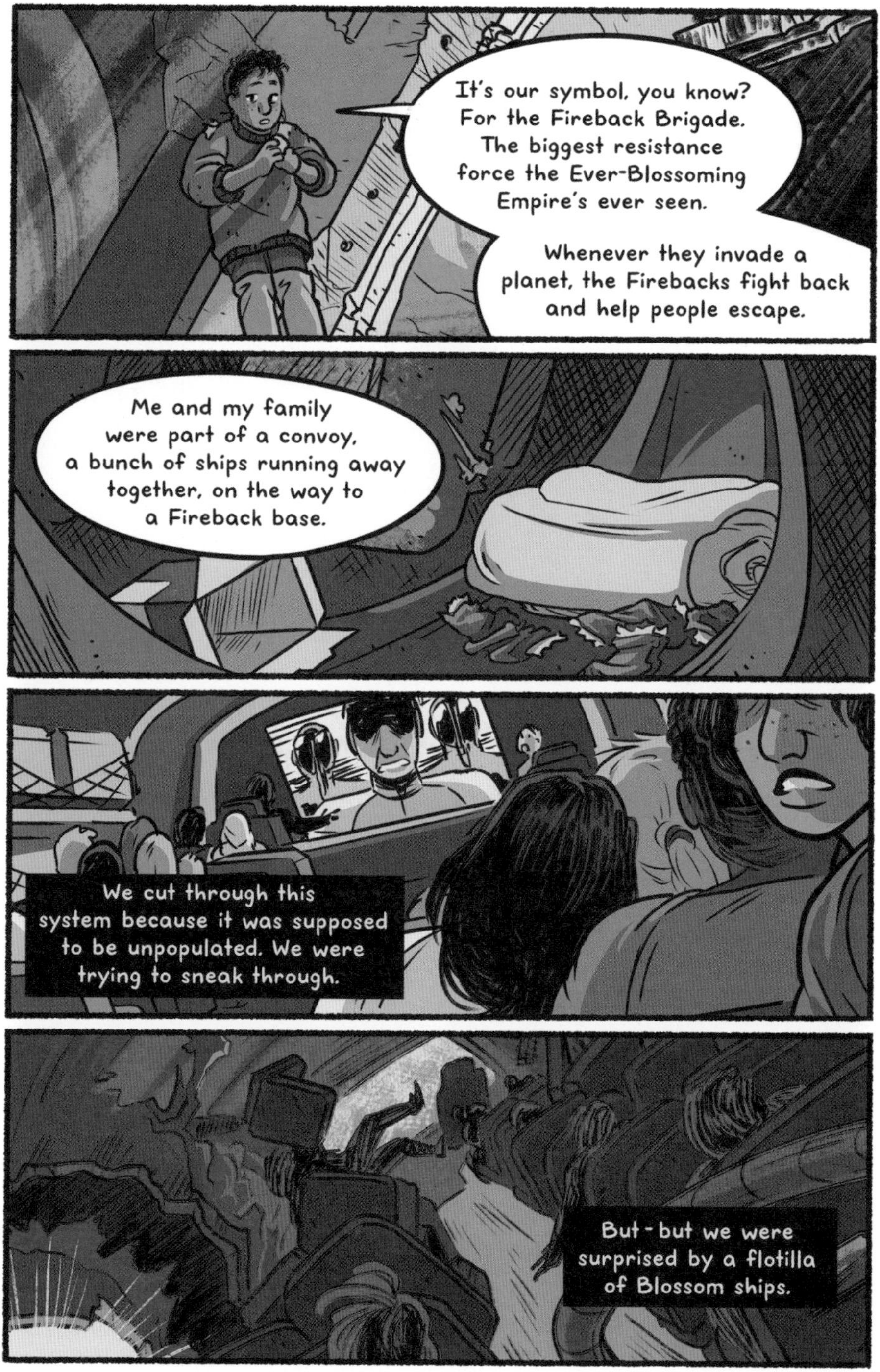
It's our symbol, you know? For the Fireback Brigade. The biggest resistance force the Ever-Blossoming Empire's ever seen.
Whenever they invade a planet, the Firebacks fight back and help people escape.
Me and my family were part of a convoy, a bunch of ships running away together, on the way to a Fireback base.
We cut through this system because it was supposed to be unpopulated. We were trying to sneak through.
But-but we were surprised by a flotilla of Blossom ships.

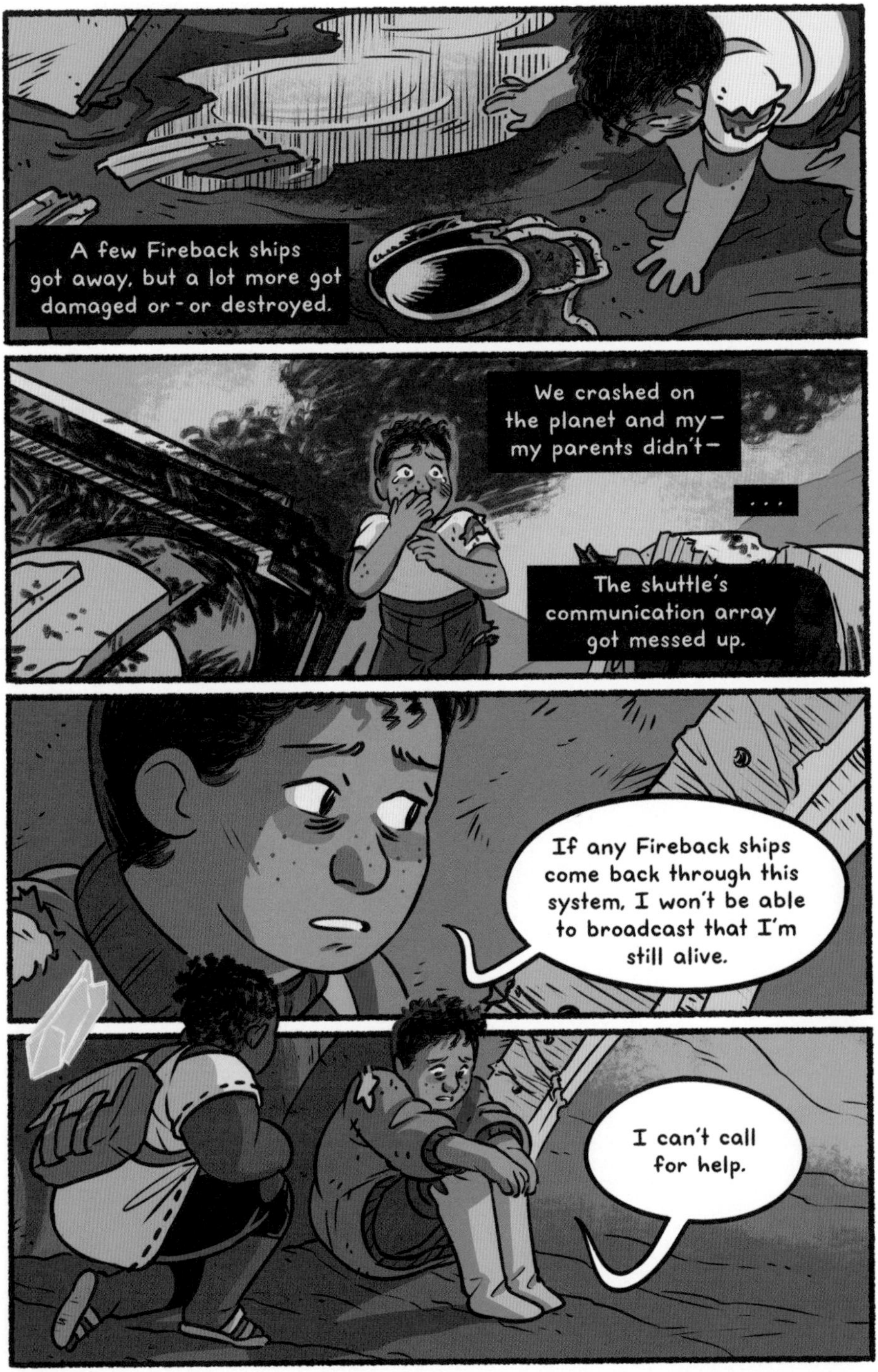

A few Fireback ships got away, but a lot more got damaged or-or destroyed.
We crashed on the planet and my— my parents didn't—
...
The shuttle's communication array got messed up.
If any Fireback ships come back through this system, I won't be able to broadcast that I'm still alive.
I can't call for help.

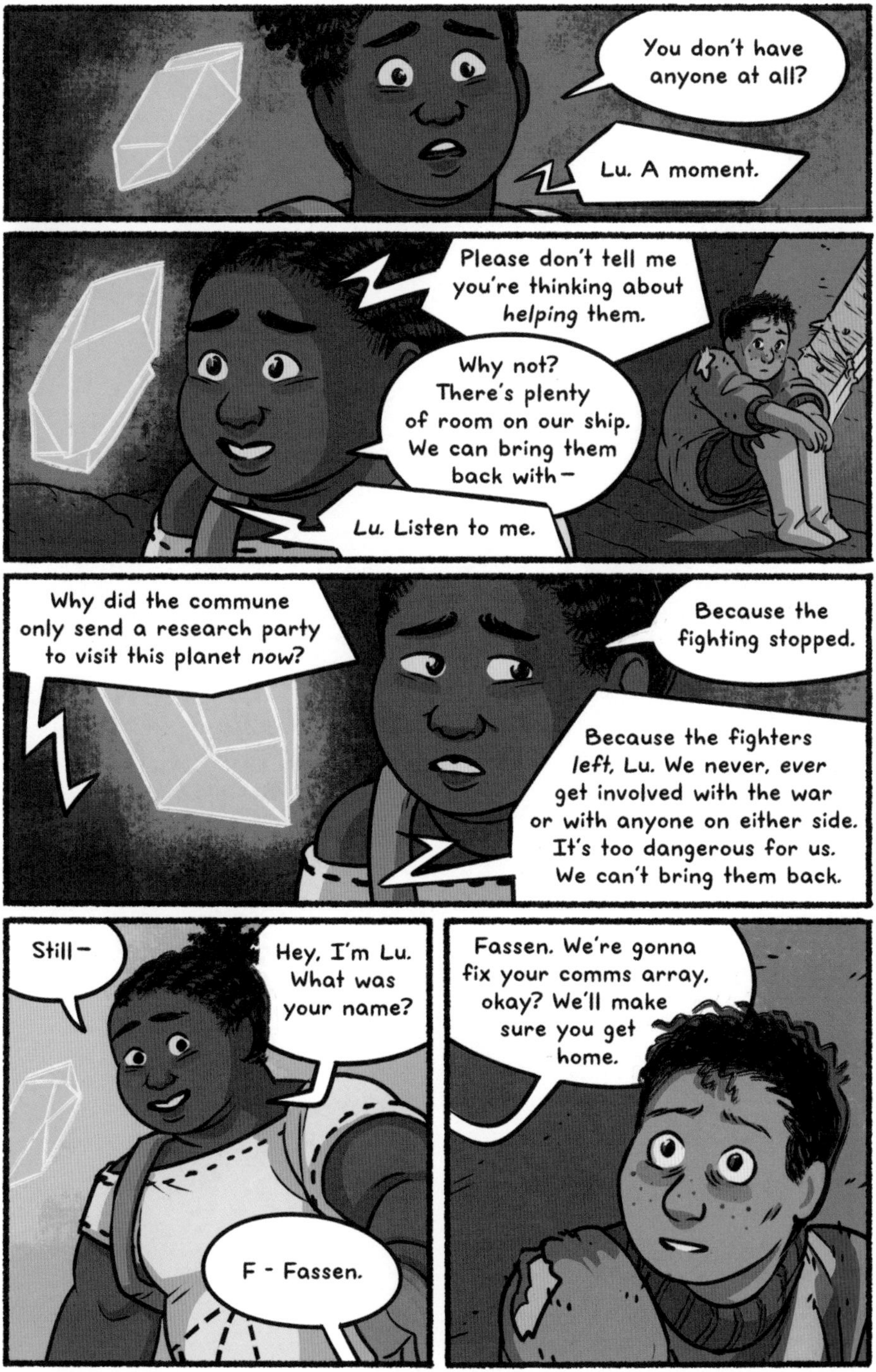

You don't have anyone at all?
Lu. A moment.
Please don't tell me you're thinking about *helping* them.
Why not? There's plenty of room on our ship. We can bring them back with—
Lu. Listen to me.
Why did the commune only send a research party to visit this planet *now*?
Because the fighting stopped.
Because the fighters *left*, Lu. We never, *ever* get involved with the war or with anyone on either side. It's too dangerous for us. We can't bring them back.
Still—
Hey, I'm Lu. What was your name?
F - Fassen.
Fassen. We're gonna fix your comms array, okay? We'll make sure you get home.

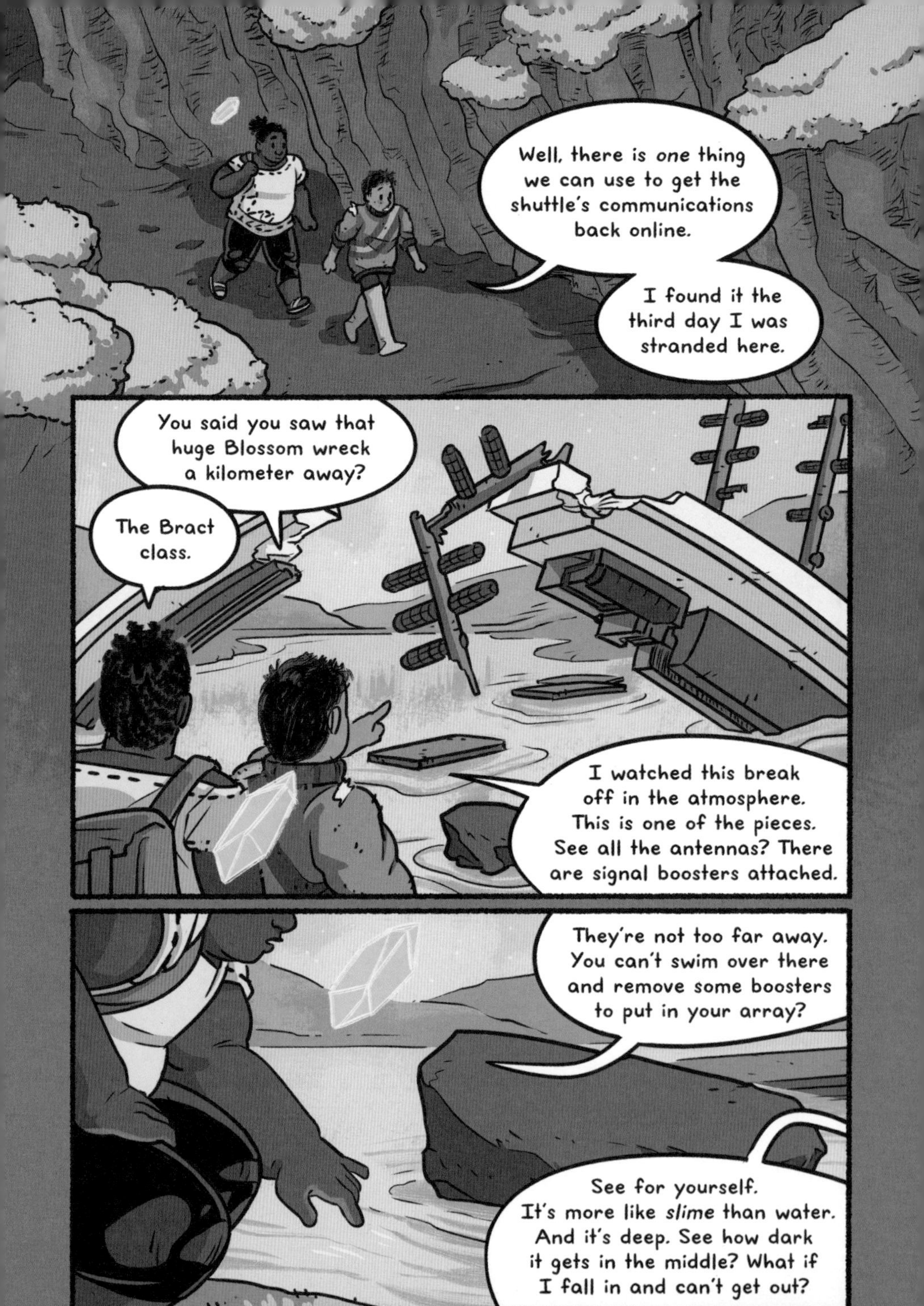
Well, there is *one* thing we can use to get the shuttle's communications back online.
I found it the third day I was stranded here.
You said you saw that huge Blossom wreck a kilometer away?
The Bract class.
I watched this break off in the atmosphere. This is one of the pieces. See all the antennas? There are signal boosters attached.
They're not too far away. You can't swim over there and remove some boosters to put in your array?
See for yourself. It's more like *slime* than water. And it's deep. See how dark it gets in the middle? What if I fall in and can't get out?

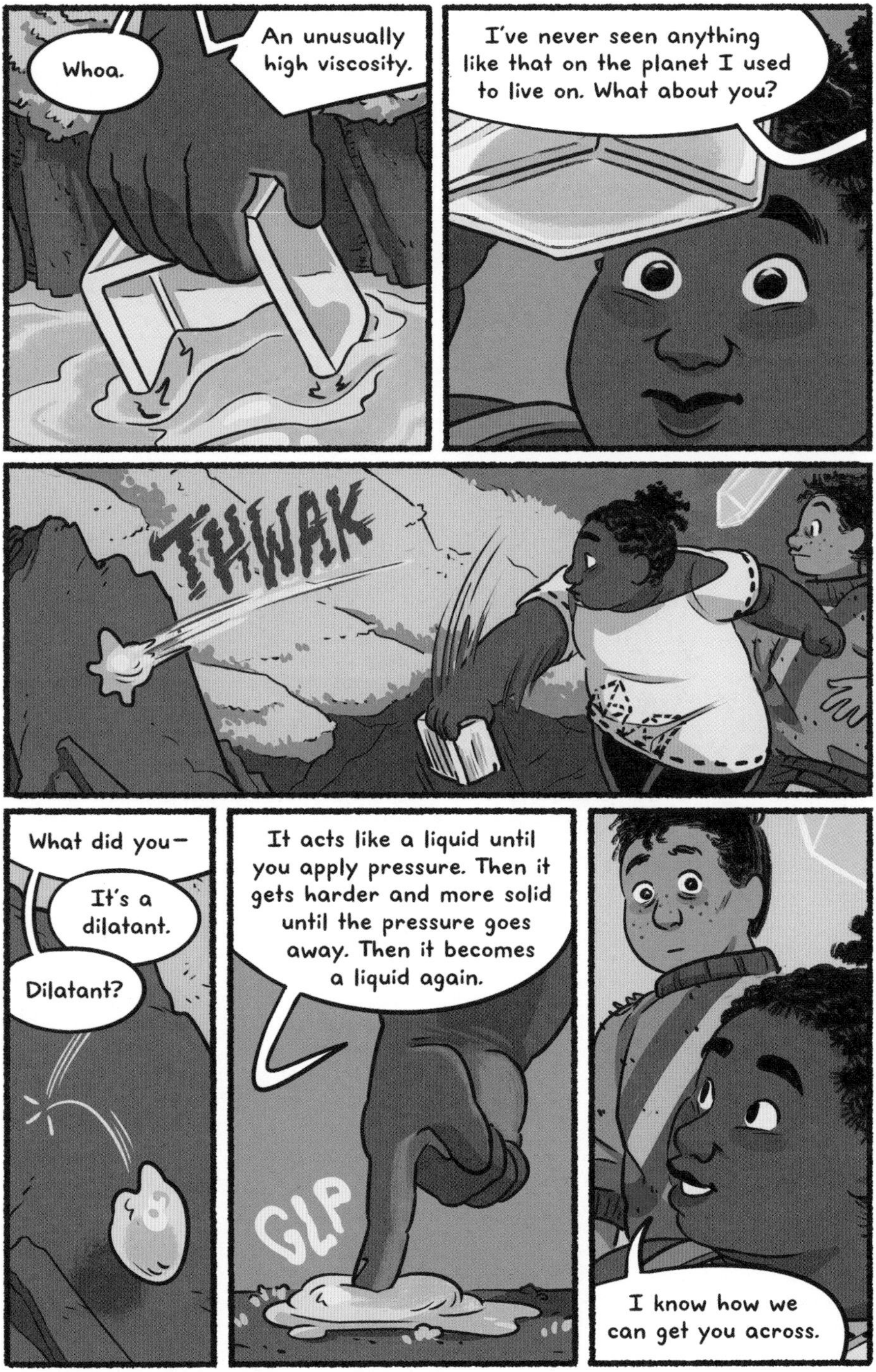
Whoa.
An unusually high viscosity.
I've never seen anything like that on the planet I used to live on. What about you?
THWAK
What did you—
It's a dilatant.
Dilatant?
It acts like a liquid until you apply pressure. Then it gets harder and more solid until the pressure goes away. Then it becomes a liquid again.
GLP
I know how we can get you across.

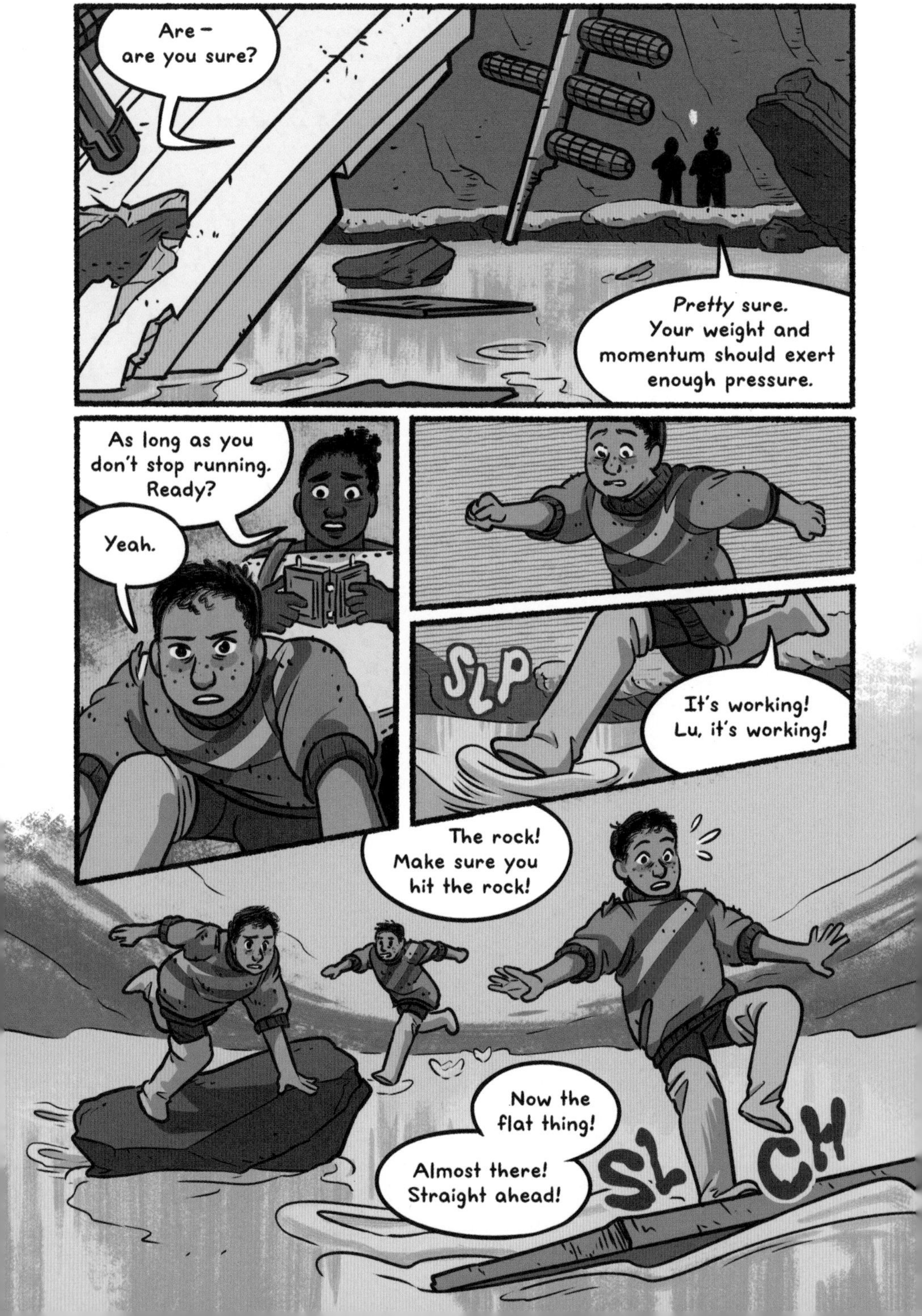
Are -
are you sure?
Pretty sure. Your weight and momentum should exert enough pressure.
As long as you don't stop running. Ready?
Yeah.
SLP
It's working! Lu, it's working!
The rock! Make sure you hit the rock!
Now the flat thing!
Almost there! Straight ahead!
SL CH

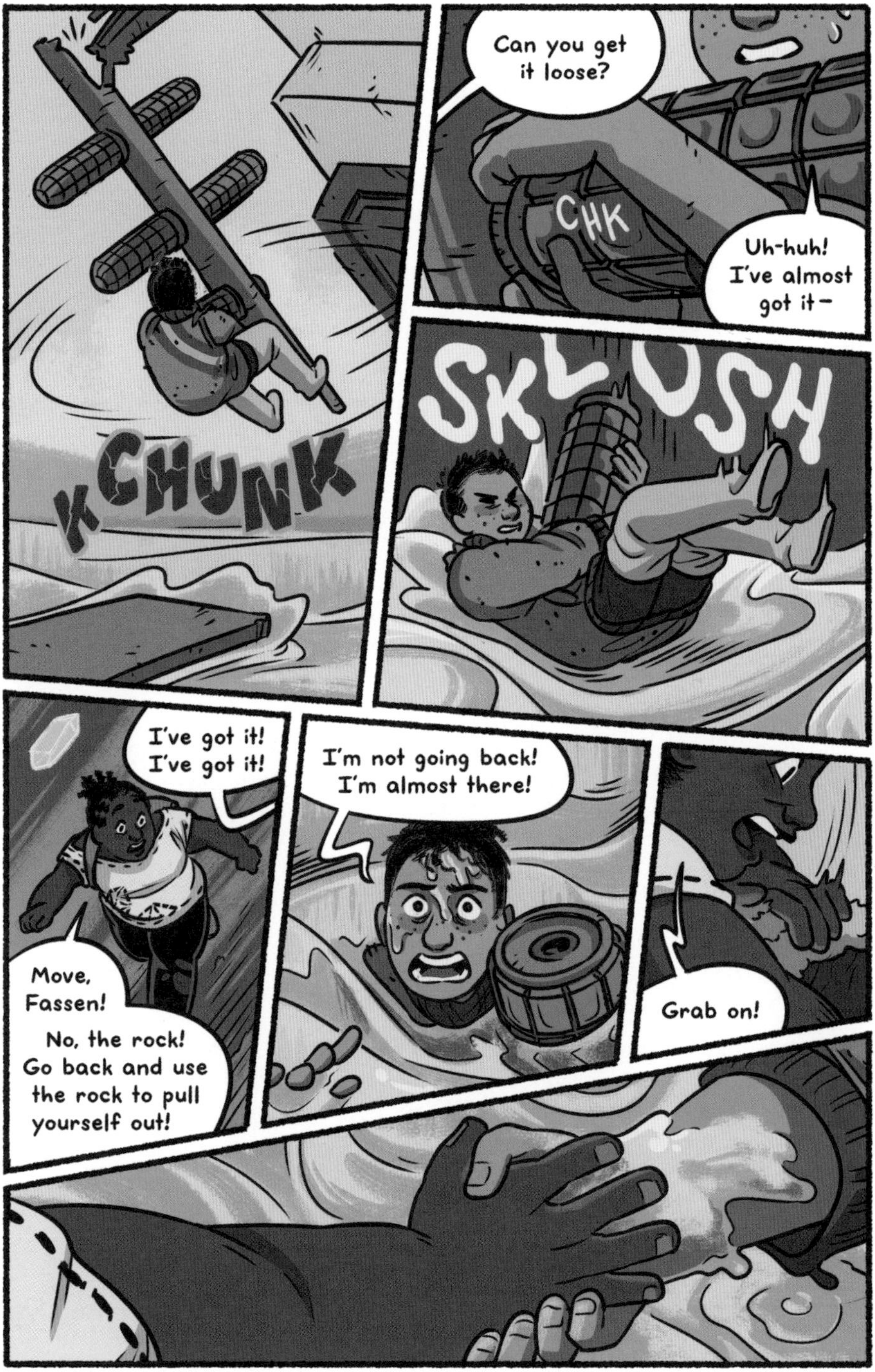
KCHUNK
Can you get it loose?
CHK
Uh-huh! I've almost got it—
SKLOSH
I've got it! I've got it!
Move, Fassen!
No, the rock! Go back and use the rock to pull yourself out!
I'm not going back! I'm almost there!
Grab on!

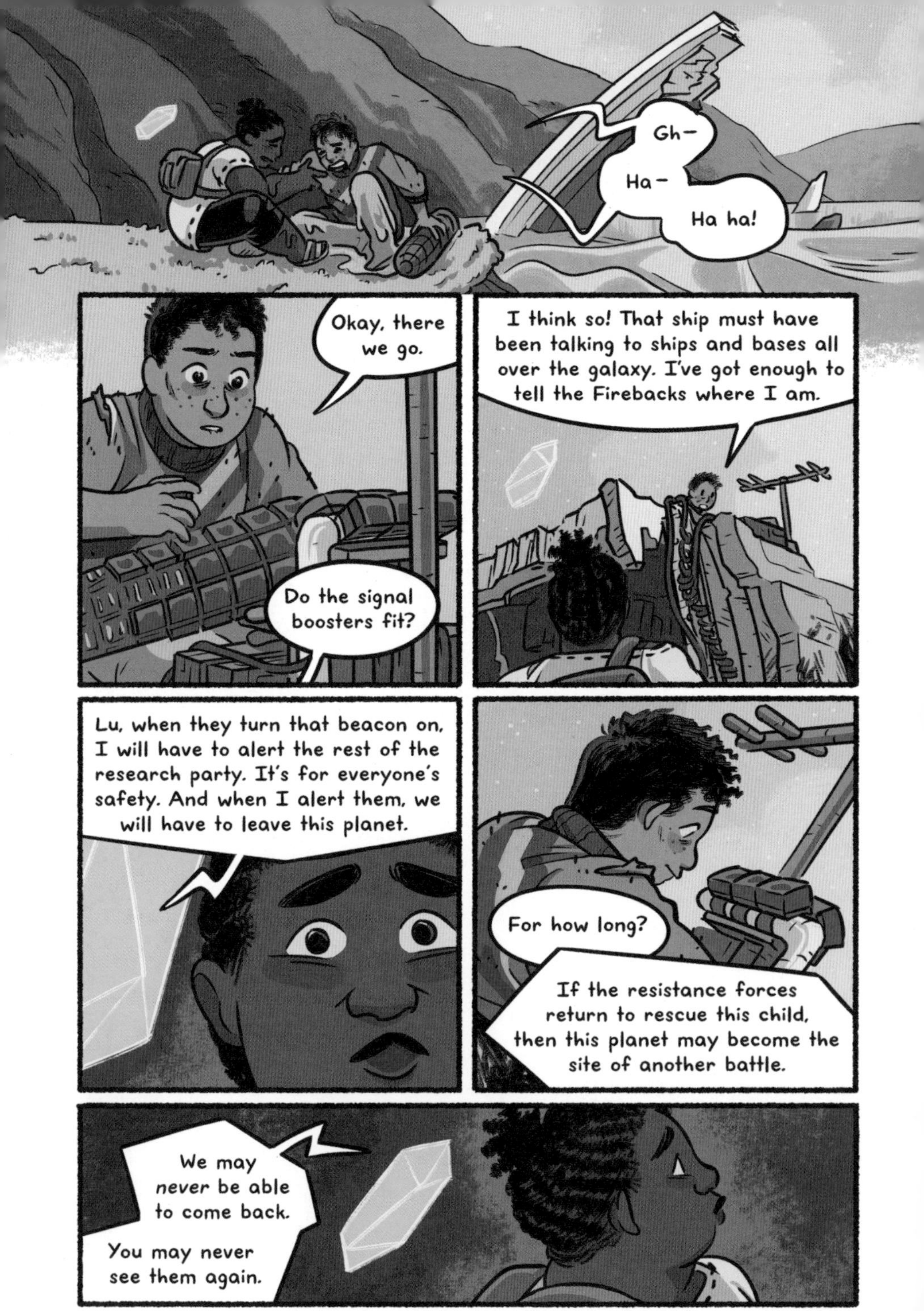
Gh—
Ha—
Ha ha!
Okay, there we go.
Do the signal boosters fit?
I think so! That ship must have been talking to ships and bases all over the galaxy. I've got enough to tell the Firebacks where I am.
Lu, when they turn that beacon on, I will have to alert the rest of the research party. It's for everyone's safety. And when I alert them, we will have to leave this planet.
For how long?
If the resistance forces return to rescue this child, then this planet may become the site of another battle.
We may *never* be able to come back.
You may never see them again.

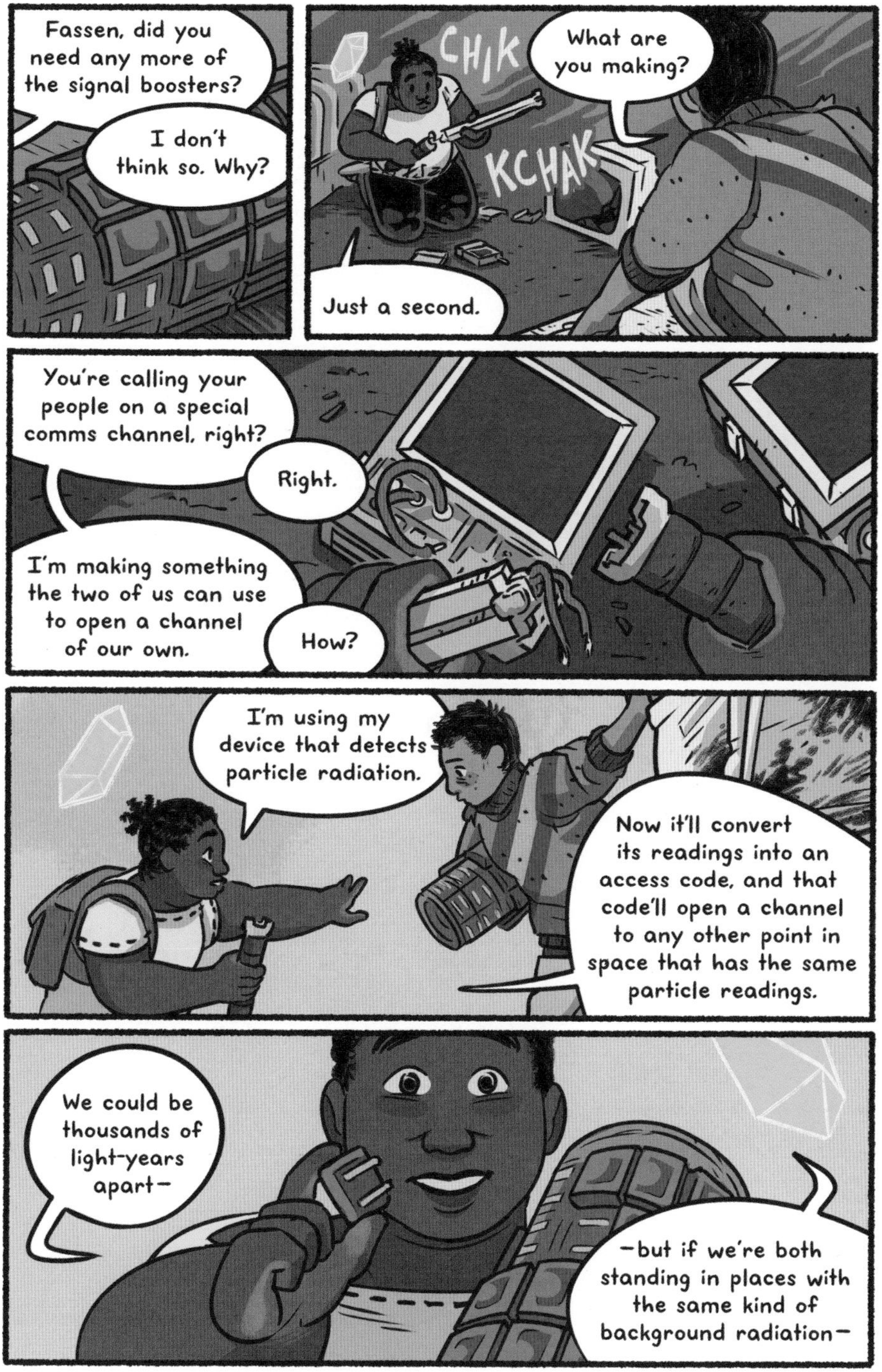
Fassen, did you need any more of the signal boosters?
I don't think so. Why?
CHIK
What are you making?
KCHAK
Just a second.
You're calling your people on a special comms channel, right?
Right.
I'm making something the two of us can use to open a channel of our own.
How?
I'm using my device that detects particle radiation.
Now it'll convert its readings into an access code, and that code'll open a channel to any other point in space that has the same particle readings.
We could be thousands of light-years apart—
—but if we're both standing in places with the same kind of background radiation—

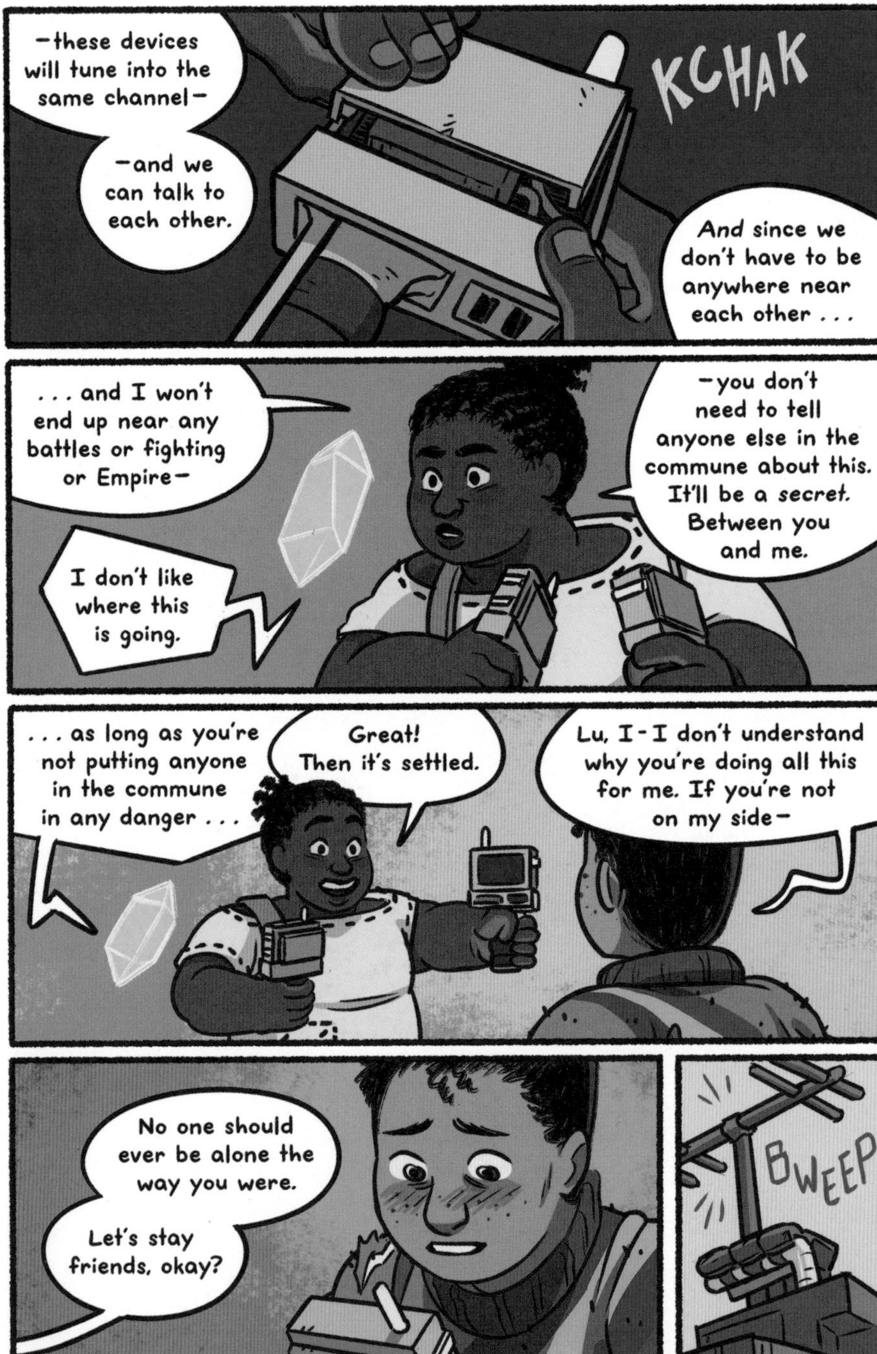
—these devices will tune into the same channel—
—and we can talk to each other.
KCHAK
And since we don't have to be anywhere near each other . . .
. . . and I won't end up near any battles or fighting or Empire—
I don't like where this is going.
—you don't need to tell anyone else in the commune about this. It'll be a *secret.* Between you and me.
. . . as long as you're not putting anyone in the commune in any danger . . .
Great! Then it's settled.
Lu, I-I don't understand why you're doing all this for me. If you're not on my side—
No one should ever be alone the way you were.
Let's stay friends, okay?
BWEEP

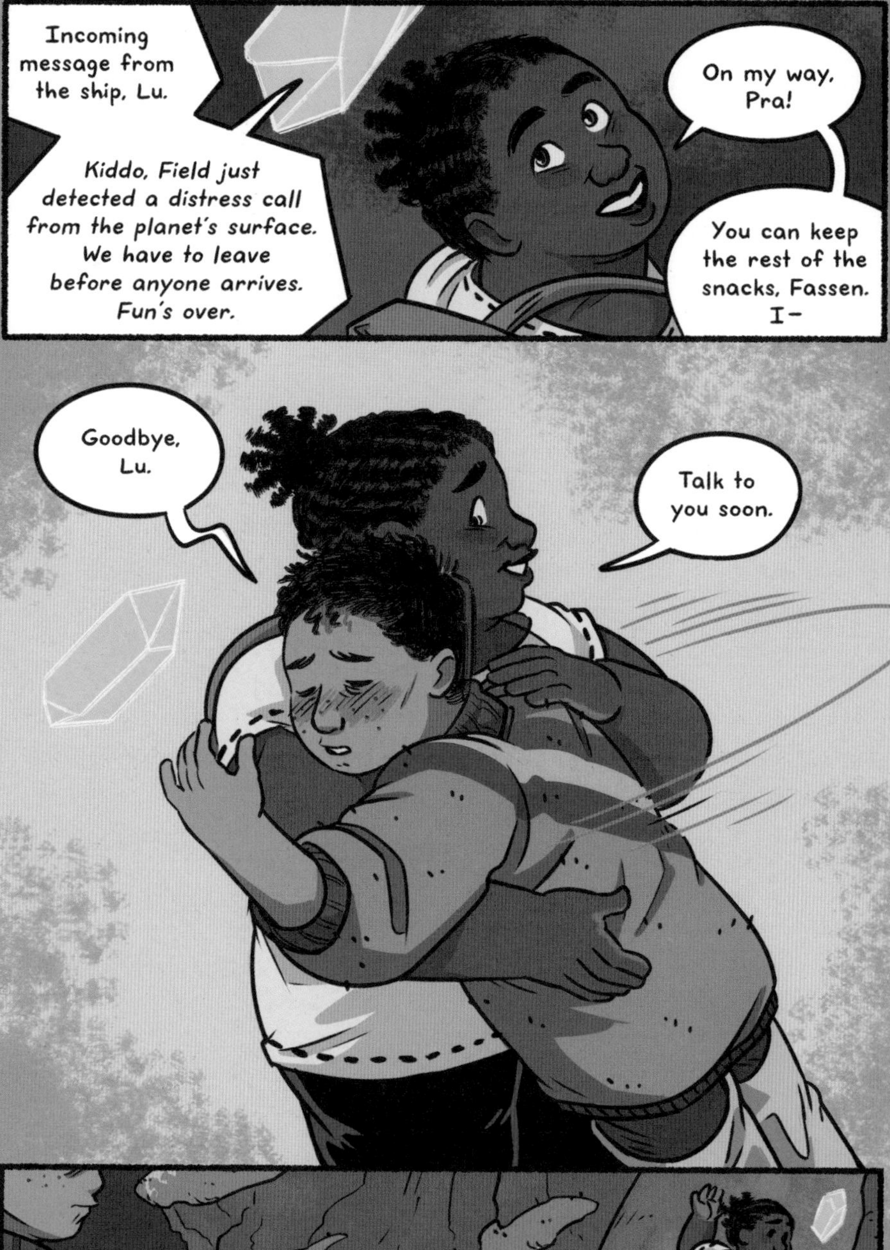
Incoming message from the ship, Lu.
Kiddo, Field just detected a distress call from the planet's surface. We have to leave before anyone arrives. Fun's over.
On my way, Pra!
You can keep the rest of the snacks, Fassen. I—
Goodbye, Lu.
Talk to you soon.

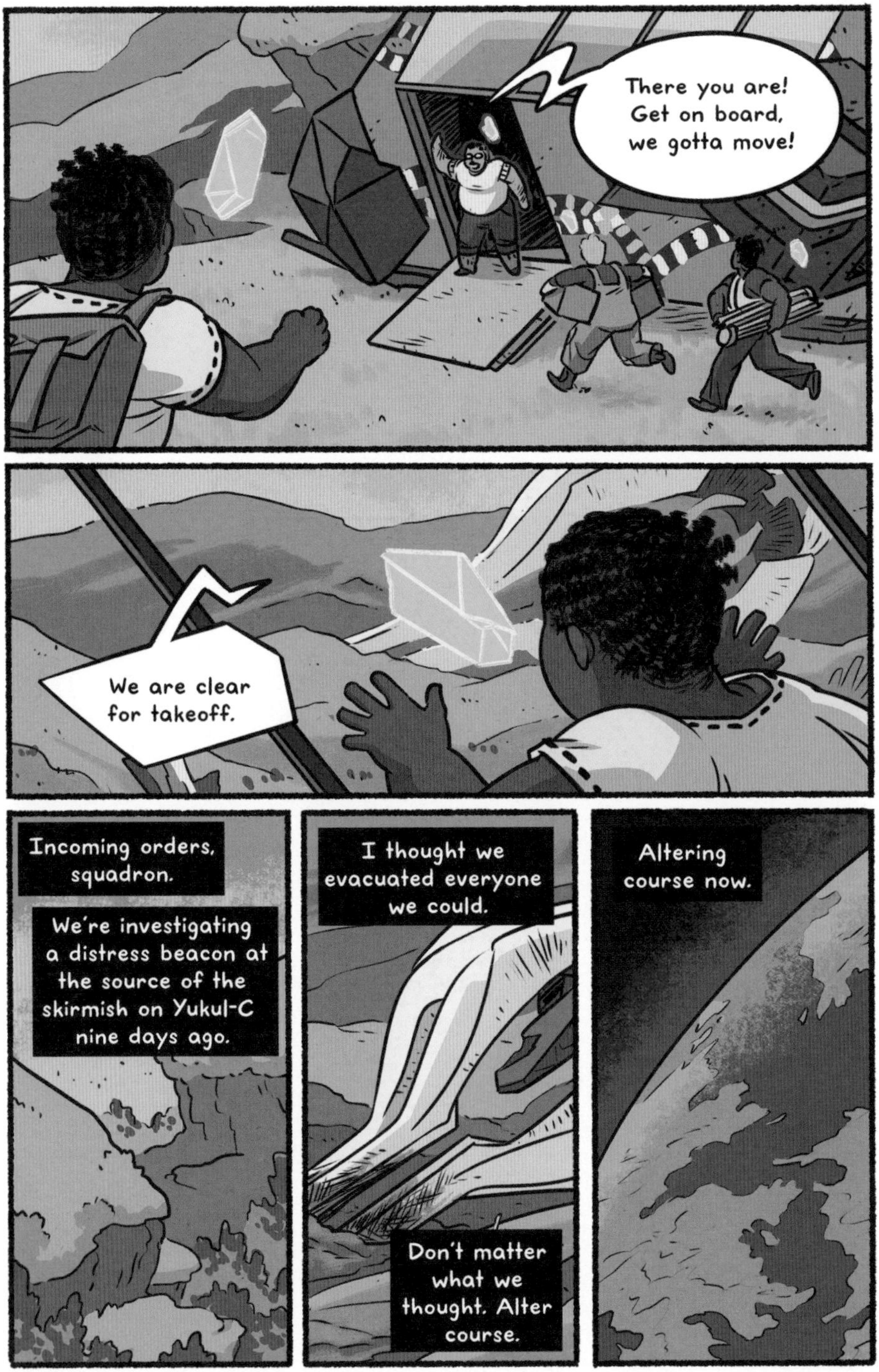
There you are! Get on board, we gotta move!
We are clear for takeoff.
Incoming orders, squadron.
We're investigating a distress beacon at the source of the skirmish on Yukul-C nine days ago.
I thought we evacuated everyone we could.
Don't matter what we thought. Alter course.
Altering course now.

Across a Field of Starlight

Blue Delliquanti

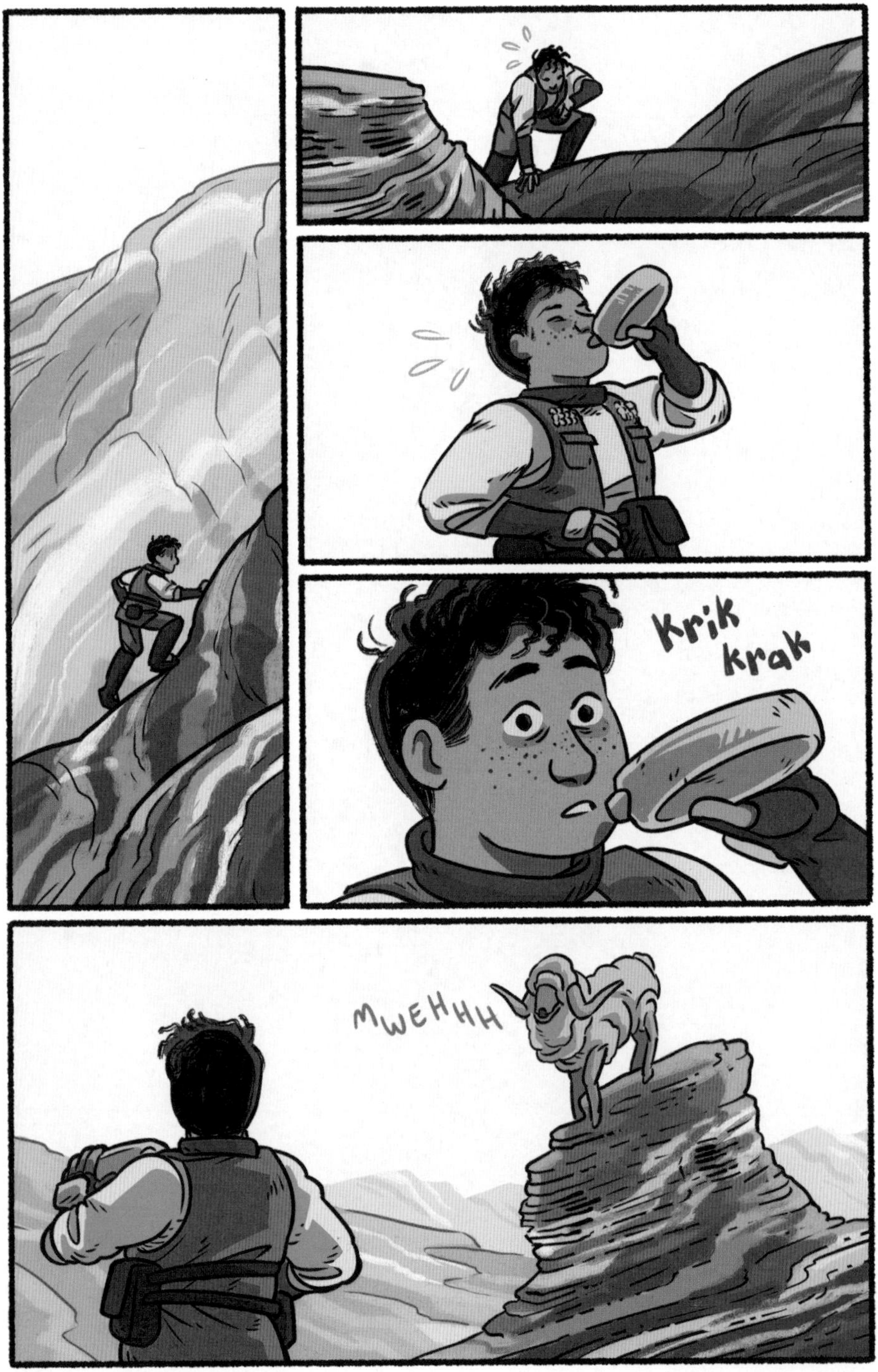
Krik
krak
MWEHHH

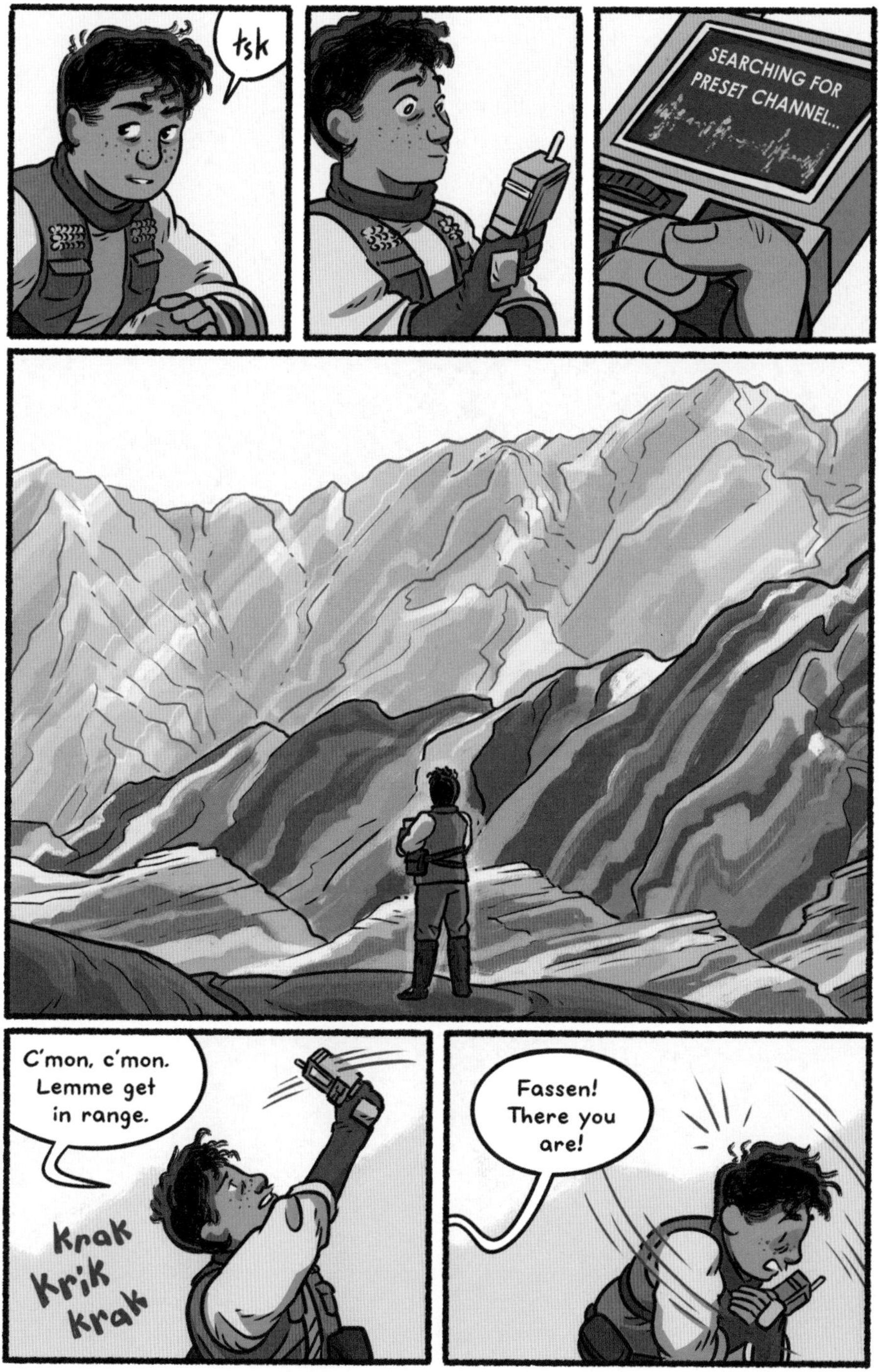
tsk
SEARCHING FOR PRESET CHANNEL...
C'mon, c'mon. Lemme get in range.
krak krik krak
Fassen! There you are!

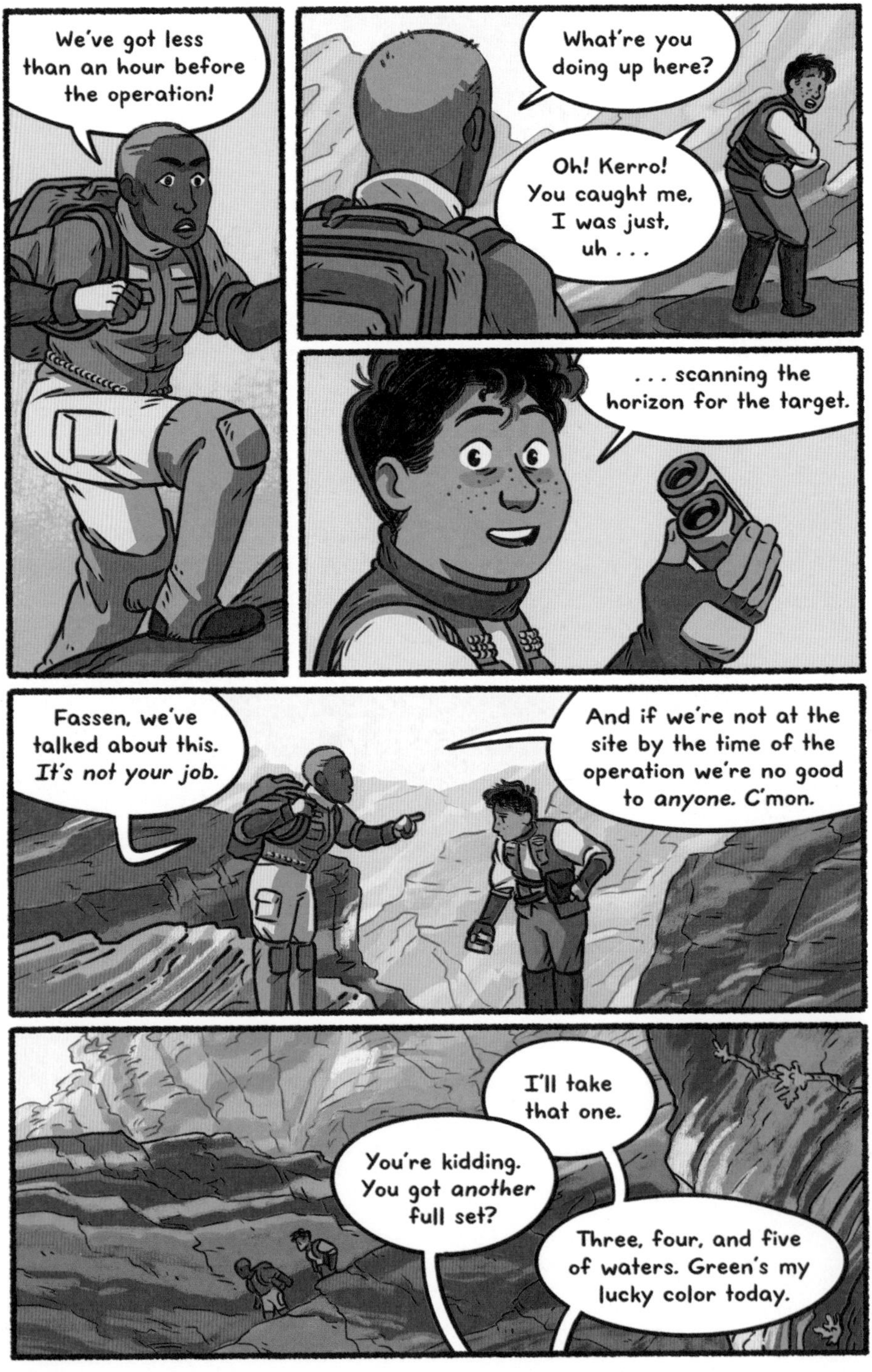
We've got less than an hour before the operation!
What're you doing up here?
Oh! Kerro! You caught me, I was just, uh . . .
. . . scanning the horizon for the target.
Fassen, we've talked about this. *It's not your job.*
And if we're not at the site by the time of the operation we're no good to *anyone*. C'mon.
I'll take that one.
You're kidding. You got *another* full set?
Three, four, and five of waters. Green's my lucky color today.

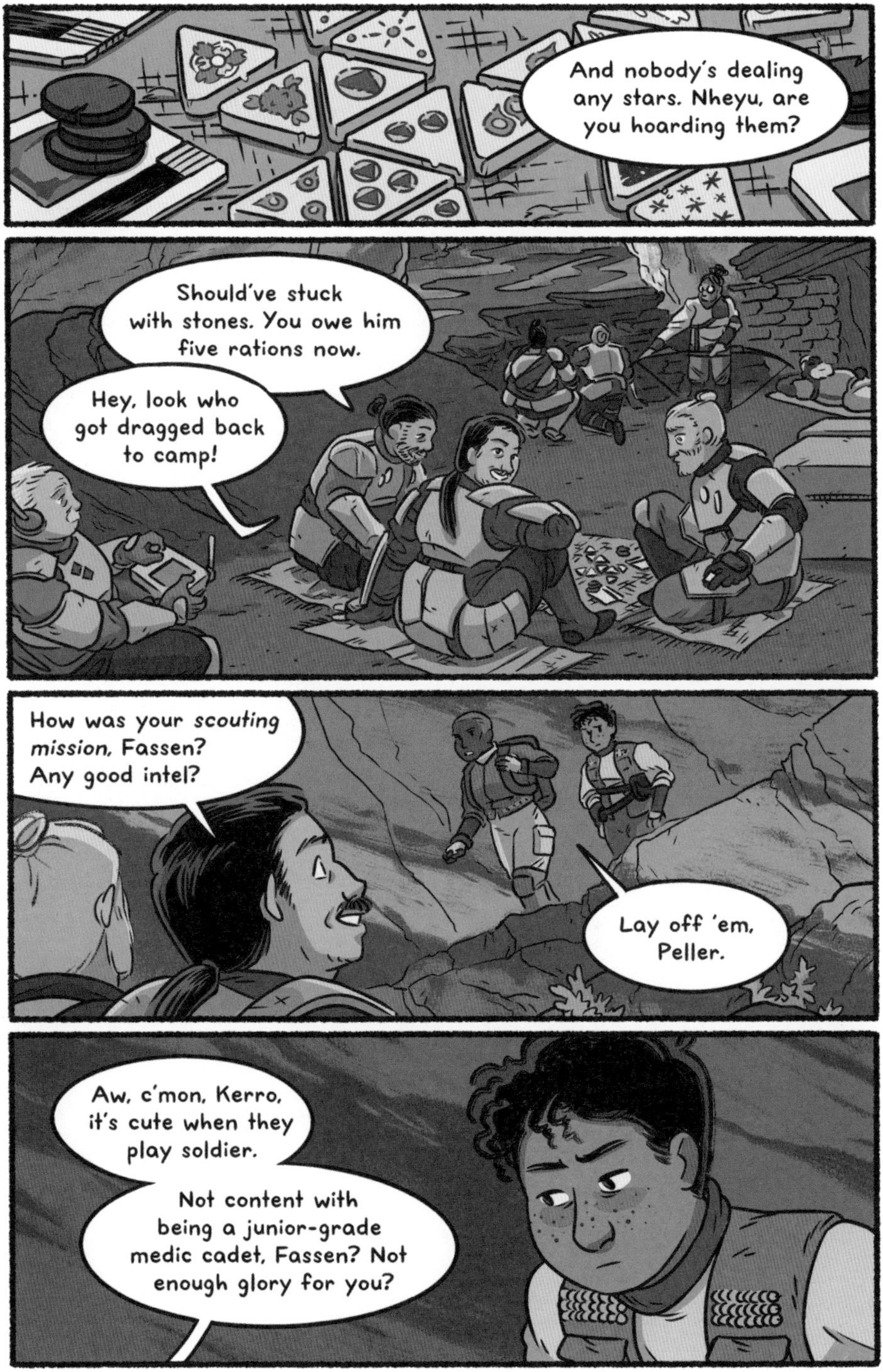
And nobody's dealing any stars. Nheyu, are you hoarding them?
Should've stuck with stones. You owe him five rations now.
Hey, look who got dragged back to camp!
How was your *scouting mission,* Fassen? Any good intel?
Lay off 'em, Peller.
Aw, c'mon, Kerro, it's cute when they play soldier.
Not content with being a junior-grade medic cadet, Fassen? Not enough glory for you?

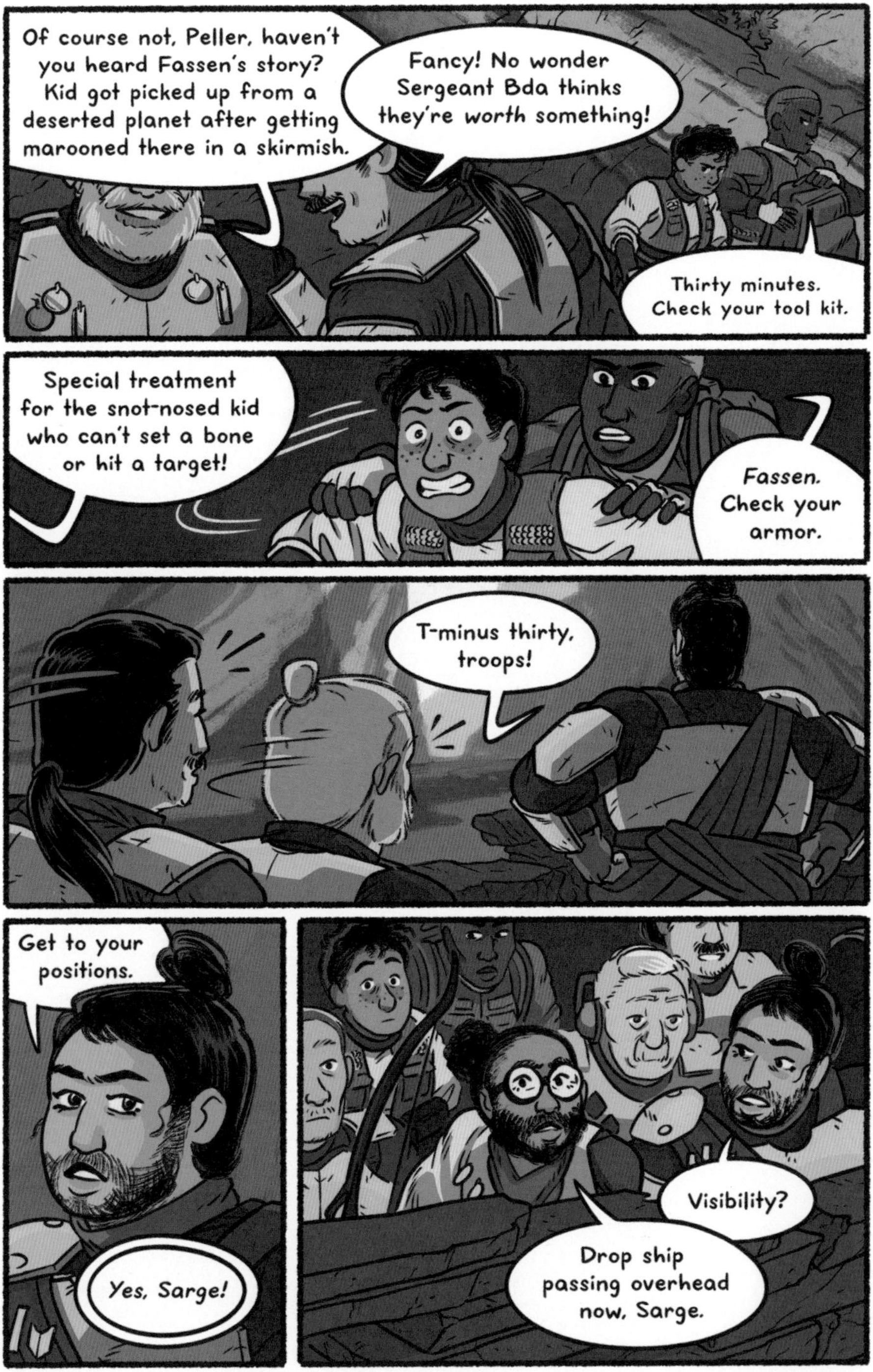
Of course not, Peller, haven't you heard Fassen's story? Kid got picked up from a deserted planet after getting marooned there in a skirmish.
Fancy! No wonder Sergeant Bda thinks they're *worth* something!
Thirty minutes. Check your tool kit.
Special treatment for the snot-nosed kid who can't set a bone or hit a target!
Fassen. Check your armor.
T-minus thirty, troops!
Get to your positions.
Yes, Sarge!
Visibility?
Drop ship passing overhead now, Sarge.

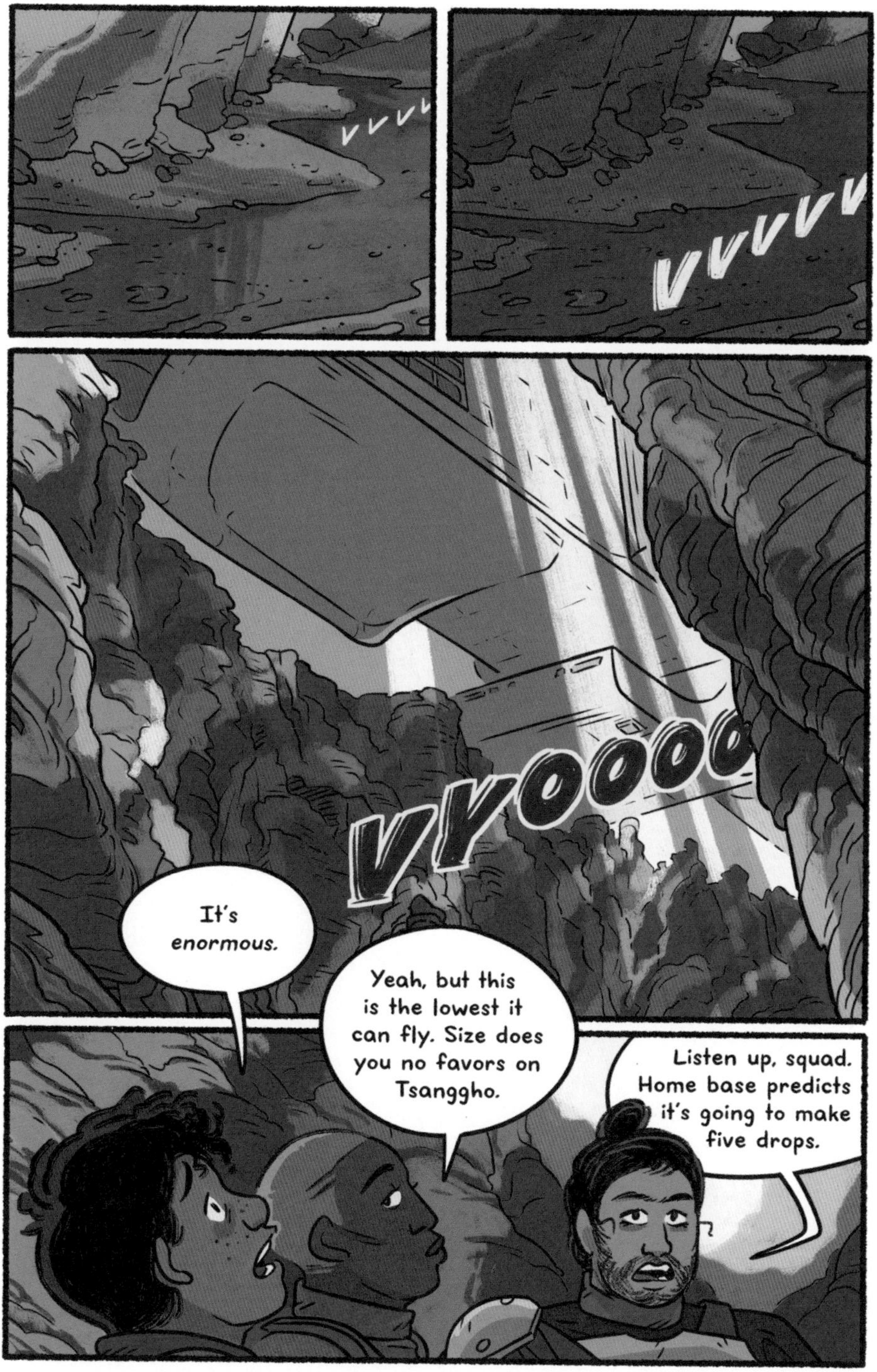
VVVV
VVVVV
VVVVV
VYOOOO
It's enormous.
Yeah, but this is the lowest it can fly. Size does you no favors on Tsanggho.
Listen up, squad. Home base predicts it's going to make five drops.

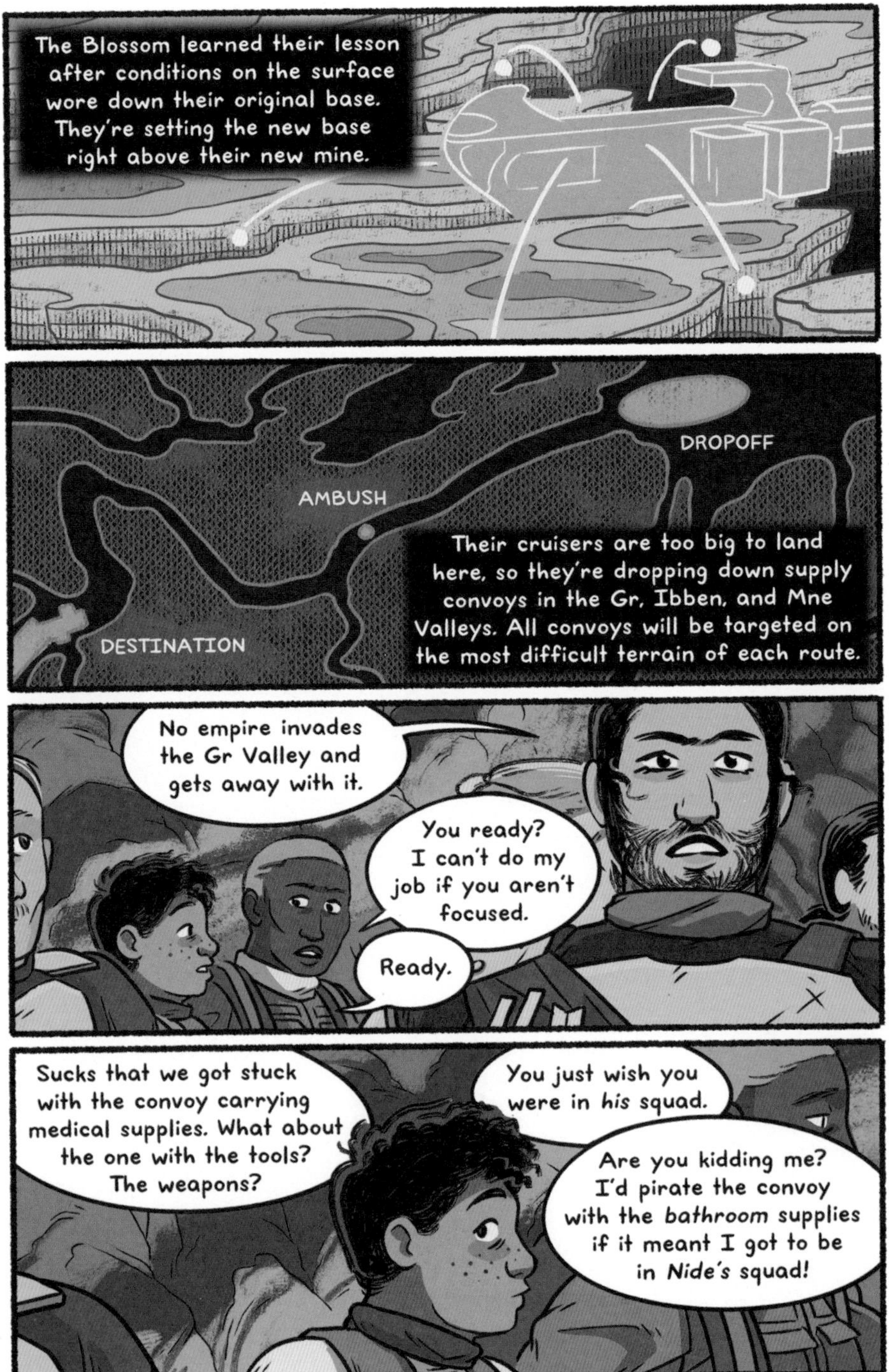
The Blossom learned their lesson after conditions on the surface wore down their original base. They're setting the new base right above their new mine.
DROPOFF
AMBUSH
DESTINATION
Their cruisers are too big to land here, so they're dropping down supply convoys in the Gr, Ibben, and Mne Valleys. All convoys will be targeted on the most difficult terrain of each route.
No empire invades the Gr Valley and gets away with it.
You ready? I can't do my job if you aren't focused.
Ready.
Sucks that we got stuck with the convoy carrying medical supplies. What about the one with the tools? The weapons?
You just wish you were in *his* squad.
Are you kidding me? I'd pirate the convoy with the *bathroom* supplies if it meant I got to be in *Nide's* squad!

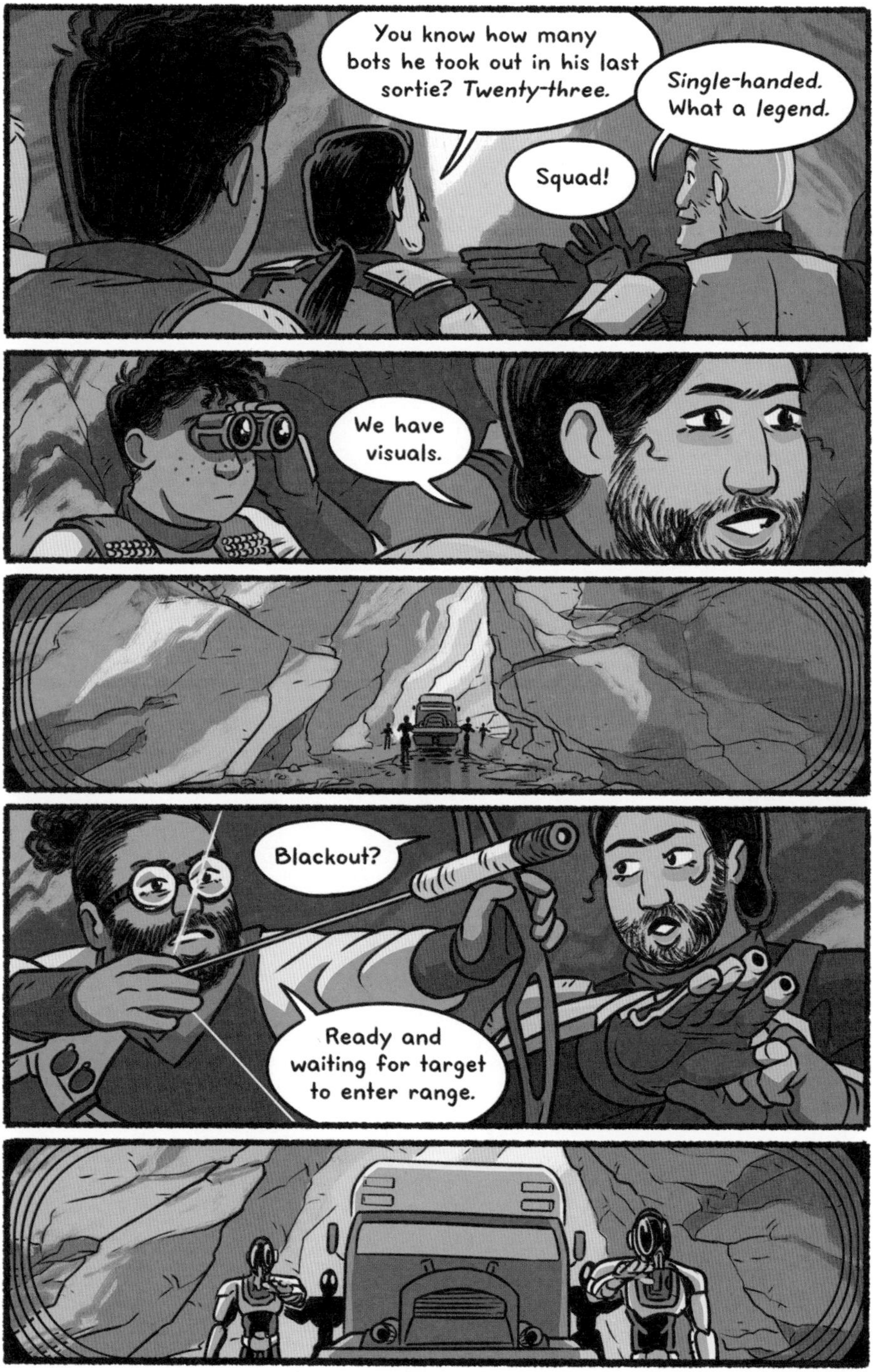
You know how many bots he took out in his last sortie? *Twenty-three.*
Single-handed. What a *legend.*
Squad!
We have visuals.
Blackout?
Ready and waiting for target to enter range.

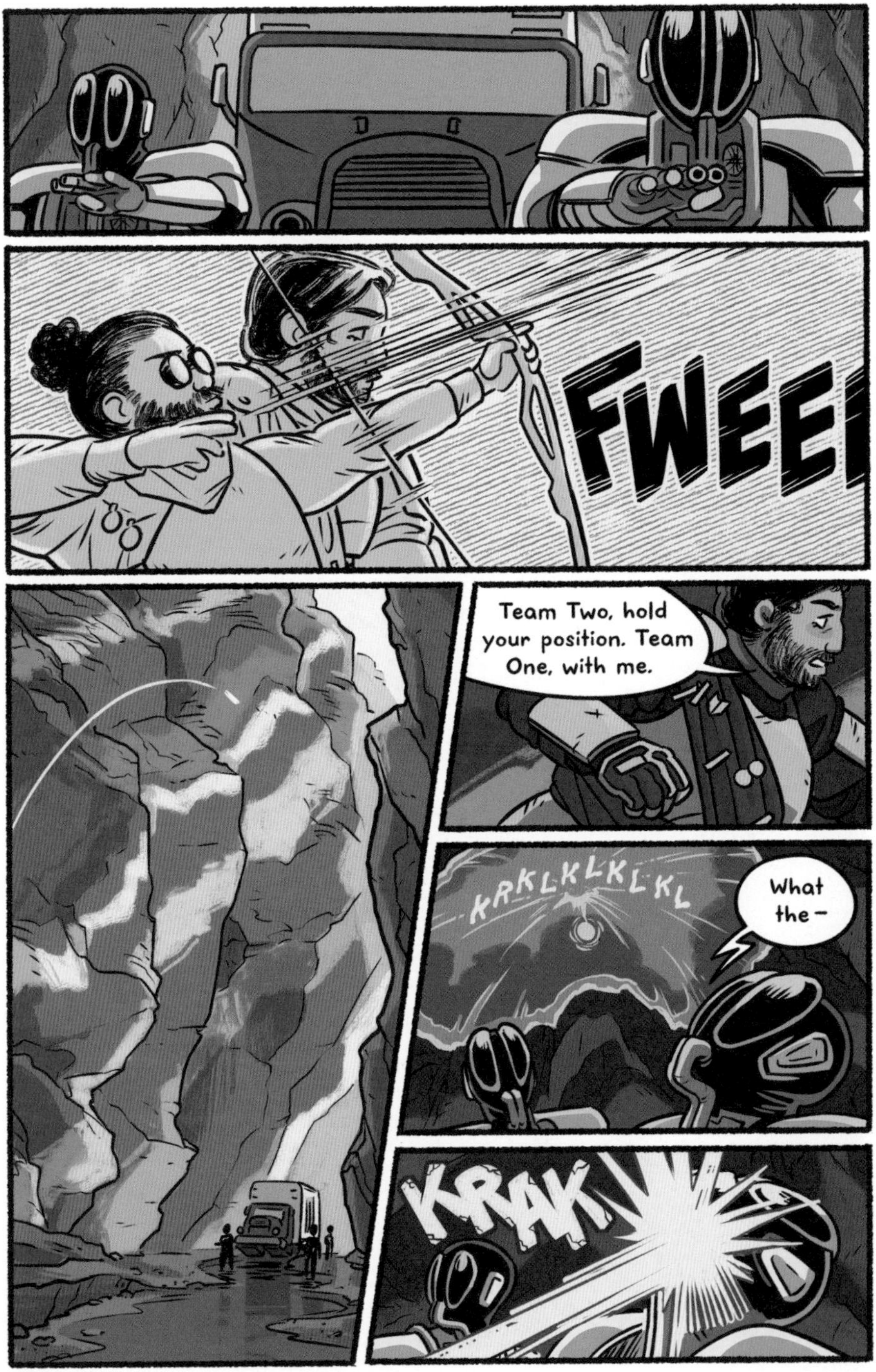
FWEE
Team Two, hold your position. Team One, with me.
KRKLKLKLKL
What the-
KRAK

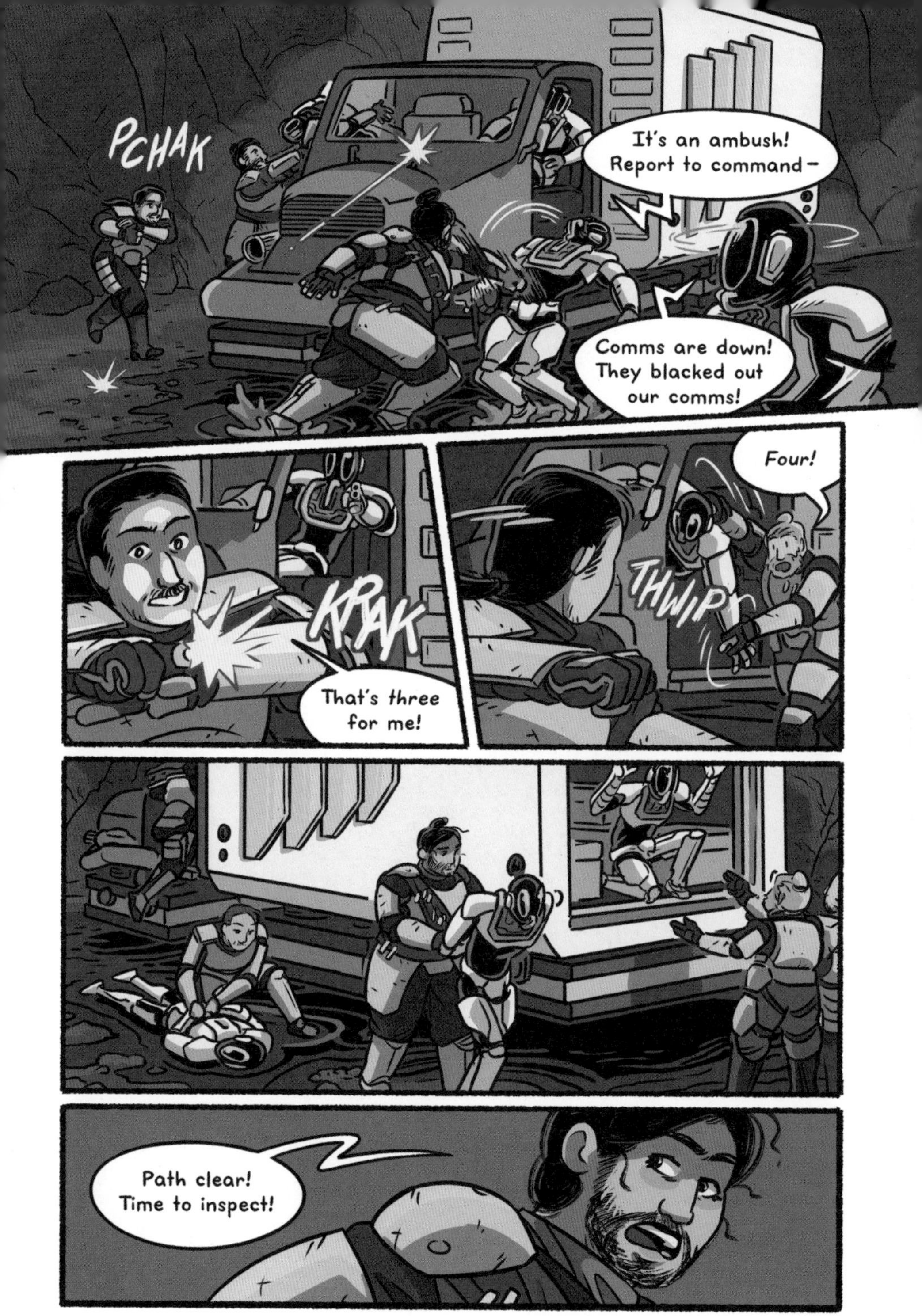
PCHAK
It's an ambush! Report to command—
Comms are down! They blacked out our comms!
KRAK
That's three for me!
THWIP
Four!
Path clear! Time to inspect!

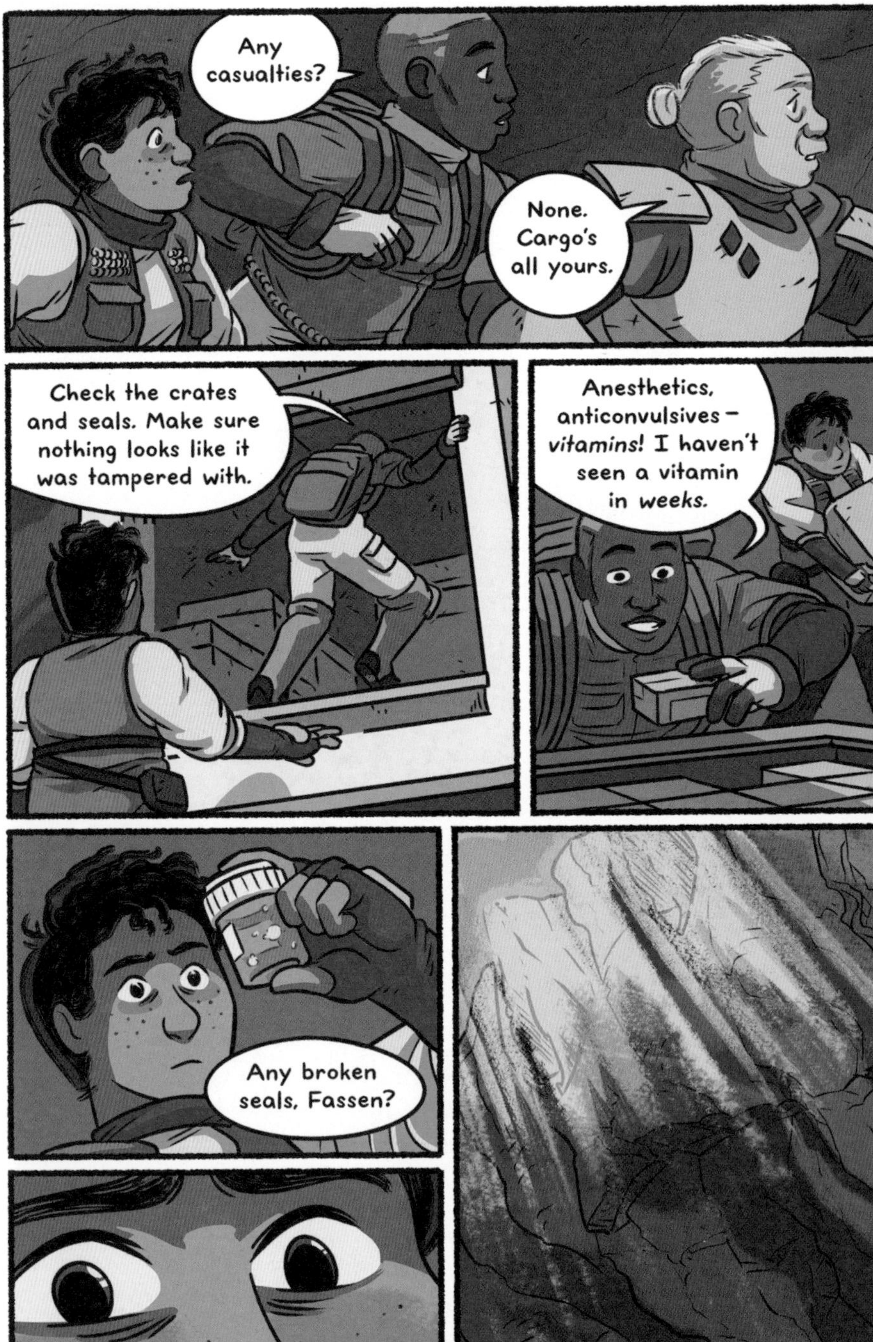
Any casualties?
None. Cargo's all yours.
Check the crates and seals. Make sure nothing looks like it was tampered with.
Anesthetics, anticonvulsives – *vitamins*! I haven't seen a vitamin in *weeks*.
Any broken seals, Fassen?

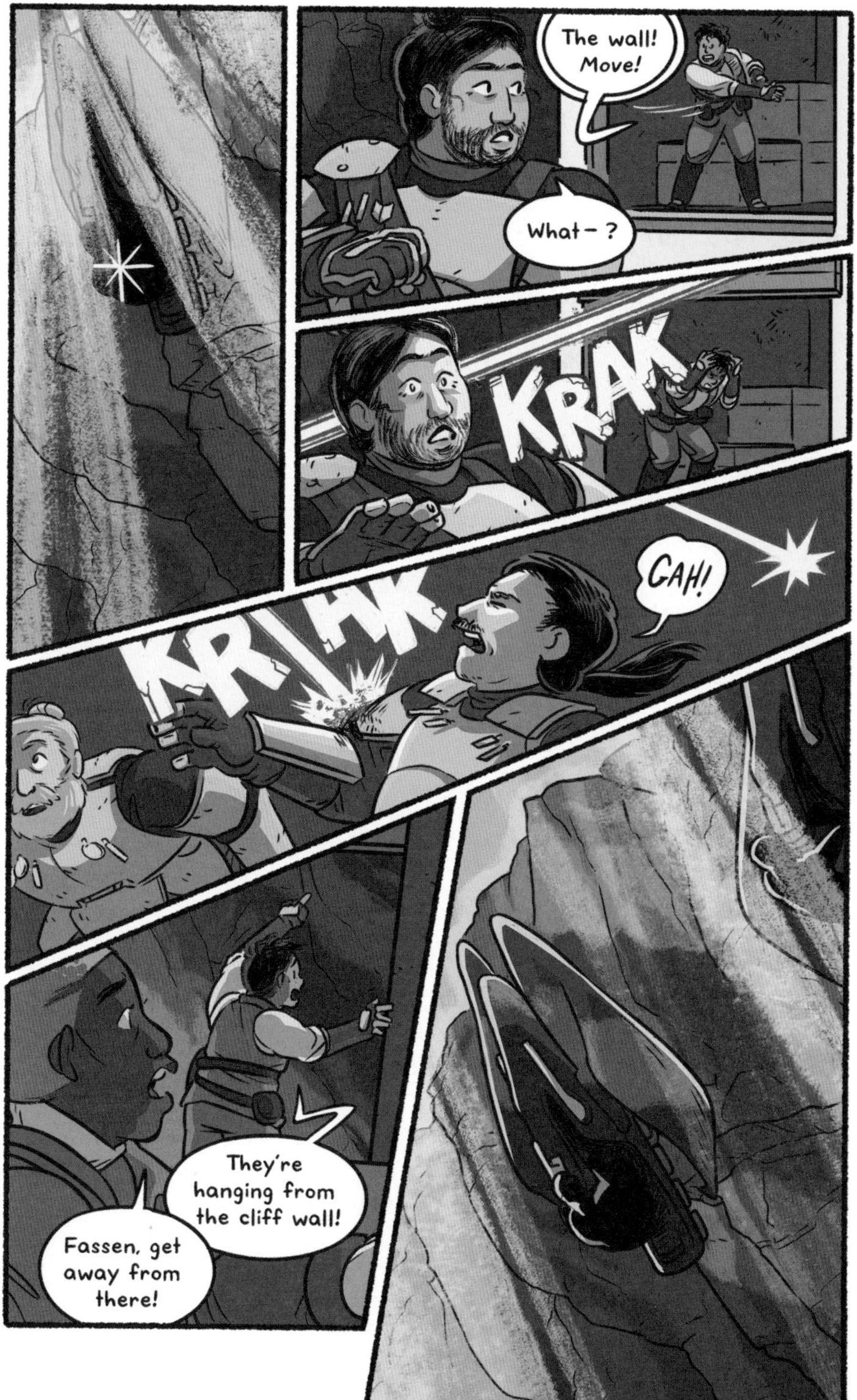
The wall! Move!
What-?
KRAK
CAH!
KRIAK
They're hanging from the cliff wall!
Fassen, get away from there!

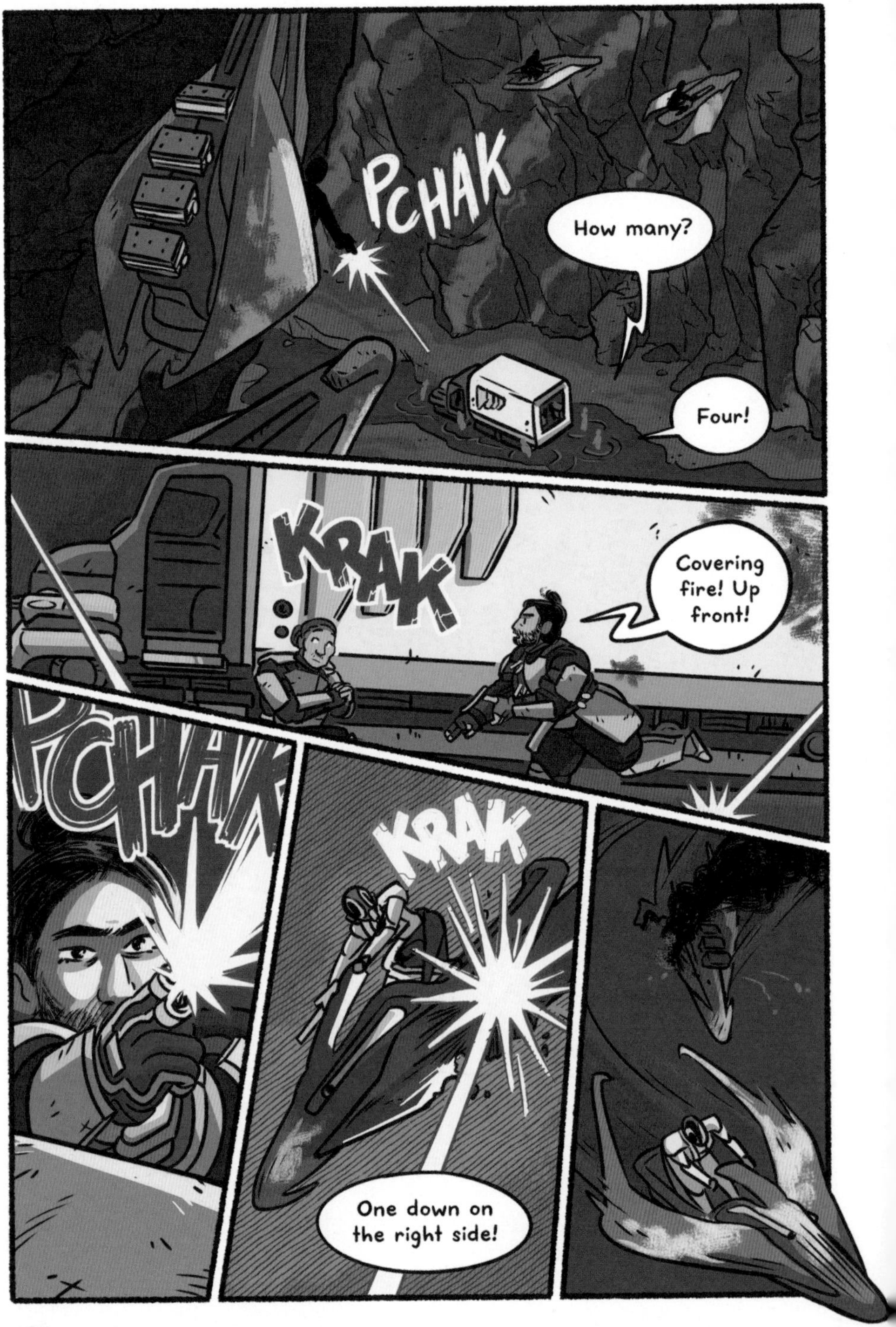
PCHAK
How many?
Four!
KRAK
Covering fire! Up front!
PCHAK
KRAK
One down on the right side!

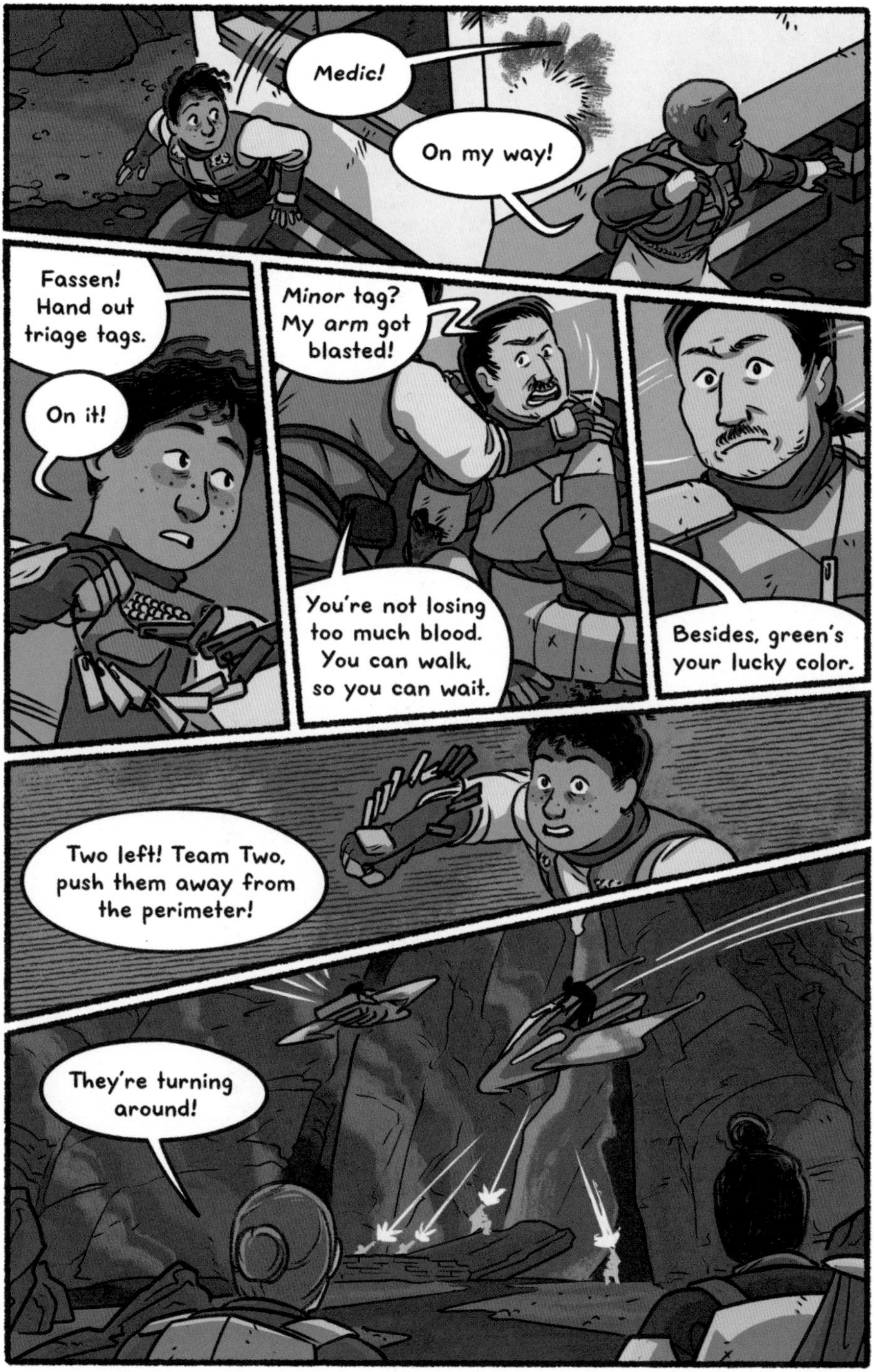
Medic!
On my way!
Fassen! Hand out triage tags.
On it!
Minor tag? My arm got blasted!
You're not losing too much blood. You can walk, so you can wait.
Besides, green's your lucky color.
Two left! Team Two, push them away from the perimeter!
They're turning around!

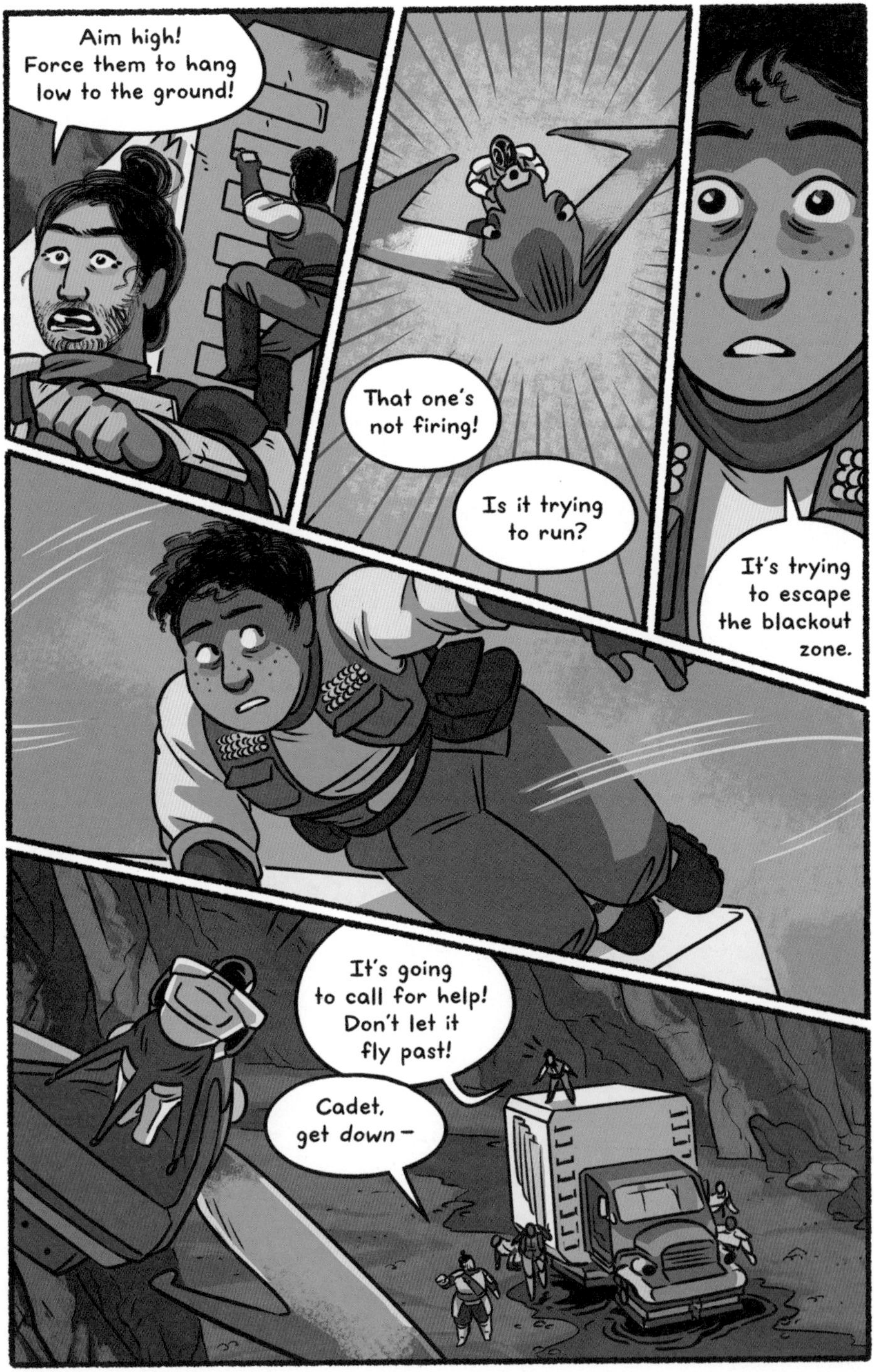
Aim high! Force them to hang low to the ground!
That one's not firing!
Is it trying to run?
It's trying to escape the blackout zone.
It's going to call for help! Don't let it fly past!
Cadet, get down—

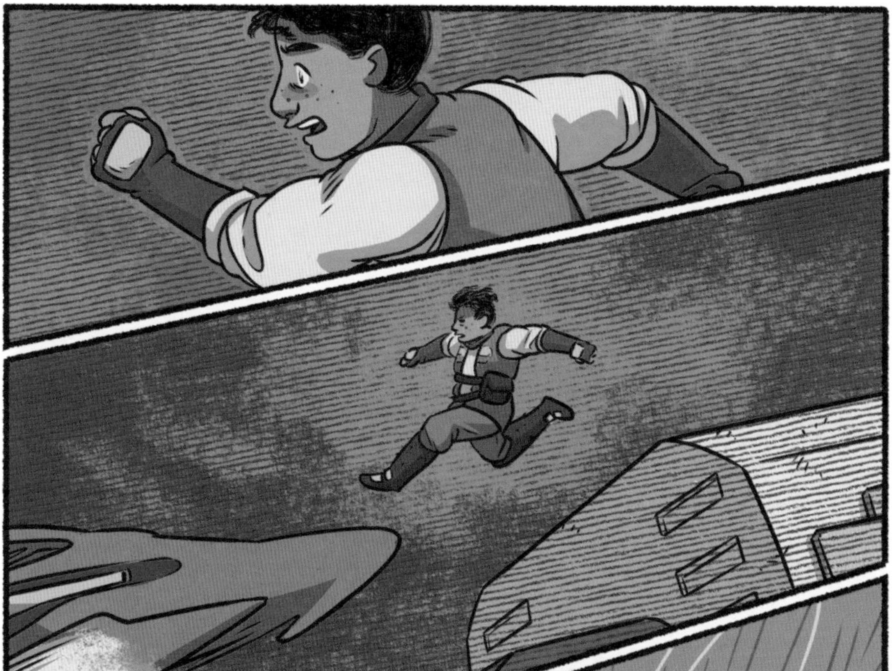
KTHUNK
The hell?

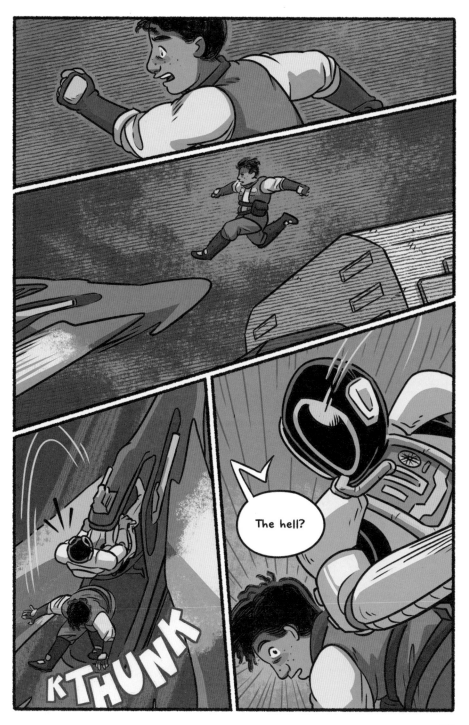

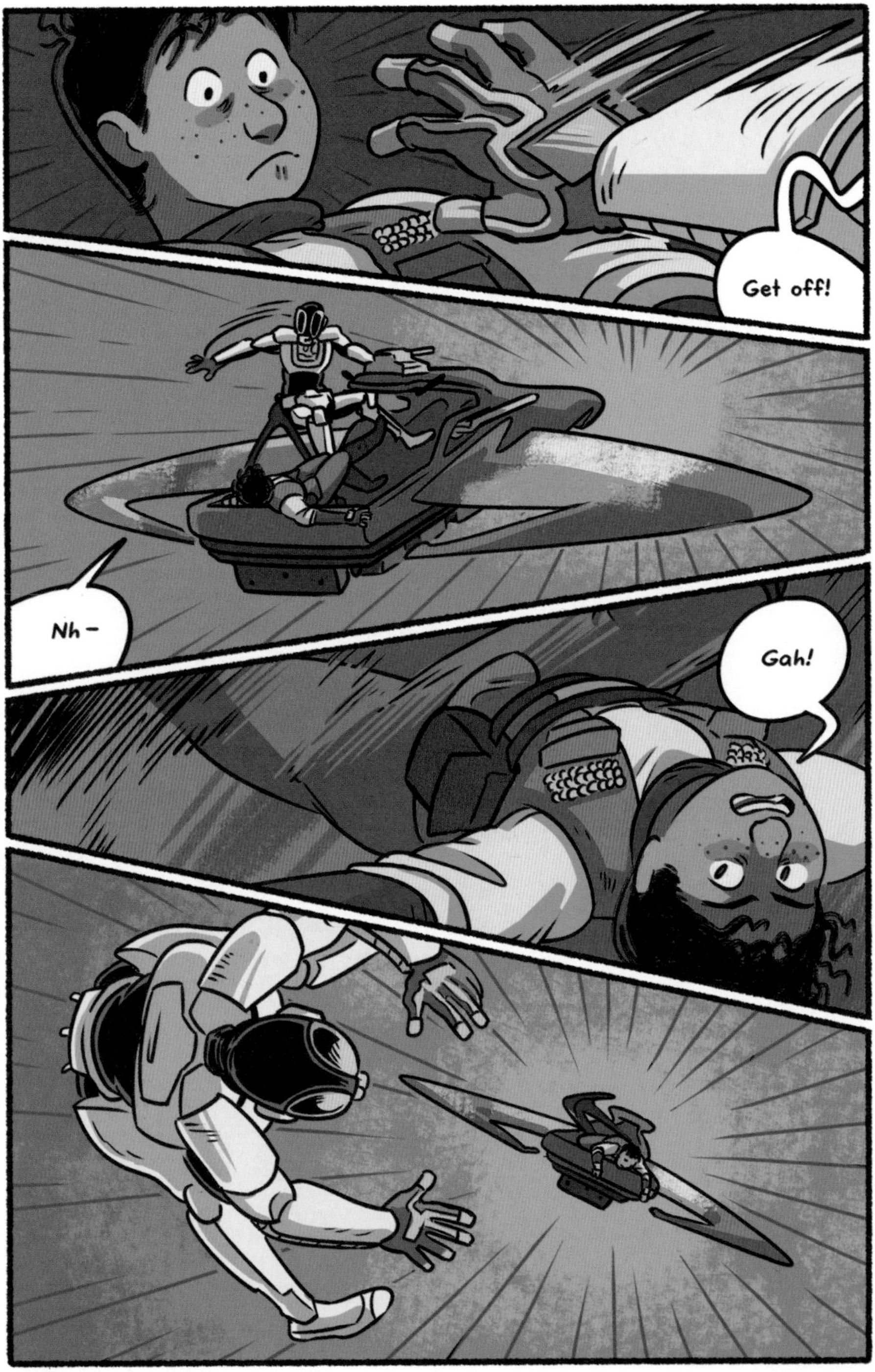
Get off!
Nh-
Gah!

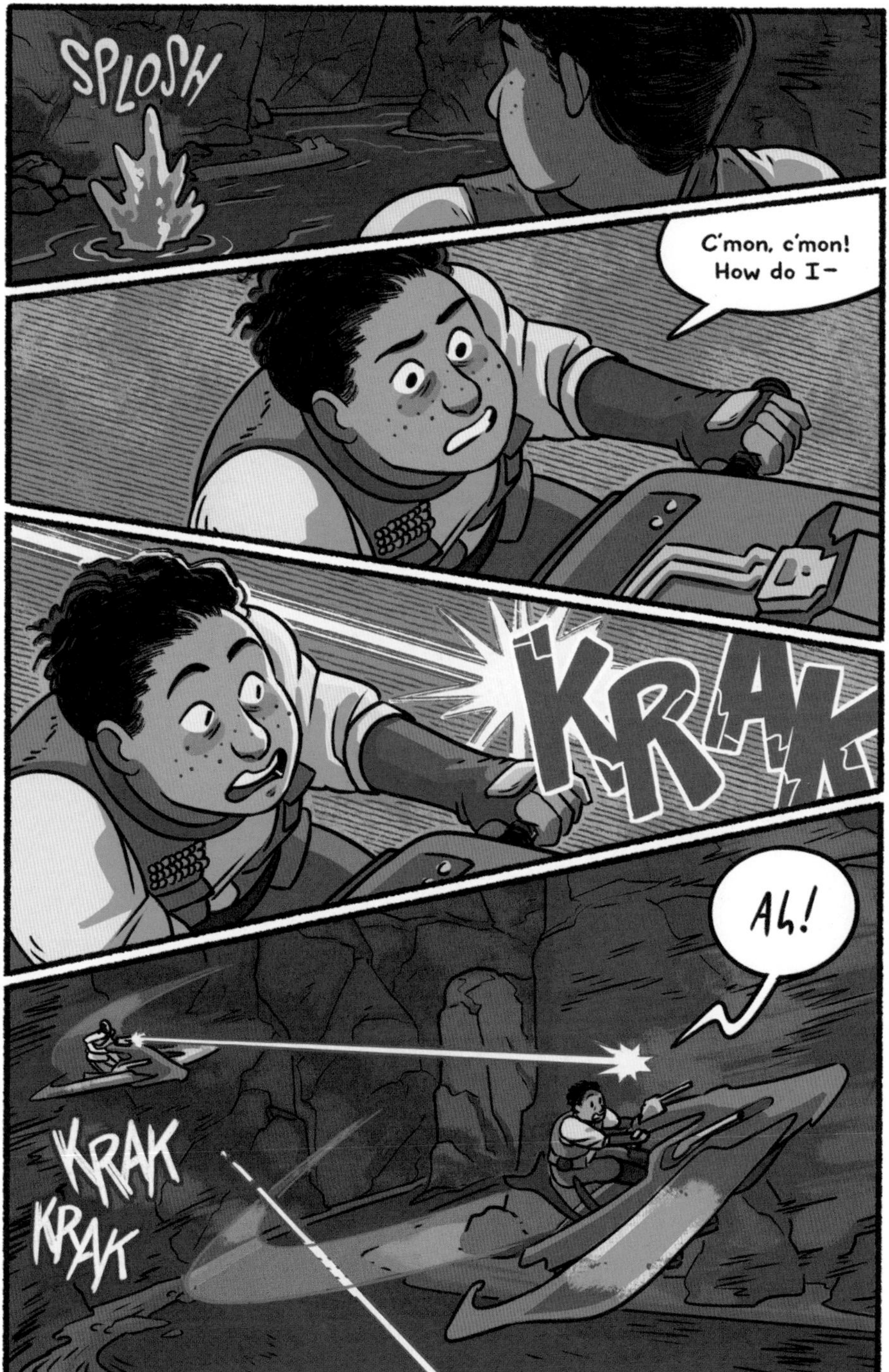
SPLOSH
C'mon, c'mon!
How do I—
KRAK
Ah!
KRAK
KRAK

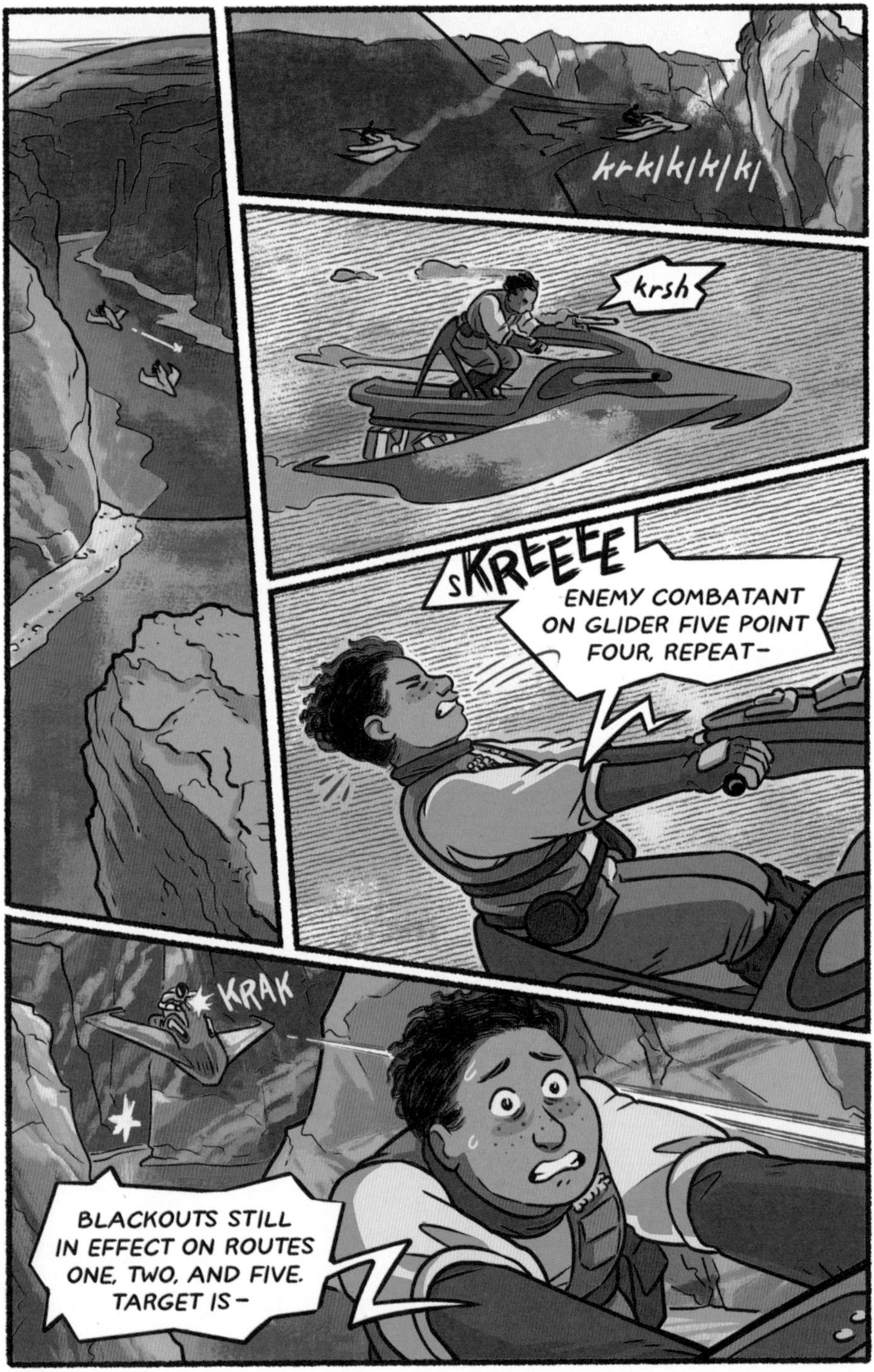
krkkkkkkk
krsh
sKREEEEE
ENEMY COMBATANT ON GLIDER FIVE POINT FOUR, REPEAT—
KRAK
BLACKOUTS STILL IN EFFECT ON ROUTES ONE, TWO, AND FIVE. TARGET IS—

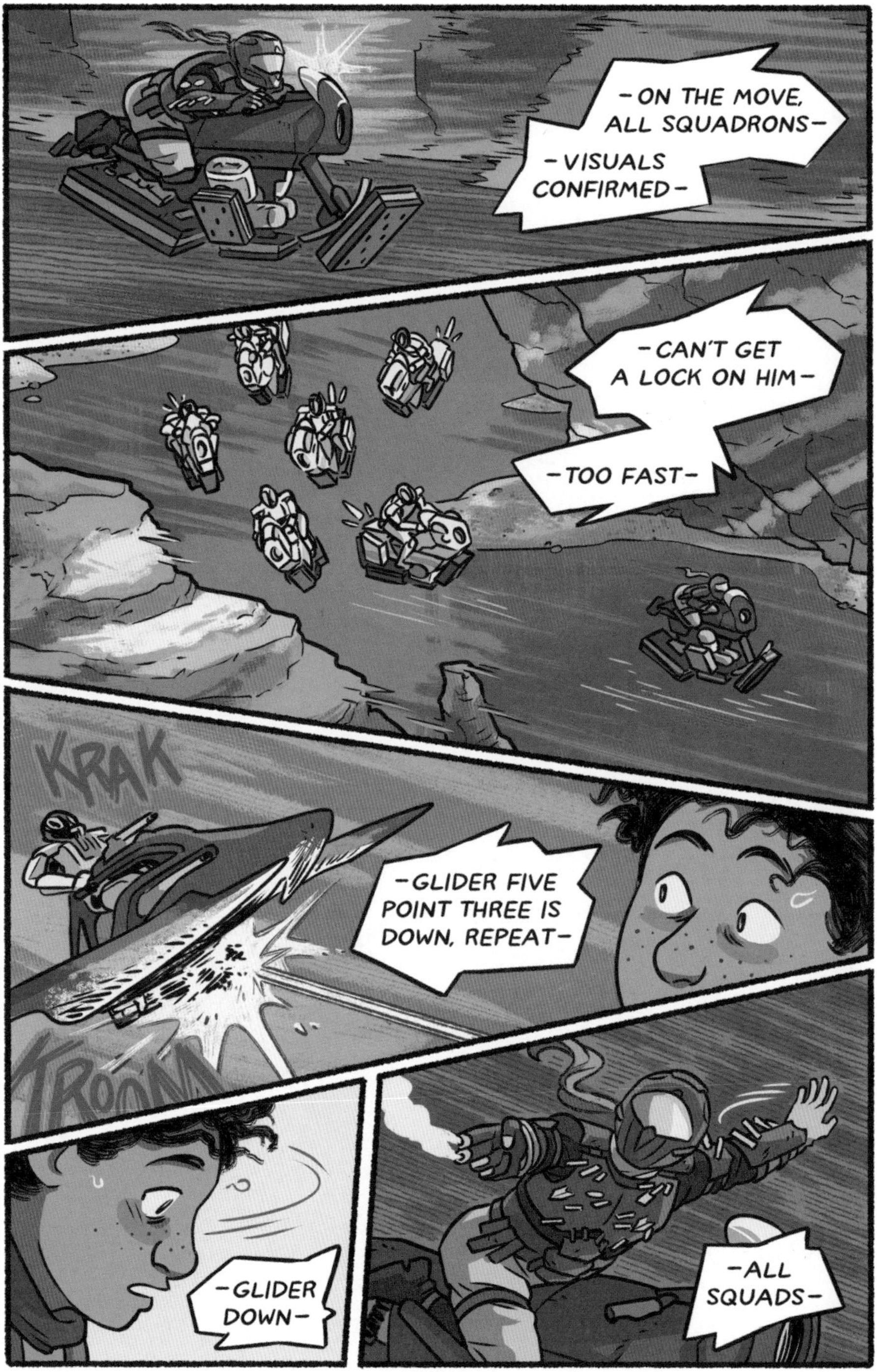
-ON THE MOVE, ALL SQUADRONS-
-VISUALS CONFIRMED-
-CAN'T GET A LOCK ON HIM-
-TOO FAST-
KRAK
-GLIDER FIVE POINT THREE IS DOWN, REPEAT-
KROOM
-GLIDER DOWN-
-ALL SQUADS-

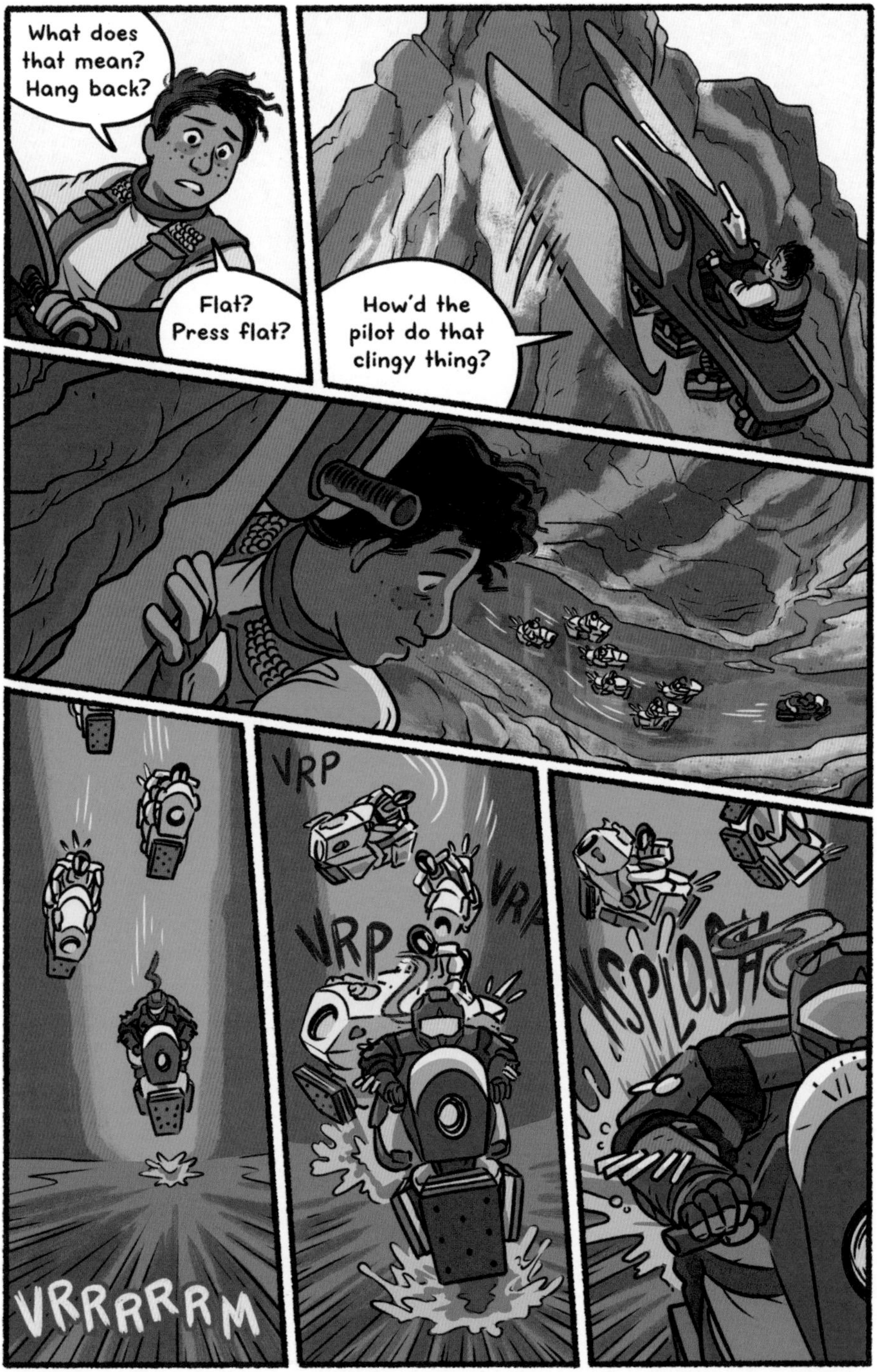

What does that mean? Hang back?
Flat? Press flat?
How'd the pilot do that clingy thing?
VRRRRRM
VRP
VRP
VRP
SPLOOSH

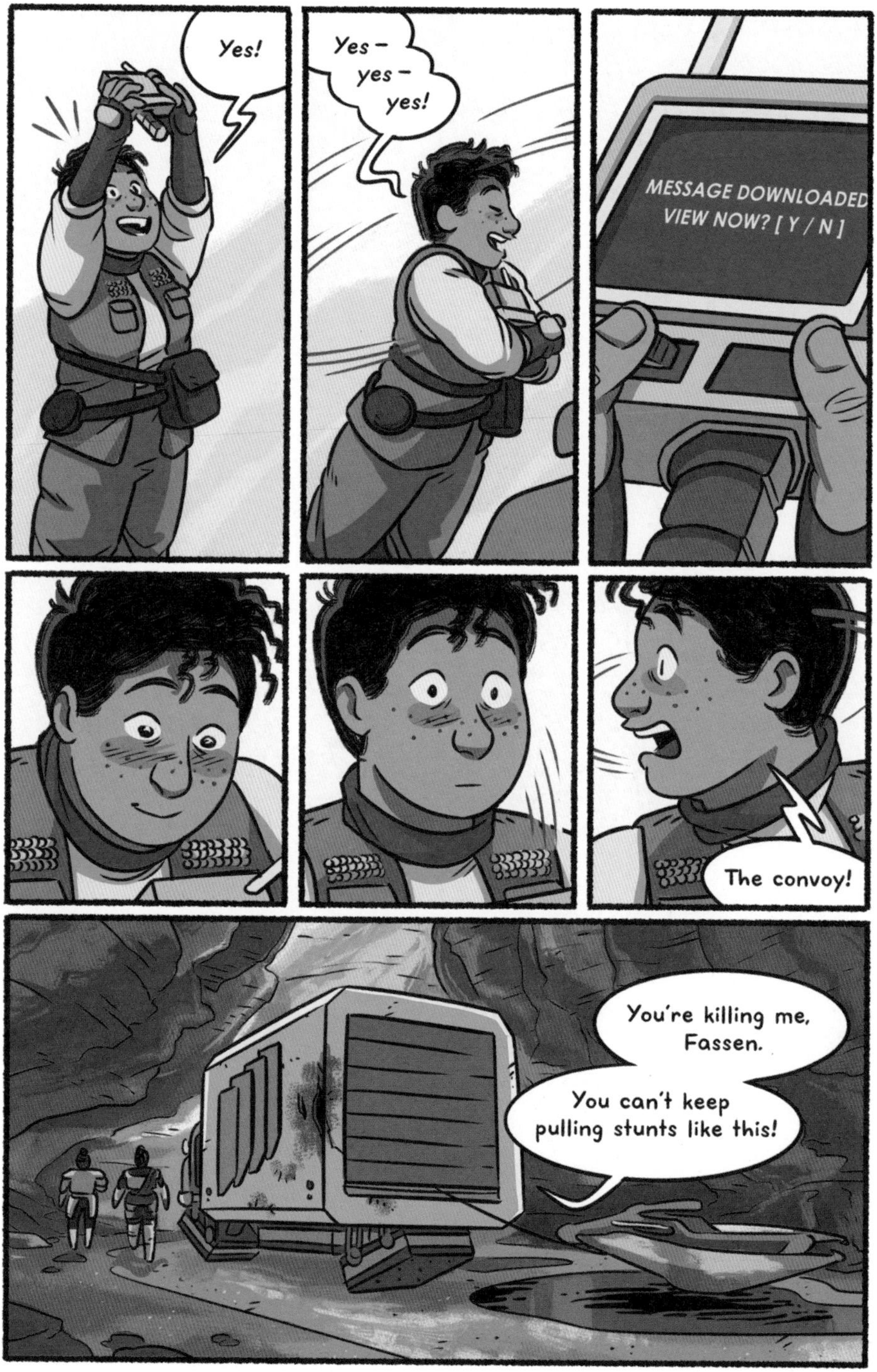
Yes!
Yes – yes – yes!
MESSAGE DOWNLOADED
VIEW NOW? [Y / N]
The convoy!
You're killing me, Fassen.
You can't keep pulling stunts like this!

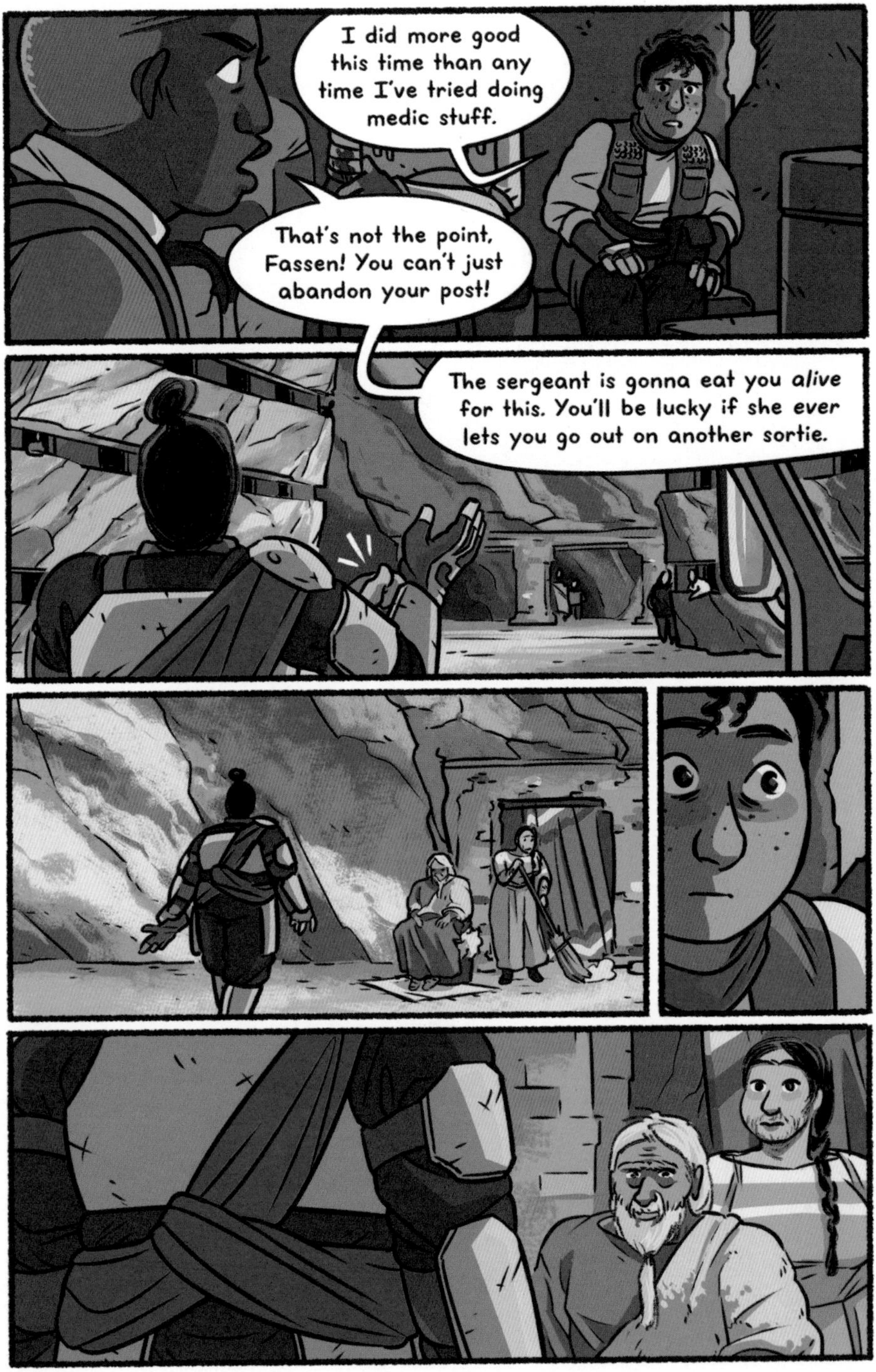
I did more good this time than any time I've tried doing medic stuff.
That's not the point, Fassen! You can't just abandon your post!
The sergeant is gonna eat you *alive* for this. You'll be lucky if she *ever* lets you go out on another sortie.

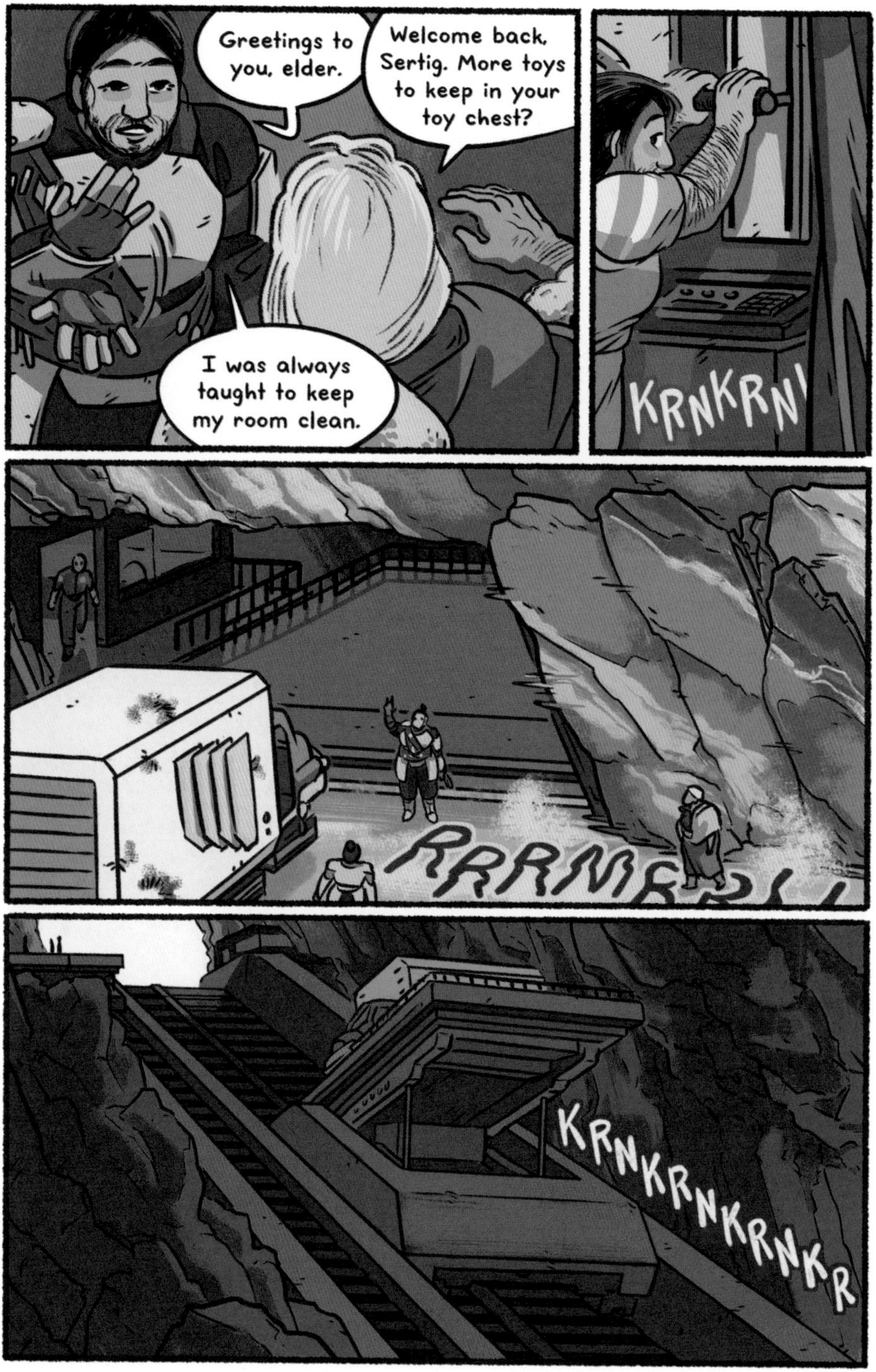
Greetings to you, elder.
Welcome back, Sertig. More toys to keep in your toy chest?
I was always taught to keep my room clean.
KRNKRN
RRRNRRRN
KRNKRNKRNKRNKR

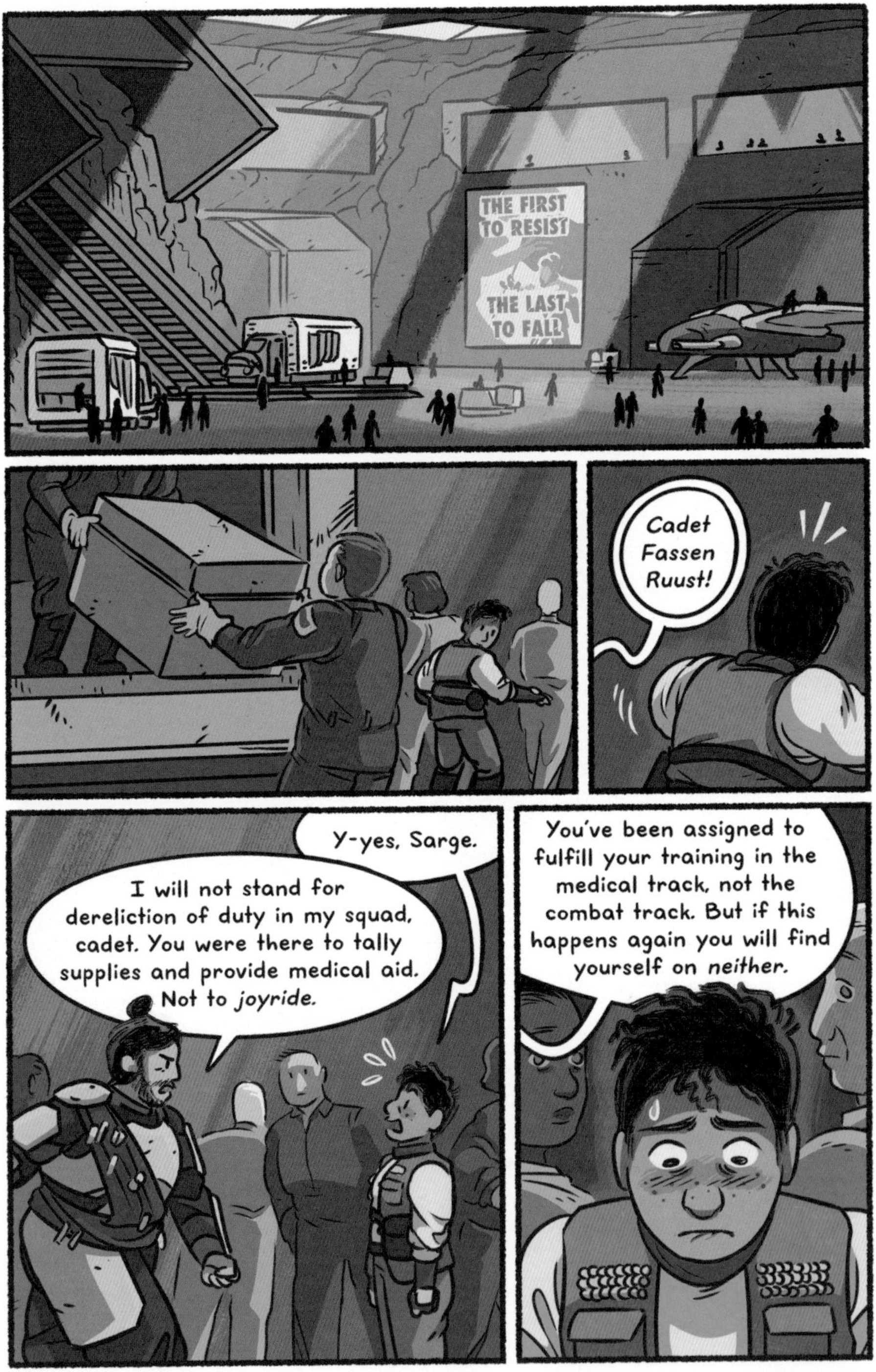
THE FIRST TO RESIST
THE LAST TO FALL
Cadet Fassen Ruust!
Y-yes, Sarge.
I will not stand for dereliction of duty in my squad, cadet. You were there to tally supplies and provide medical aid. Not to *joyride*.
You've been assigned to fulfill your training in the medical track, not the combat track. But if this happens again you will find yourself on *neither*.

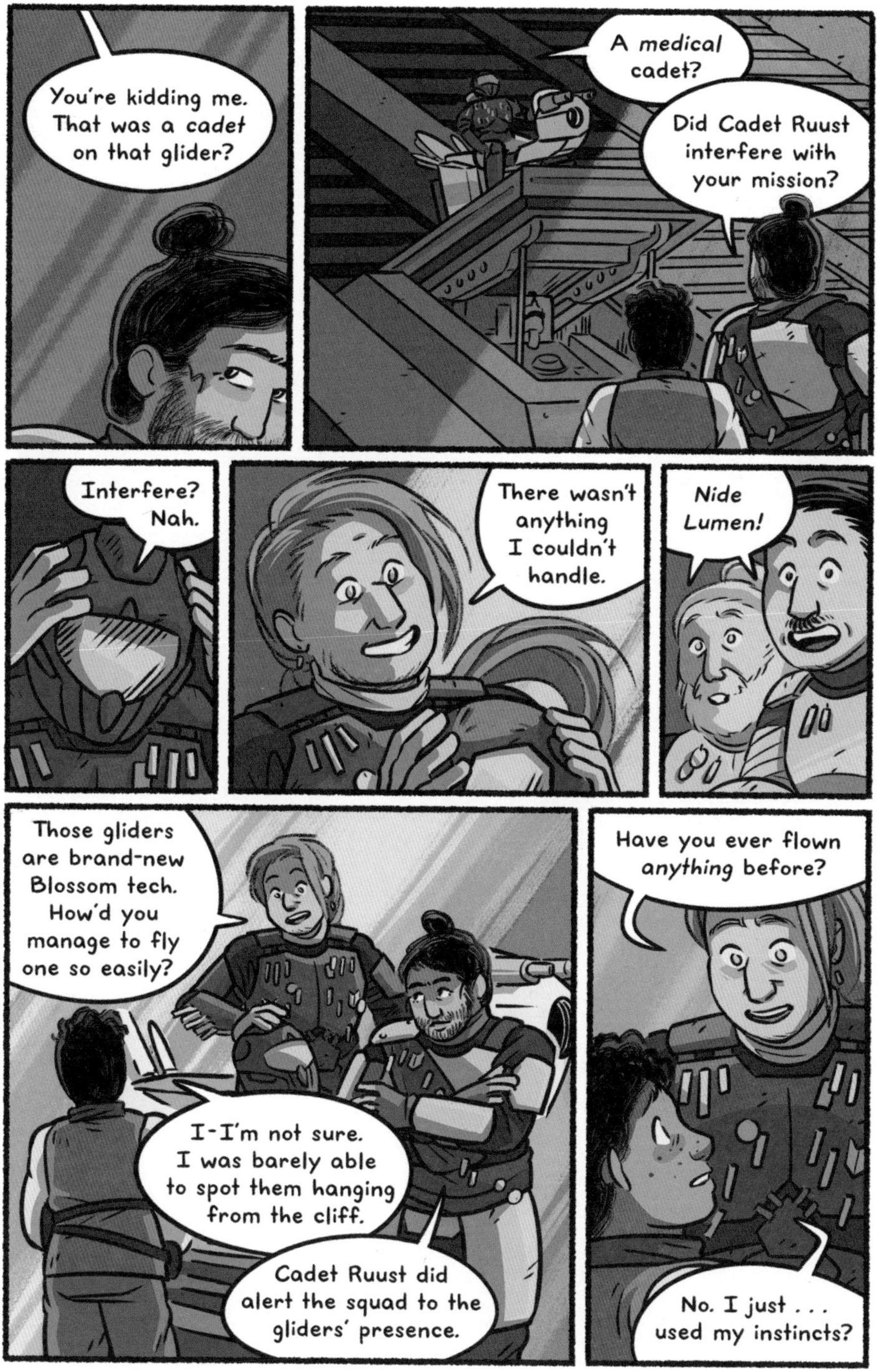
You're kidding me. That was a *cadet* on that glider?
A *medical* cadet?
Did Cadet Ruust interfere with your mission?
Interfere? Nah.
There wasn't anything I couldn't handle.
Nide Lumen!
Those gliders are brand-new Blossom tech. How'd you manage to fly one so easily?
I-I'm not sure. I was barely able to spot them hanging from the cliff.
Cadet Ruust did alert the squad to the gliders' presence.
Have you ever flown *anything* before?
No. I just . . . used my instincts?

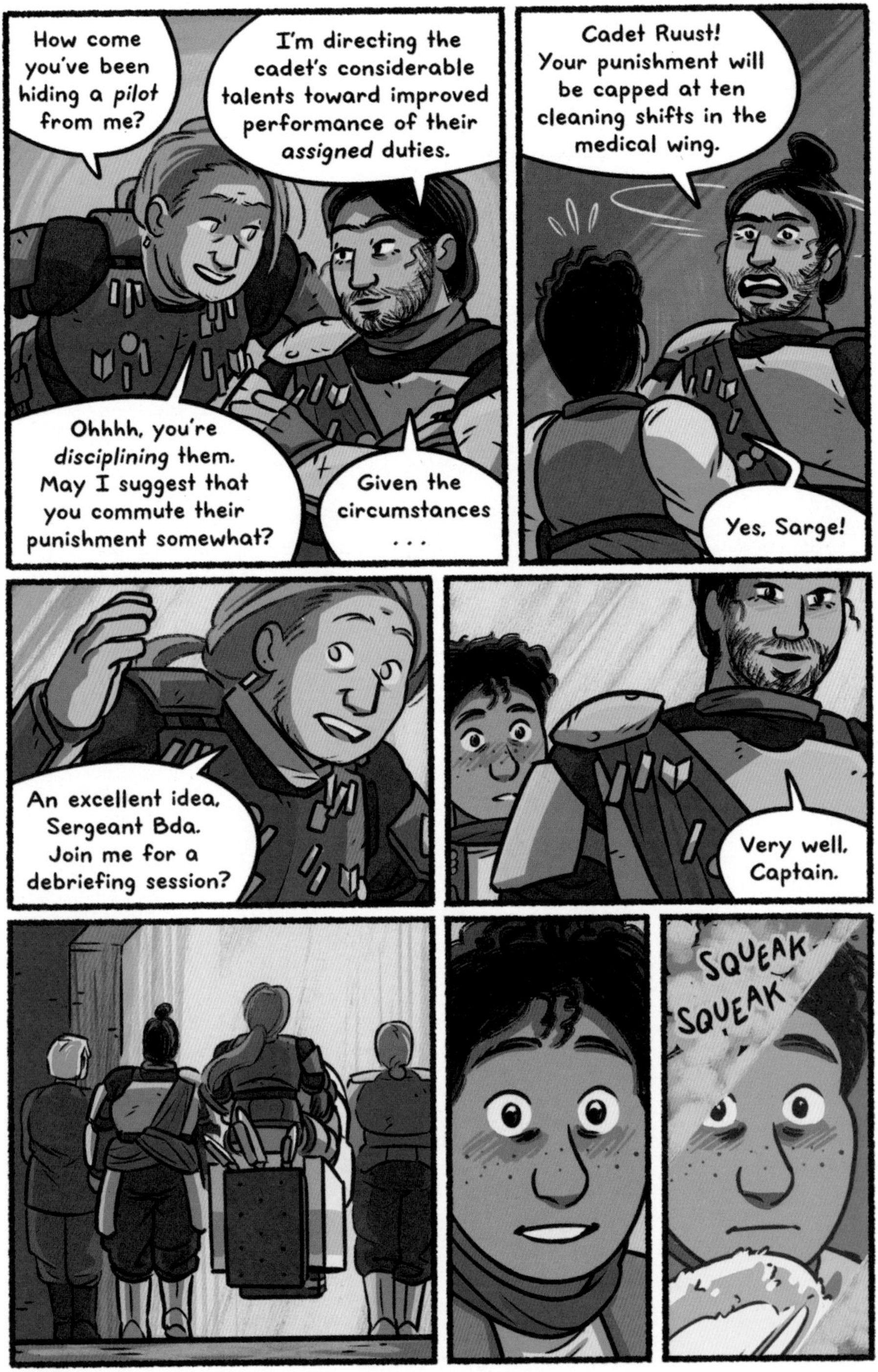
How come you've been hiding a *pilot* from me?
I'm directing the cadet's considerable talents toward improved performance of their *assigned* duties.
Ohhhh, you're *disciplining* them. May I suggest that you commute their punishment somewhat?
Given the circumstances . . .
Cadet Ruust! Your punishment will be capped at ten cleaning shifts in the medical wing.
Yes, Sarge!
An excellent idea, Sergeant Bda. Join me for a debriefing session?
Very well, Captain.
SQUEAK
SQUEAK

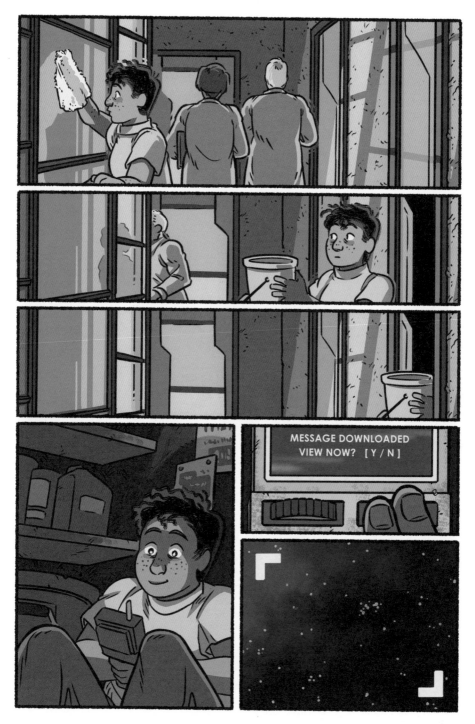

MESSAGE DOWNLOADED
VIEW NOW? [Y / N]

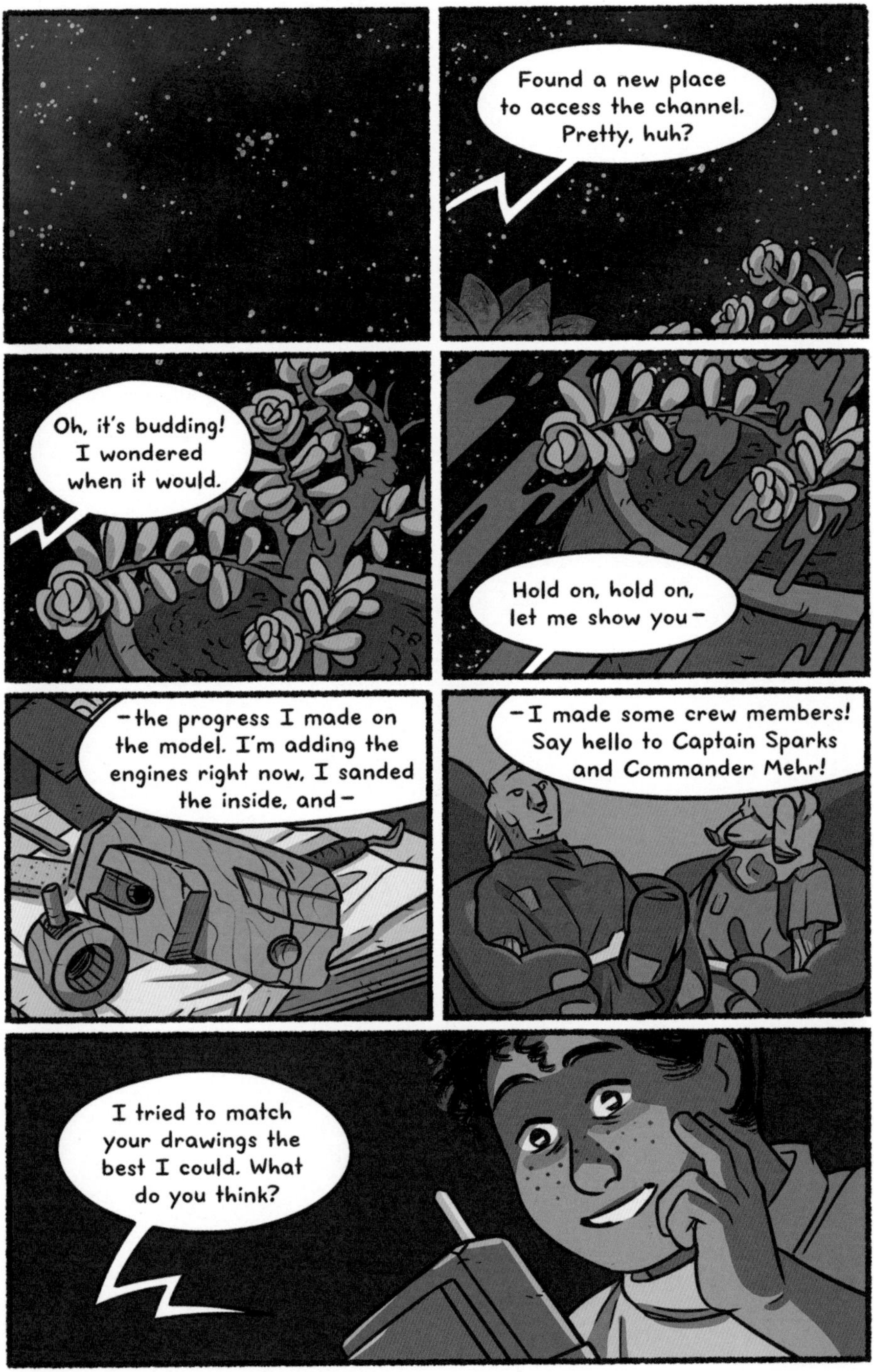
Found a new place
to access the channel.
Pretty, huh?
Oh, it's budding!
I wondered
when it would.
Hold on, hold on,
let me show you—
—the progress I made on
the model. I'm adding the
engines right now. I sanded
the inside, and—
—I made some crew members!
Say hello to Captain Sparks
and Commander Mehr!
I tried to match
your drawings the
best I could. What
do you think?

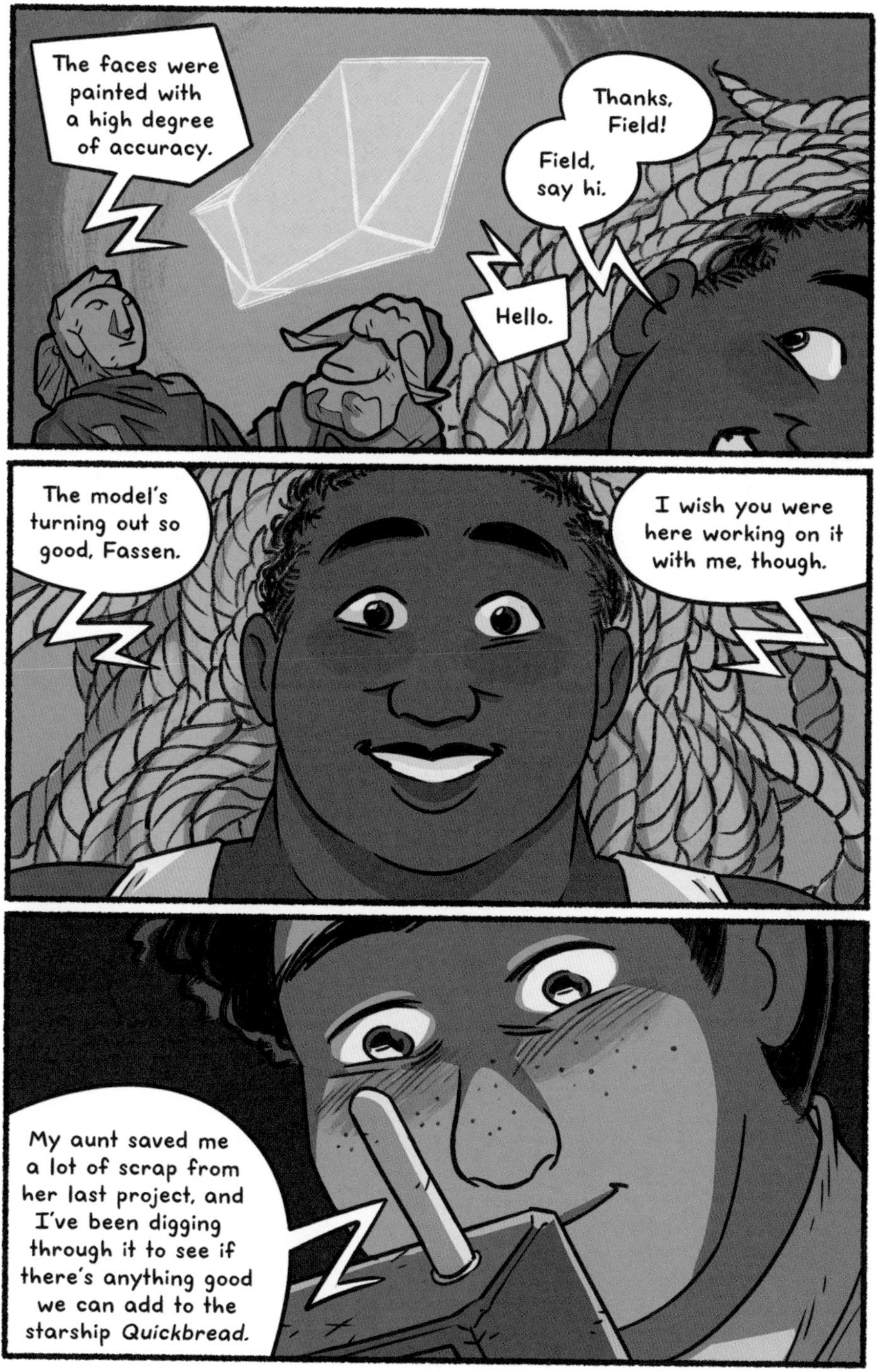
The faces were painted with a high degree of accuracy.
Thanks, Field!
Field, say hi.
Hello.
The model's turning out so good, Fassen.
I wish you were here working on it with me, though.
My aunt saved me a lot of scrap from her last project, and I've been digging through it to see if there's anything good we can add to the starship *Quickbread.*

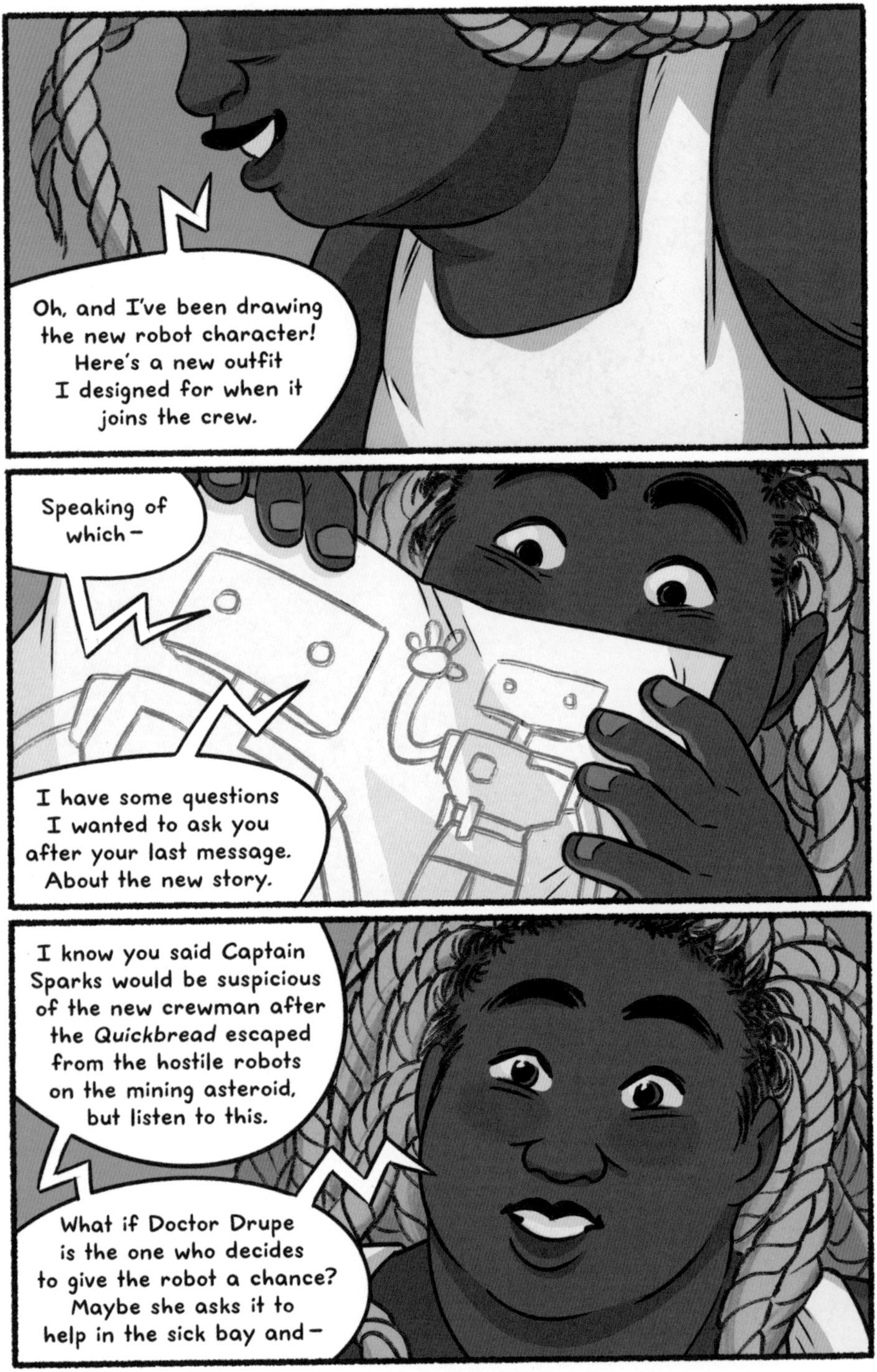
Oh, and I've been drawing the new robot character! Here's a new outfit I designed for when it joins the crew.
Speaking of which–
I have some questions I wanted to ask you after your last message. About the new story.
I know you said Captain Sparks would be suspicious of the new crewman after the *Quickbread* escaped from the hostile robots on the mining asteroid, but listen to this.
What if Doctor Drupe is the one who decides to give the robot a chance? Maybe she asks it to help in the sick bay and–

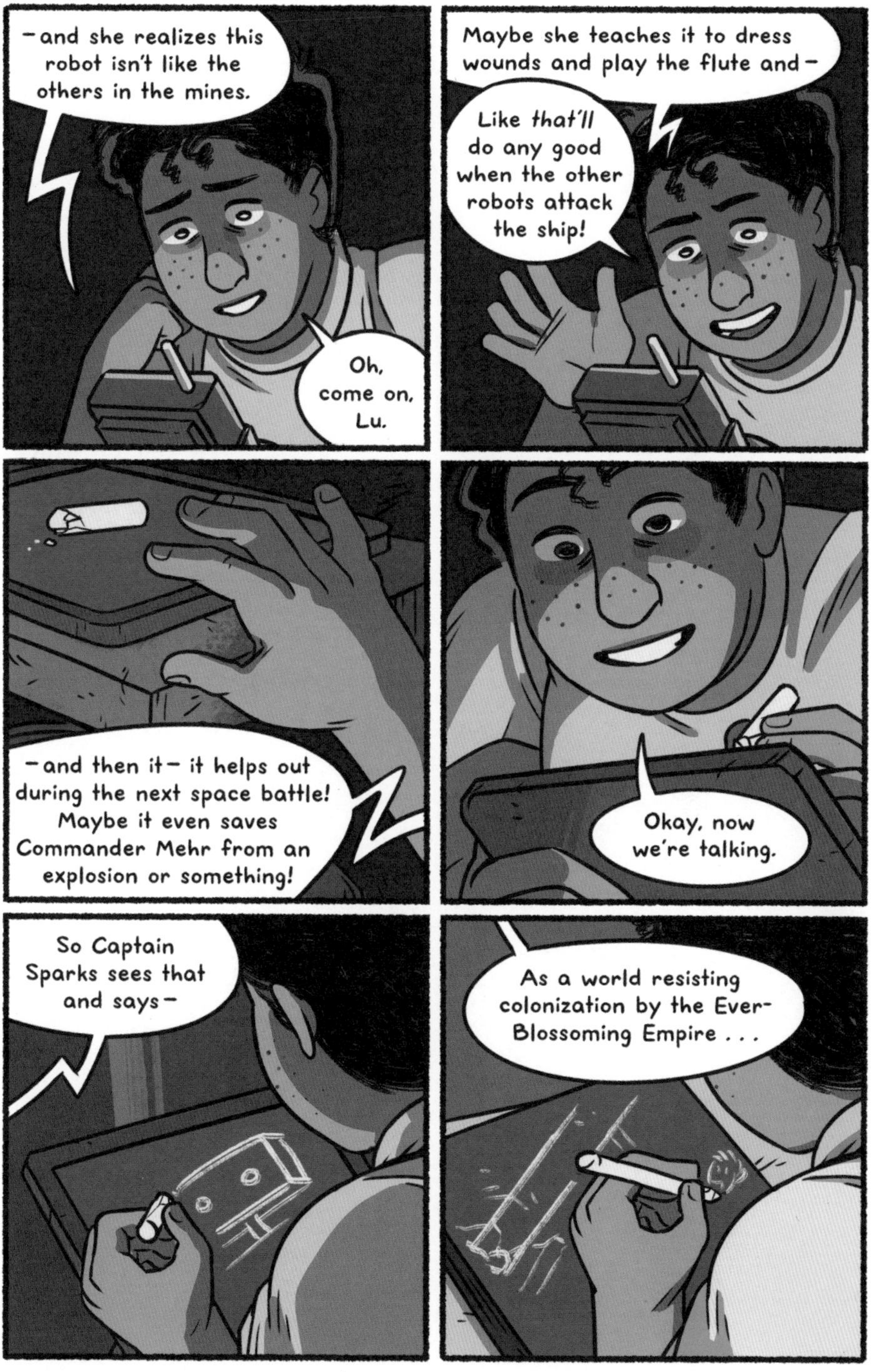
—and she realizes this robot isn't like the others in the mines.
Oh, come on, Lu.
Maybe she teaches it to dress wounds and play the flute and—
Like that'll do any good when the other robots attack the ship!
—and then it— it helps out during the next space battle! Maybe it even saves Commander Mehr from an explosion or something!
Okay, now we're talking.
So Captain Sparks sees that and says—
As a world resisting colonization by the Ever-Blossoming Empire . . .

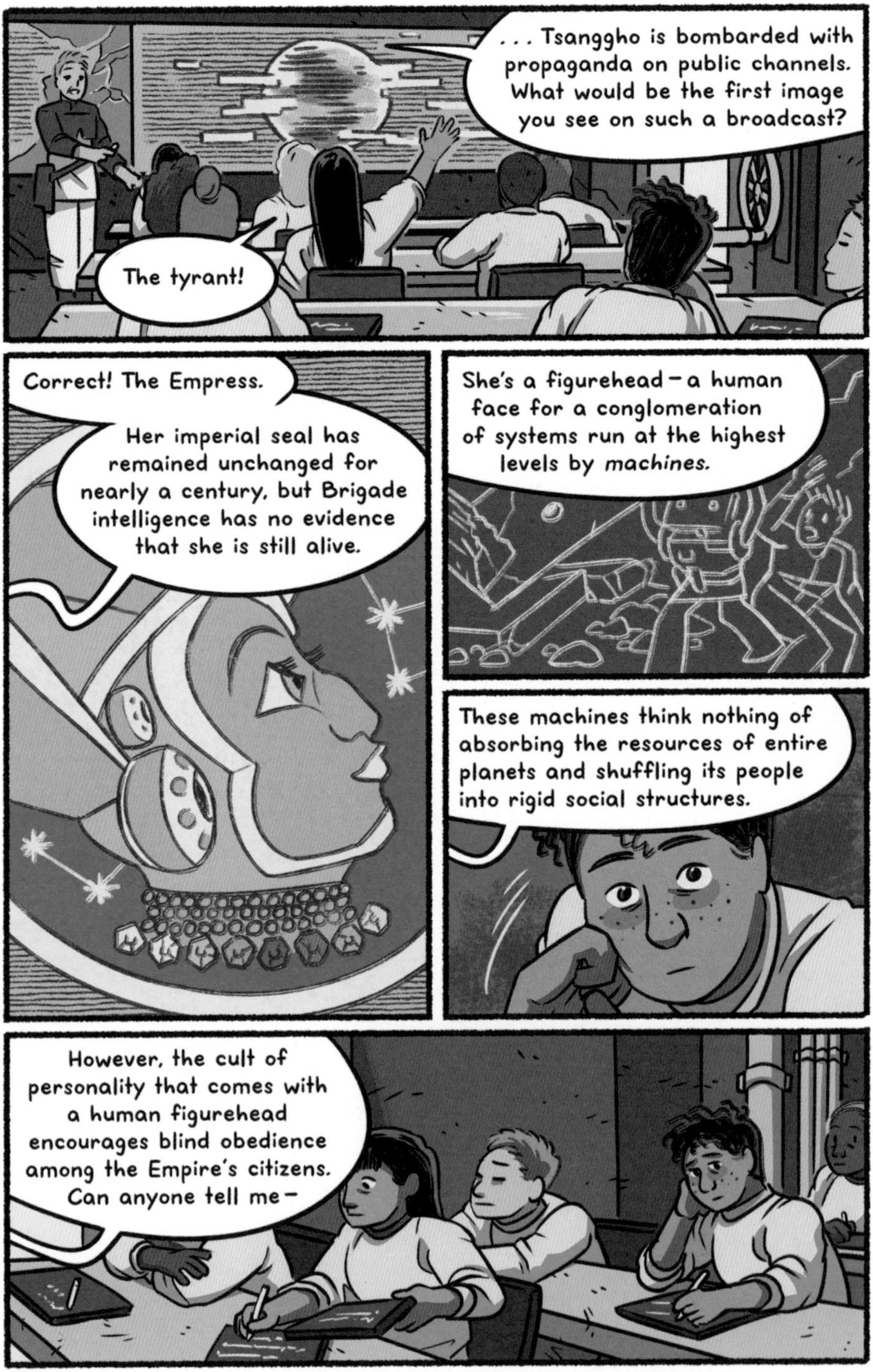
. . . Tsanggho is bombarded with propaganda on public channels. What would be the first image you see on such a broadcast?
The tyrant!
Correct! The Empress.
Her imperial seal has remained unchanged for nearly a century, but Brigade intelligence has no evidence that she is still alive.
She's a figurehead—a human face for a conglomeration of systems run at the highest levels by *machines.*
These machines think nothing of absorbing the resources of entire planets and shuffling its people into rigid social structures.
However, the cult of personality that comes with a human figurehead encourages blind obedience among the Empire's citizens. Can anyone tell me—

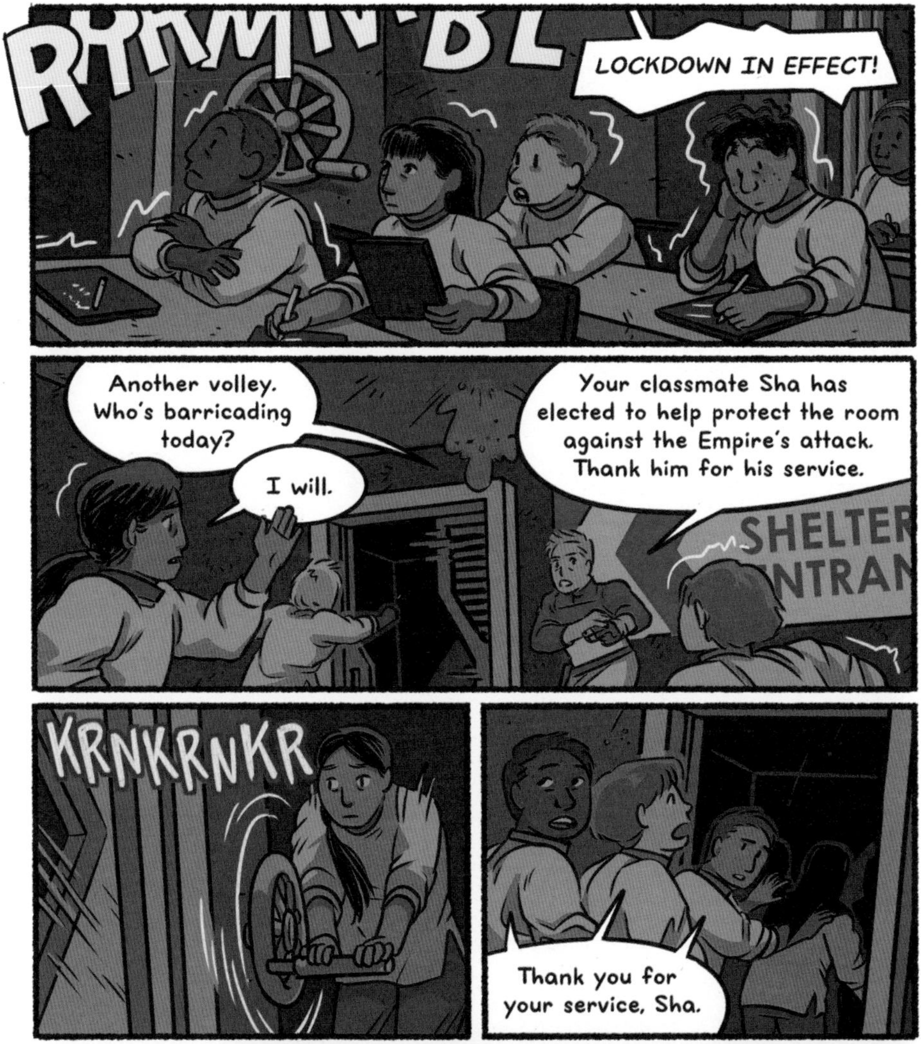

LOCKDOWN IN EFFECT!
Another volley. Who's barricading today?
I will.
Your classmate Sha has elected to help protect the room against the Empire's attack. Thank him for his service.
SHELTER
KRNKRNKR
Thank you for your service, Sha.
Man, and it was almost lunchtime, too.
Betcha this one only lasts an hour.
Don't get my hopes up.

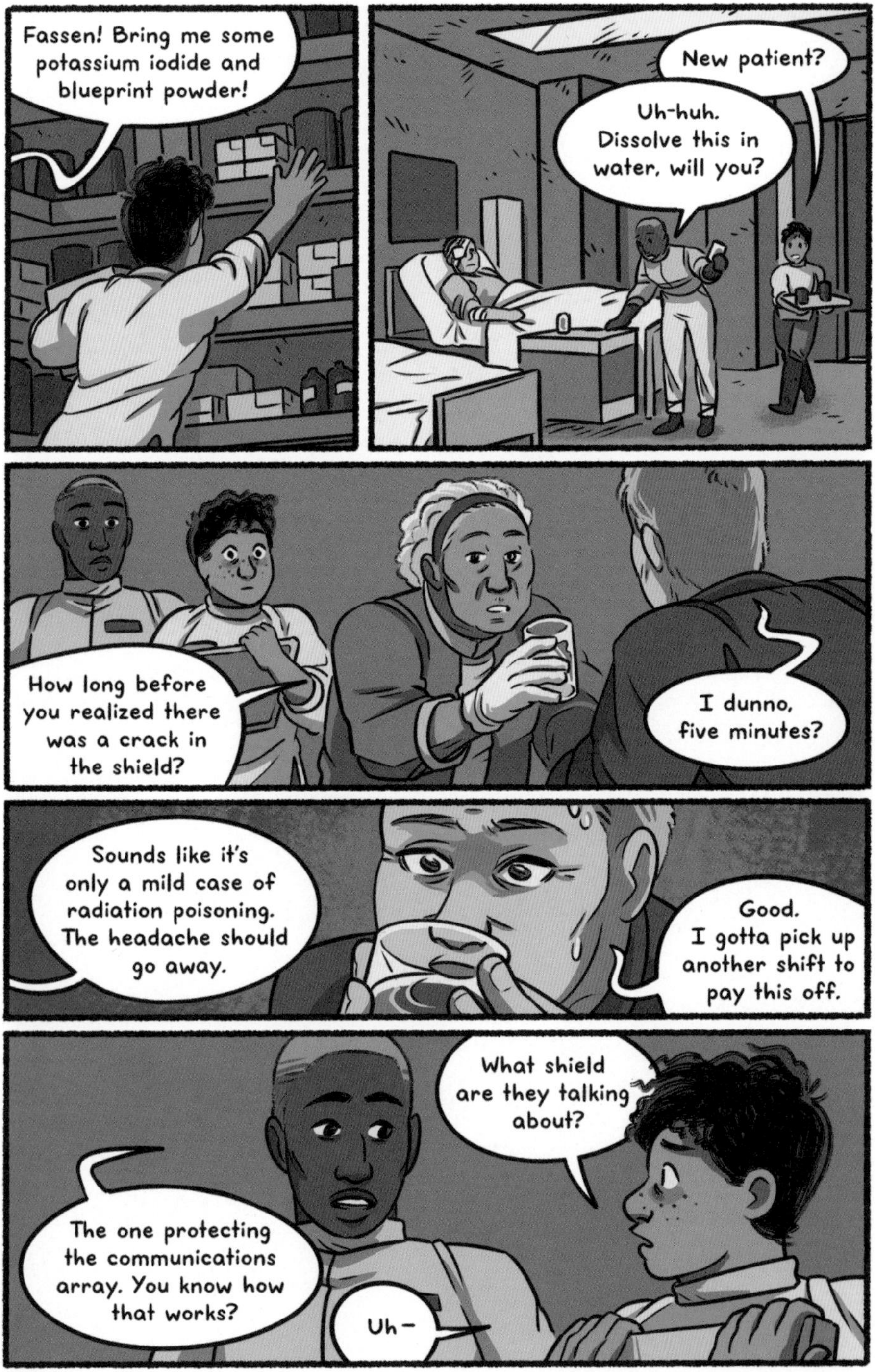
Fassen! Bring me some potassium iodide and blueprint powder!
New patient?
Uh-huh. Dissolve this in water, will you?
How long before you realized there was a crack in the shield?
I dunno, five minutes?
Sounds like it's only a mild case of radiation poisoning. The headache should go away.
Good. I gotta pick up another shift to pay this off.
What shield are they talking about?
The one protecting the communications array. You know how that works?
Uh-

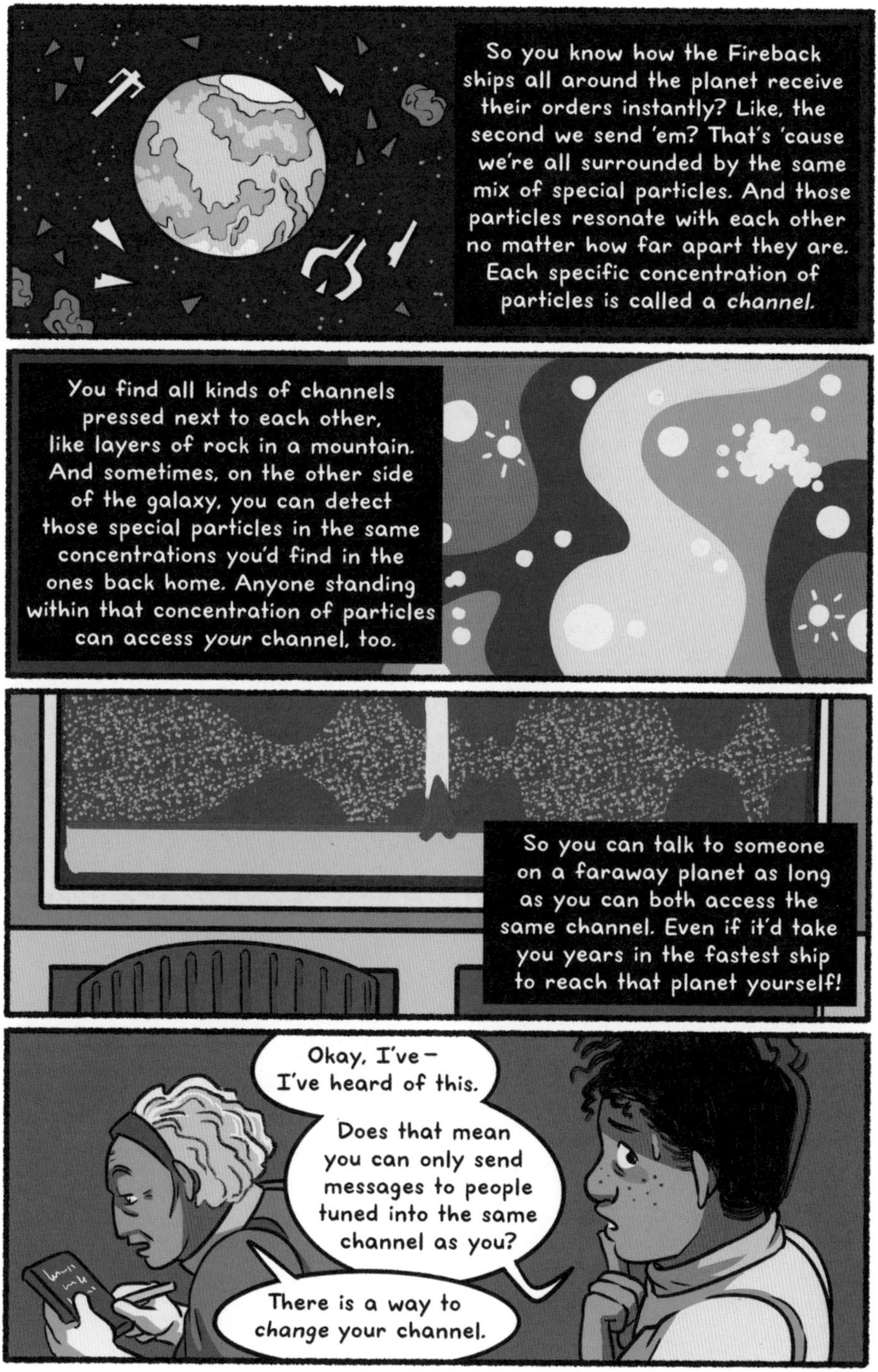

So you know how the Fireback ships all around the planet receive their orders instantly? Like, the second we send 'em? That's 'cause we're all surrounded by the same mix of special particles. And those particles resonate with each other no matter how far apart they are. Each specific concentration of particles is called a *channel*.

You find all kinds of channels pressed next to each other, like layers of rock in a mountain. And sometimes, on the other side of the galaxy, you can detect those special particles in the same concentrations you'd find in the ones back home. Anyone standing within that concentration of particles can access *your* channel, too.

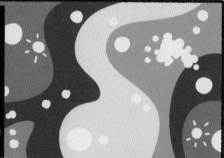

So you can talk to someone on a faraway planet as long as you can both access the same channel. Even if it'd take you years in the fastest ship to reach that planet yourself!

Okay, I've— I've heard of this.

Does that mean you can only send messages to people tuned into the same channel as you?

There is a way to change your channel.

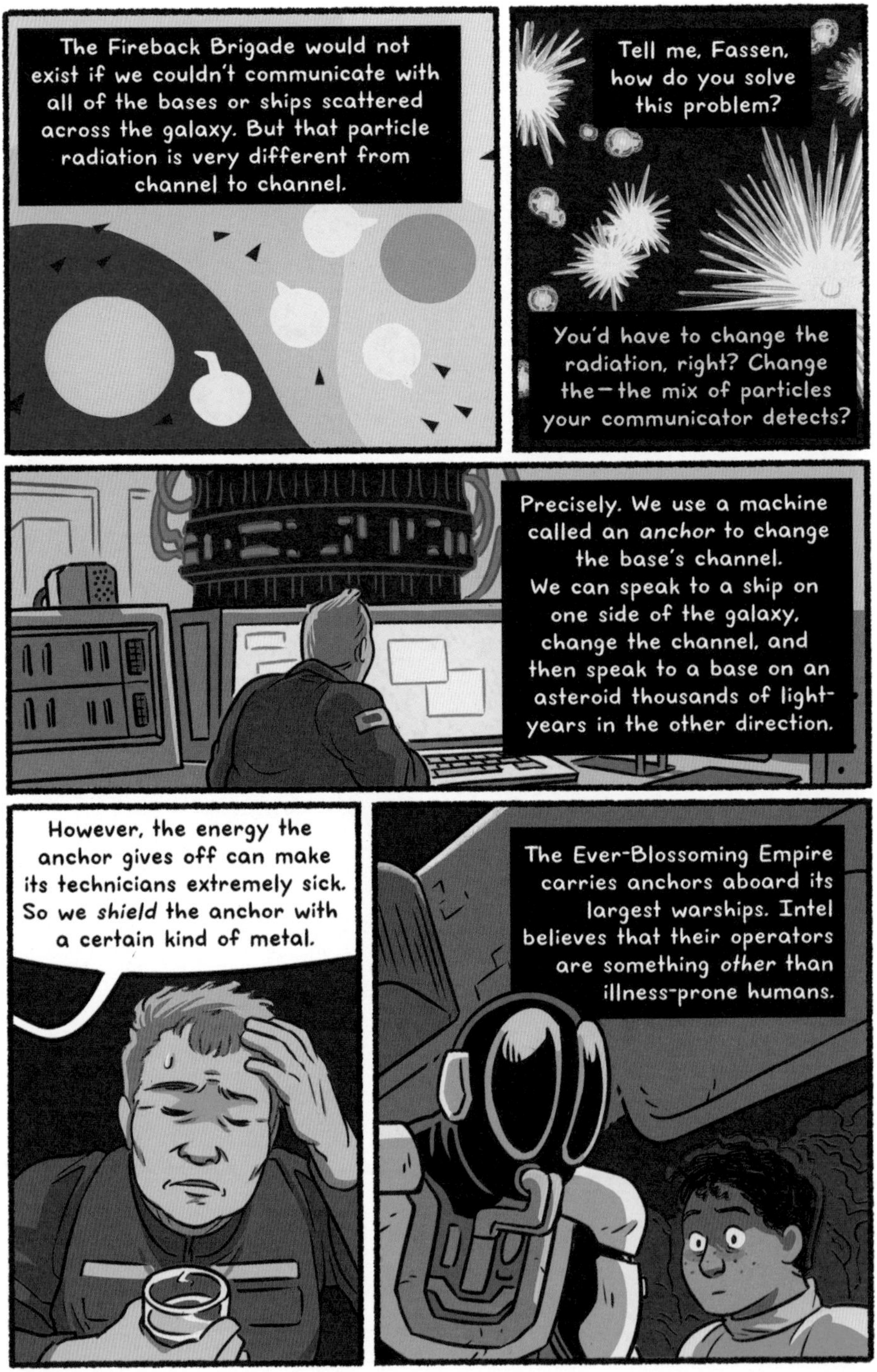
The Fireback Brigade would not exist if we couldn't communicate with all of the bases or ships scattered across the galaxy. But that particle radiation is very different from channel to channel.
Tell me, Fassen, how do you solve this problem?
You'd have to change the radiation, right? Change the—the mix of particles your communicator detects?
Precisely. We use a machine called an *anchor* to change the base's channel.
We can speak to a ship on one side of the galaxy, change the channel, and then speak to a base on an asteroid thousands of light-years in the other direction.
However, the energy the anchor gives off can make its technicians extremely sick. So we *shield* the anchor with a certain kind of metal.
The Ever-Blossoming Empire carries anchors aboard its largest warships. Intel believes that their operators are something *other* than illness-prone humans.

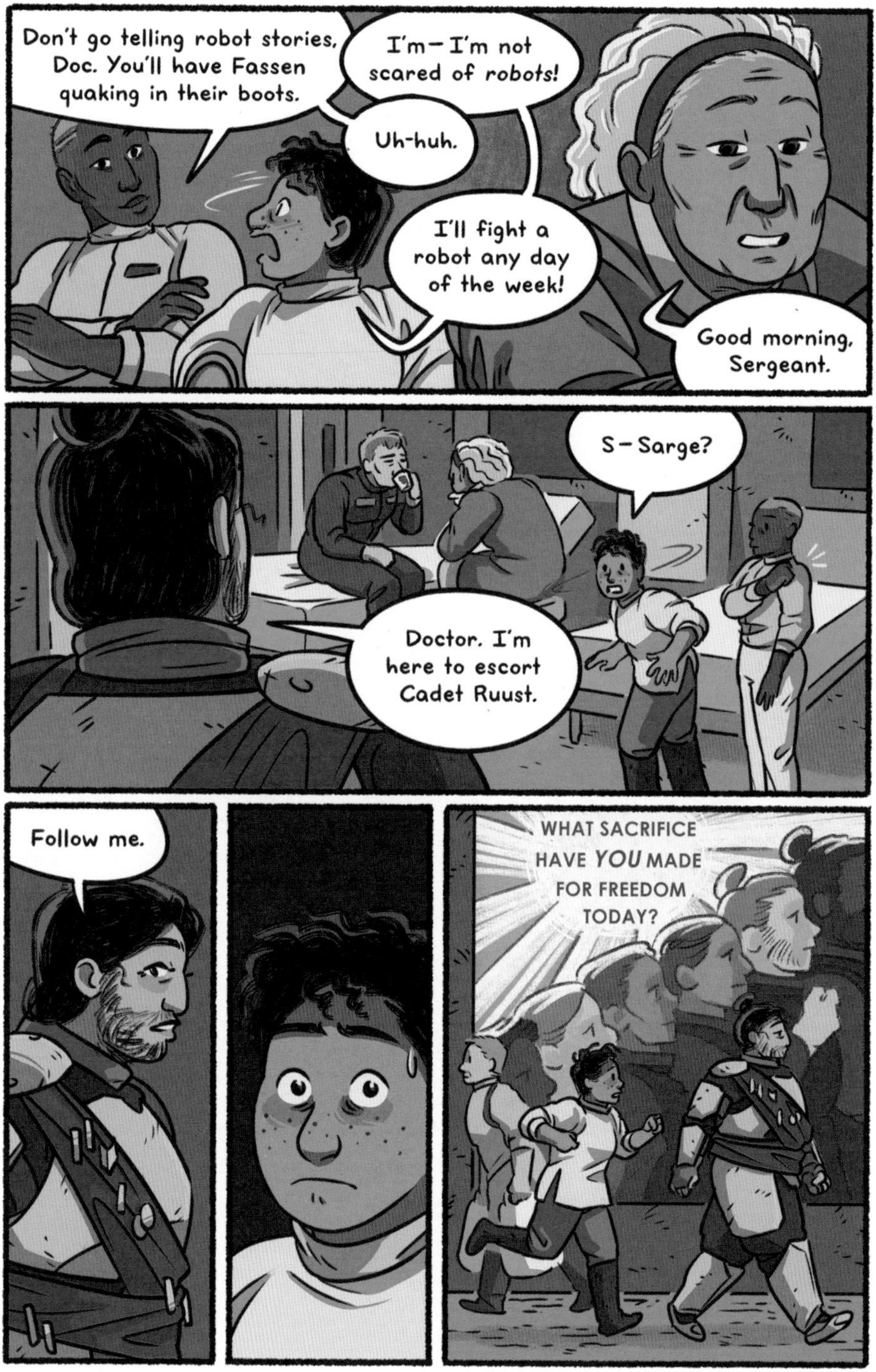
Don't go telling robot stories, Doc. You'll have Fassen quaking in their boots.
I'm—I'm not scared of *robots*!
Uh-huh.
I'll fight a robot any day of the week!
Good morning, Sergeant.
S—Sarge?
Doctor. I'm here to escort Cadet Ruust.
Follow me.
WHAT SACRIFICE HAVE *YOU* MADE FOR FREEDOM TODAY?

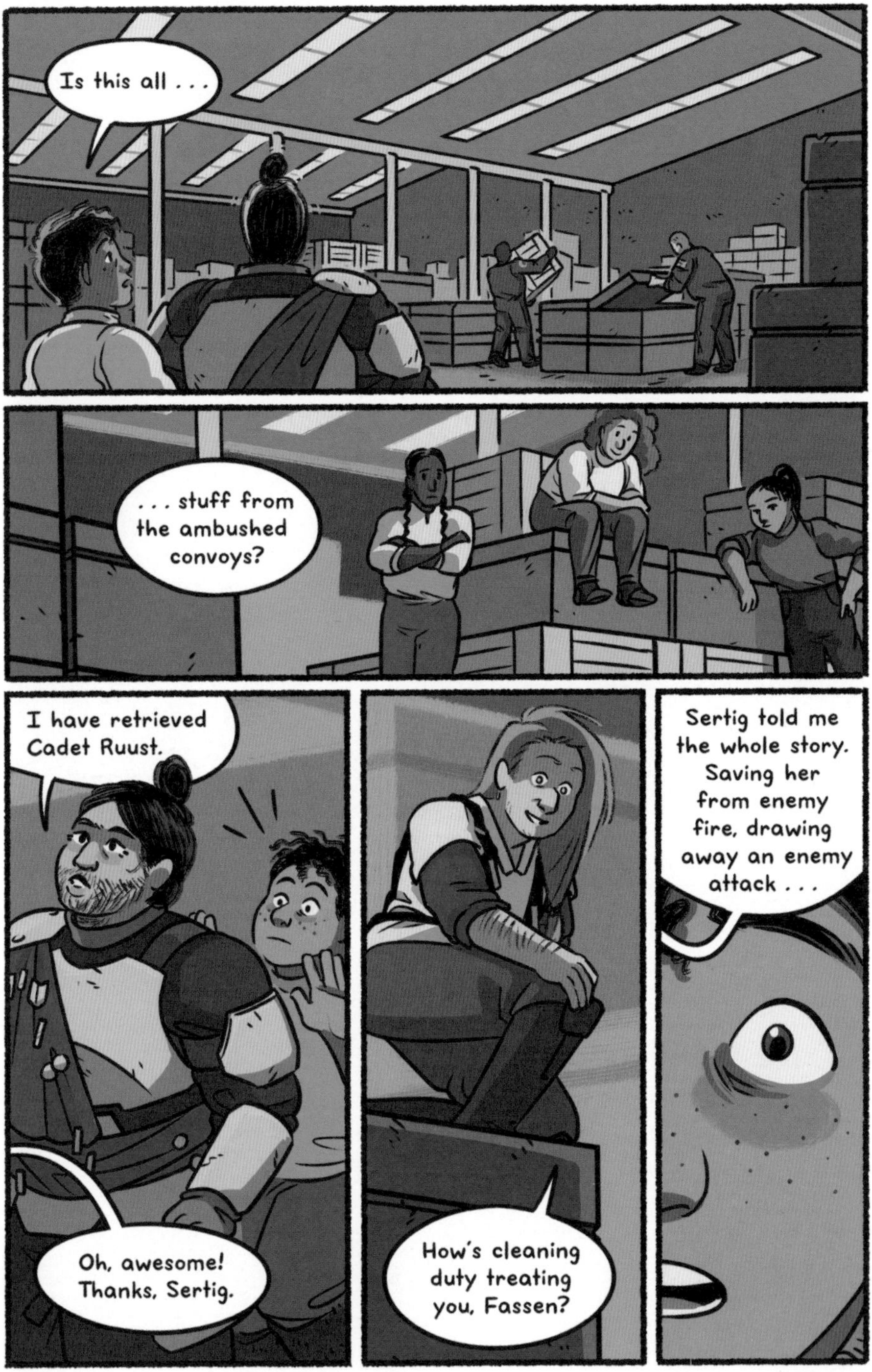
Is this all . . .
. . . stuff from the ambushed convoys?
I have retrieved Cadet Ruust.
Oh, awesome! Thanks, Sertig.
How's cleaning duty treating you, Fassen?
Sertig told me the whole story. Saving her from enemy fire, drawing away an enemy attack . . .

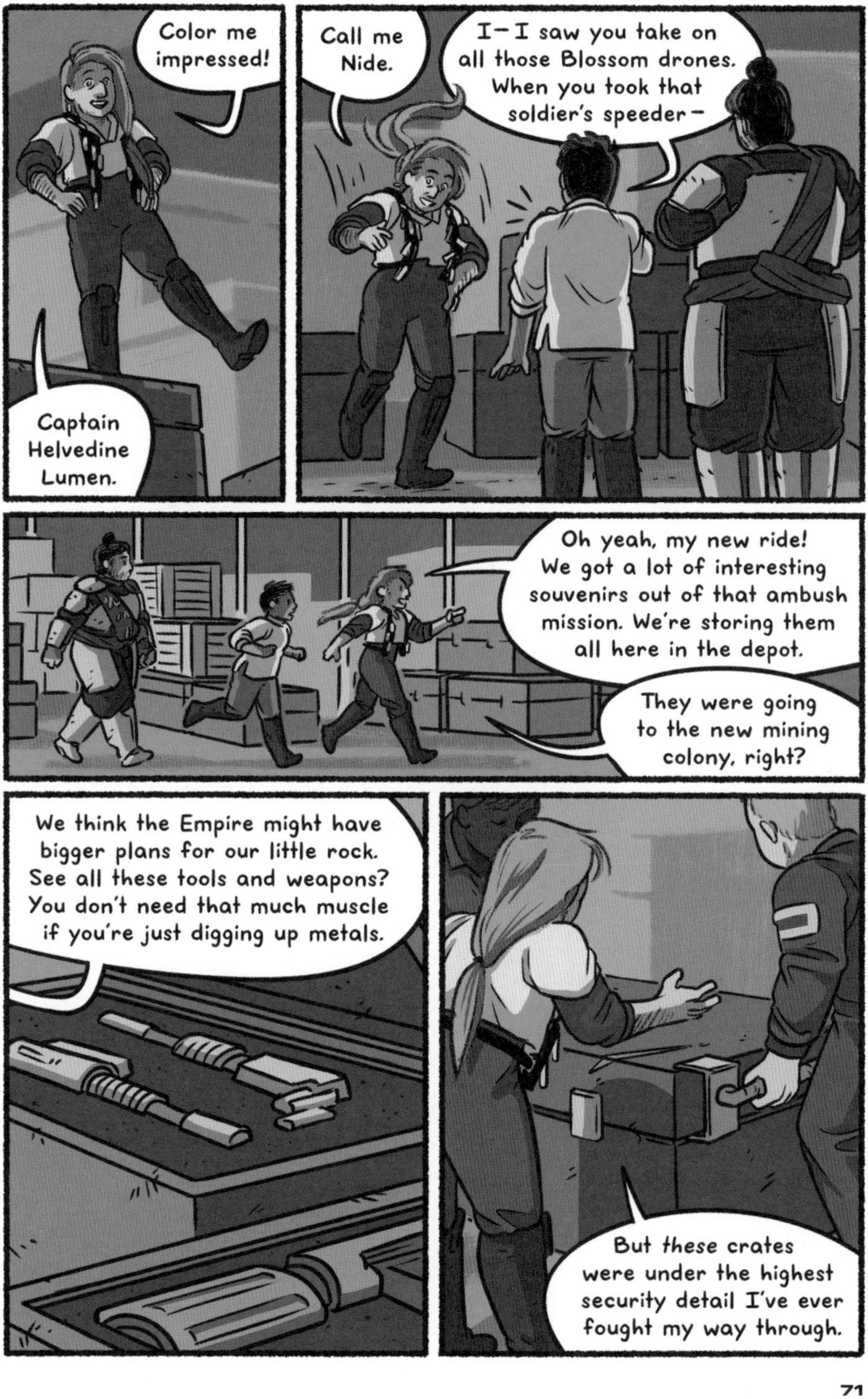
Color me impressed!
Captain Helvedine Lumen.
Call me Nide.
I—I saw you take on all those Blossom drones. When you took that soldier's speeder—
Oh yeah, my new ride! We got a lot of interesting souvenirs out of that ambush mission. We're storing them all here in the depot.
They were going to the new mining colony, right?
We think the Empire might have bigger plans for our little rock. See all these tools and weapons? You don't need that much muscle if you're just digging up metals.
But *these* crates were under the highest security detail I've ever fought my way through.

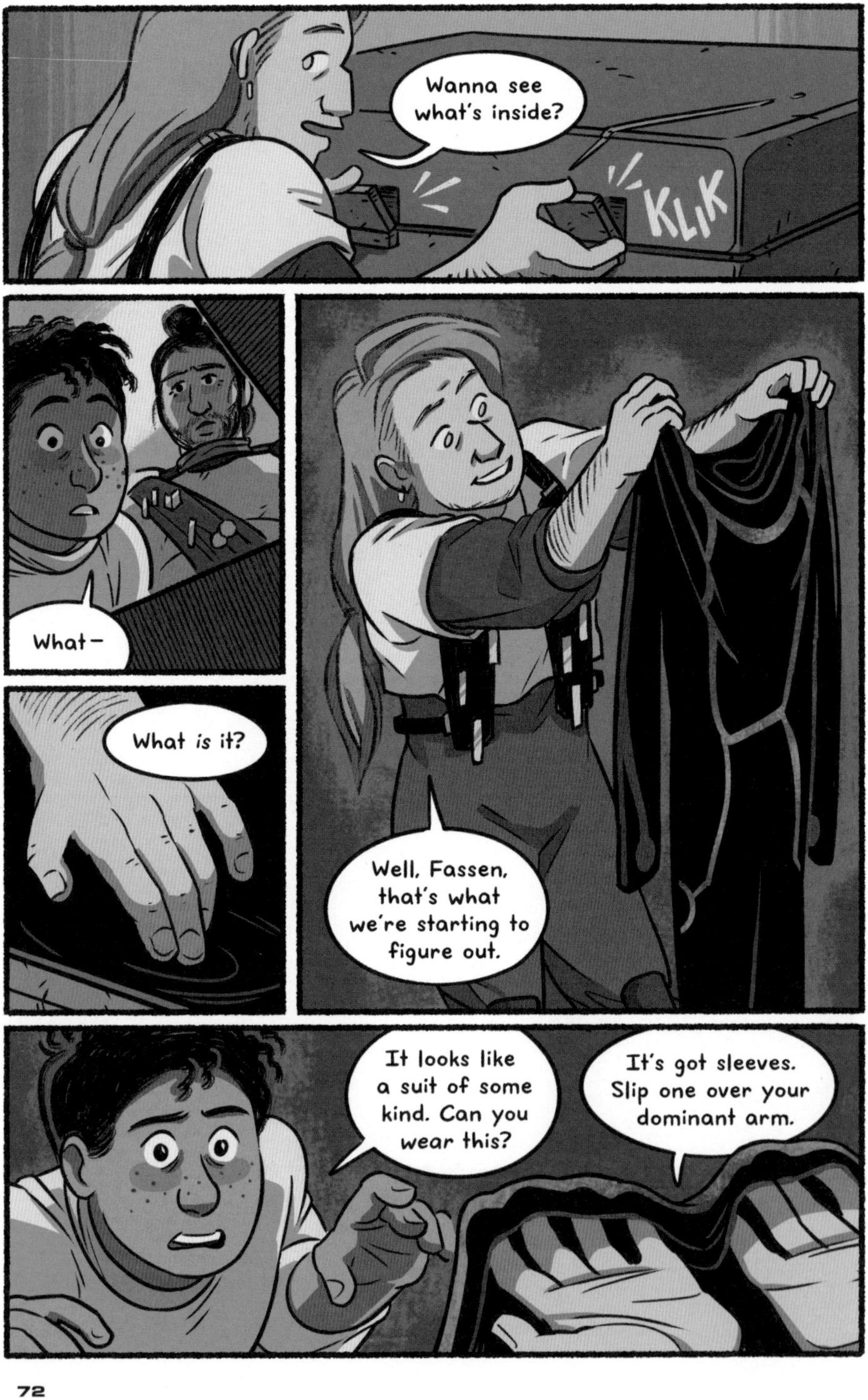
Wanna see what's inside?
KLIK
What–
What *is* it?
Well, Fassen, that's what we're starting to figure out.
It looks like a suit of some kind. Can you wear this?
It's got sleeves. Slip one over your dominant arm.

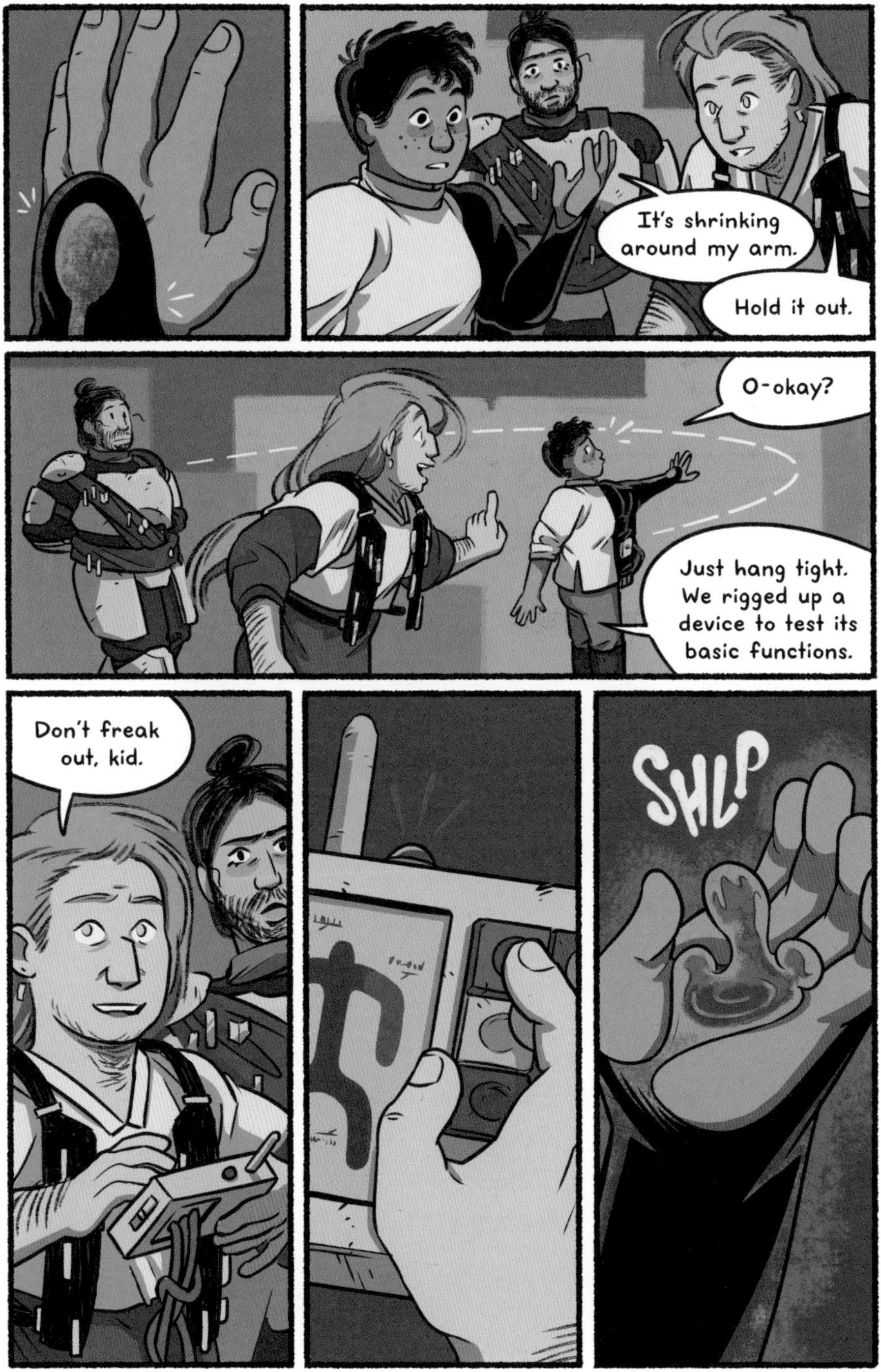
It's shrinking around my arm.
Hold it out.
O-okay?
Just hang tight. We rigged up a device to test its basic functions.
Don't freak out, kid.
SHLP

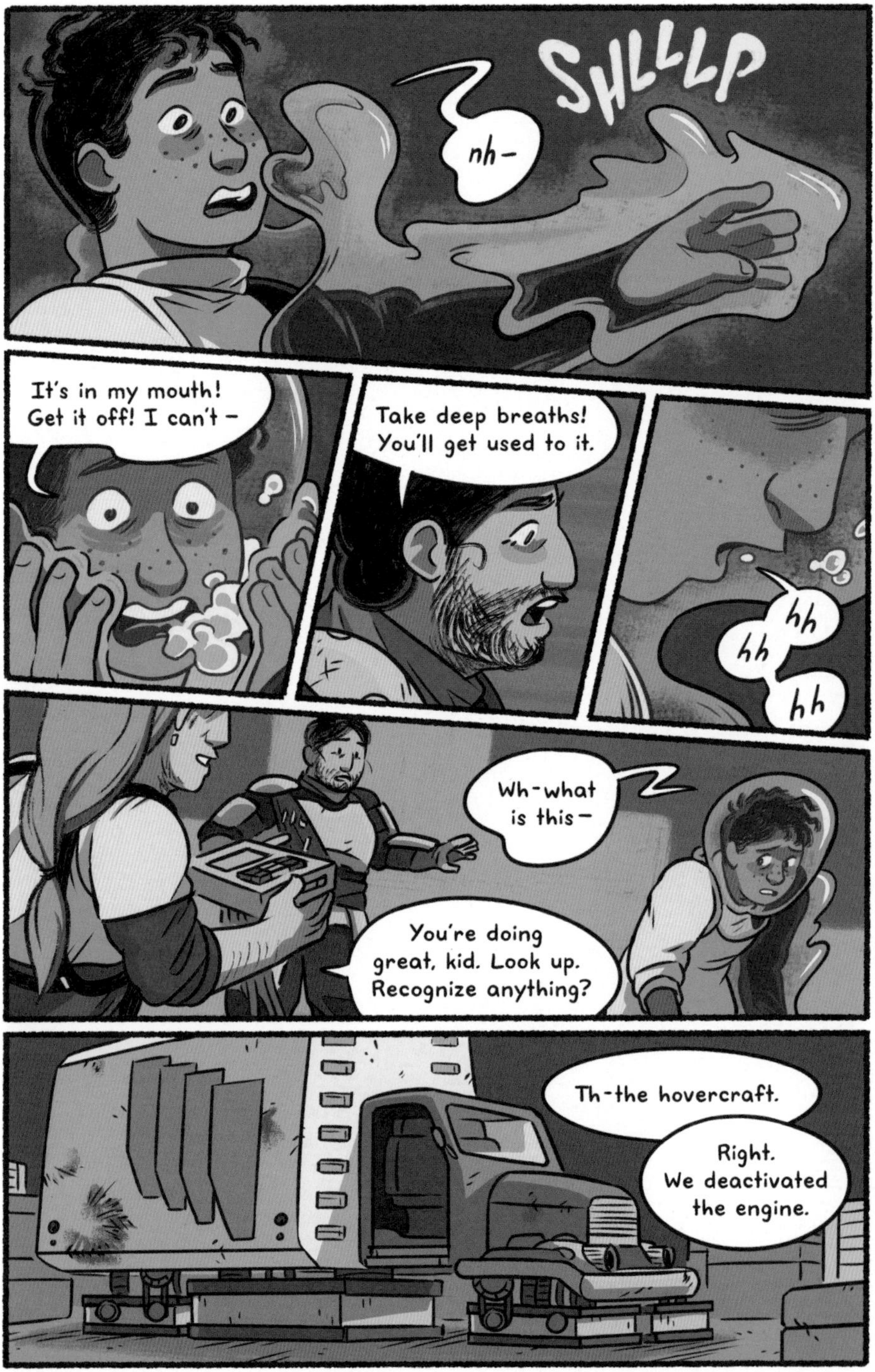
SHLLLP
nh-
It's in my mouth! Get it off! I can't -
Take deep breaths! You'll get used to it.
hh
hh
hh
Wh-what is this-
You're doing great, kid. Look up. Recognize anything?
Th-the hovercraft.
Right. We deactivated the engine.

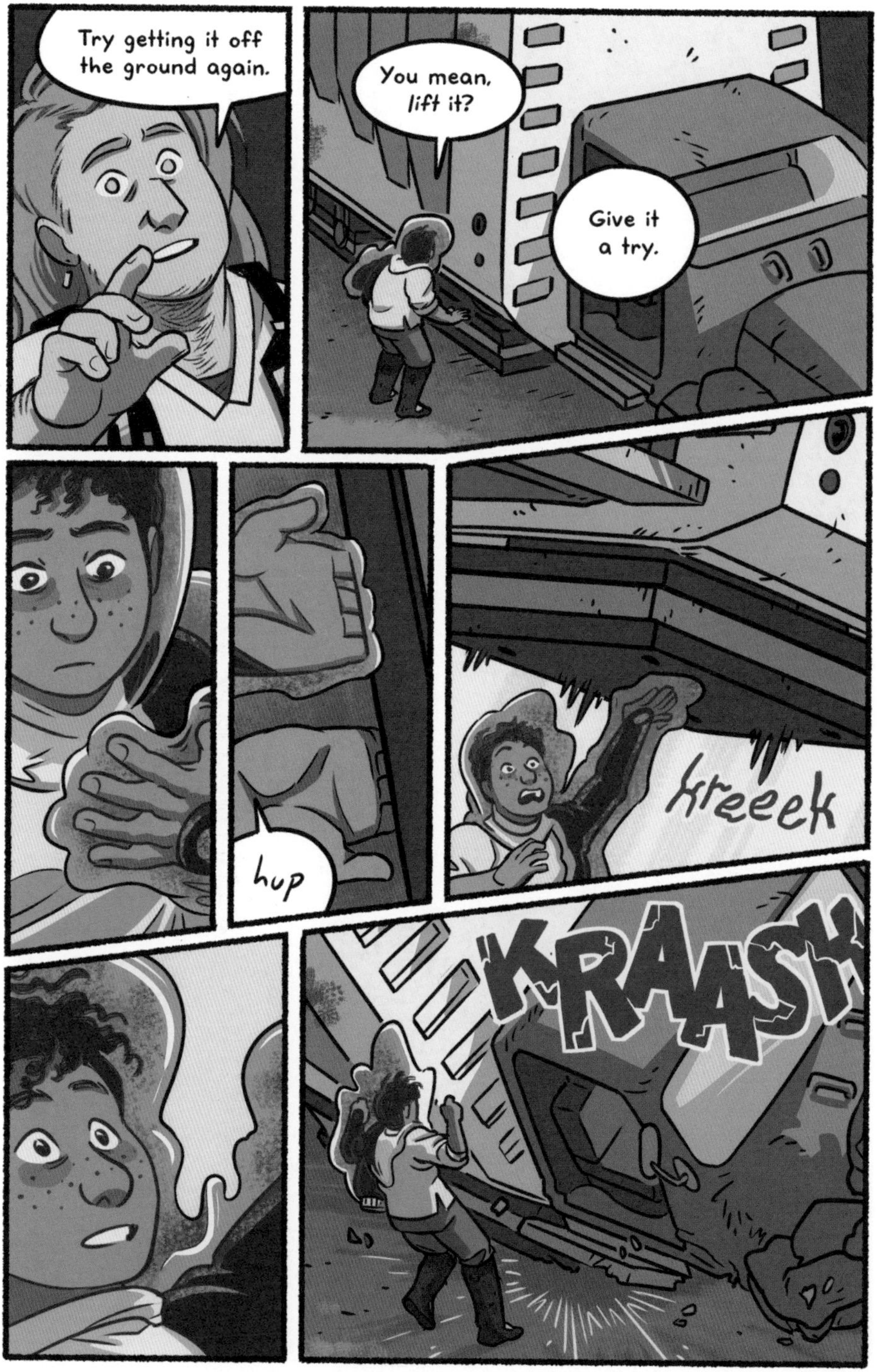
Try getting it off the ground again.
You mean, lift it?
Give it a try.
hup
kreeek
KRAASH

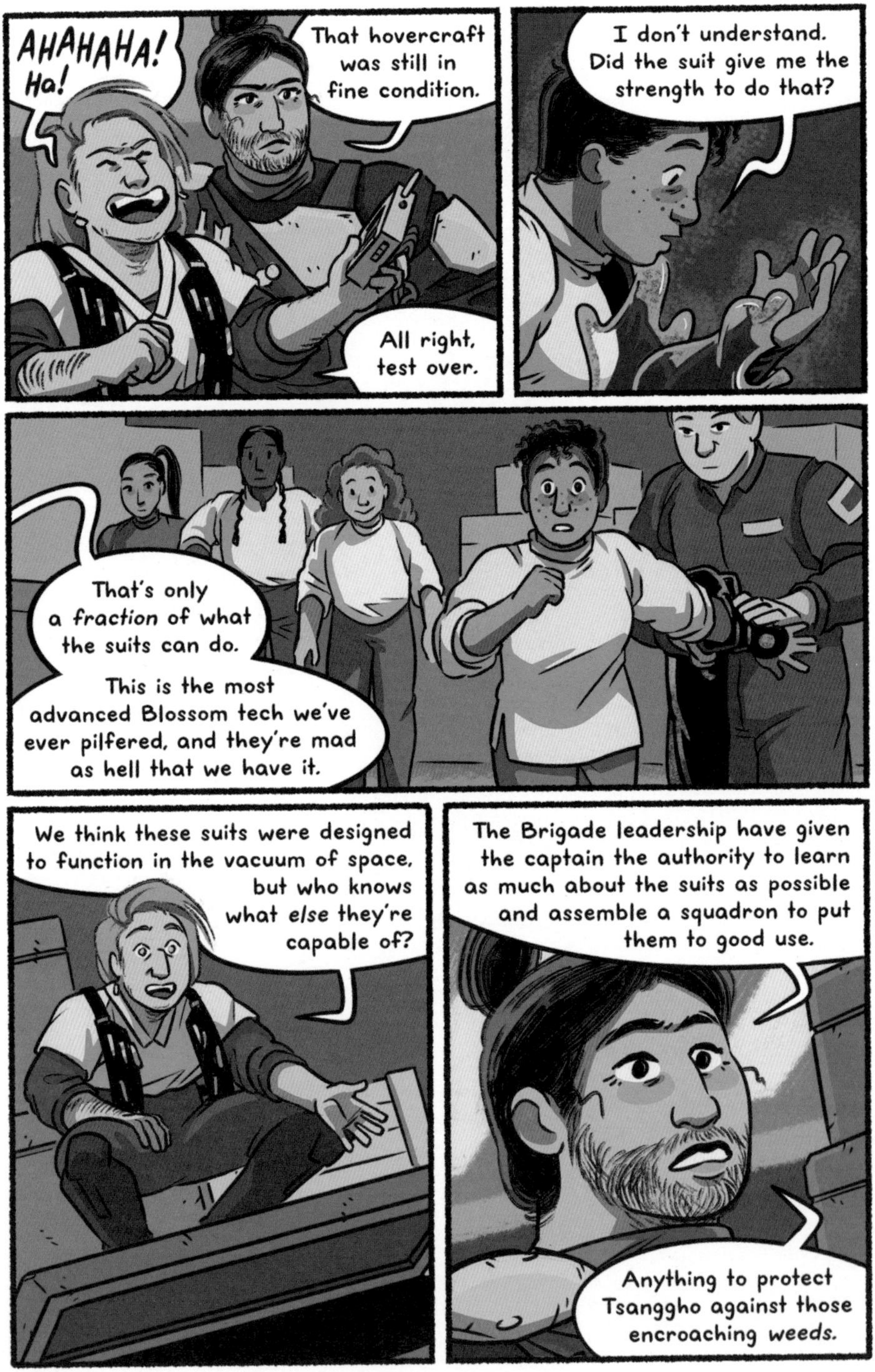
AHAHAHA! Ha!
That hovercraft was still in fine condition.
All right, test over.
I don't understand. Did the suit give me the strength to do that?
That's only a *fraction* of what the suits can do.
This is the most advanced Blossom tech we've ever pilfered, and they're mad as hell that we have it.
We think these suits were designed to function in the vacuum of space, but who knows what *else* they're capable of?
The Brigade leadership have given the captain the authority to learn as much about the suits as possible and assemble a squadron to put them to good use.
Anything to protect Tsanggho against those encroaching *weeds.*

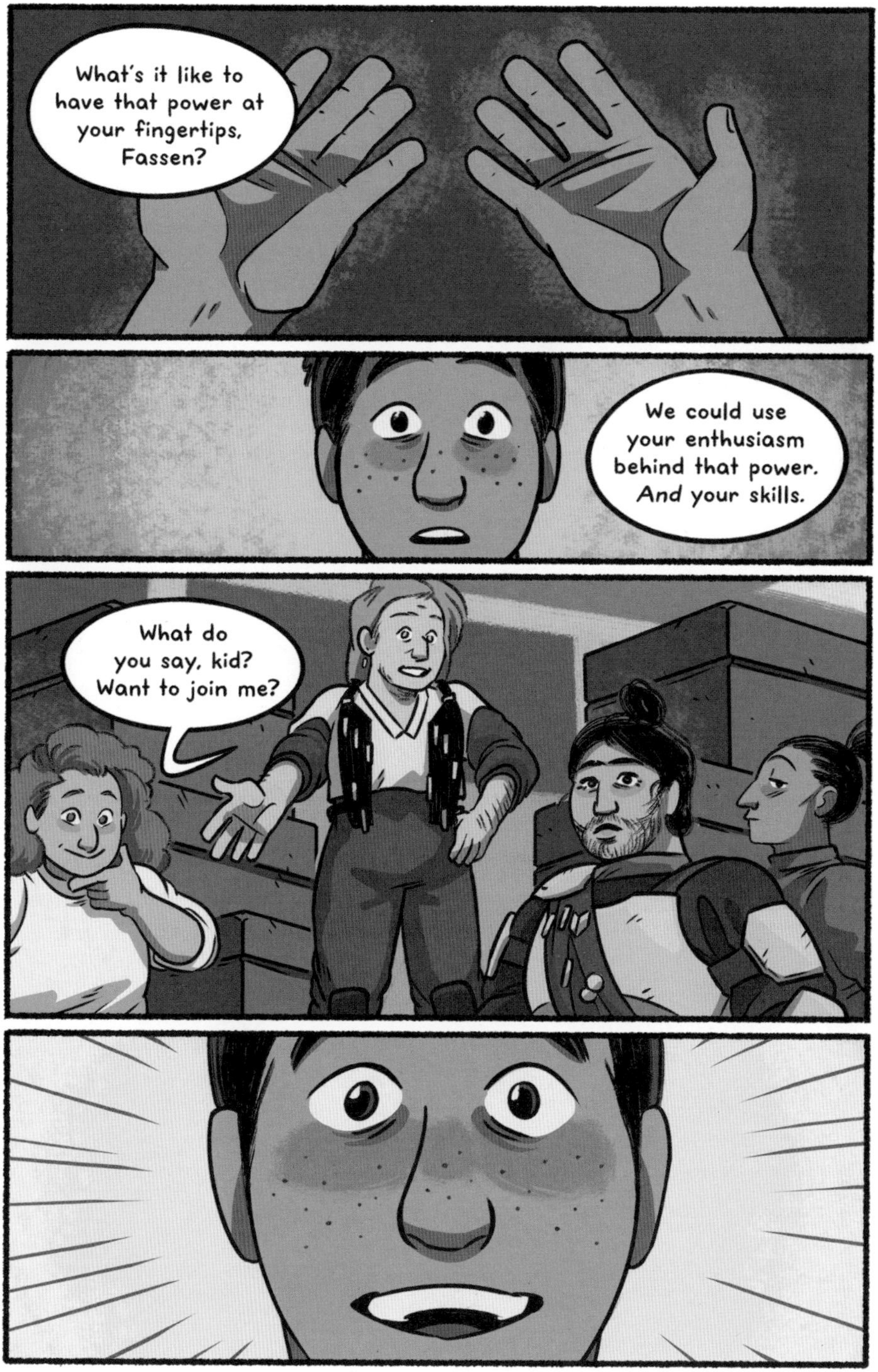
What's it like to have that power at your fingertips, Fassen?
We could use your enthusiasm behind that power. And your skills.
What do you say, kid? Want to join me?

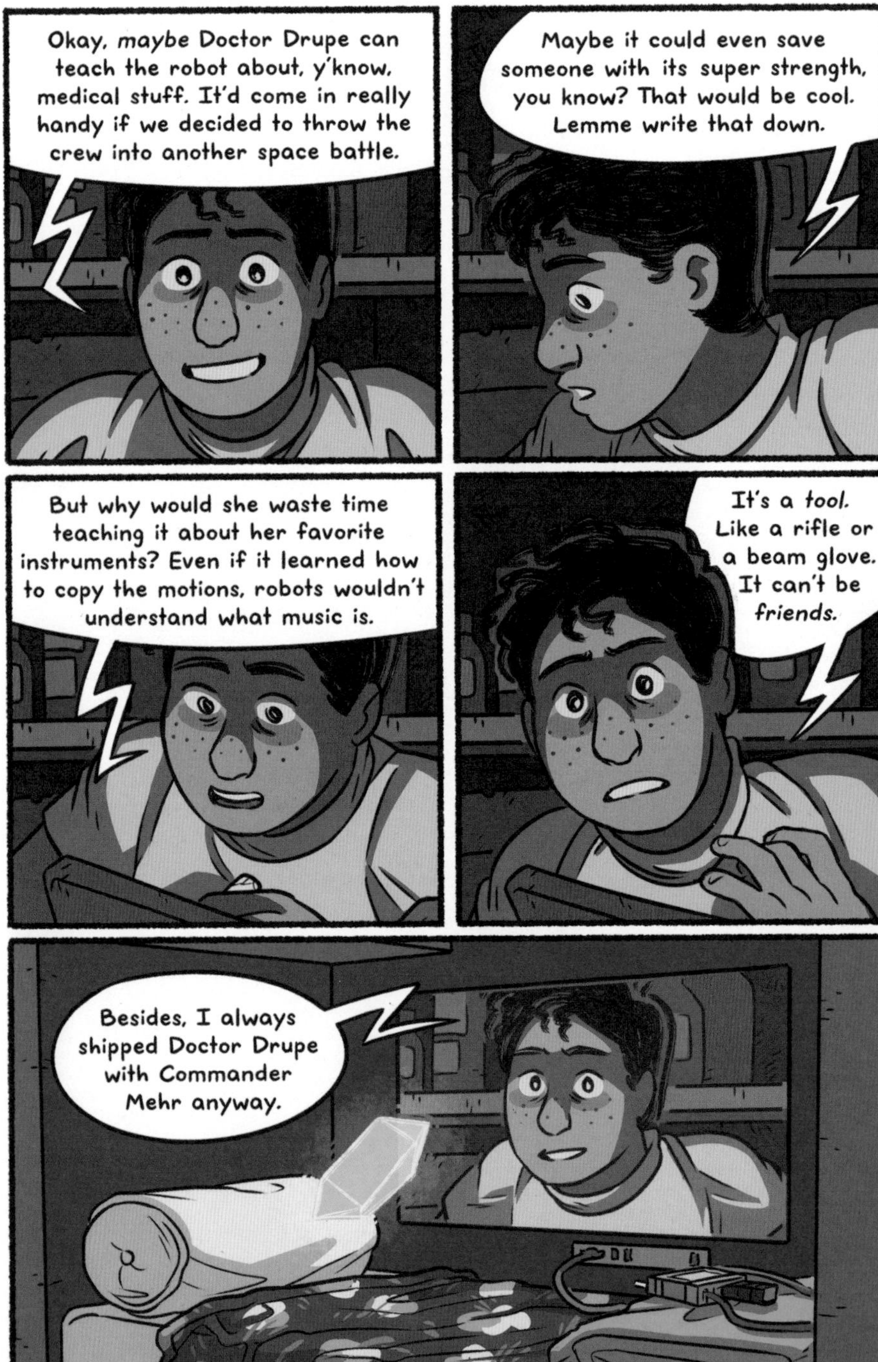
Okay, *maybe* Doctor Drupe can teach the robot about, y'know, medical stuff. It'd come in really handy if we decided to throw the crew into another space battle.
Maybe it could even save someone with its super strength, you know? That would be cool. Lemme write that down.
But why would she waste time teaching it about her favorite instruments? Even if it learned how to copy the motions, robots wouldn't understand what music is.
It's a *tool.* Like a rifle or a beam glove. It can't be *friends.*
Besides, I always shipped Doctor Drupe with Commander Mehr anyway.

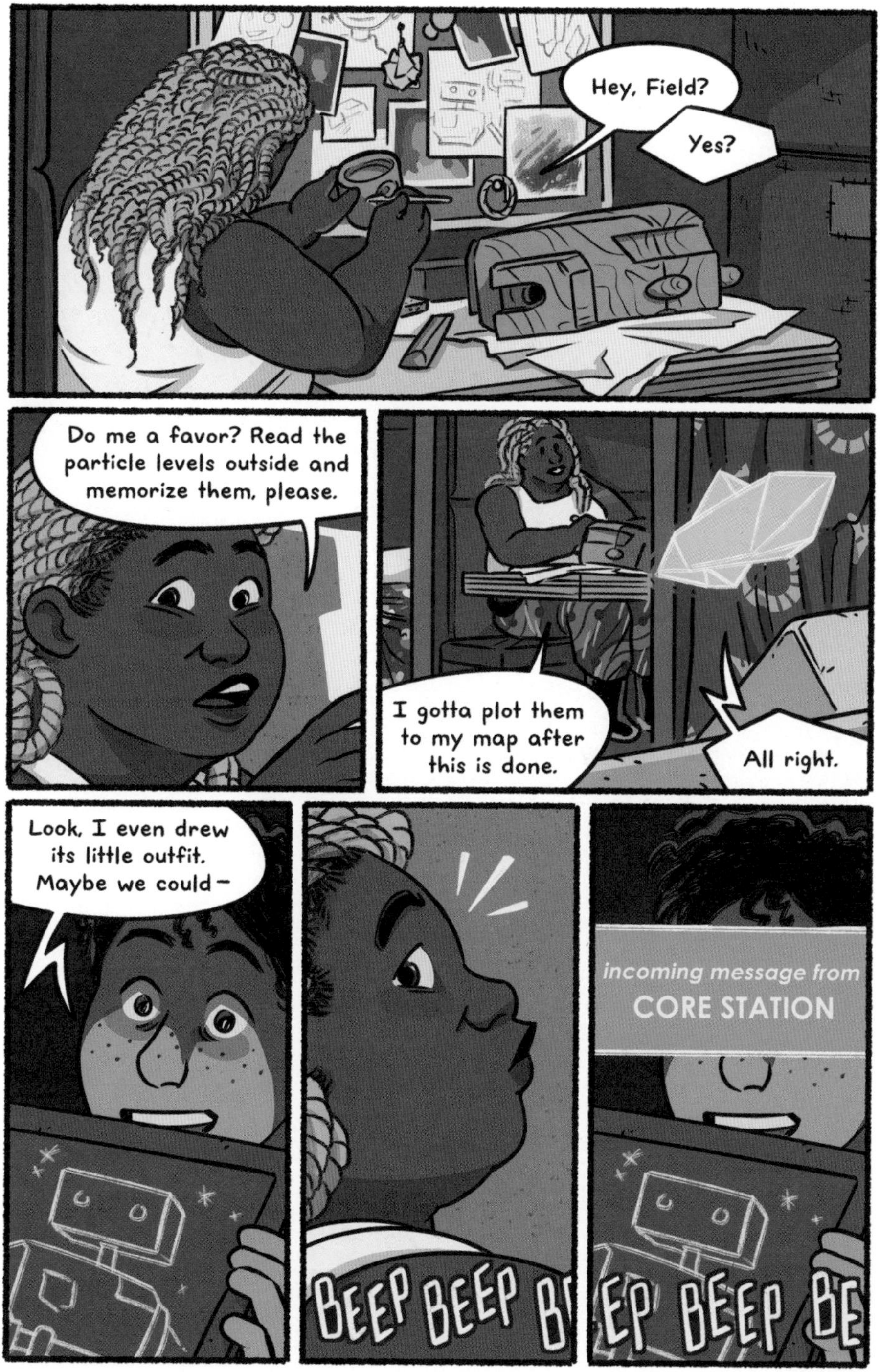
Hey, Field?
Yes?
Do me a favor? Read the particle levels outside and memorize them, please.
I gotta plot them to my map after this is done.
All right.
Look, I even drew its little outfit. Maybe we could—
BEEP BEEP
incoming message from
CORE STATION
BEEP BEEP

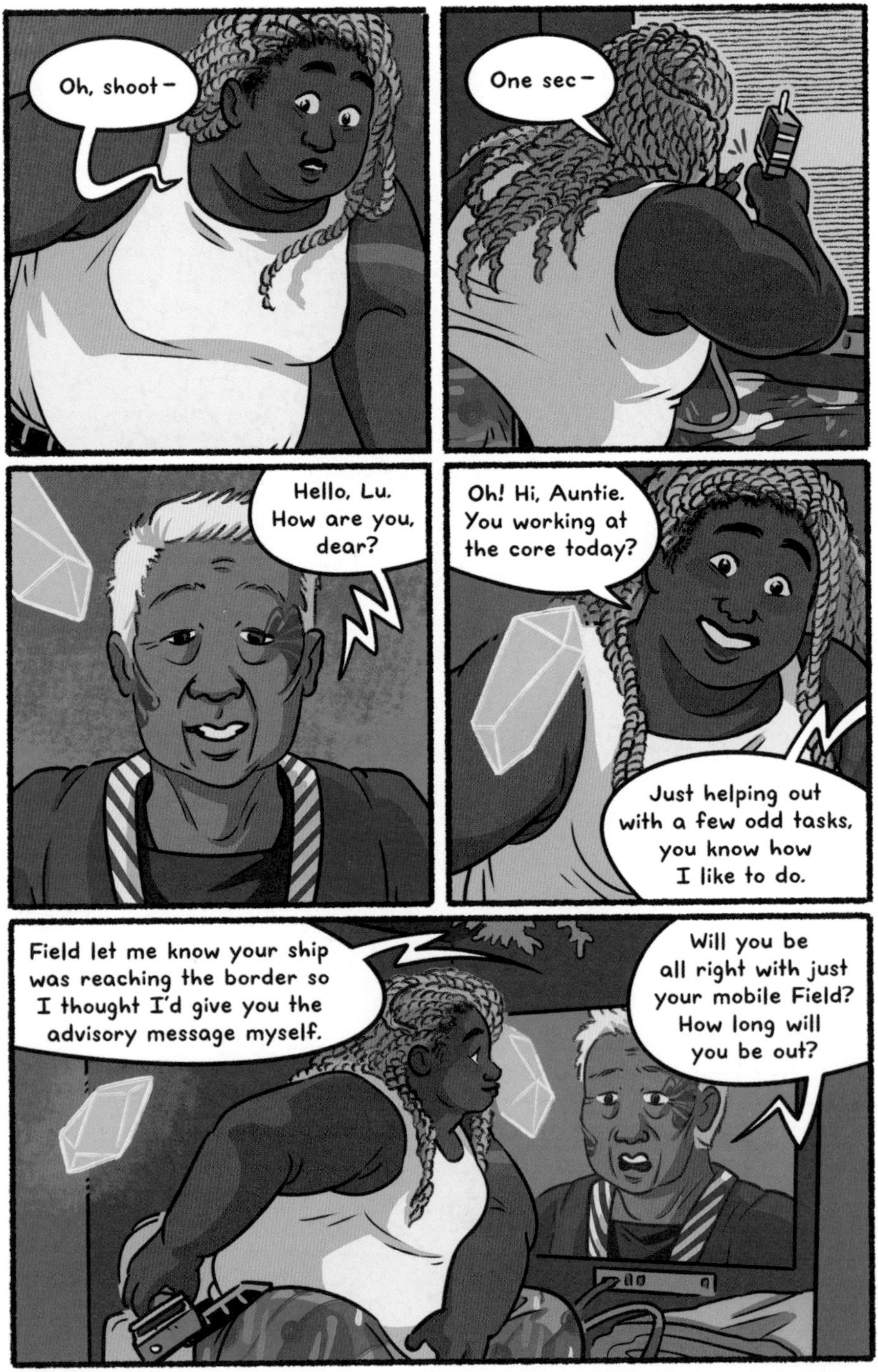
Oh, shoot-
One sec-
Hello, Lu. How are you, dear?
Oh! Hi, Auntie. You working at the core today?
Just helping out with a few odd tasks, you know how I like to do.
Field let me know your ship was reaching the border so I thought I'd give you the advisory message myself.
Will you be all right with just your mobile Field? How long will you be out?

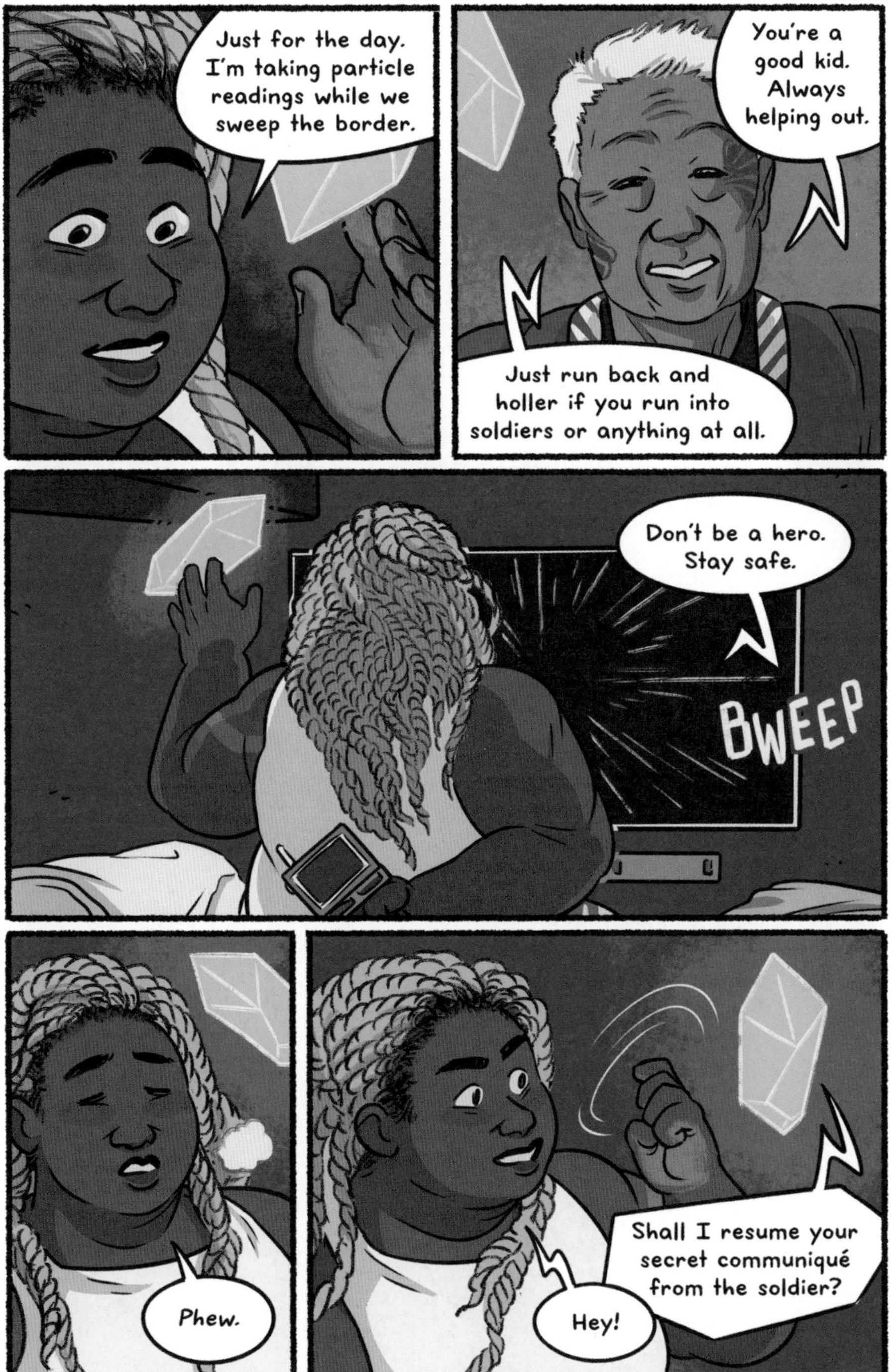
Just for the day. I'm taking particle readings while we sweep the border.
You're a good kid. Always helping out.
Just run back and holler if you run into soldiers or anything at all.
Don't be a hero. Stay safe.
BWEEP
Phew.
Hey!
Shall I resume your secret communiqué from the soldier?

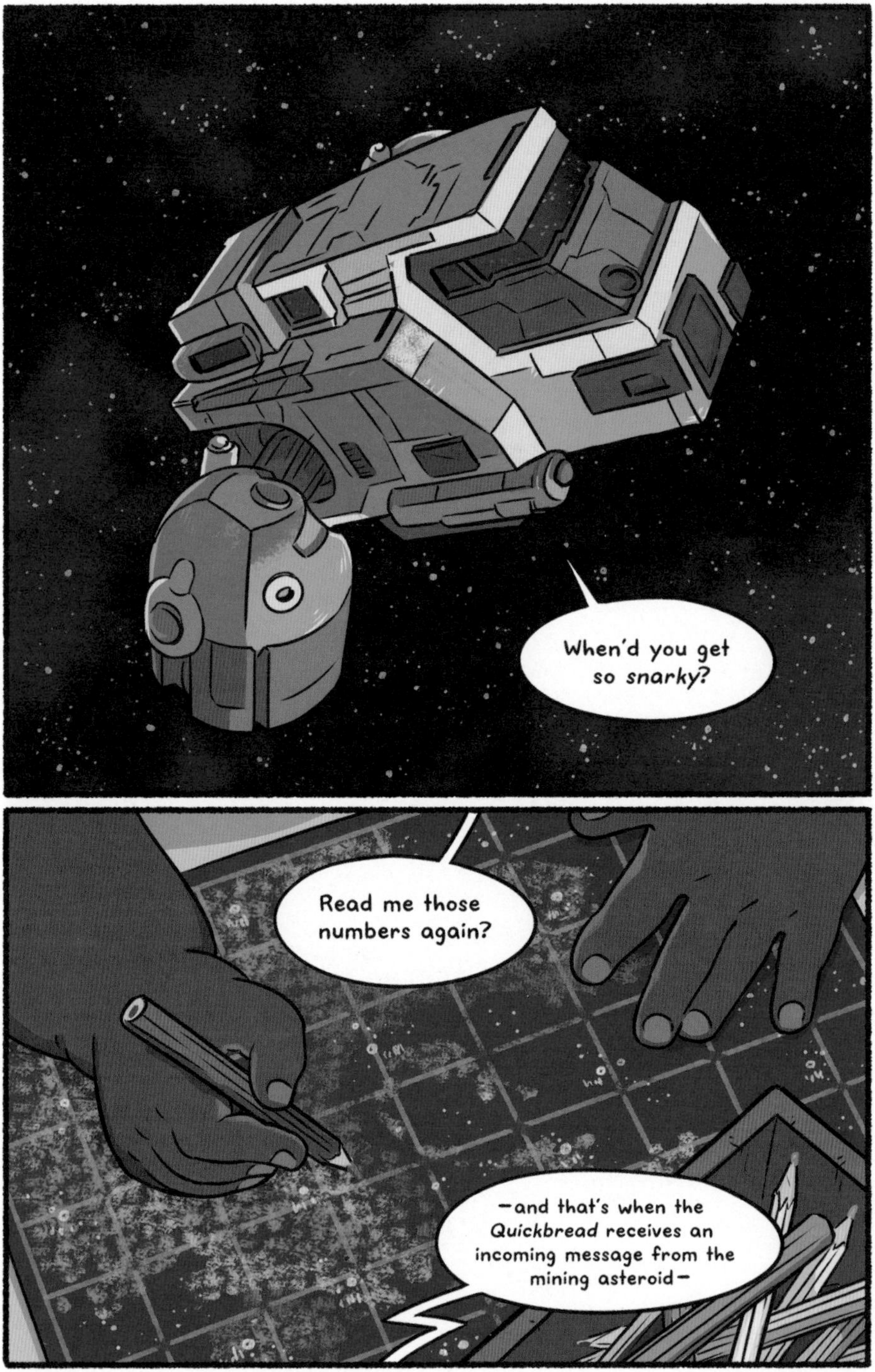
When'd you get so *snarky?*
Read me those numbers again?
—and that's when the *Quickbread* receives an incoming message from the mining asteroid—

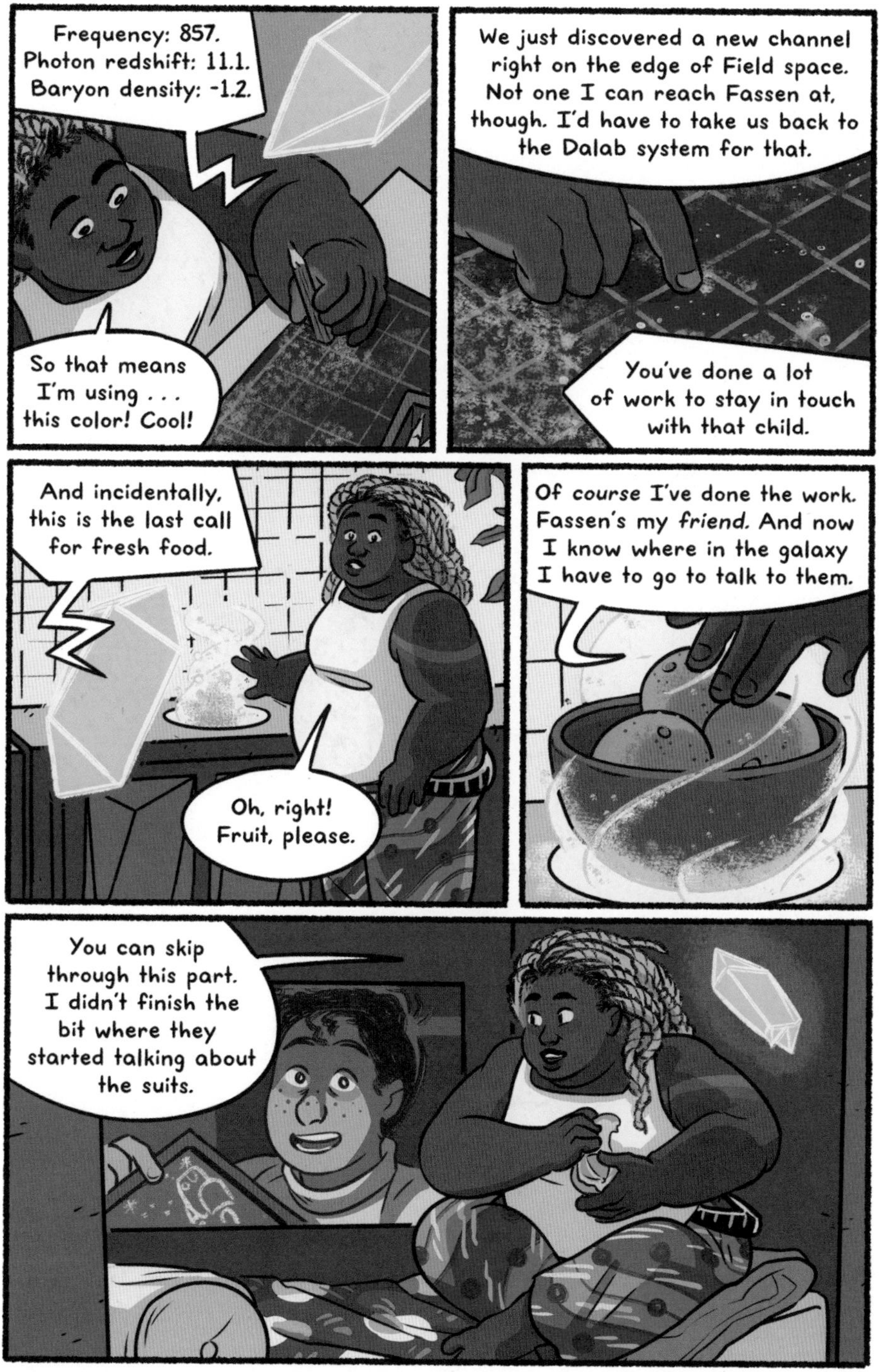
Frequency: 857.
Photon redshift: 11.1.
Baryon density: -1.2.
So that means
I'm using . . .
this color! Cool!
We just discovered a new channel right on the edge of Field space. Not one I can reach Fassen at, though. I'd have to take us back to the Dalab system for that.
You've done a lot of work to stay in touch with that child.
And incidentally, this is the last call for fresh food.
Oh, right! Fruit, please.
Of *course* I've done the work. Fassen's my *friend.* And now I know where in the galaxy I have to go to talk to them.
You can skip through this part. I didn't finish the bit where they started talking about the suits.

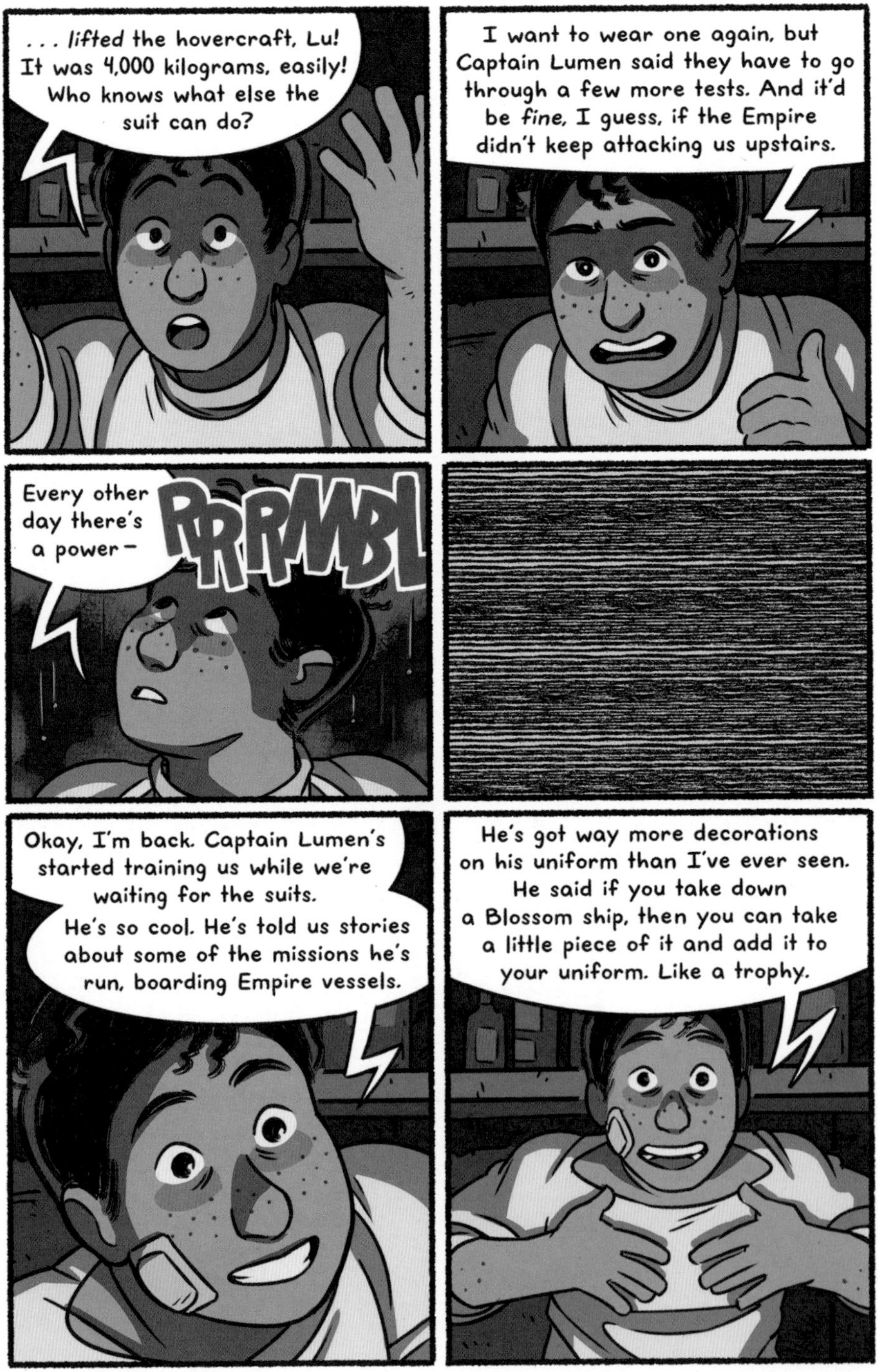

. . . *lifted* the hovercraft, Lu! It was 4,000 kilograms, easily! Who knows what else the suit can do?
I want to wear one again, but Captain Lumen said they have to go through a few more tests. And it'd be *fine*, I guess, if the Empire didn't keep attacking us upstairs.
Every other day there's a power—
RRRMBL
Okay, I'm back. Captain Lumen's started training us while we're waiting for the suits.
He's so cool. He's told us stories about some of the missions he's run, boarding Empire vessels.
He's got way more decorations on his uniform than I've ever seen. He said if you take down a Blossom ship, then you can take a little piece of it and add it to your uniform. Like a trophy.

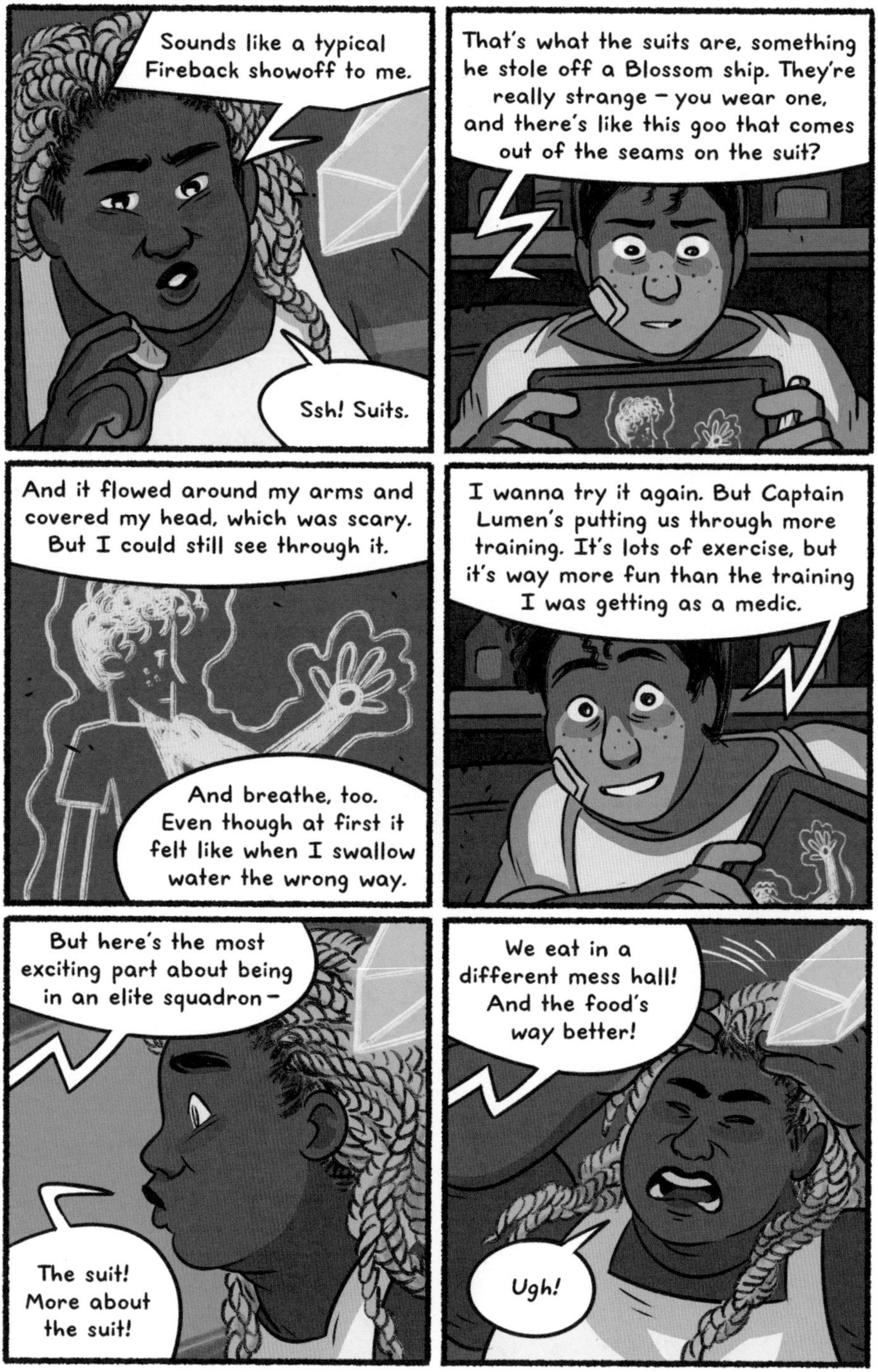
Sounds like a typical Fireback showoff to me.
Ssh! Suits.
That's what the suits are, something he stole off a Blossom ship. They're really strange – you wear one, and there's like this goo that comes out of the seams on the suit?
And it flowed around my arms and covered my head, which was scary. But I could still see through it.
And breathe, too. Even though at first it felt like when I swallow water the wrong way.
I wanna try it again. But Captain Lumen's putting us through more training. It's lots of exercise, but it's way more fun than the training I was getting as a medic.
But here's the most exciting part about being in an elite squadron–
The suit! More about the suit!
We eat in a different mess hall! And the food's way better!
Ugh!

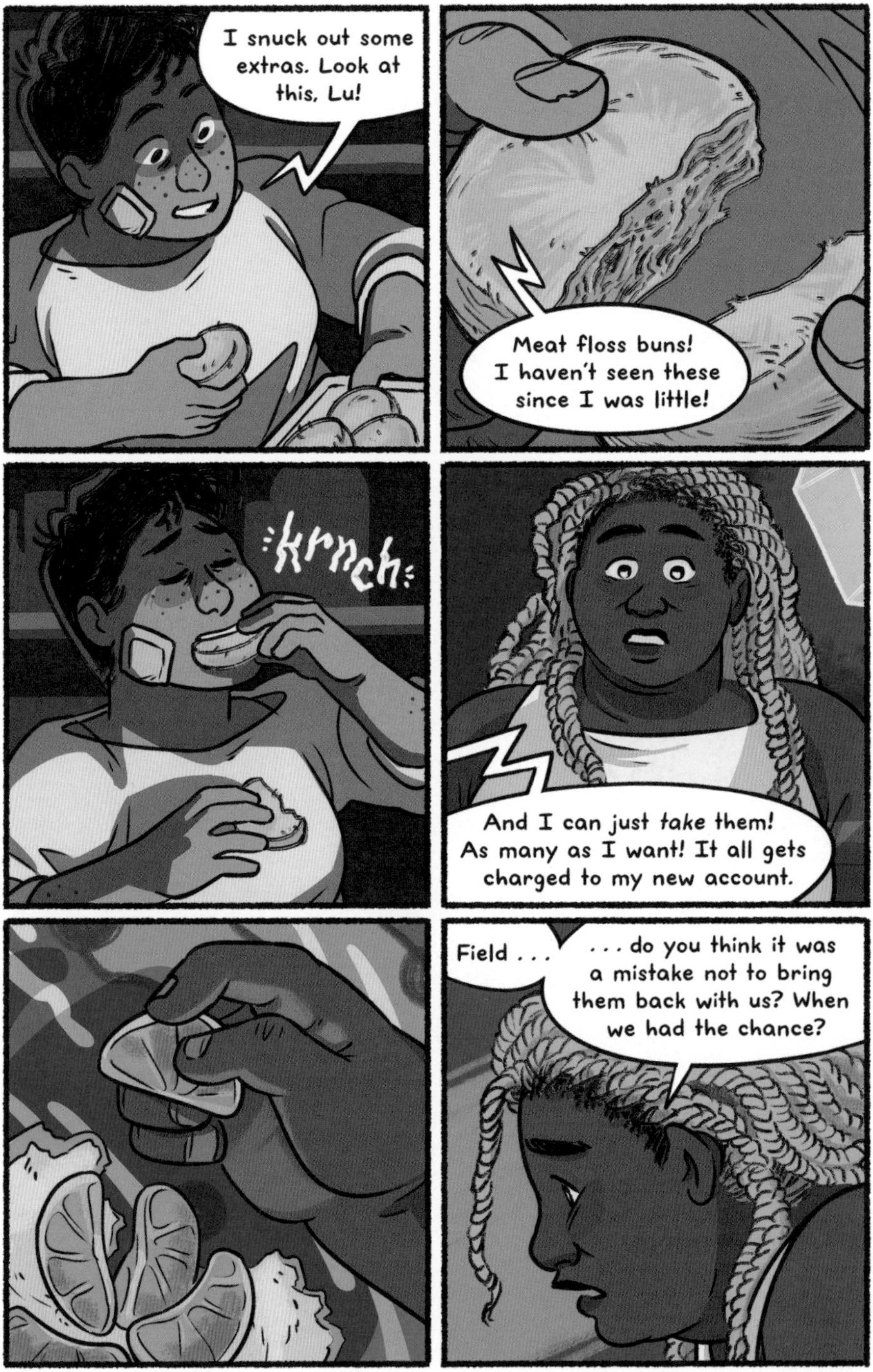
I snuck out some extras. Look at this, Lu!
Meat floss buns! I haven't seen these since I was little!
krnch
And I can just *take* them! As many as I want! It all gets charged to my new account.
Field . . .
. . . do you think it was a mistake not to bring them back with us? When we had the chance?

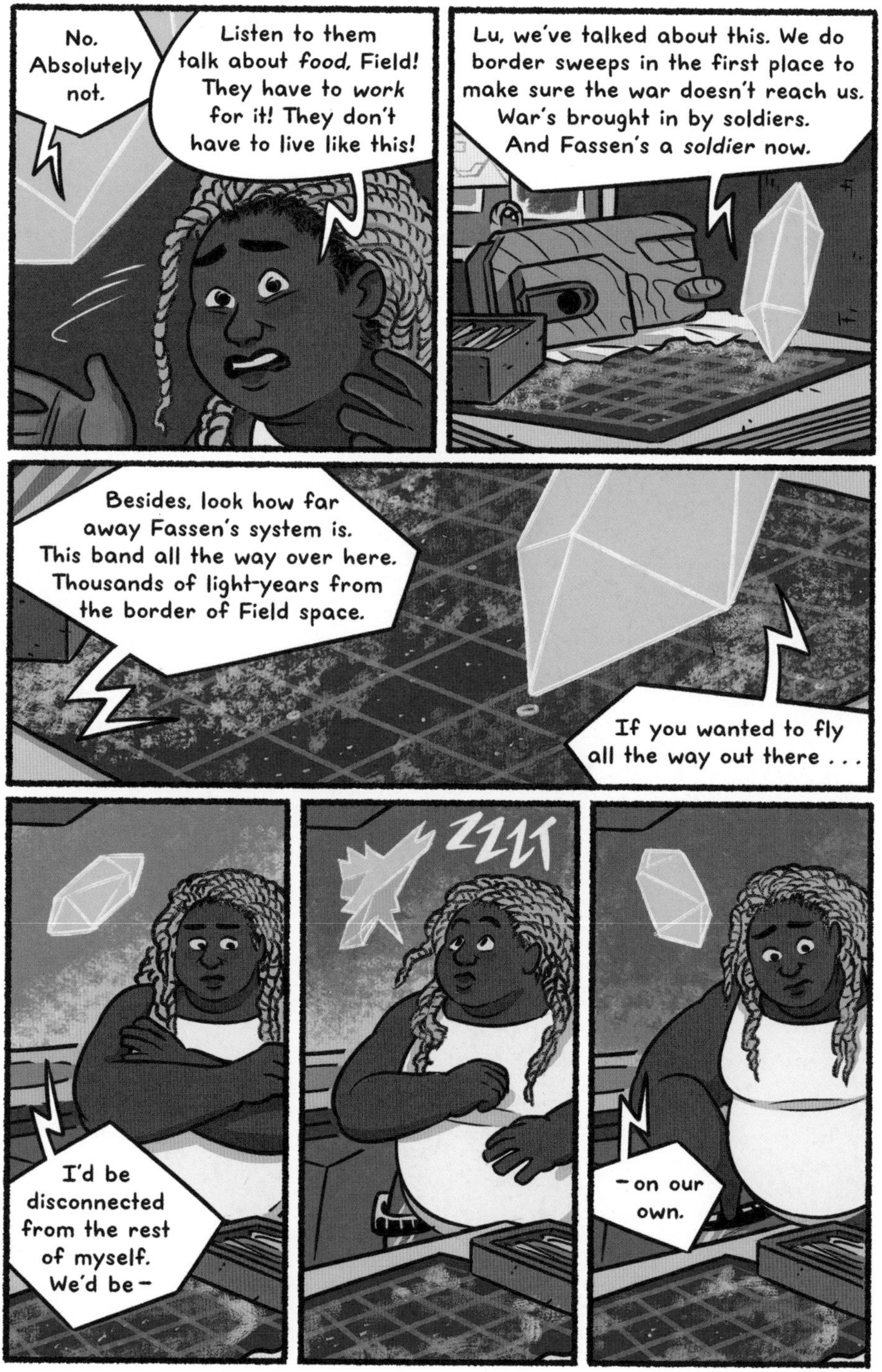
No. Absolutely not.
Listen to them talk about *food*, Field! They have to *work* for it! They don't have to live like this!
Lu, we've talked about this. We do border sweeps in the first place to make sure the war doesn't reach us. War's brought in by soldiers. And Fassen's a *soldier* now.
Besides, look how far away Fassen's system is. This band all the way over here. Thousands of light-years from the border of Field space.
If you wanted to fly all the way out there . . .
I'd be disconnected from the rest of myself. We'd be—
ZZZT
—on our own.

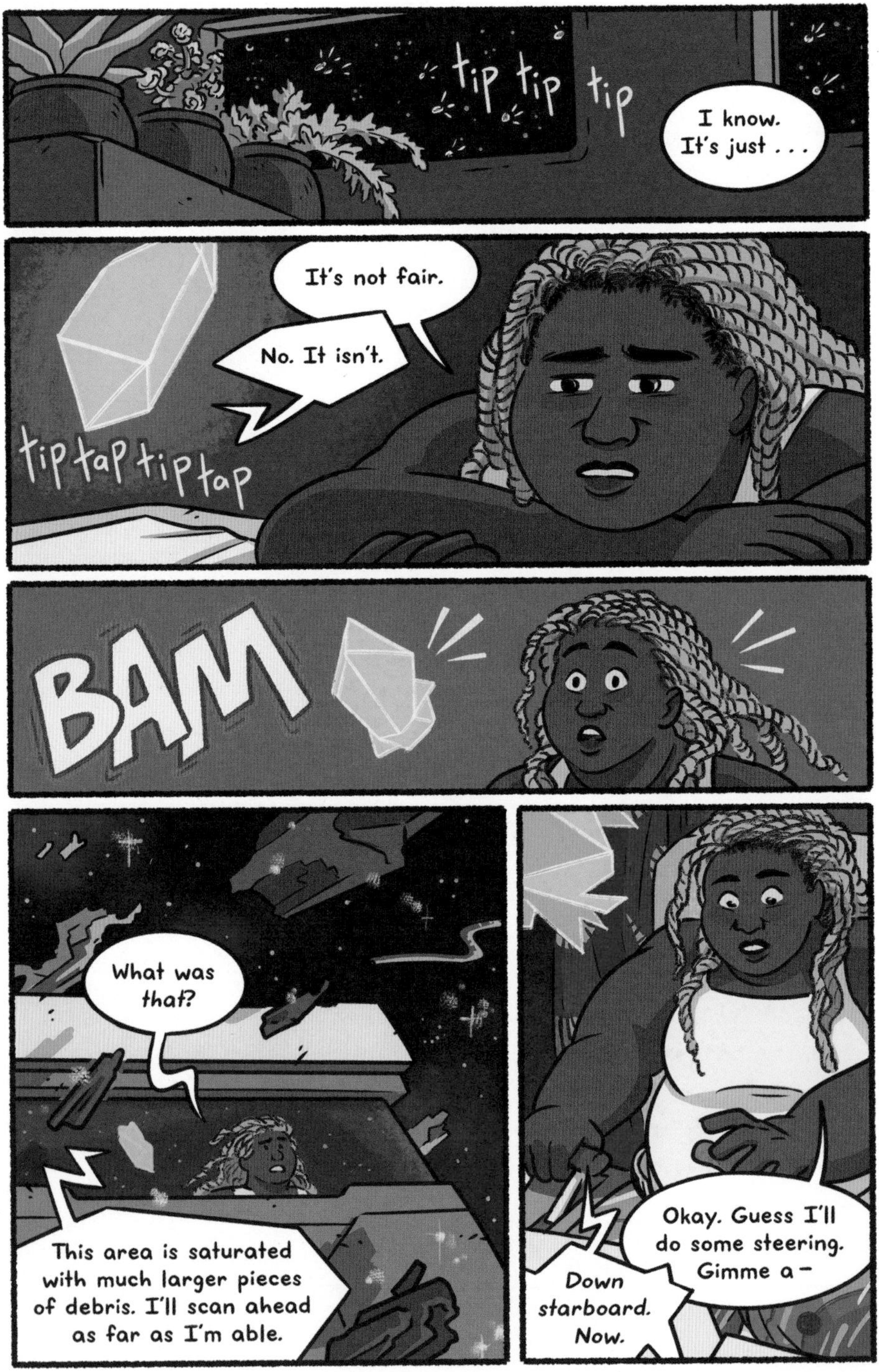
tip tip tip
I know. It's just . . .
It's not fair.
No. It isn't.
tip tap tip tap
BAM
What was that?
This area is saturated with much larger pieces of debris. I'll scan ahead as far as I'm able.
Okay. Guess I'll do some steering. Gimme a—
Down starboard. Now.

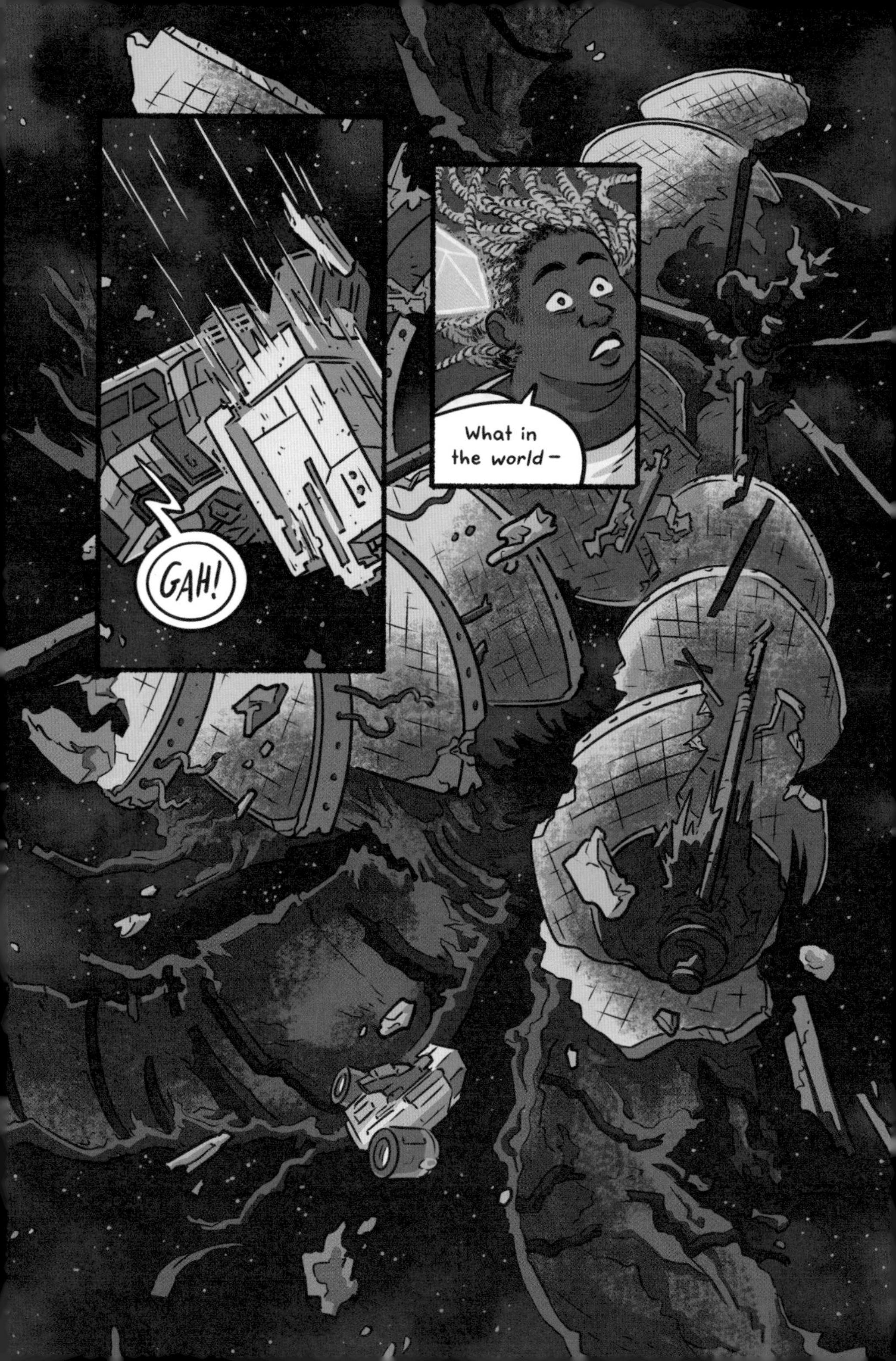
GAH!
What in the world—

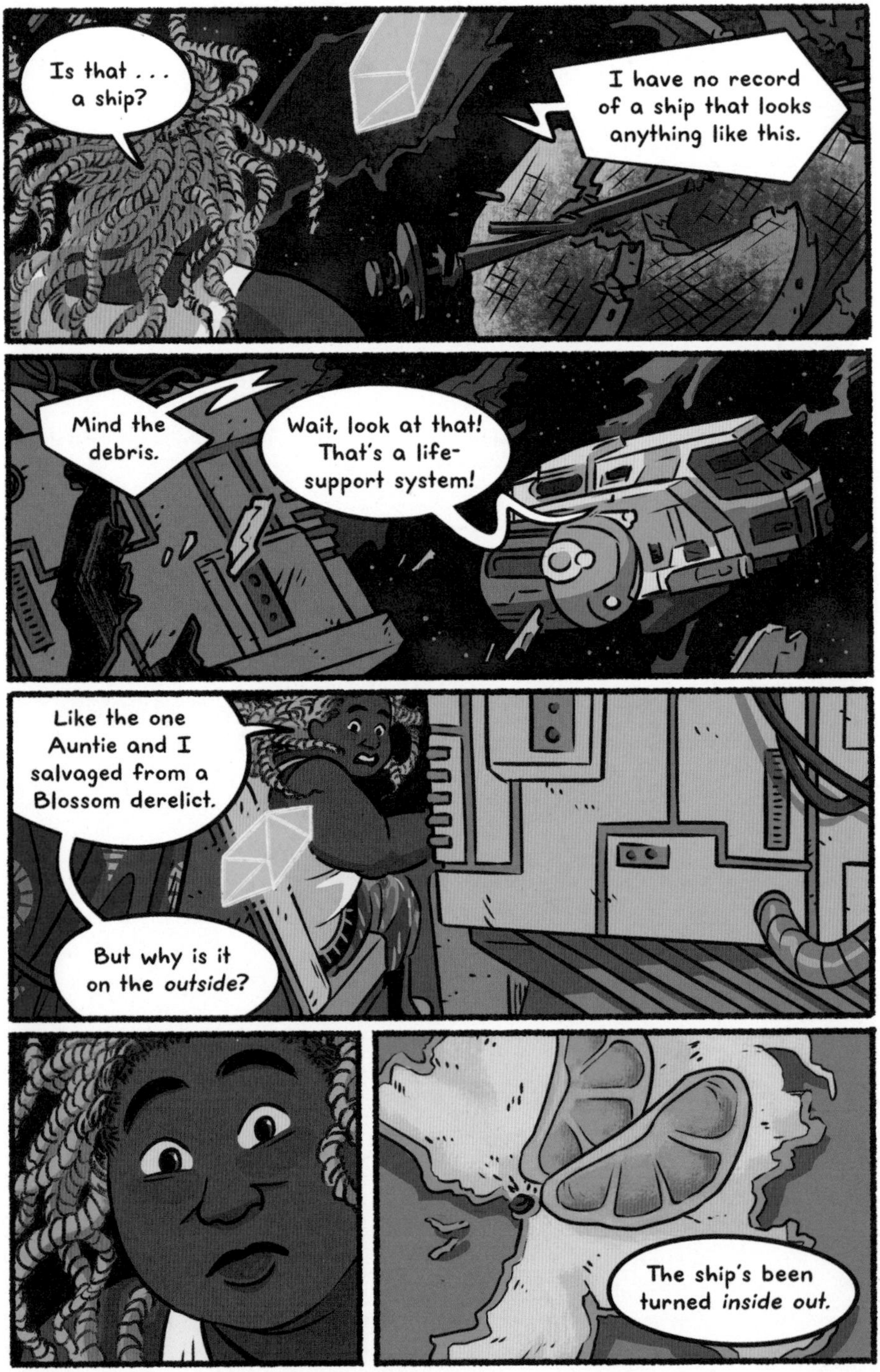

Is that . . . a ship?
I have no record of a ship that looks anything like this.
Mind the debris.
Wait, look at that! That's a life-support system!
Like the one Auntie and I salvaged from a Blossom derelict.
But why is it on the *outside?*
The ship's been turned *inside out.*

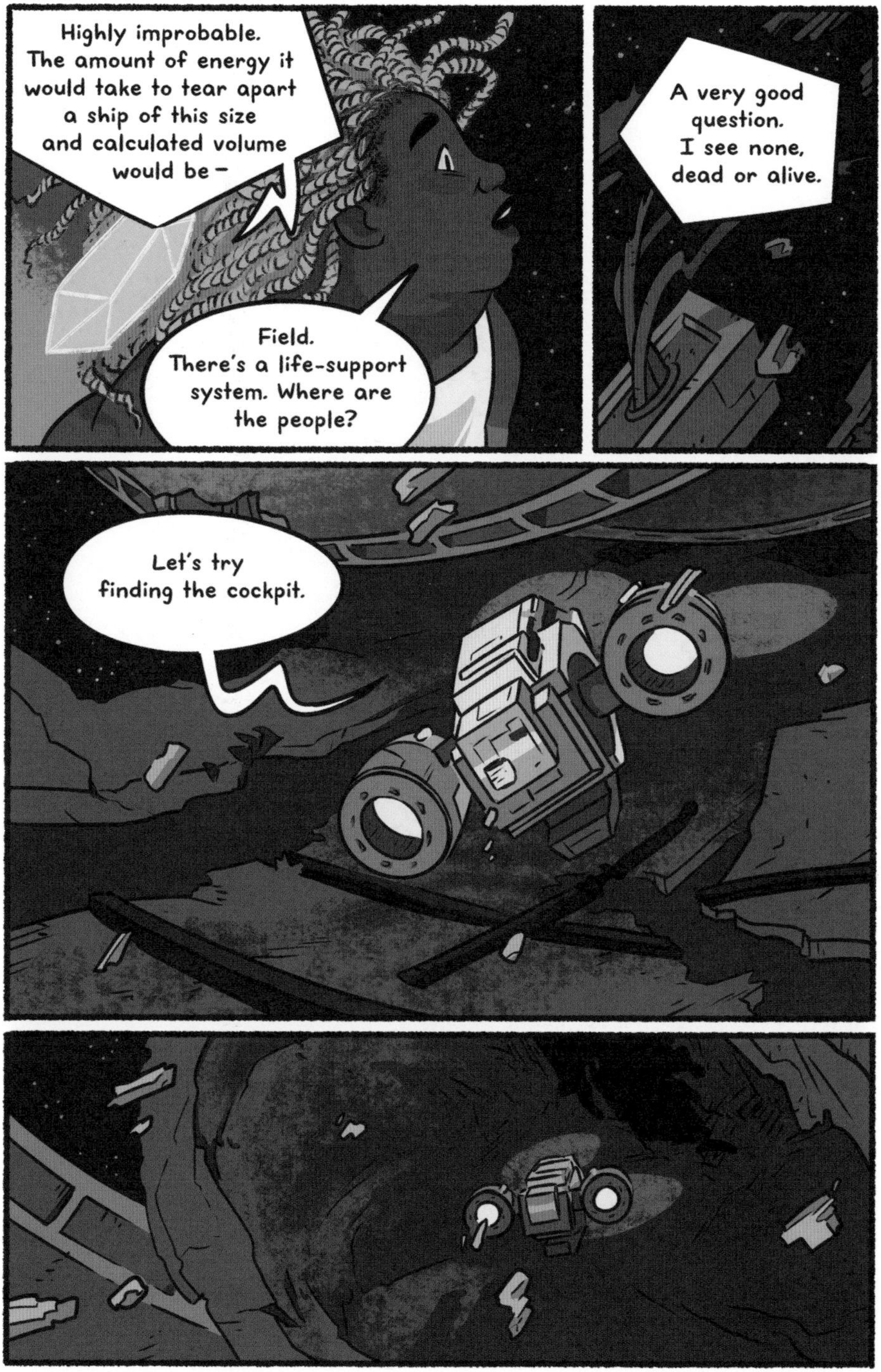

Highly improbable. The amount of energy it would take to tear apart a ship of this size and calculated volume would be –
Field. There's a life-support system. Where are the people?
A very good question. I see none, dead or alive.
Let's try finding the cockpit.

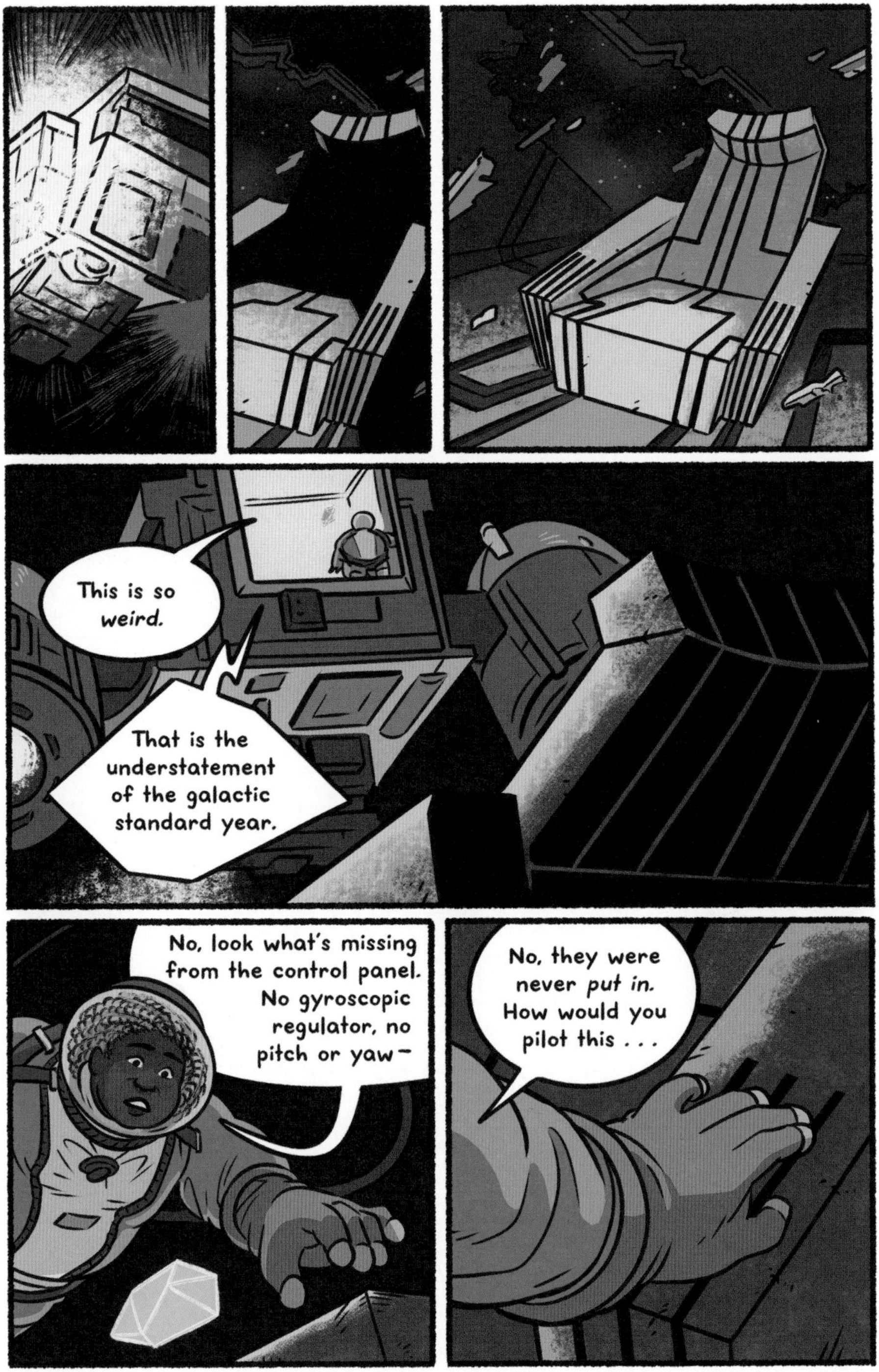
This is so *weird.*
That is the understatement of the galactic standard year.
No, look what's missing from the control panel. No gyroscopic regulator, no pitch or yaw—
No, they were never *put in.* How would you pilot this . . .

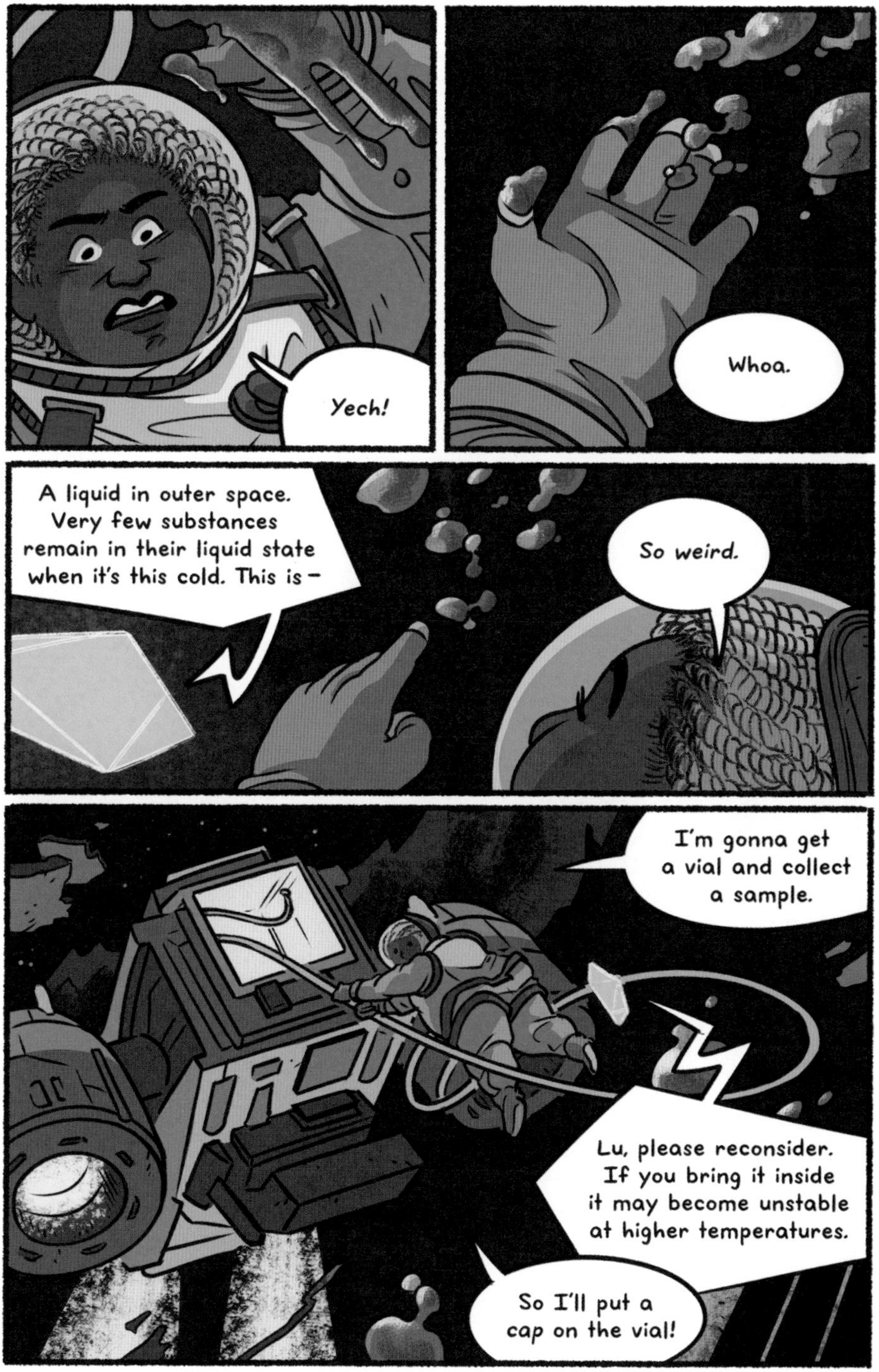
Yech!
Whoa.
A liquid in outer space. Very few substances remain in their liquid state when it's this cold. This is—
So weird.
I'm gonna get a vial and collect a sample.
Lu, please reconsider. If you bring it inside it may become unstable at higher temperatures.
So I'll put a cap on the vial!

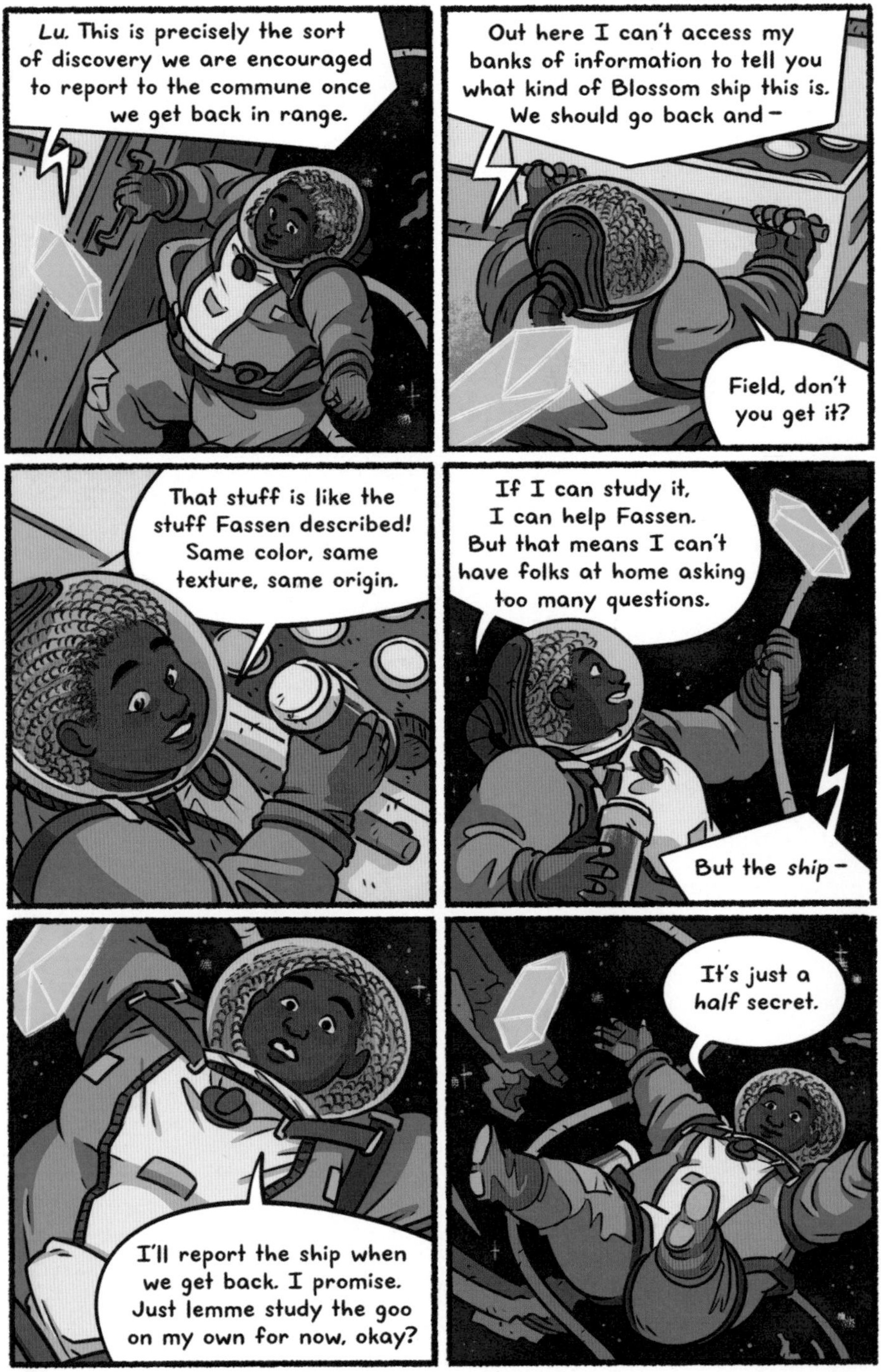
Lu. This is precisely the sort of discovery we are encouraged to report to the commune once we get back in range.
Out here I can't access my banks of information to tell you what kind of Blossom ship this is. We should go back and—
Field, don't you get it?
That stuff is like the stuff Fassen described! Same color, same texture, same origin.
If I can study it, I can help Fassen. But that means I can't have folks at home asking too many questions.
But the *ship*—
I'll report the ship when we get back. I promise. Just lemme study the goo on my own for now, okay?
It's just a *half* secret.

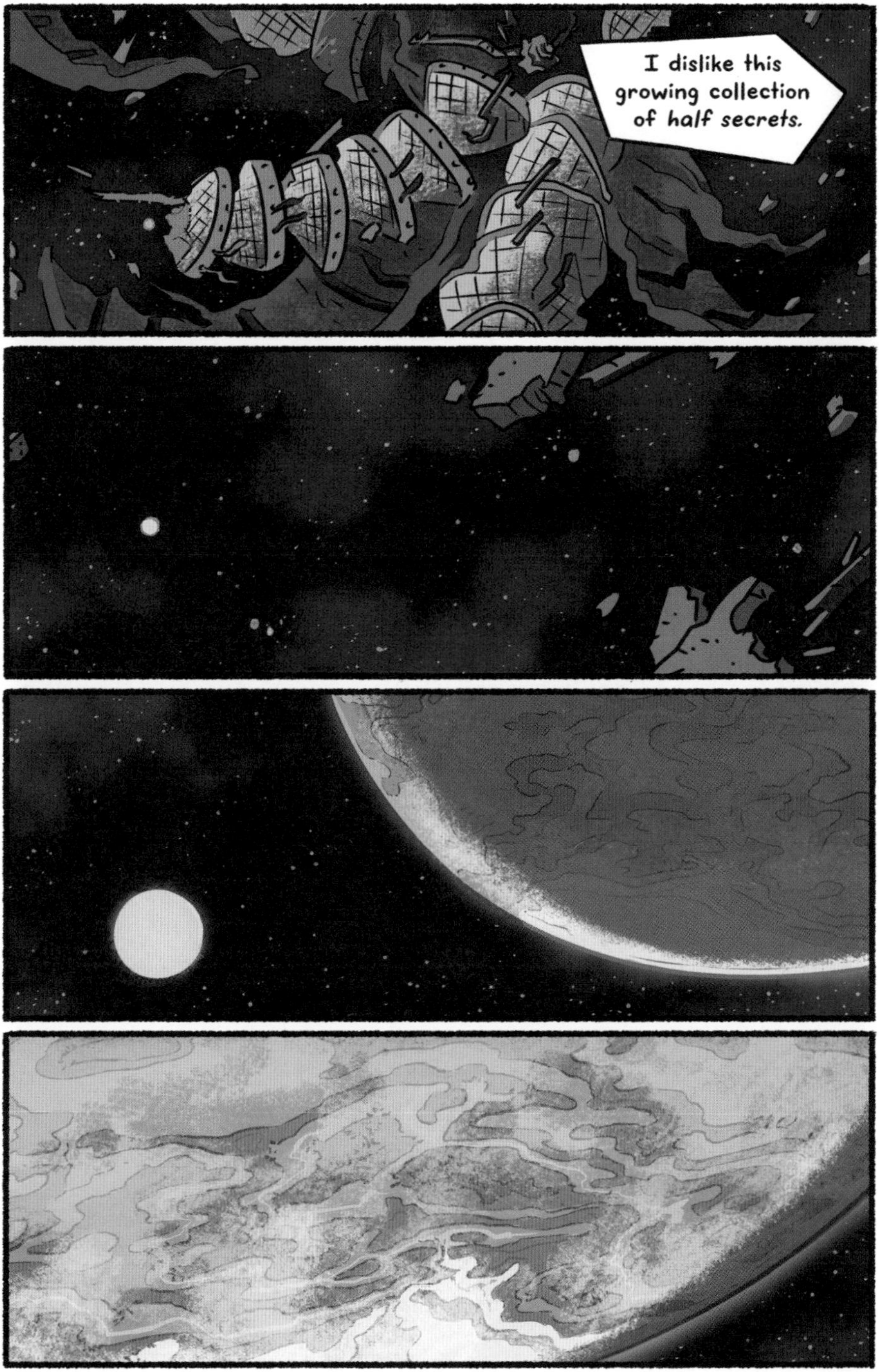
I dislike this growing collection of half secrets.

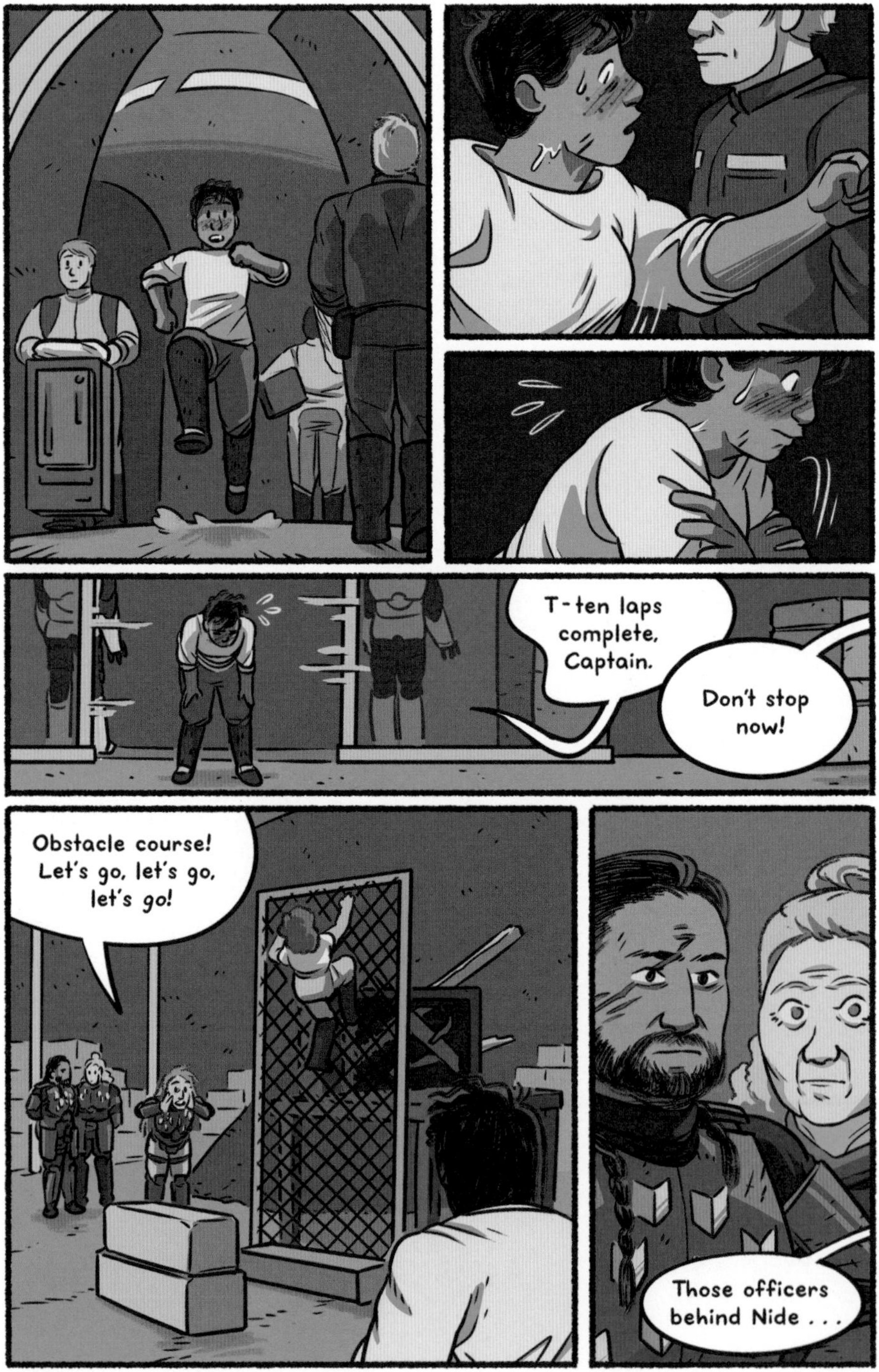
T-ten laps complete, Captain.
Don't stop now!
Obstacle course! Let's go, let's go, let's go!
Those officers behind Nide . . .

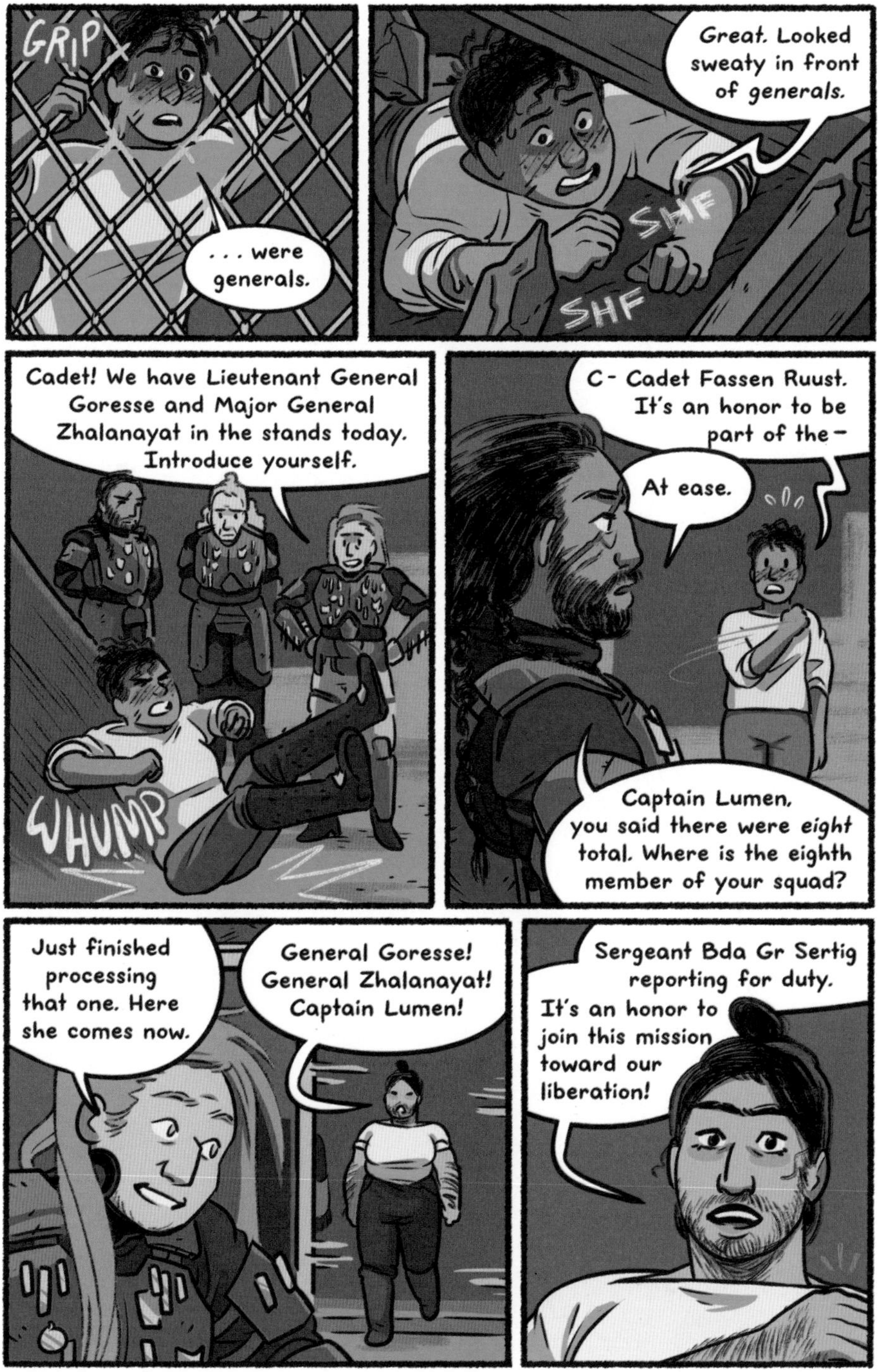

GRIP
. . . were generals.
Great. Looked sweaty in front of generals.
SHF
SHF
Cadet! We have Lieutenant General Goresse and Major General Zhalanayat in the stands today. Introduce yourself.
WHUMP
C- Cadet Fassen Ruust. It's an honor to be part of the—
At ease.
Captain Lumen, you said there were *eight* total. Where is the eighth member of your squad?
Just finished processing that one. Here she comes now.
General Goresse! General Zhalanayat! Captain Lumen!
Sergeant Bda Gr Sertig reporting for duty.
It's an honor to join this mission toward our liberation!

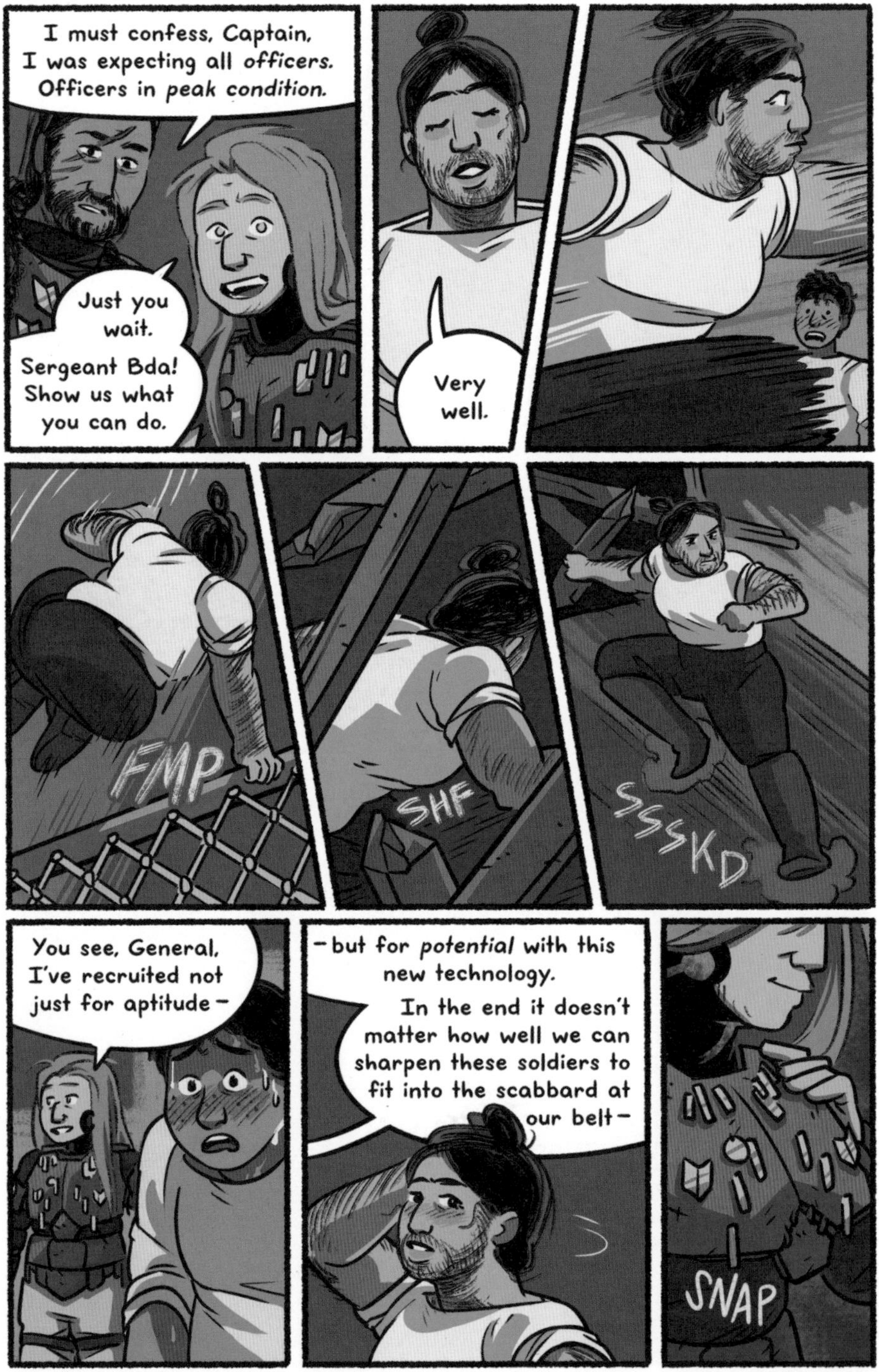
I must confess, Captain, I was expecting all *officers*. Officers in *peak condition*.
Just you wait.
Sergeant Bda! Show us what you can do.
Very well.
FMP
SHF
SSSKD
You see, General, I've recruited not just for aptitude—
—but for *potential* with this new technology.
In the end it doesn't matter how well we can sharpen these soldiers to fit into the scabbard at our belt—
SNAP

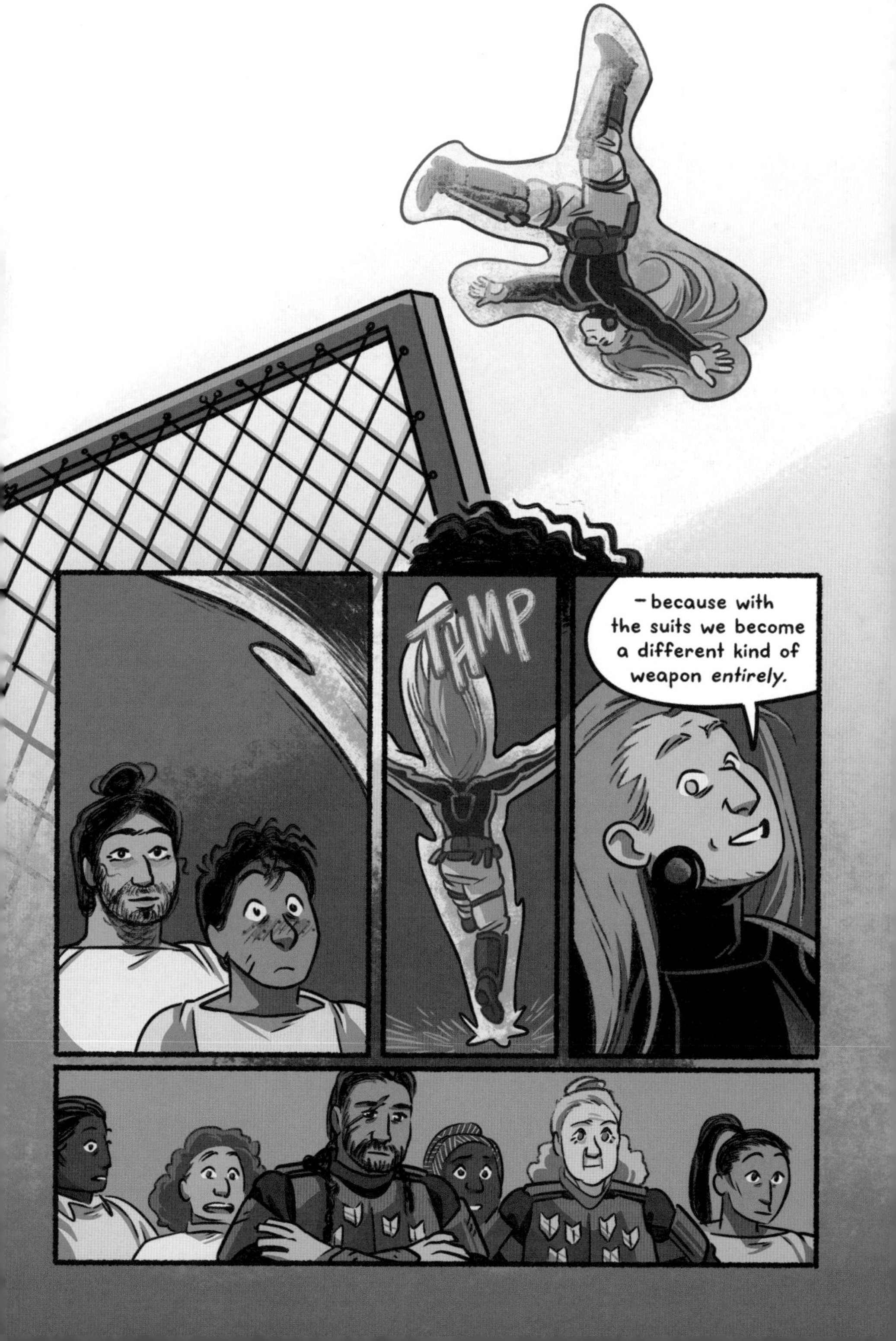
THMP
–because with the suits we become a different kind of weapon *entirely*.

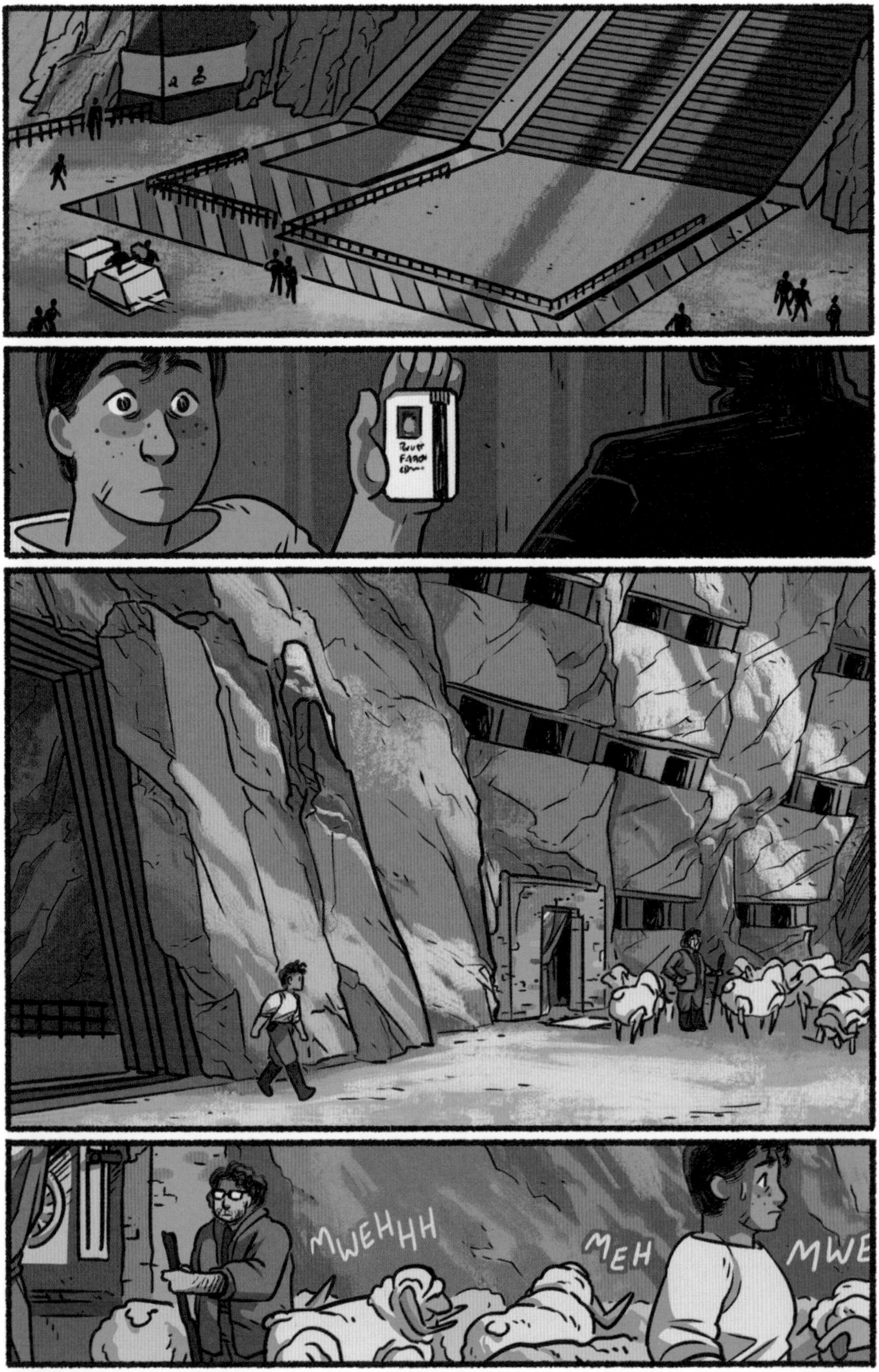
MWEHHH
MEH
MWE

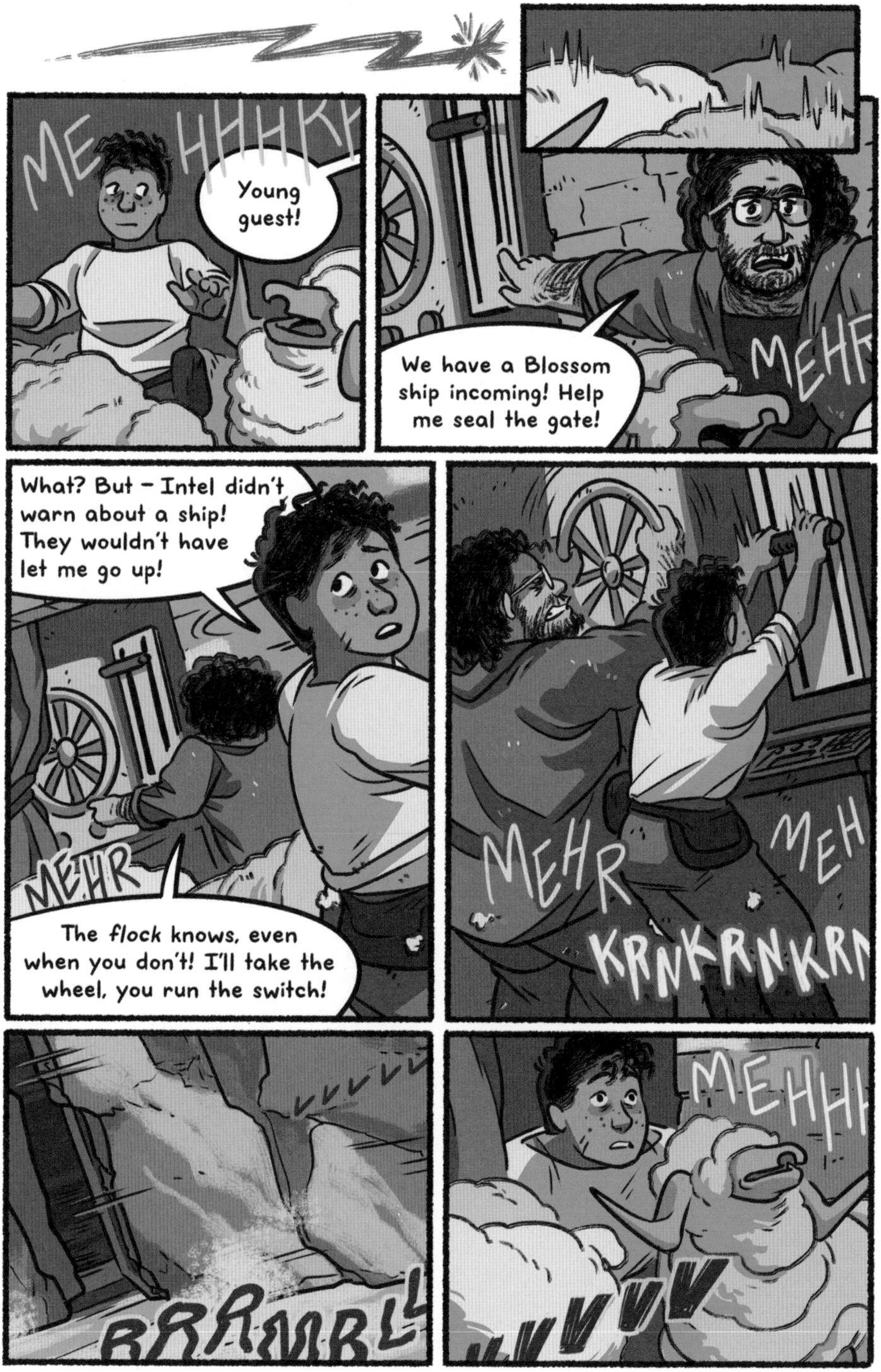
MEHHHHKH
Young guest!
We have a Blossom ship incoming! Help me seal the gate!
MEHR
What? But — Intel didn't warn about a ship! They wouldn't have let me go up!
MEHR
The *flock* knows, even when you don't! I'll take the wheel, you run the switch!
MEHR
MEH
KRNKRNKRN
BRRMBL
MEHHH

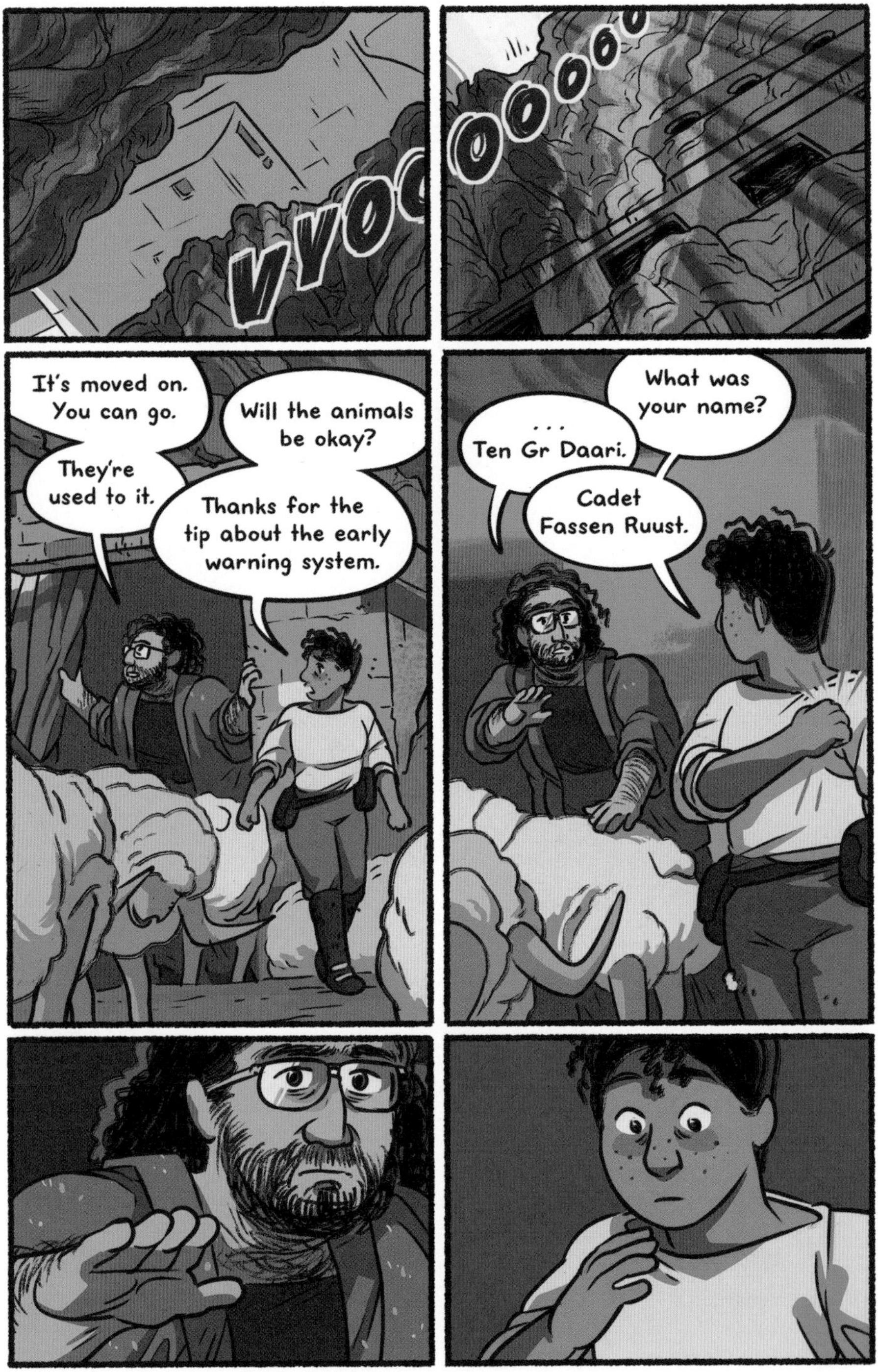
VVOOOOOOOO
It's moved on. You can go.
Will the animals be okay?
They're used to it.
Thanks for the tip about the early warning system.
What was your name?
. . .
Ten Gr Daari.
Cadet Fassen Ruust.

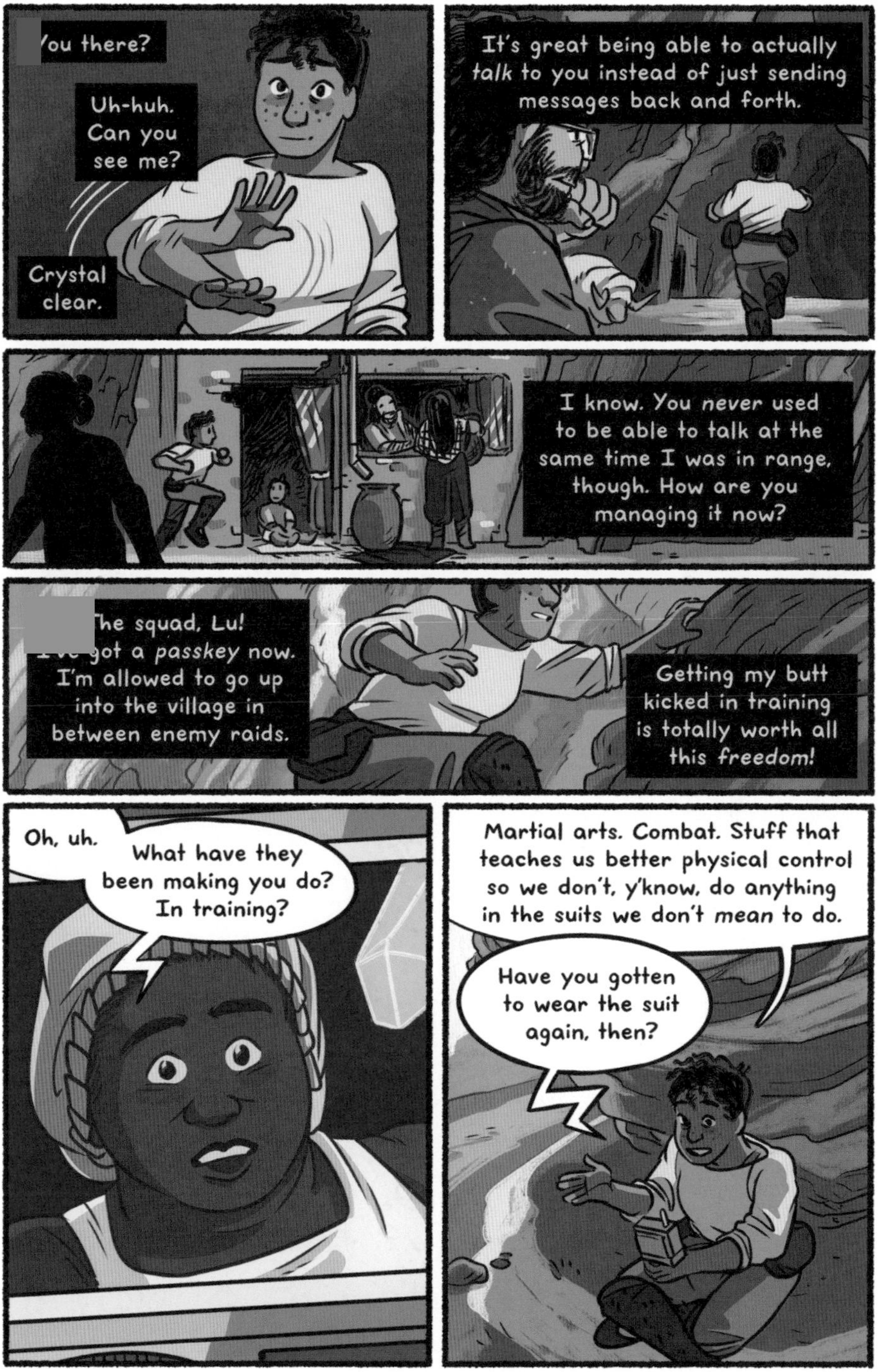

[redacted]ou there?
Uh-huh. Can you see me?
Crystal clear.
It's great being able to actually *talk* to you instead of just sending messages back and forth.
I know. You *never* used to be able to talk at the same time I was in range, though. How are you managing it now?
[redacted]he squad, Lu!
[redacted]got a *passkey* now. I'm allowed to go up into the village in between enemy raids.
Getting my butt kicked in training is totally worth all this *freedom!*
Oh, uh.
What have they been making you do? In training?
Martial arts. Combat. Stuff that teaches us better physical control so we don't, y'know, do anything in the suits we don't *mean* to do.
Have you gotten to wear the suit again, then?

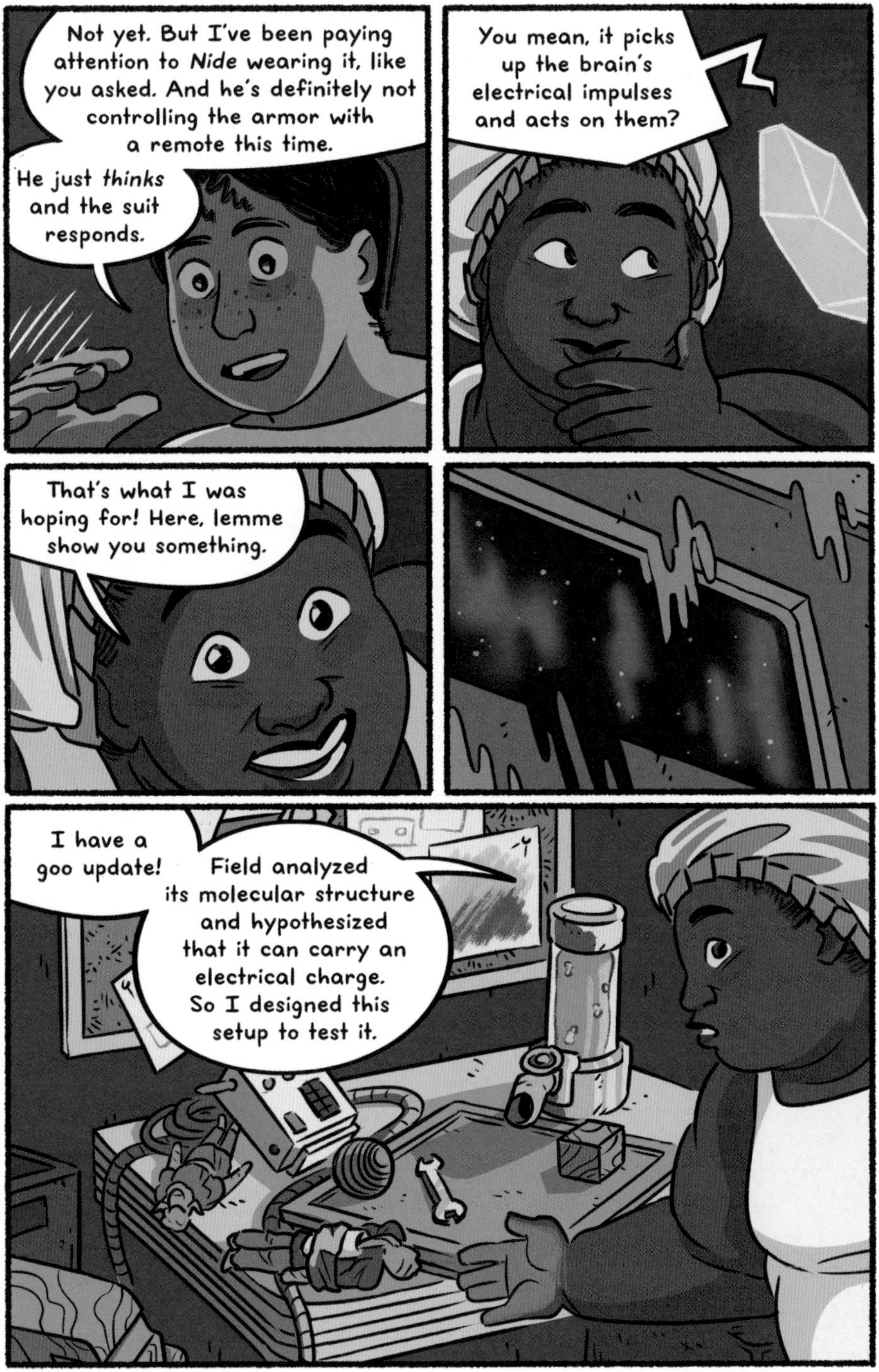
Not yet. But I've been paying attention to *Nide* wearing it, like you asked. And he's definitely not controlling the armor with a remote this time.
He just *thinks* and the suit responds.
You mean, it picks up the brain's electrical impulses and acts on them?
That's what I was hoping for! Here, lemme show you something.
I have a goo update!
Field analyzed its molecular structure and hypothesized that it can carry an electrical charge. So I designed this setup to test it.

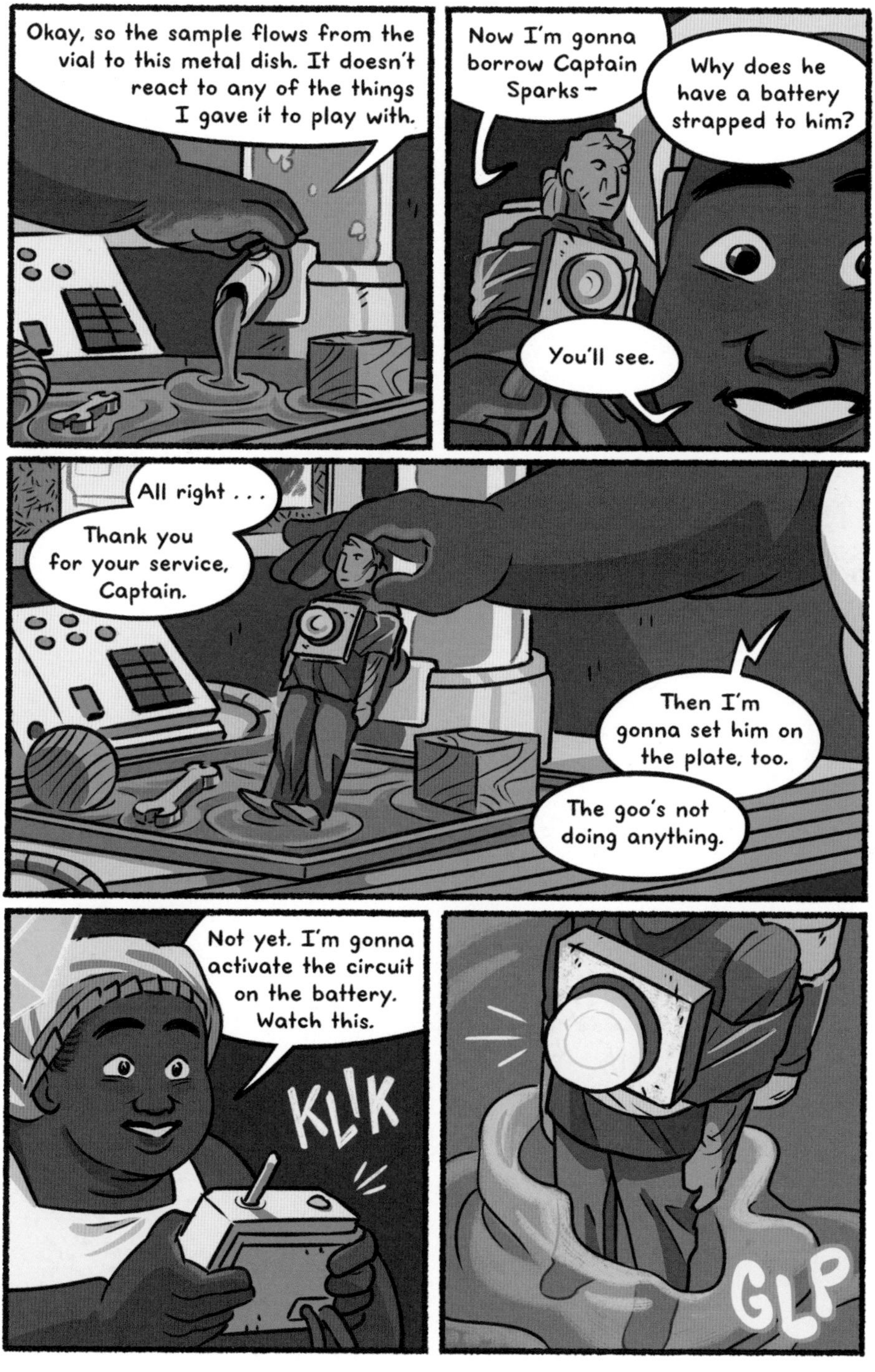
Okay, so the sample flows from the vial to this metal dish. It doesn't react to any of the things I gave it to play with.
Now I'm gonna borrow Captain Sparks—
Why does he have a battery strapped to him?
You'll see.
All right . . .
Thank you for your service, Captain.
Then I'm gonna set him on the plate, too.
The goo's not doing anything.
Not yet. I'm gonna activate the circuit on the battery. Watch this.
KLIK
GLP

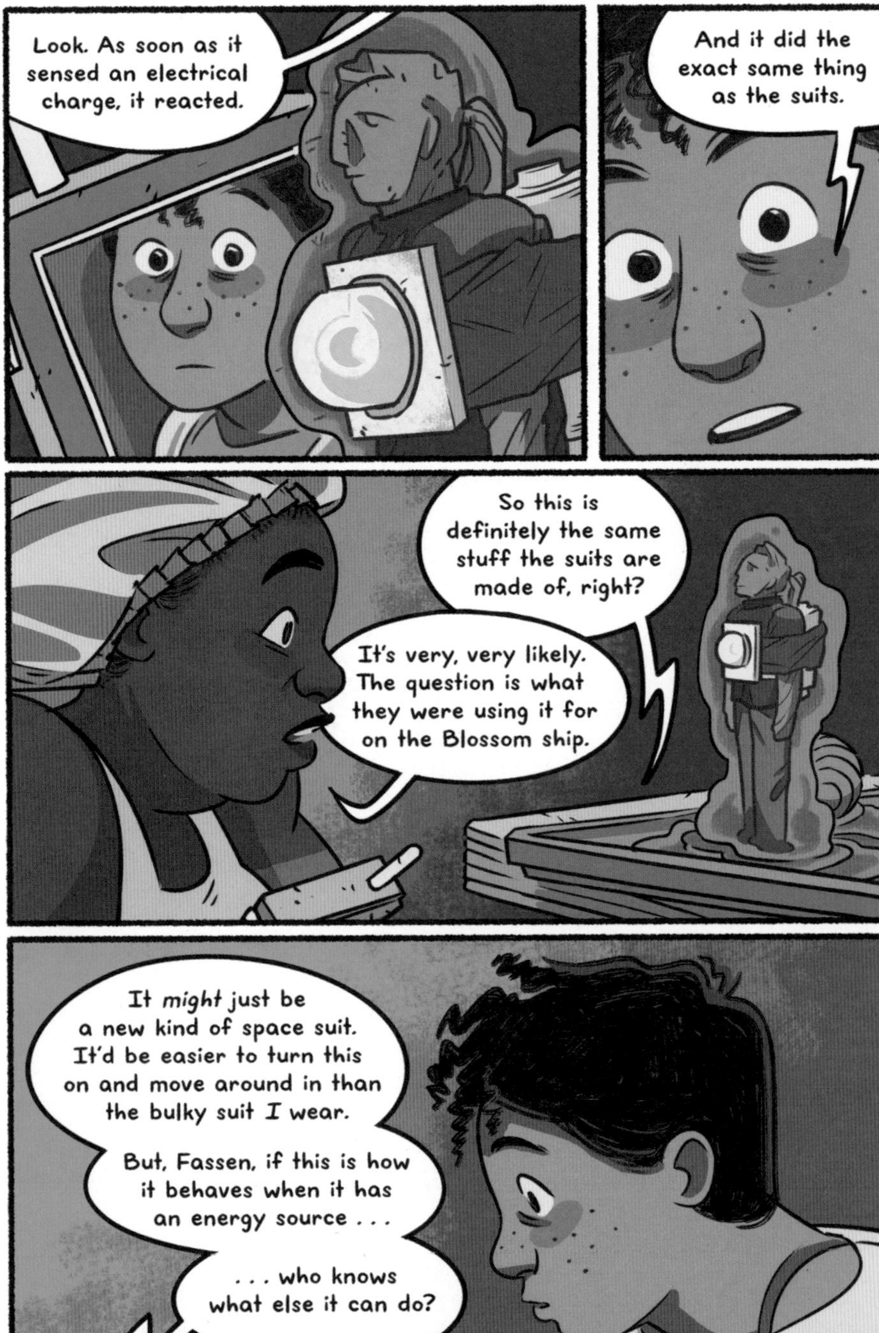
Look. As soon as it sensed an electrical charge, it reacted.
And it did the exact same thing as the suits.
So this is definitely the same stuff the suits are made of, right?
It's very, very likely. The question is what they were using it for on the Blossom ship.
It *might* just be a new kind of space suit. It'd be easier to turn this on and move around in than the bulky suit *I* wear.
But, Fassen, if this is how it behaves when it has an energy source . . .
. . . who knows what else it can do?

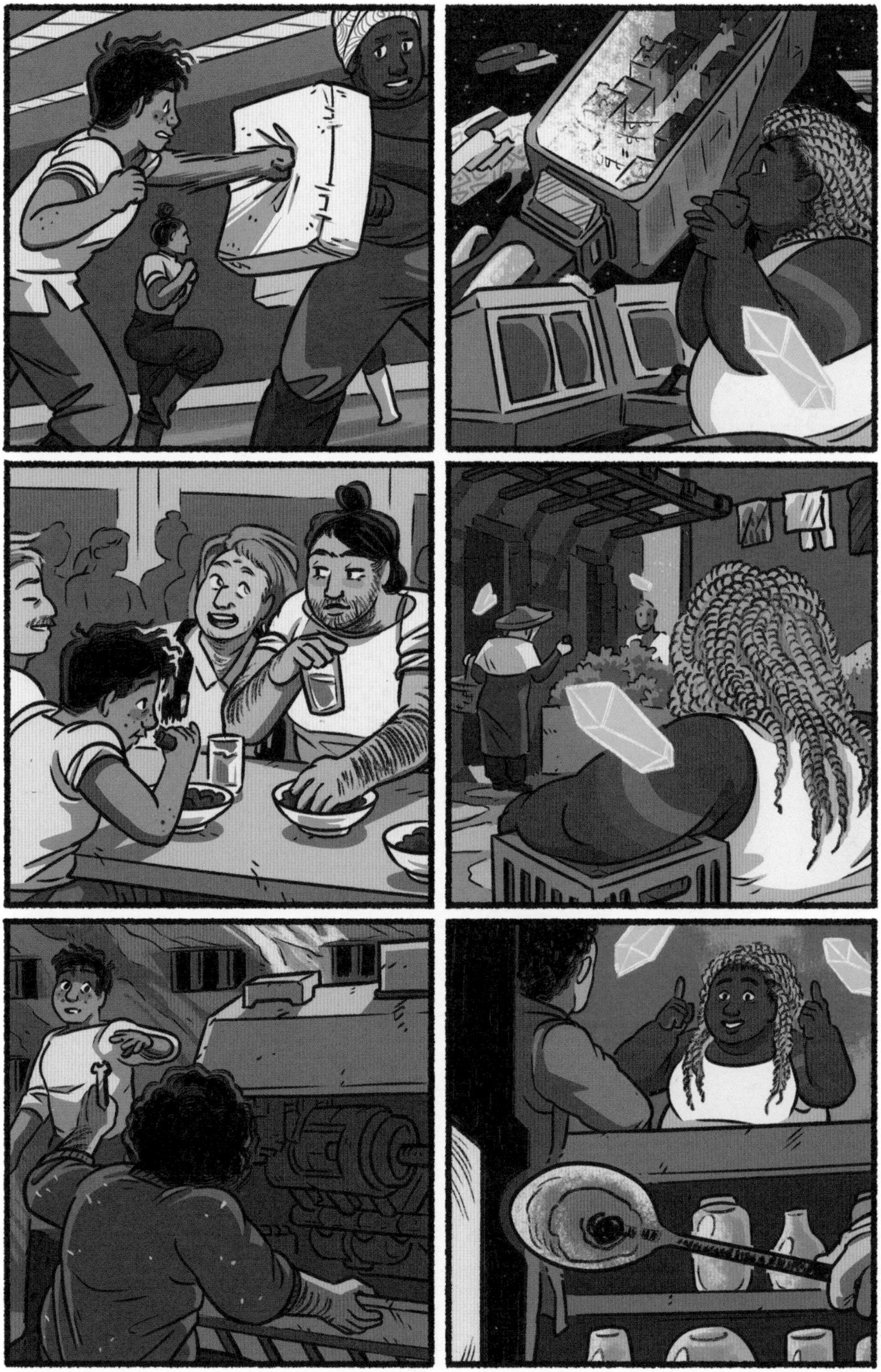

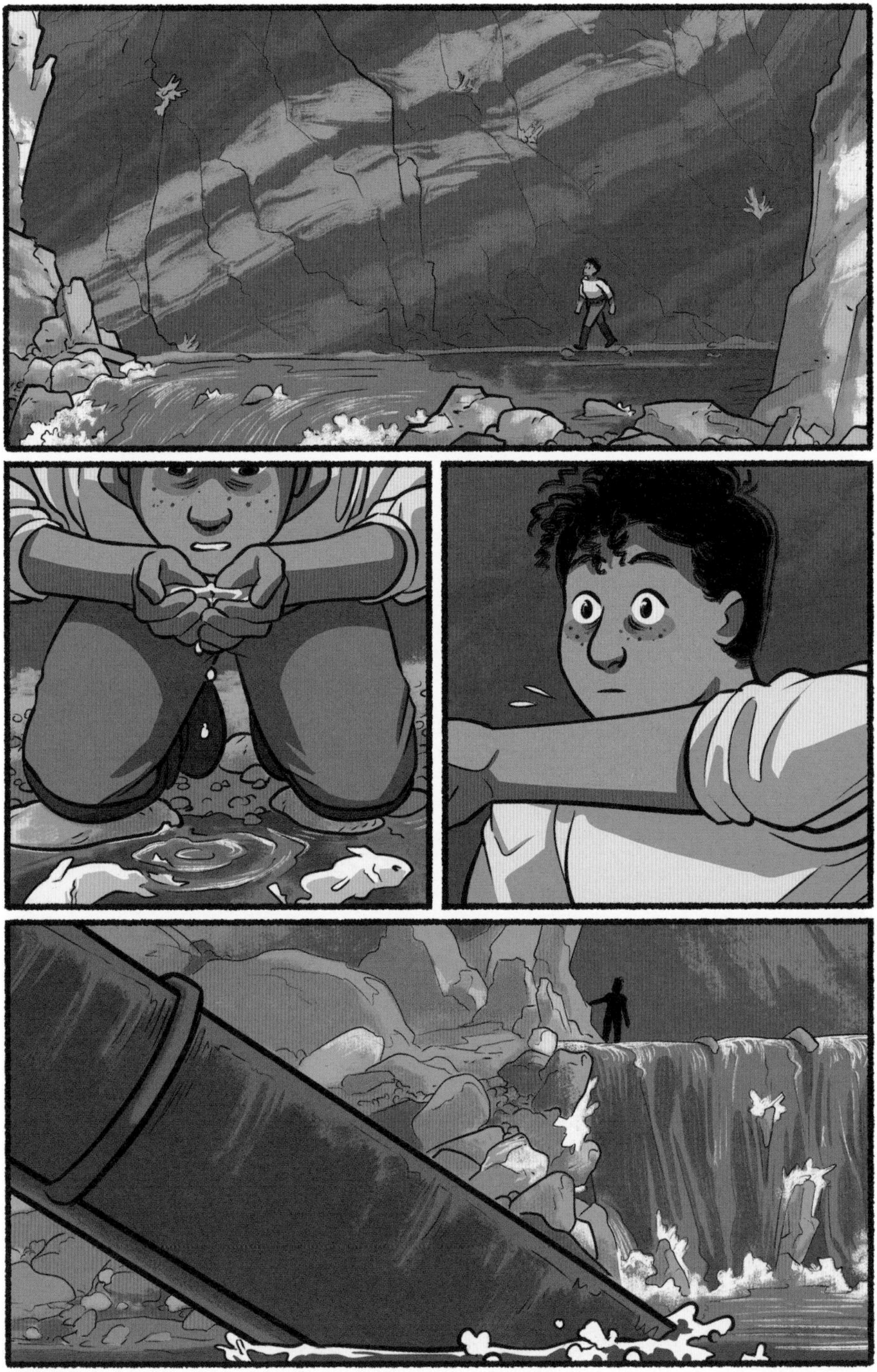

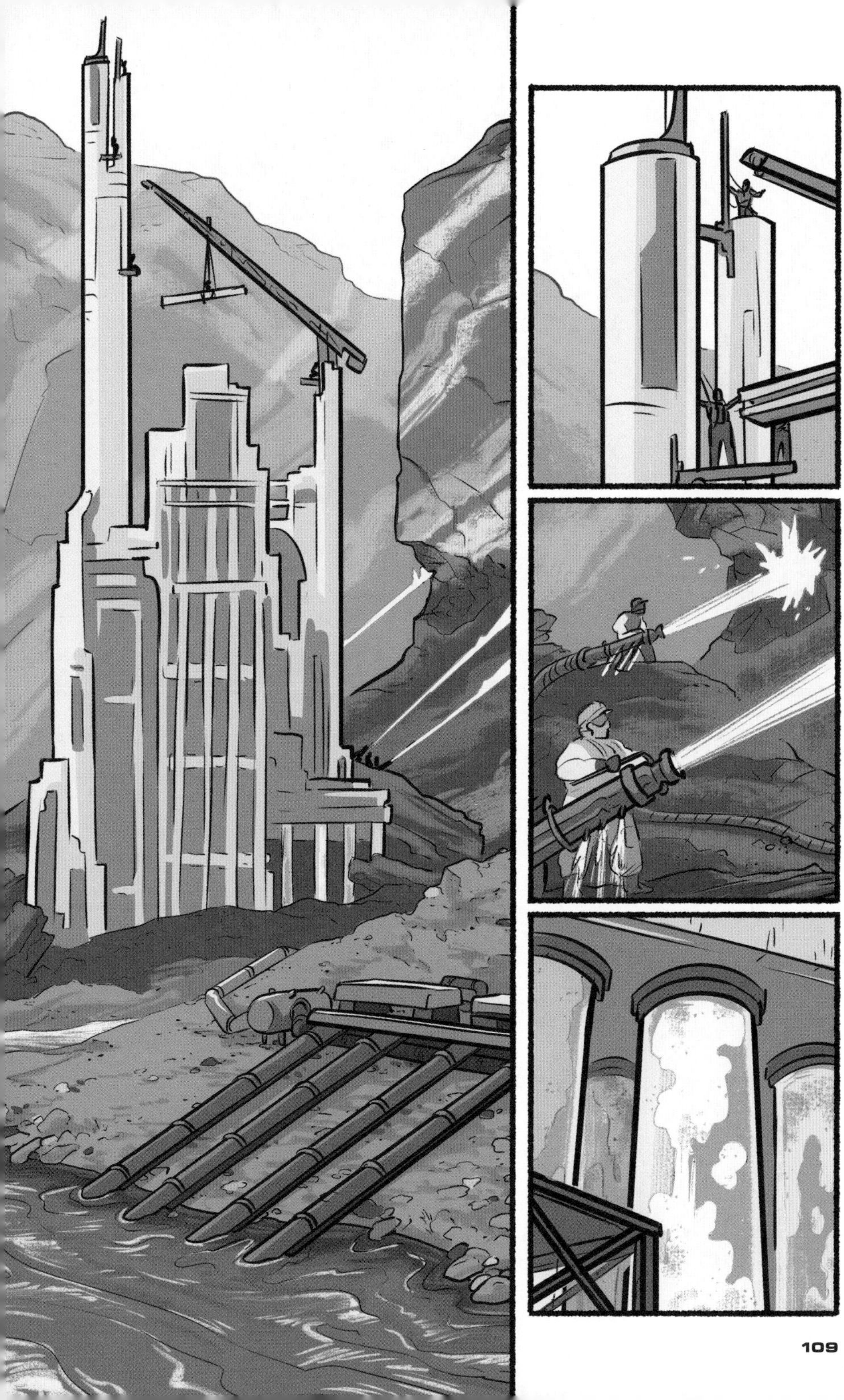

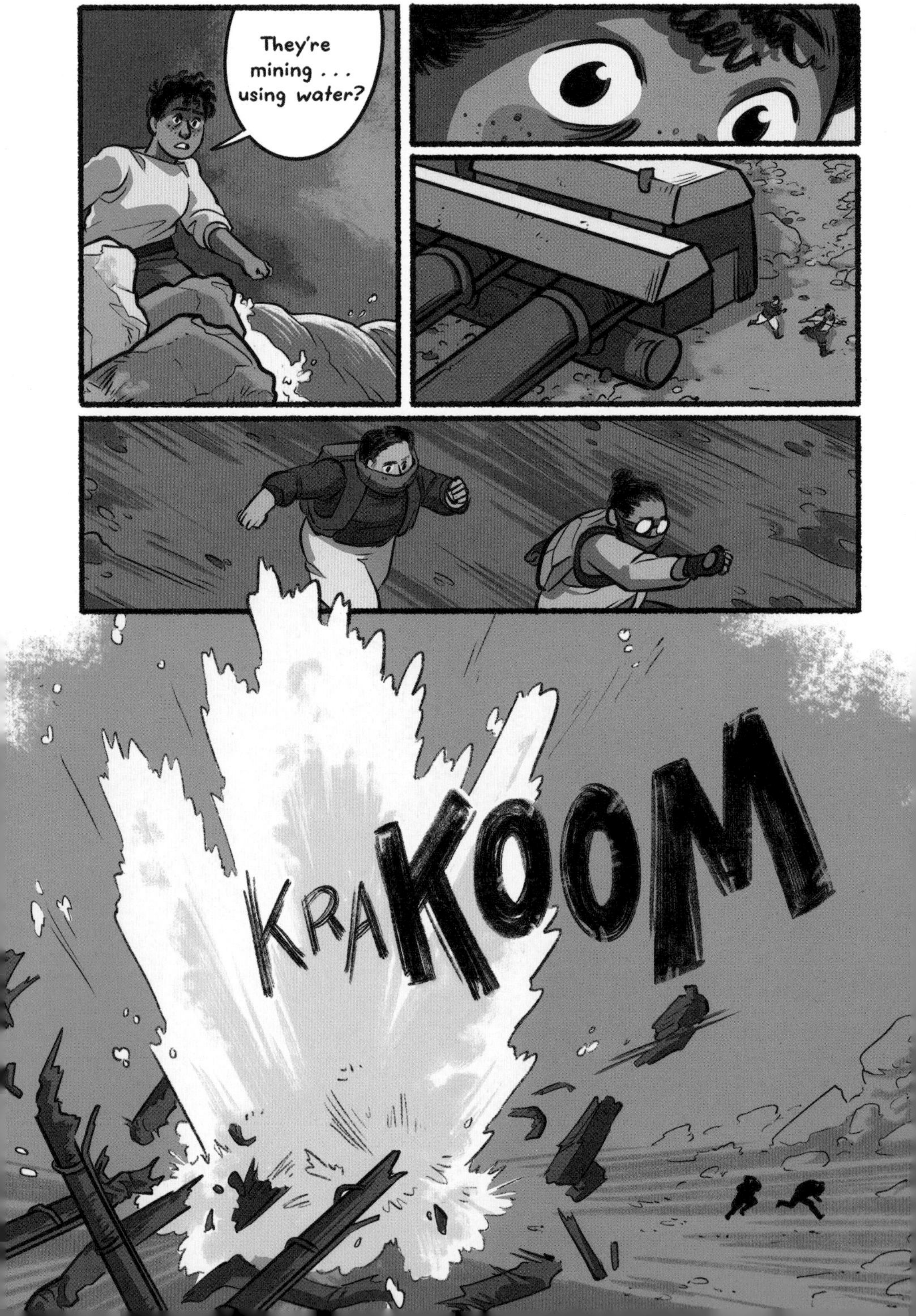
They're mining . . . using water?
KRAKOOM

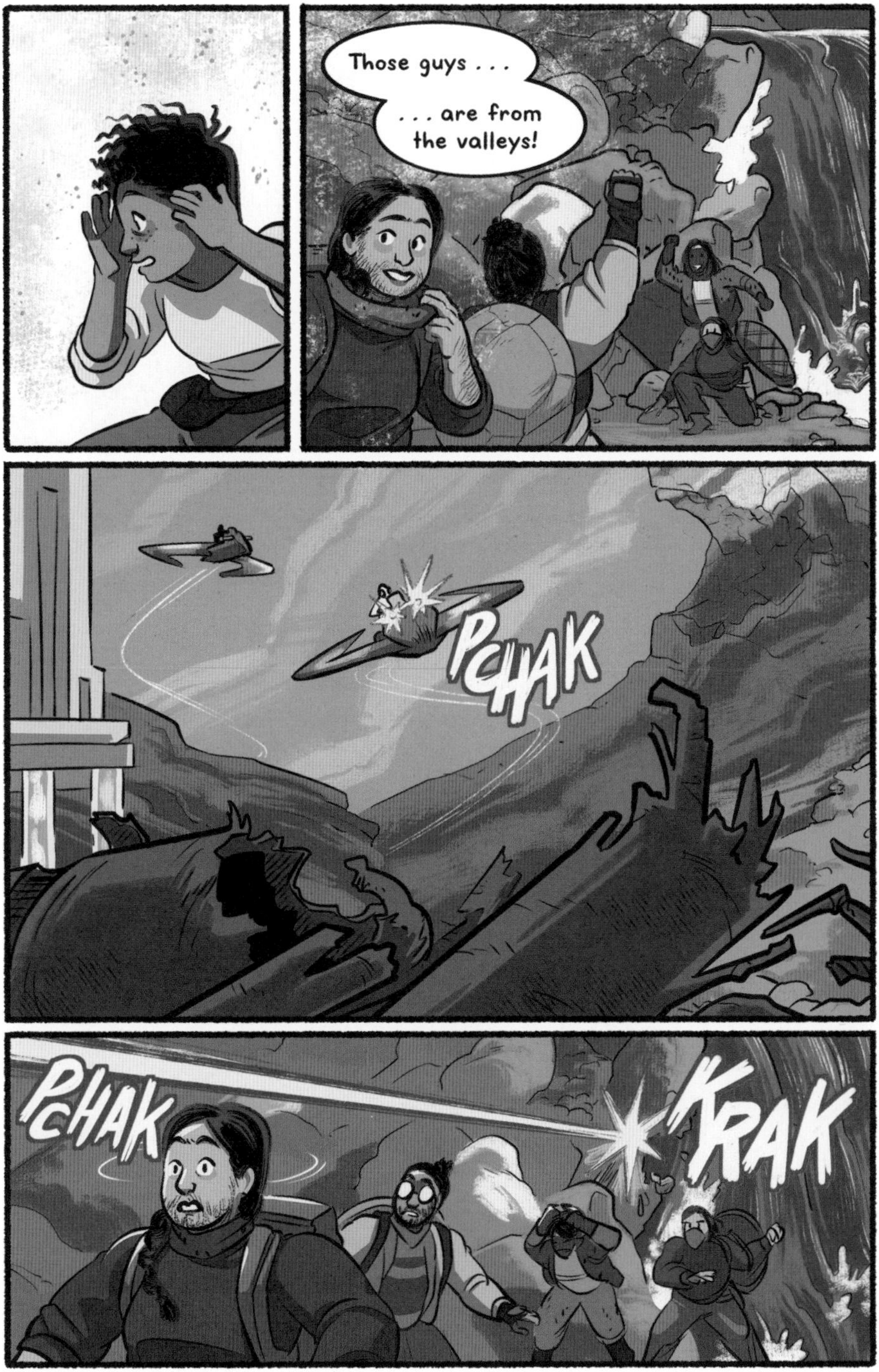
Those guys . . .
. . . are from the valleys!
PCHAK
PCHAK
KRAK

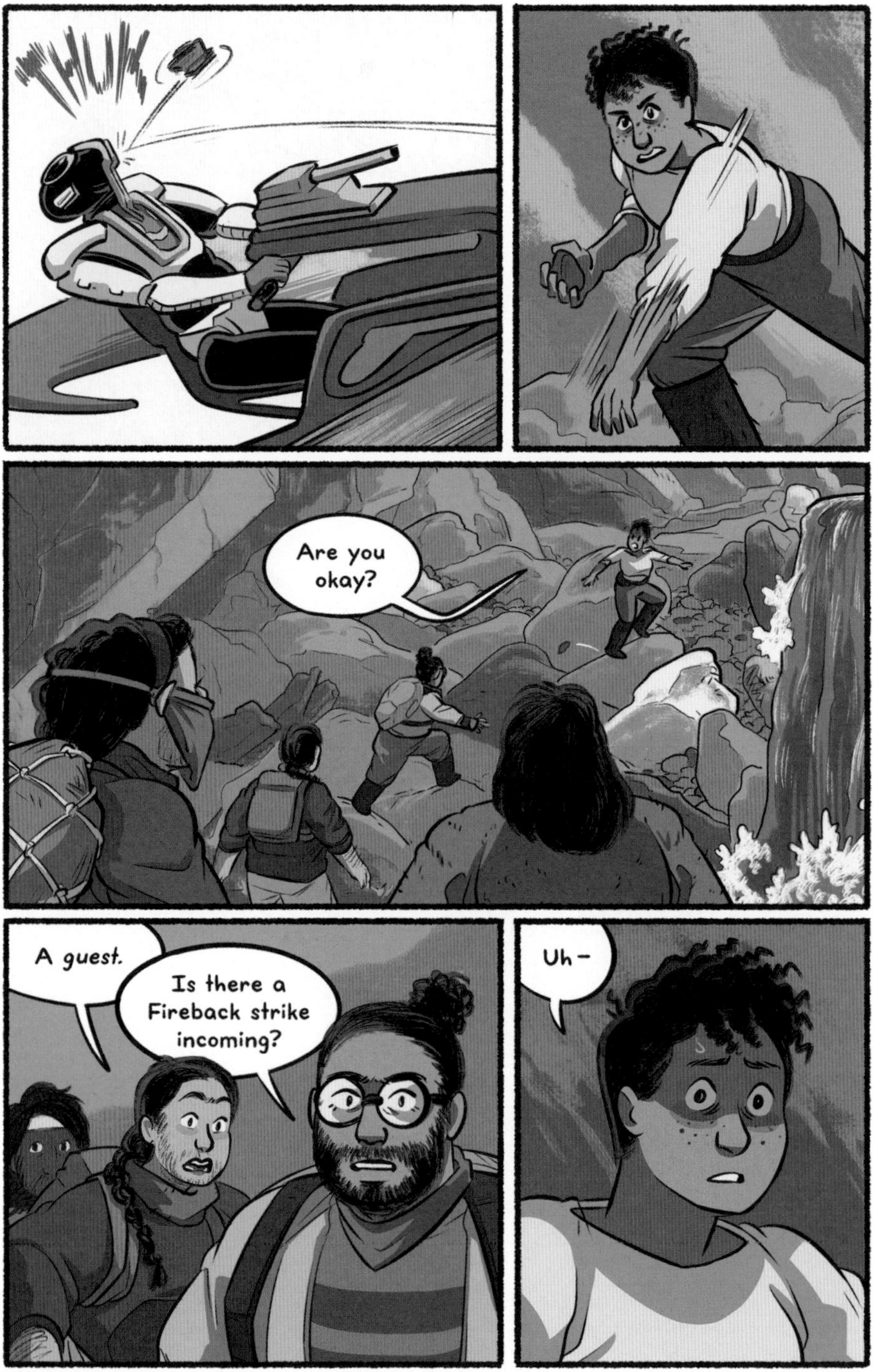
THUK
Are you okay?
A guest.
Is there a Fireback strike incoming?
Uh-

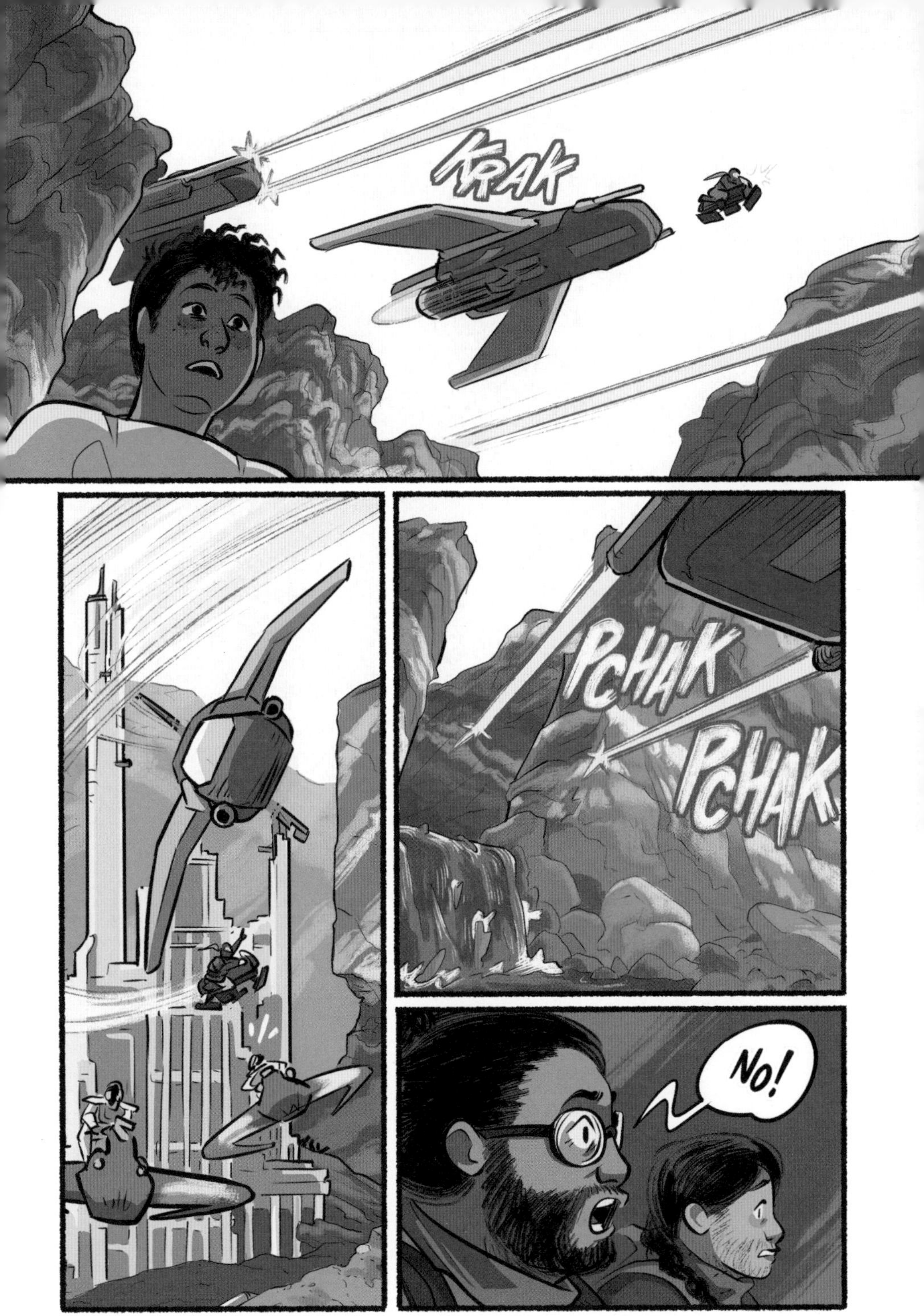
KRAK
PCHAK
PCHAK
No!

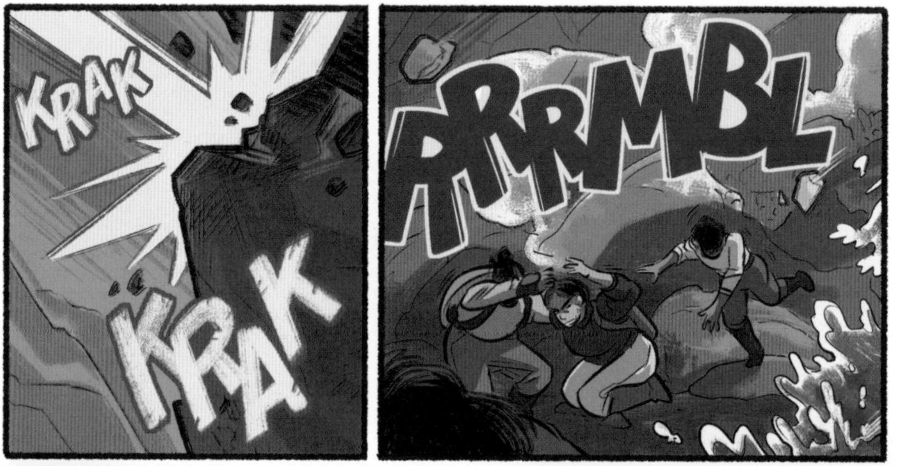
KRAK
KRAK
RRRMBL

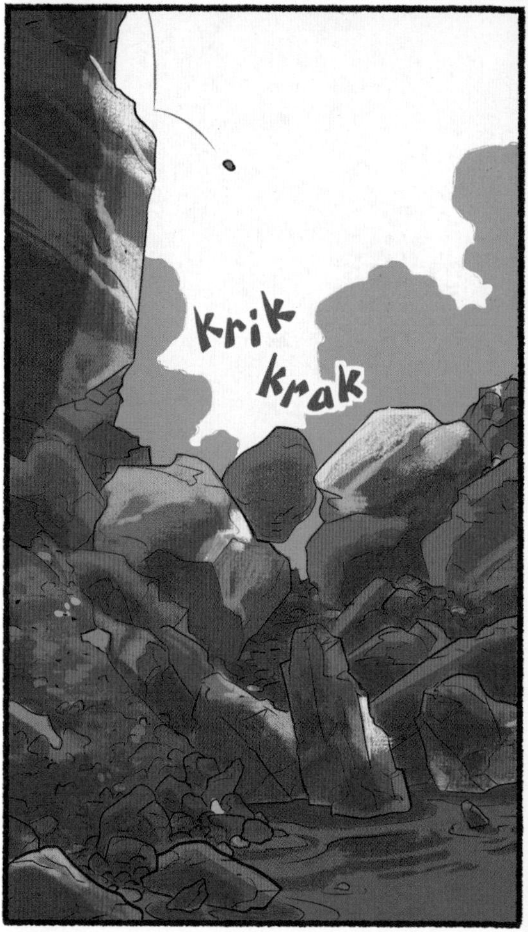
krik
krak

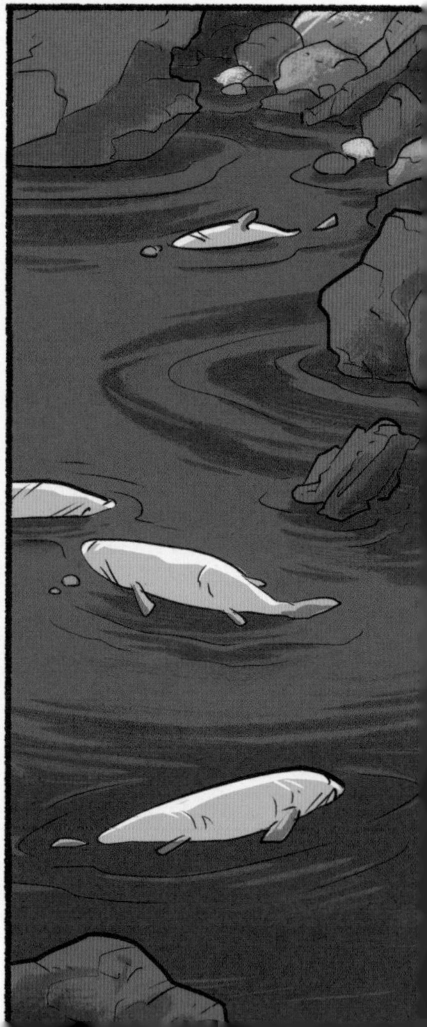

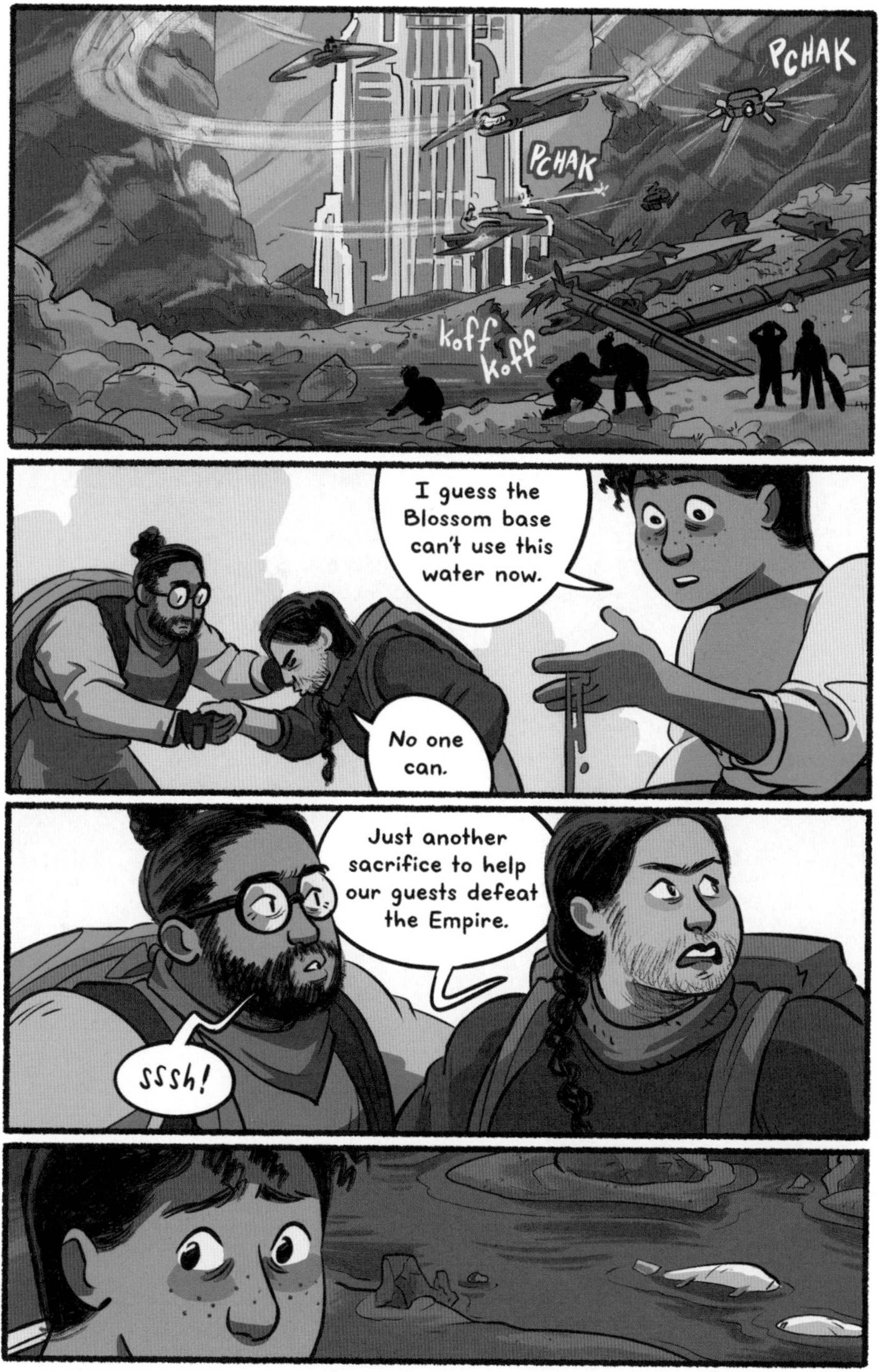
PCHAK
PCHAK
koff koff
I guess the Blossom base can't use this water now.
No one can.
Just another sacrifice to help our guests defeat the Empire.
sssh!

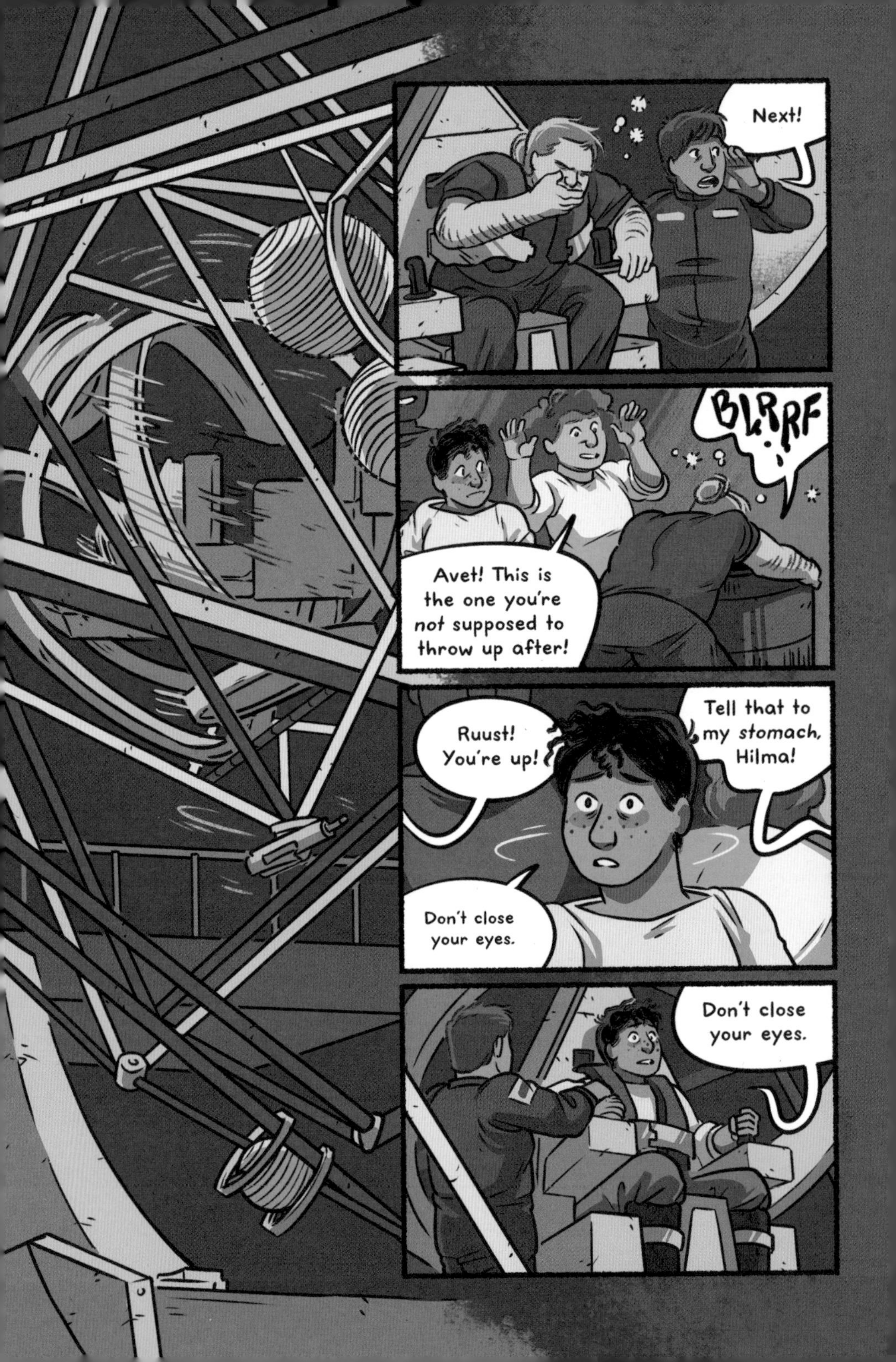
Next!
BLRRF
Avet! This is the one you're *not* supposed to throw up after!
Ruust! You're up!
Tell that to my *stomach*, Hilma!
Don't close your eyes.
Don't close your eyes.

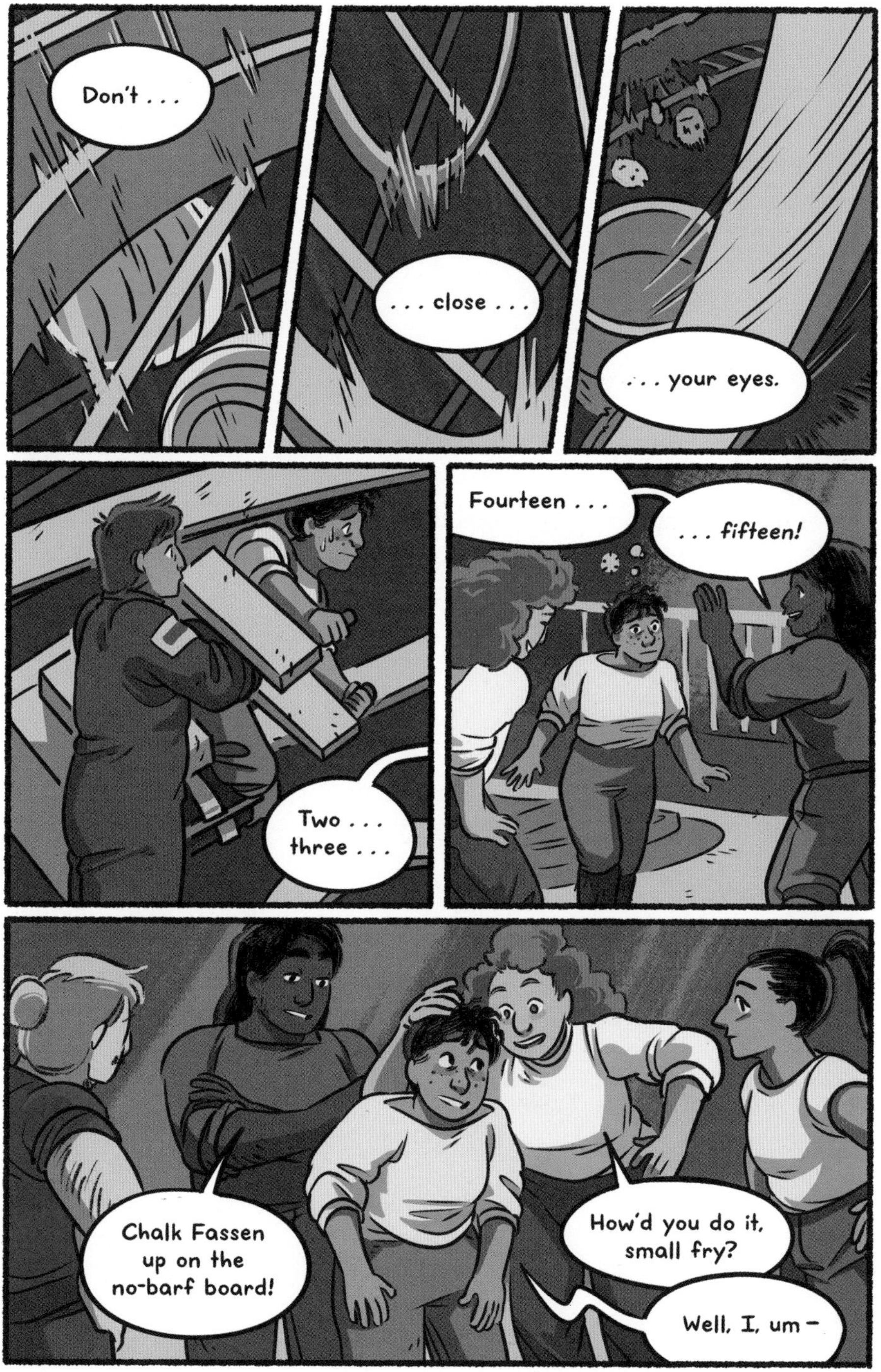
Don't . . .
. . . close . . .
. . . your eyes.
Two . . .
three . . .
Fourteen . . .
. . . fifteen!
Chalk Fassen up on the no-barf board!
How'd you do it, small fry?
Well, I, um—

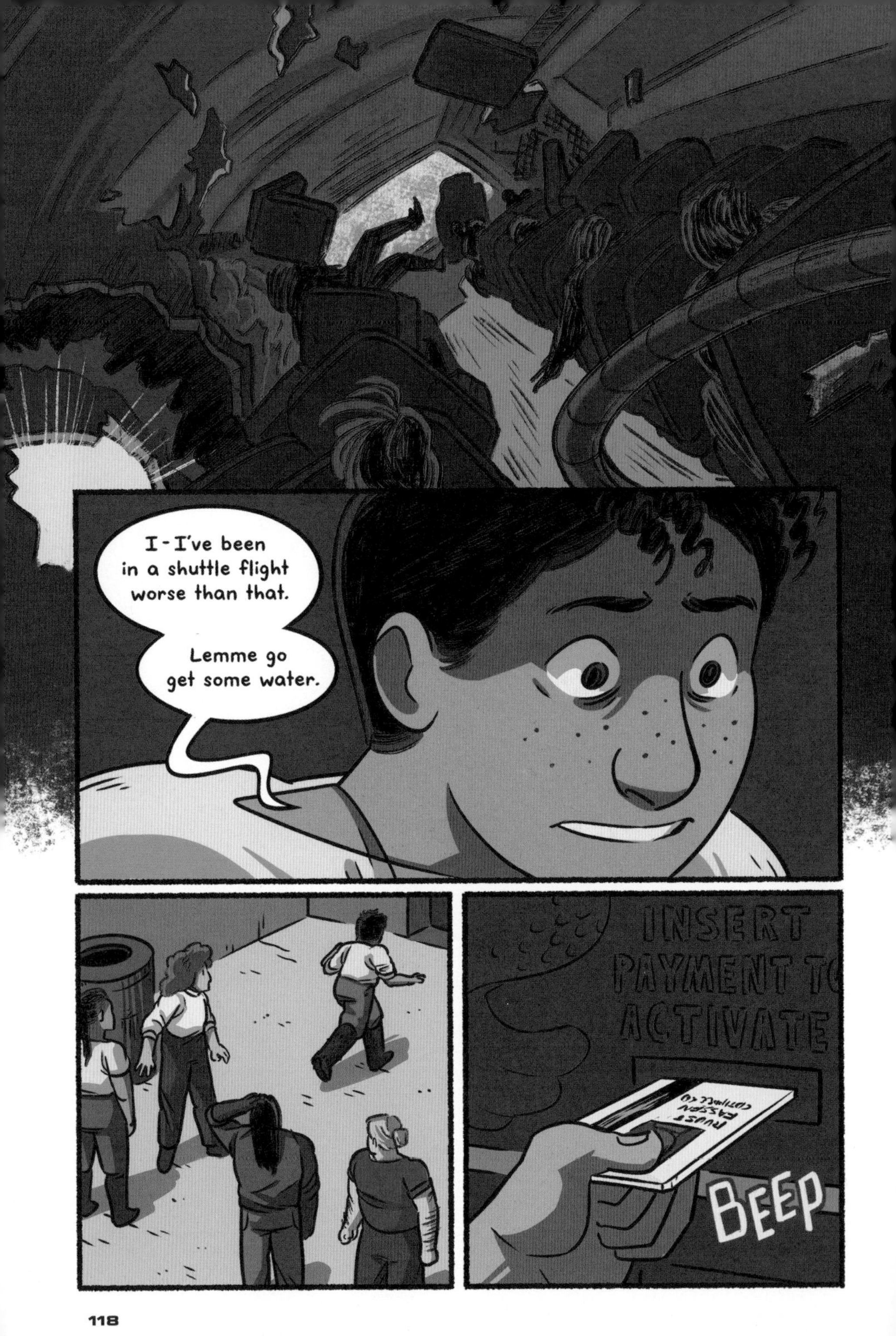
I-I've been in a shuttle flight worse than that.
Lemme go get some water.
INSERT PAYMENT TO ACTIVATE
BEEP

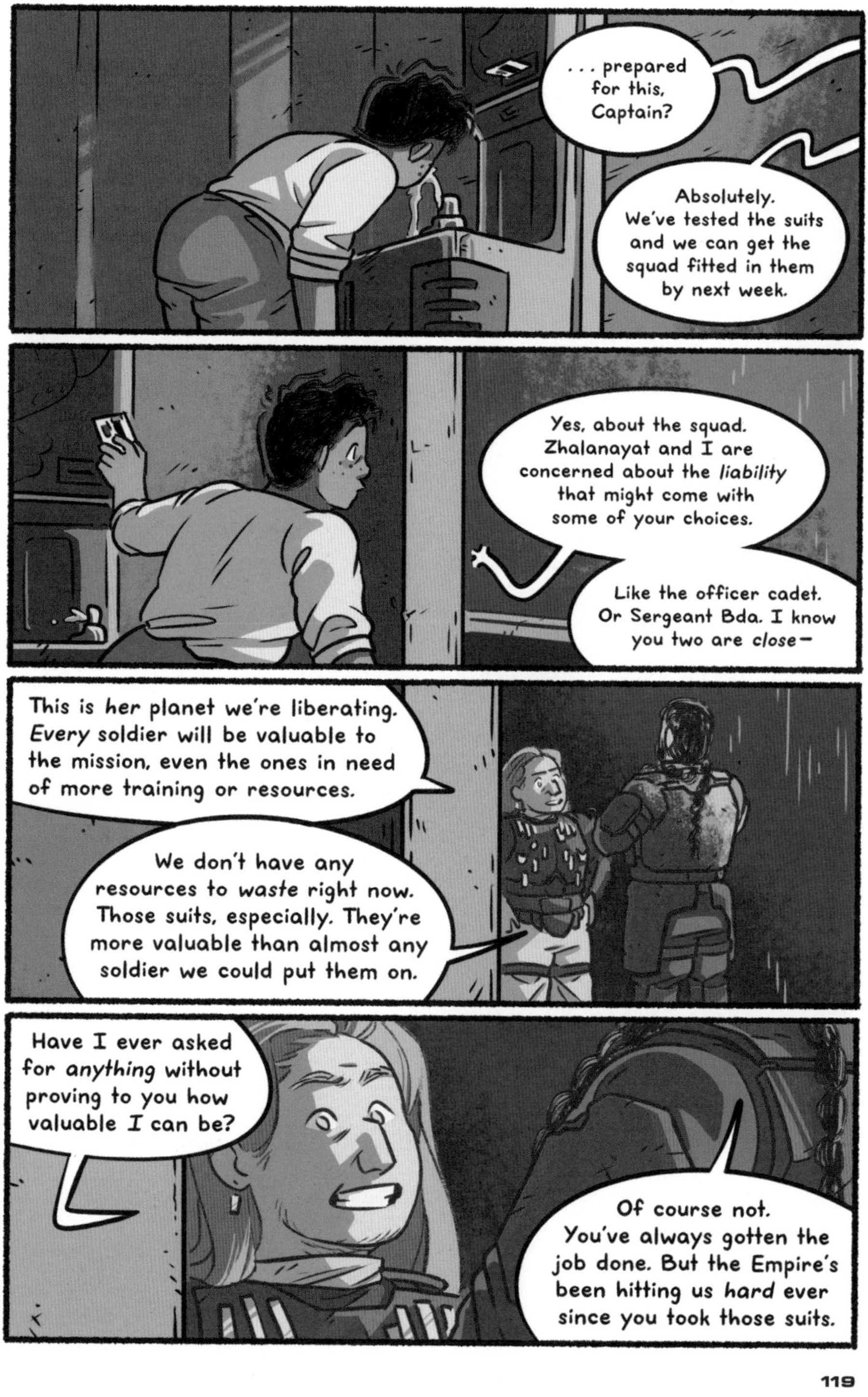
. . . prepared for this, Captain?
Absolutely. We've tested the suits and we can get the squad fitted in them by next week.
Yes, about the squad. Zhalanayat and I are concerned about the *liability* that might come with some of your choices.
Like the officer cadet. Or Sergeant Bda. I know you two are *close*—
This is *her* planet we're liberating. *Every* soldier will be valuable to the mission, even the ones in need of more training or resources.
We don't have any resources to *waste* right now. Those suits, especially. They're more valuable than almost any soldier we could put them on.
Have I ever asked for *anything* without proving to you how valuable *I* can be?
Of course not. You've always gotten the job done. But the Empire's been hitting us *hard* ever since you took those suits.

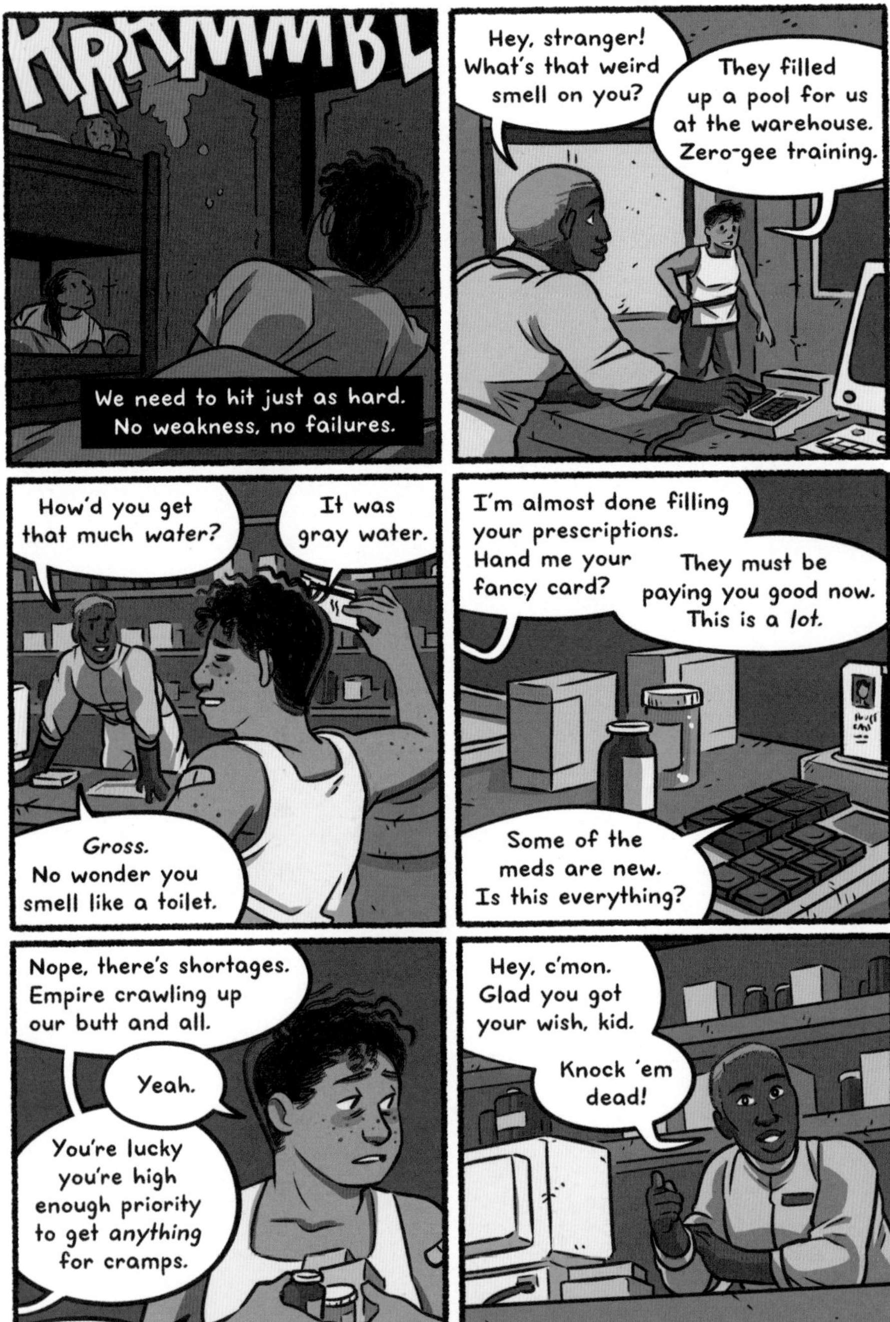
KRRMMBL
We need to hit just as hard. No weakness, no failures.
Hey, stranger! What's that weird smell on you?
They filled up a pool for us at the warehouse. Zero-gee training.
How'd you get that much *water?*
It was gray water.
Gross. No wonder you smell like a toilet.
I'm almost done filling your prescriptions. Hand me your fancy card?
They must be paying you good now. This is a *lot.*
Some of the meds are new. Is this everything?
Nope, there's shortages. Empire crawling up our butt and all.
Yeah.
You're lucky you're high enough priority to get *anything* for cramps.
. . . yeah.
Hey, c'mon. Glad you got your wish, kid.
Knock 'em dead!

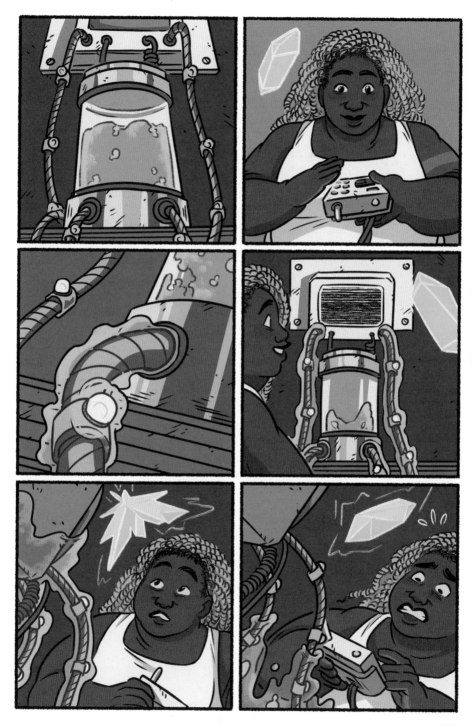

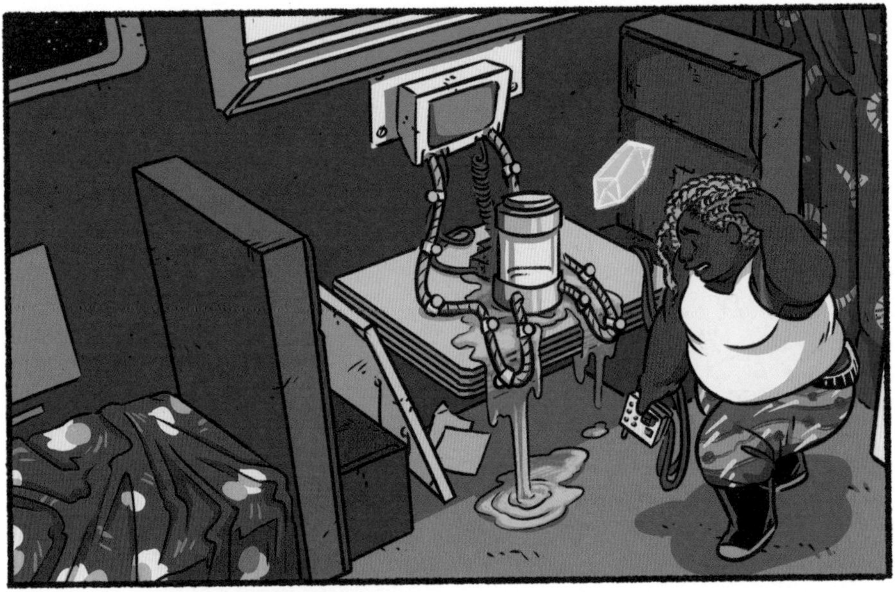

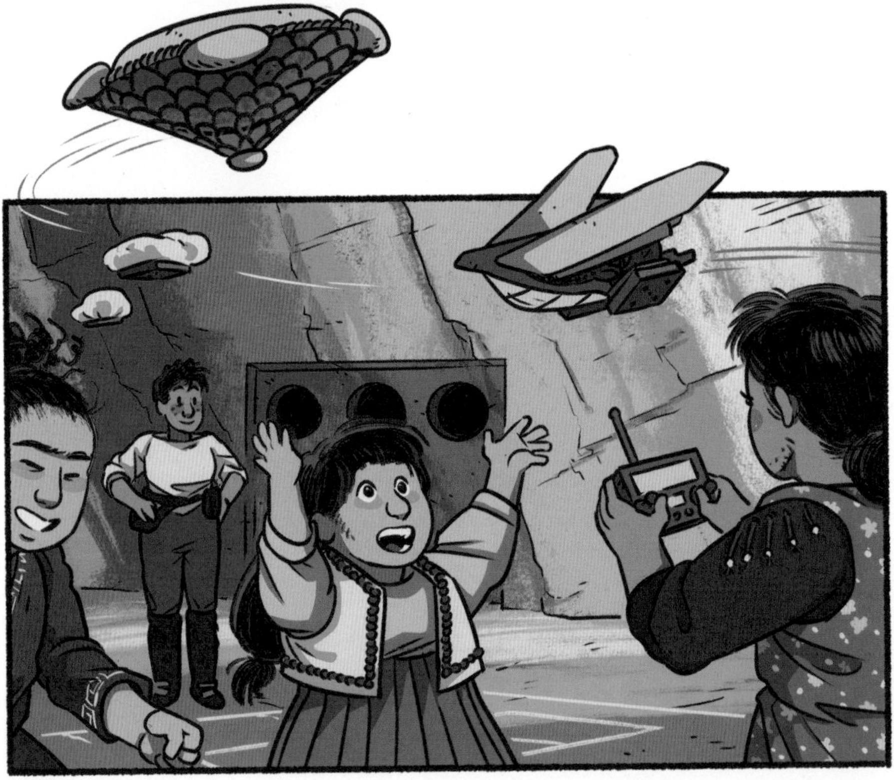

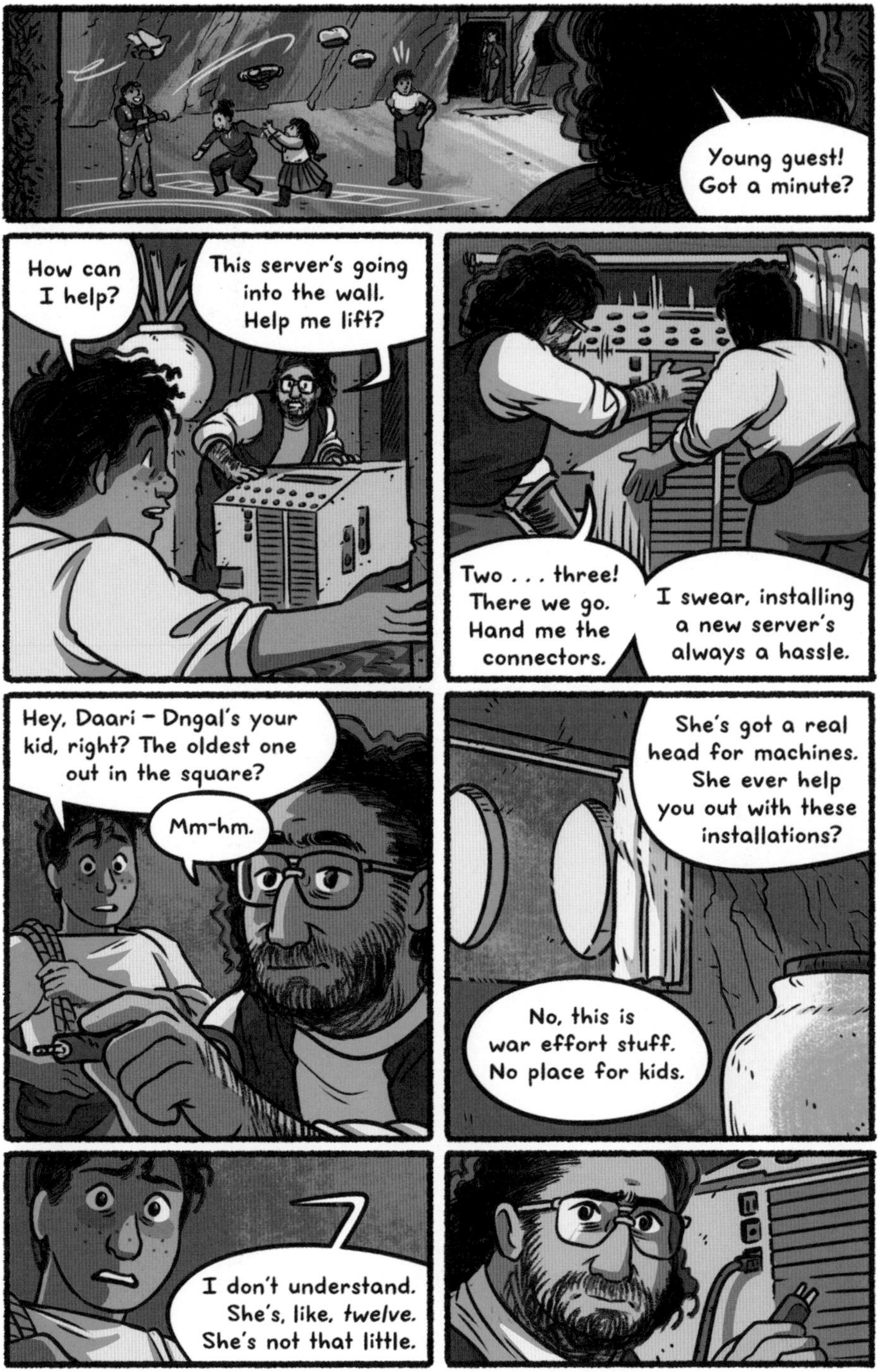
Young guest! Got a minute?
How can I help?
This server's going into the wall. Help me lift?
Two . . . three! There we go. Hand me the connectors.
I swear, installing a new server's always a hassle.
Hey, Daari – Dngal's your kid, right? The oldest one out in the square?
Mm-hm.
She's got a real head for machines. She ever help you out with these installations?
No, this is war effort stuff. No place for kids.
I don't understand. She's, like, *twelve.* She's not that little.

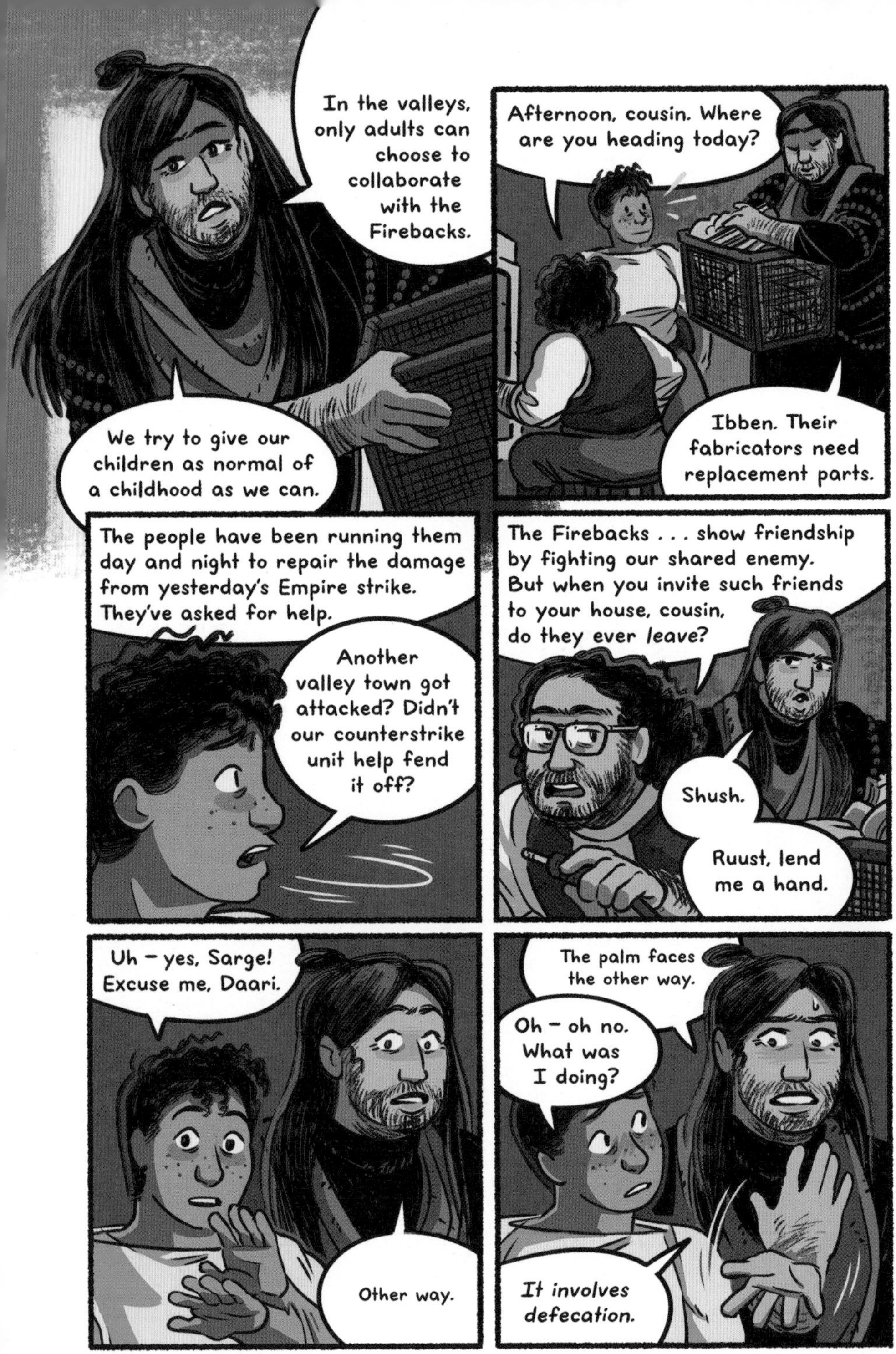
In the valleys, only adults can choose to collaborate with the Firebacks.
We try to give our children as normal of a childhood as we can.
Afternoon, cousin. Where are you heading today?
Ibben. Their fabricators need replacement parts.
The people have been running them day and night to repair the damage from yesterday's Empire strike. They've asked for help.
Another valley town got attacked? Didn't our counterstrike unit help fend it off?
The Firebacks . . . show friendship by fighting our shared enemy. But when you invite such friends to your house, cousin, do they ever *leave*?
Shush.
Ruust, lend me a hand.
Uh – yes, Sarge! Excuse me, Daari.
Other way.
The palm faces the other way.
Oh – oh no. What was I doing?
It involves defecation.

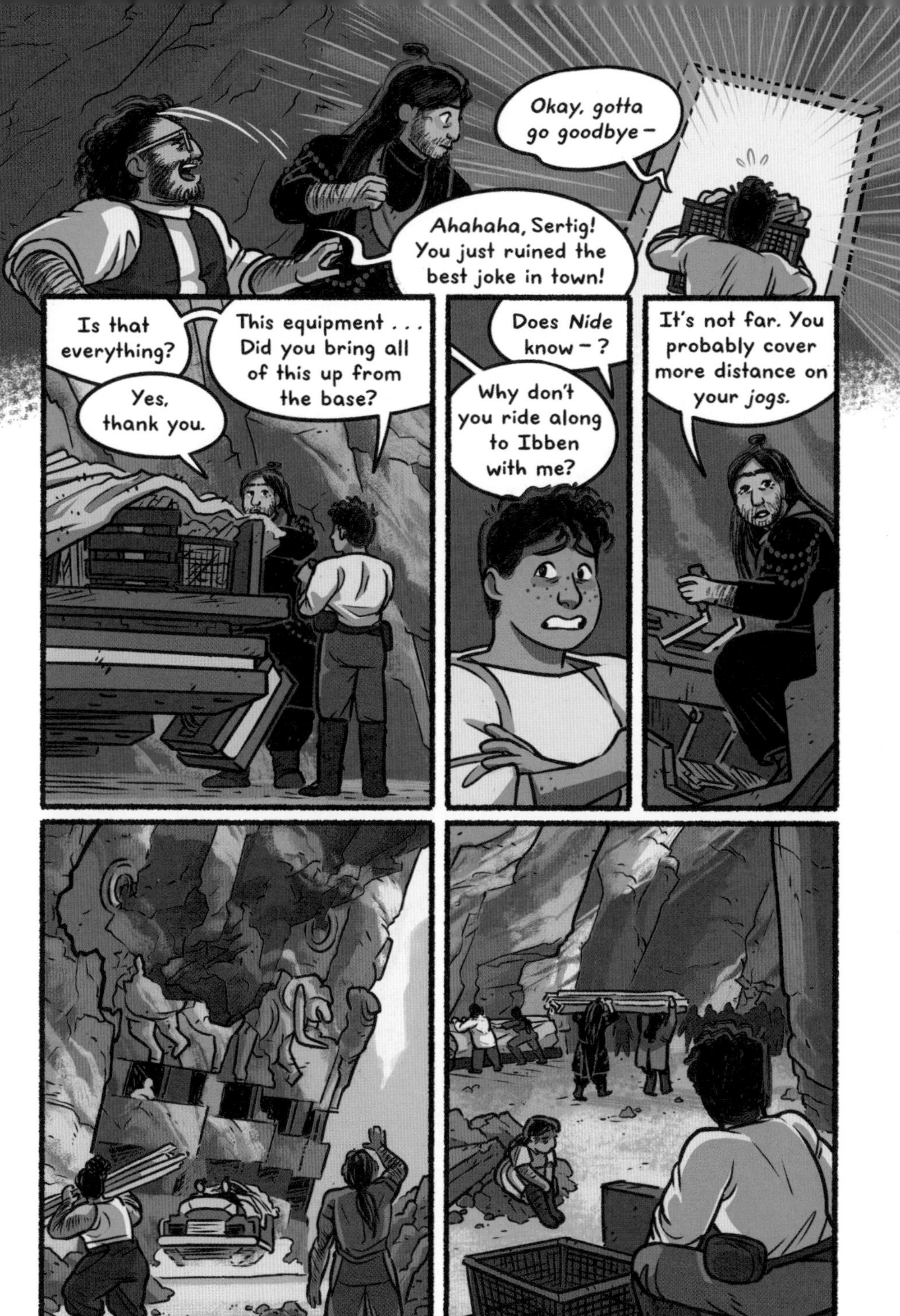
Okay, gotta go goodbye—
Ahahaha, Sertig! You just ruined the best joke in town!
Is that everything?
Yes, thank you.
This equipment . . . Did you bring all of this up from the base?
Does *Nide* know—?
Why don't you ride along to Ibben with me?
It's not far. You probably cover more distance on your *jogs*.

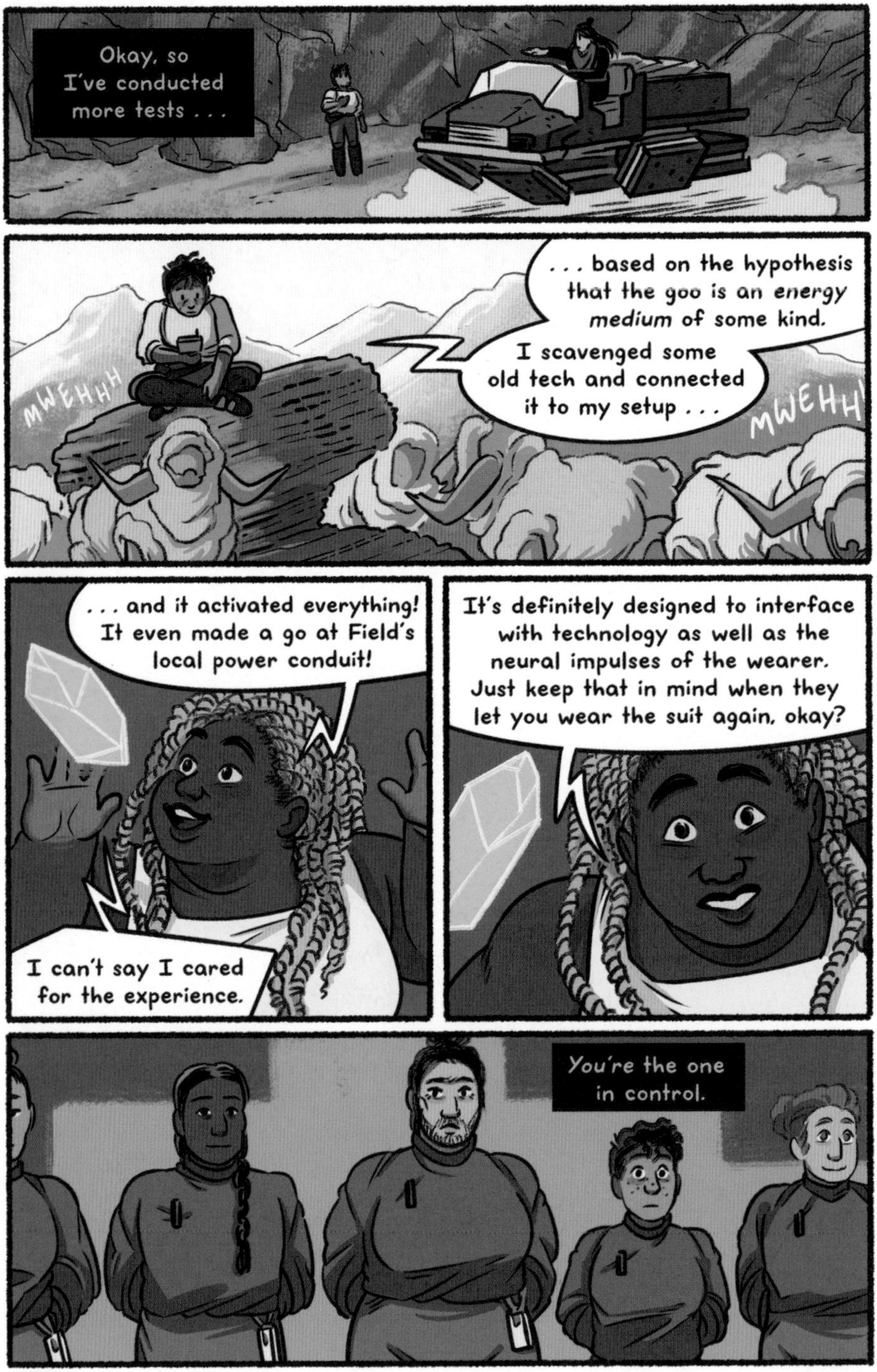
Okay, so I've conducted more tests . . .
. . . based on the hypothesis that the goo is an *energy medium* of some kind.
I scavenged some old tech and connected it to my setup . . .
MWEHHH
MWEHHH
. . . and it activated everything! It even made a go at Field's local power conduit!
I can't say I cared for the experience.
It's definitely designed to interface with technology as well as the neural impulses of the wearer. Just keep that in mind when they let you wear the suit again, okay?
You're the one in control.

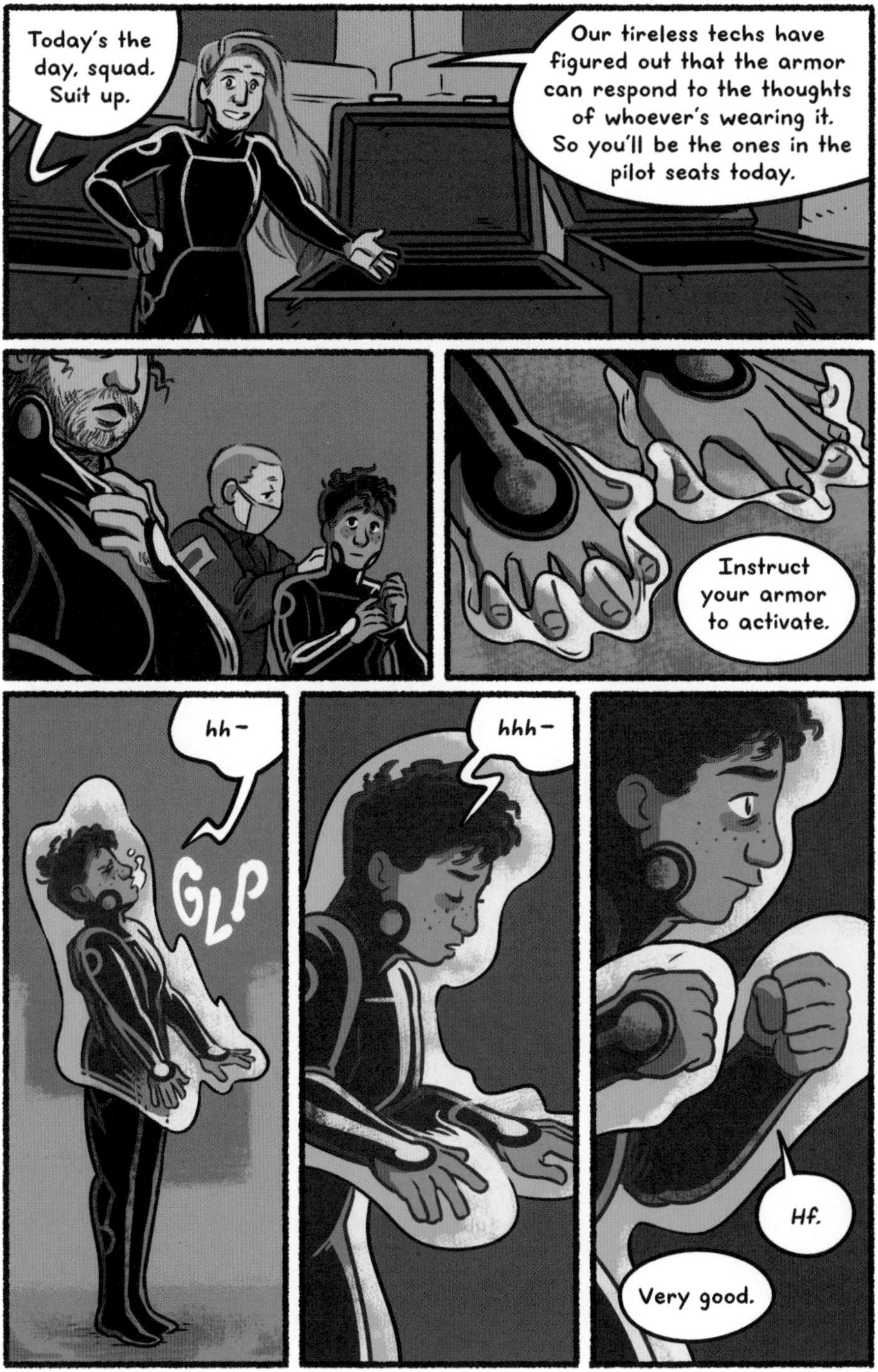
Today's the day, squad. Suit up.
Our tireless techs have figured out that the armor can respond to the thoughts of whoever's wearing it. So you'll be the ones in the pilot seats today.
Instruct your armor to activate.
hh-
GLP
hhh-
Hf.
Very good.

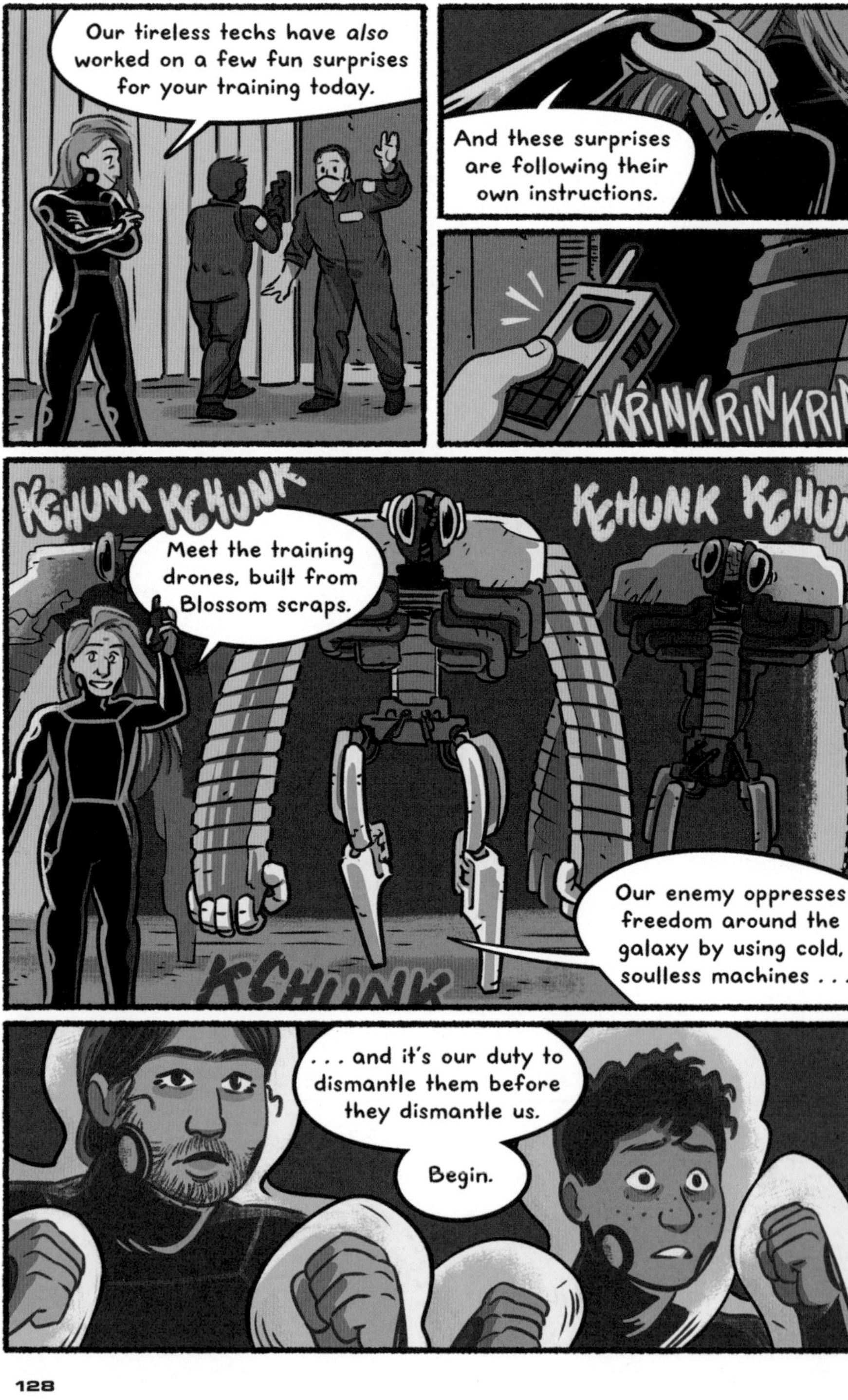
Our tireless techs have *also* worked on a few fun surprises for your training today.
And these surprises are following their own instructions.
KRINKRINKRIN
KCHUNK KCHUNK
KCHUNK KCHUN
Meet the training drones, built from Blossom scraps.
KCHUNK
Our enemy oppresses freedom around the galaxy by using cold, soulless machines . . .
. . . and it's our duty to dismantle them before they dismantle us.
Begin.

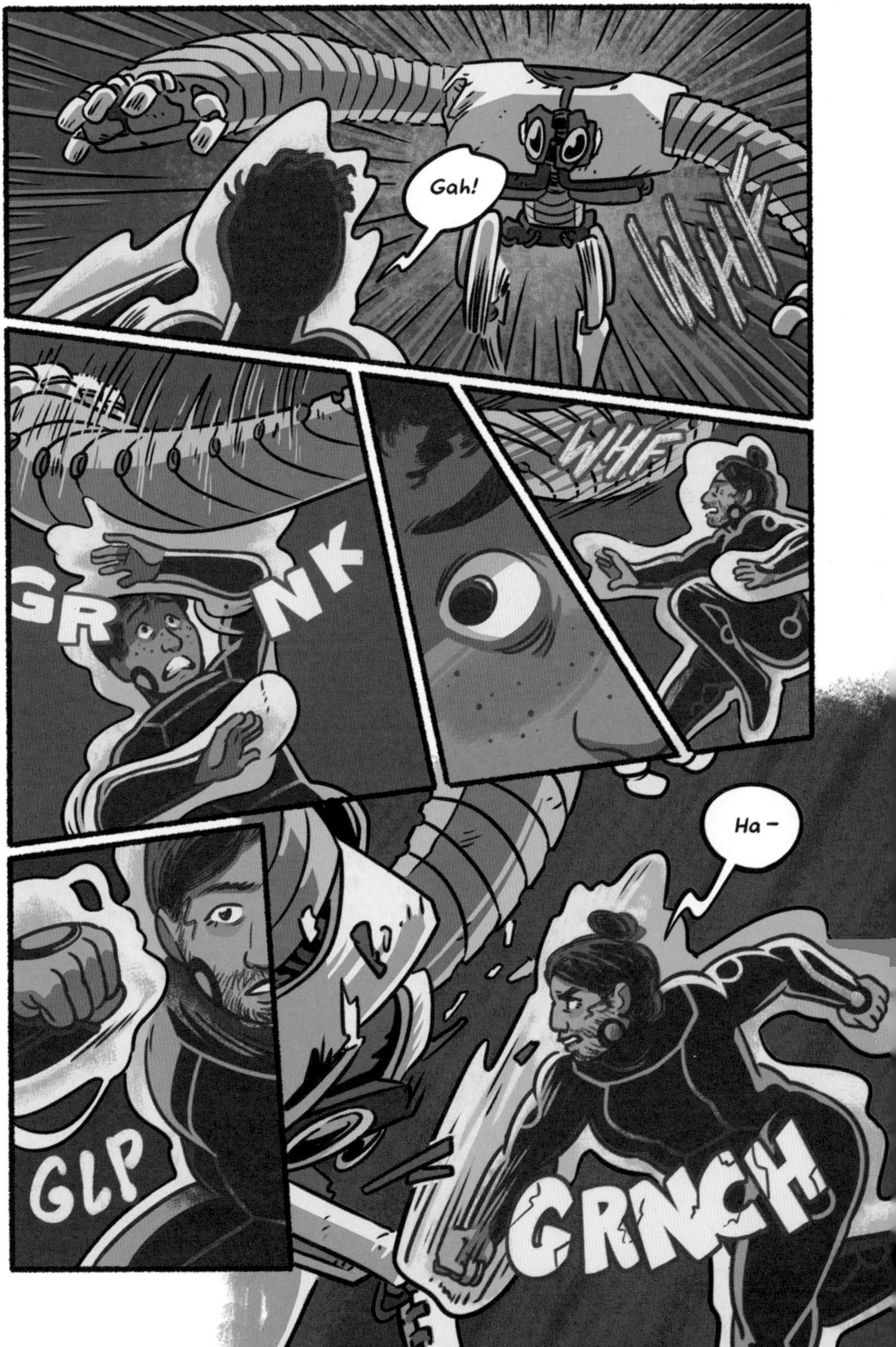
Gah!
WHX
GRNK
WHF
Ha—
GLP
GRNCH

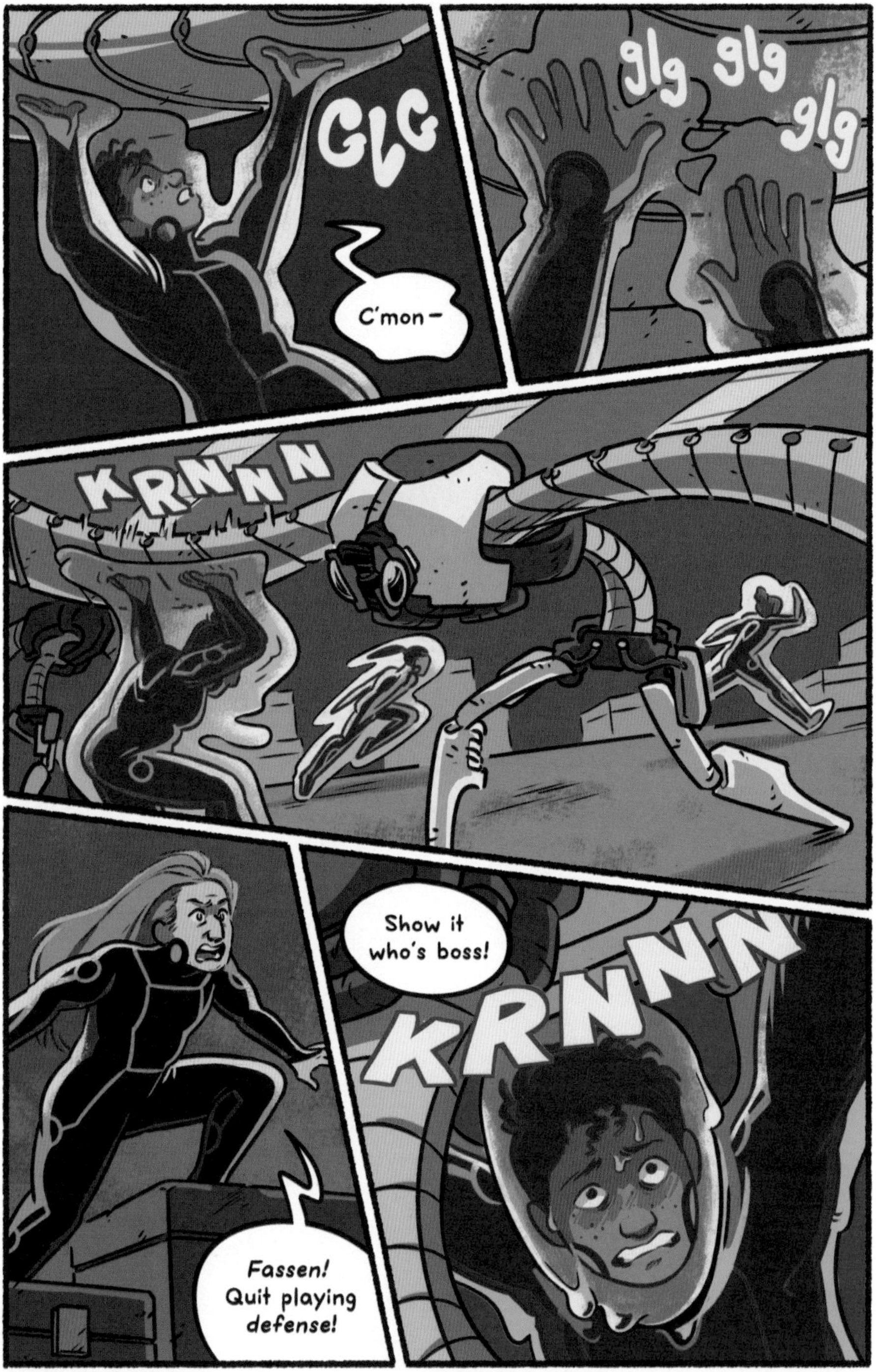
GLG
C'mon—
glg glg
glg
KRNNN
Show it who's boss!
KRNNN
Fassen! Quit playing defense!

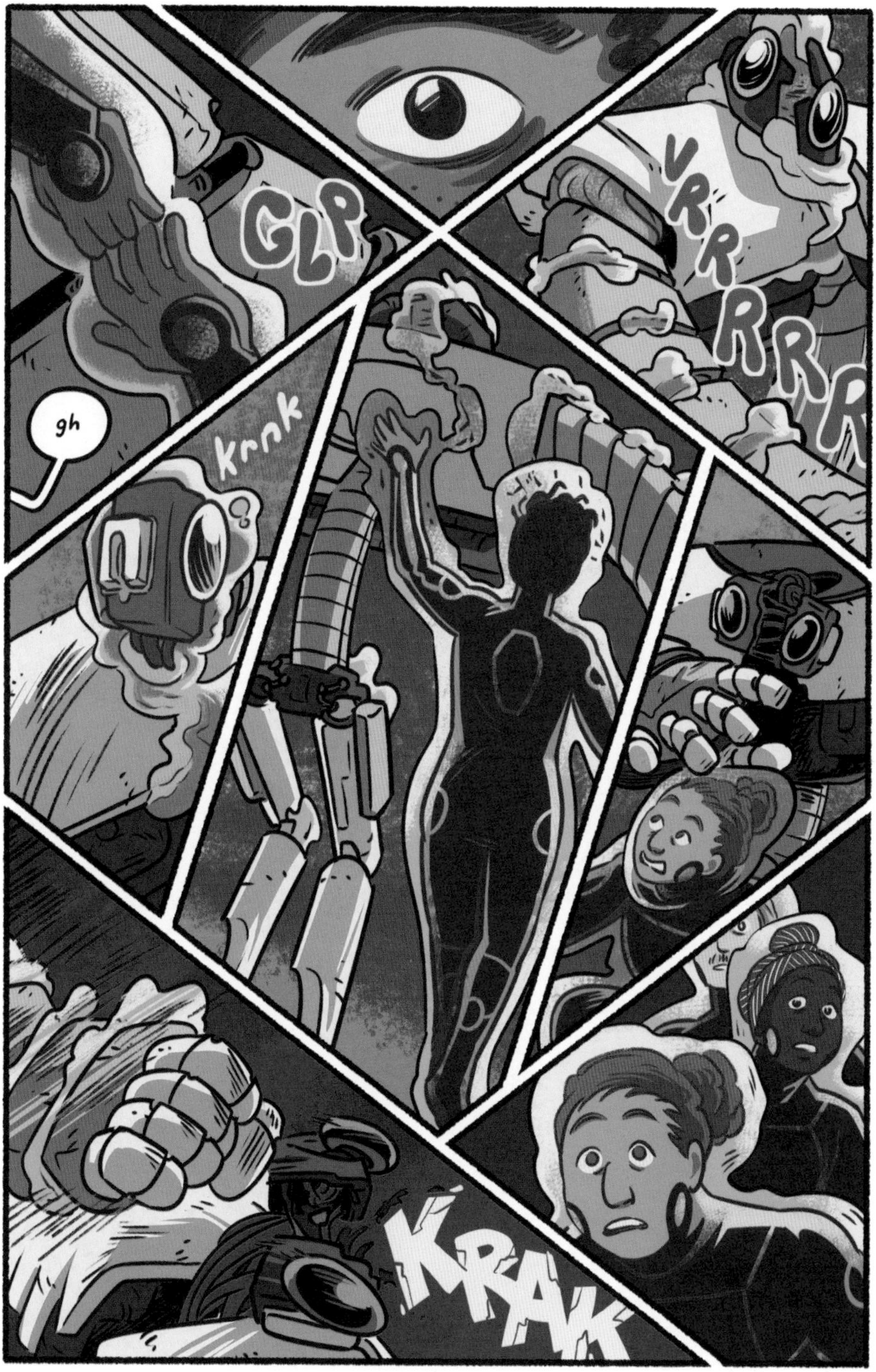
GLP
VRRRRRR
gh
krnk
KRAK

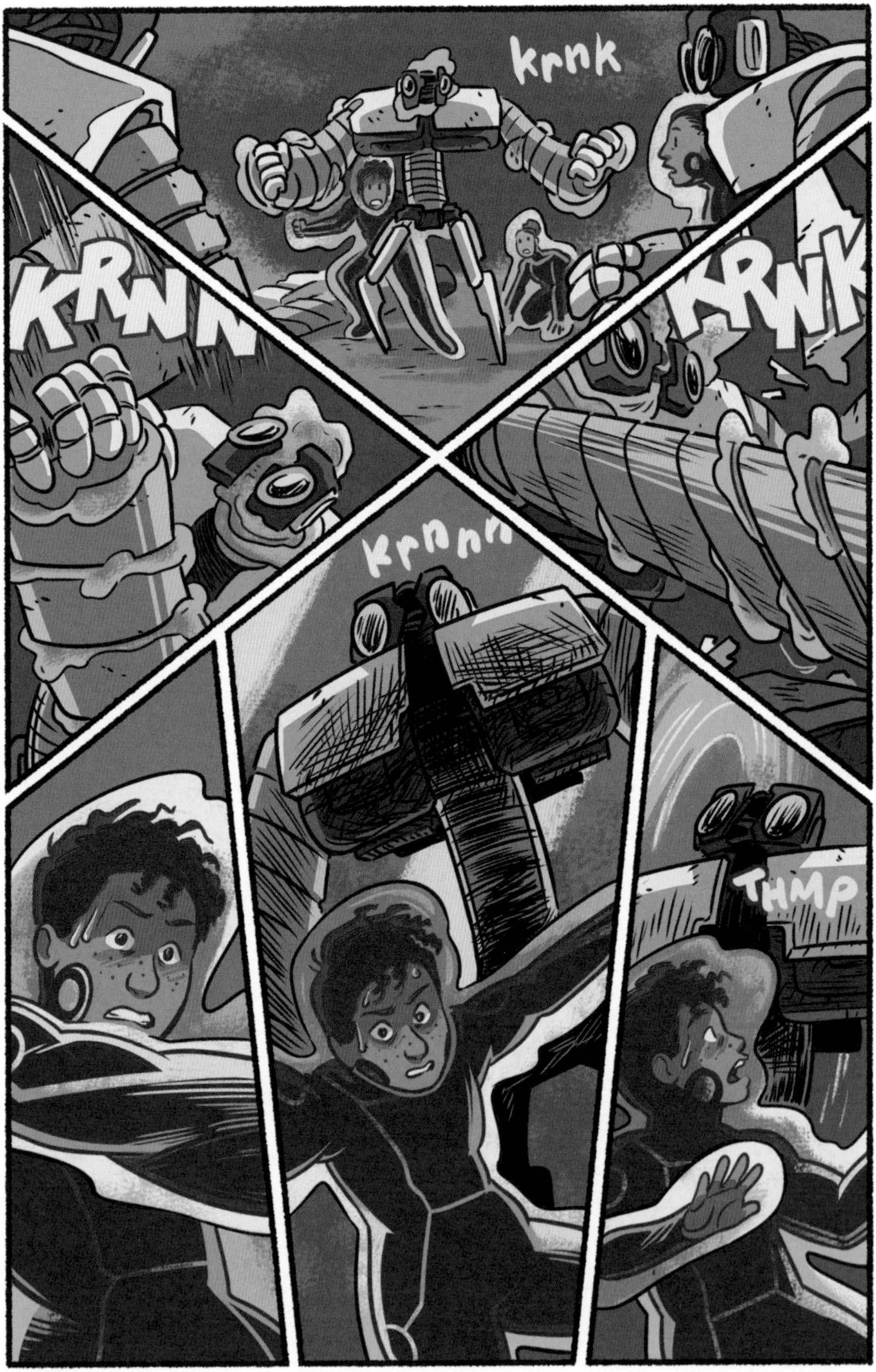
krnk
KRNN
KRNK
krnnn
THMP

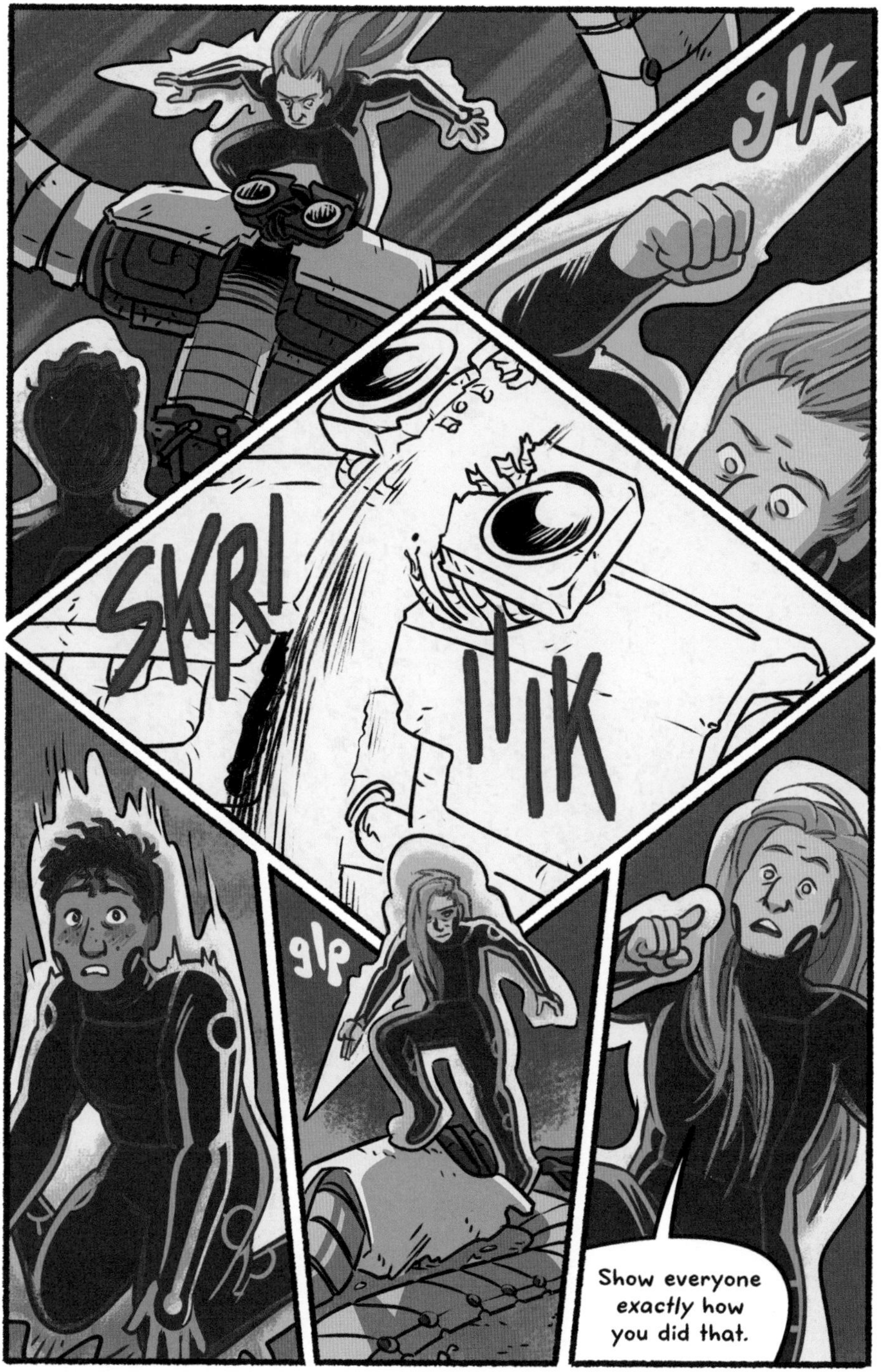
g'k
SKRI
IIIK
glp
Show everyone exactly how you did that.

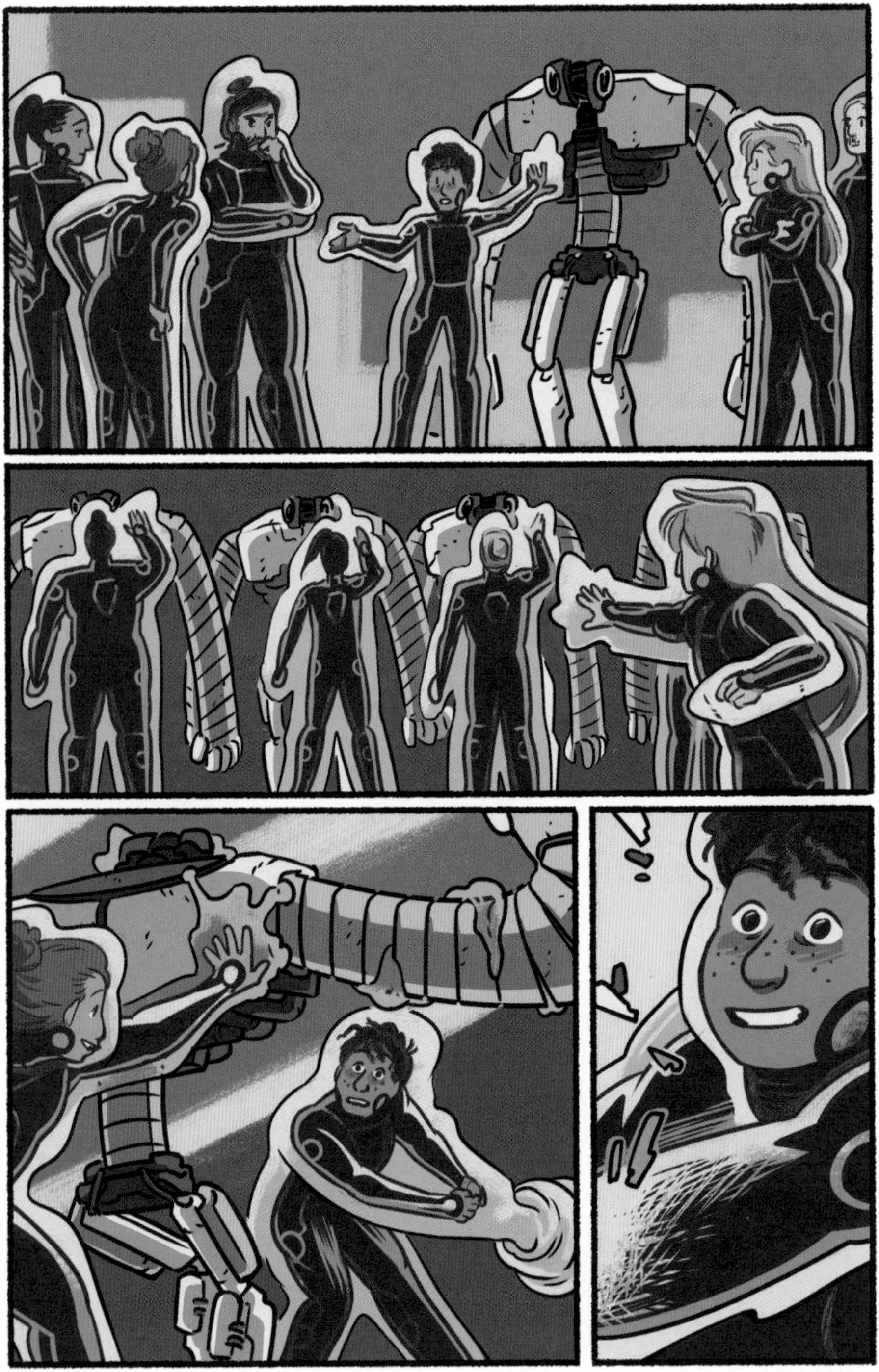

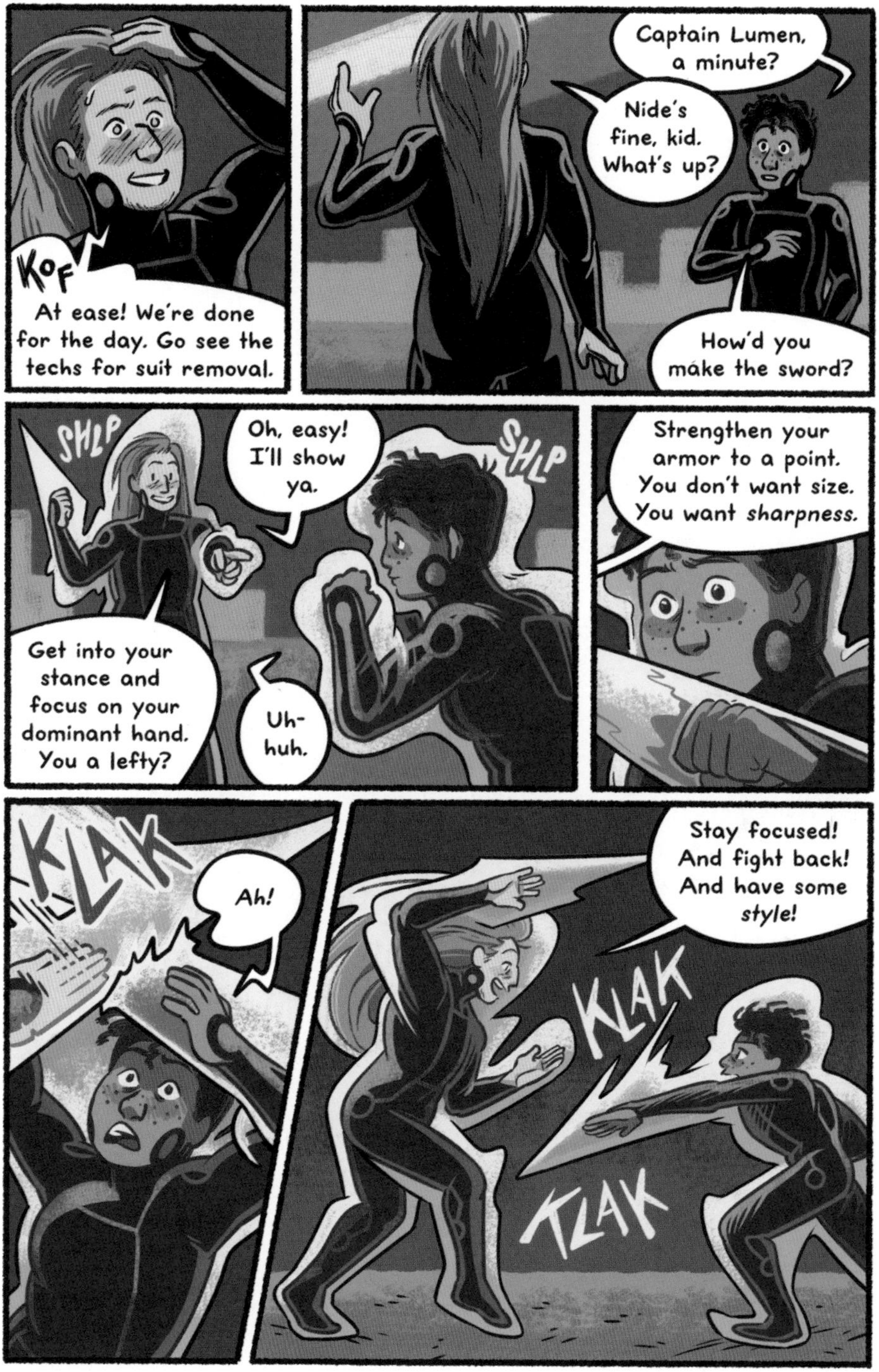
KOF
At ease! We're done for the day. Go see the techs for suit removal.
Captain Lumen, a minute?
Nide's fine, kid. What's up?
How'd you make the sword?
SHLP
Oh, easy! I'll show ya.
SHLP
Get into your stance and focus on your dominant hand. You a lefty?
Uh-huh.
Strengthen your armor to a point. You don't want size. You want *sharpness.*
KLAK
Ah!
Stay focused! And fight back! And have some *style!*
KLAK
KLAK

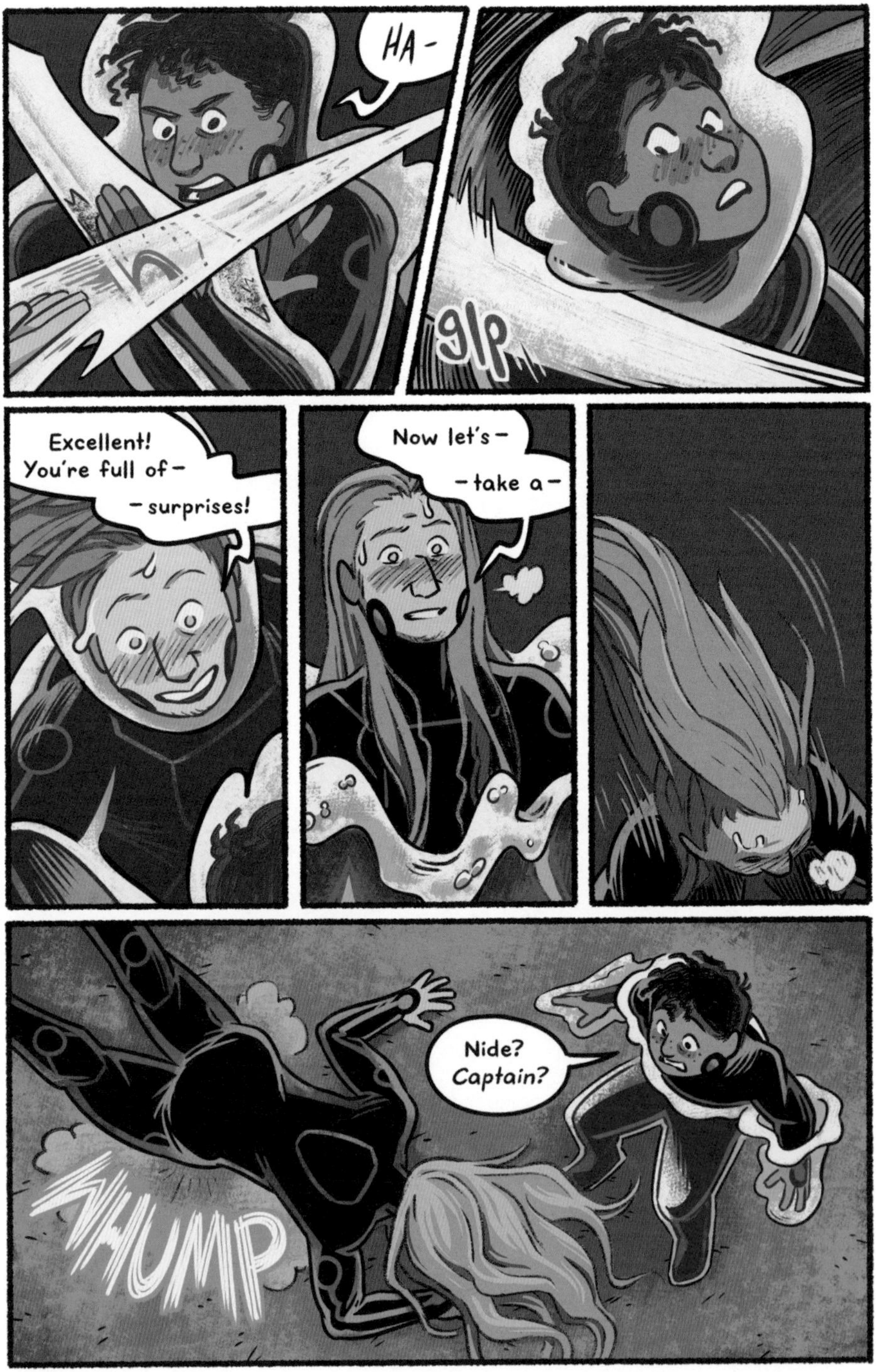
HA-
glp
Excellent! You're full of-
-surprises!
Now let's-
-take a-
Nide? Captain?
WHUMP

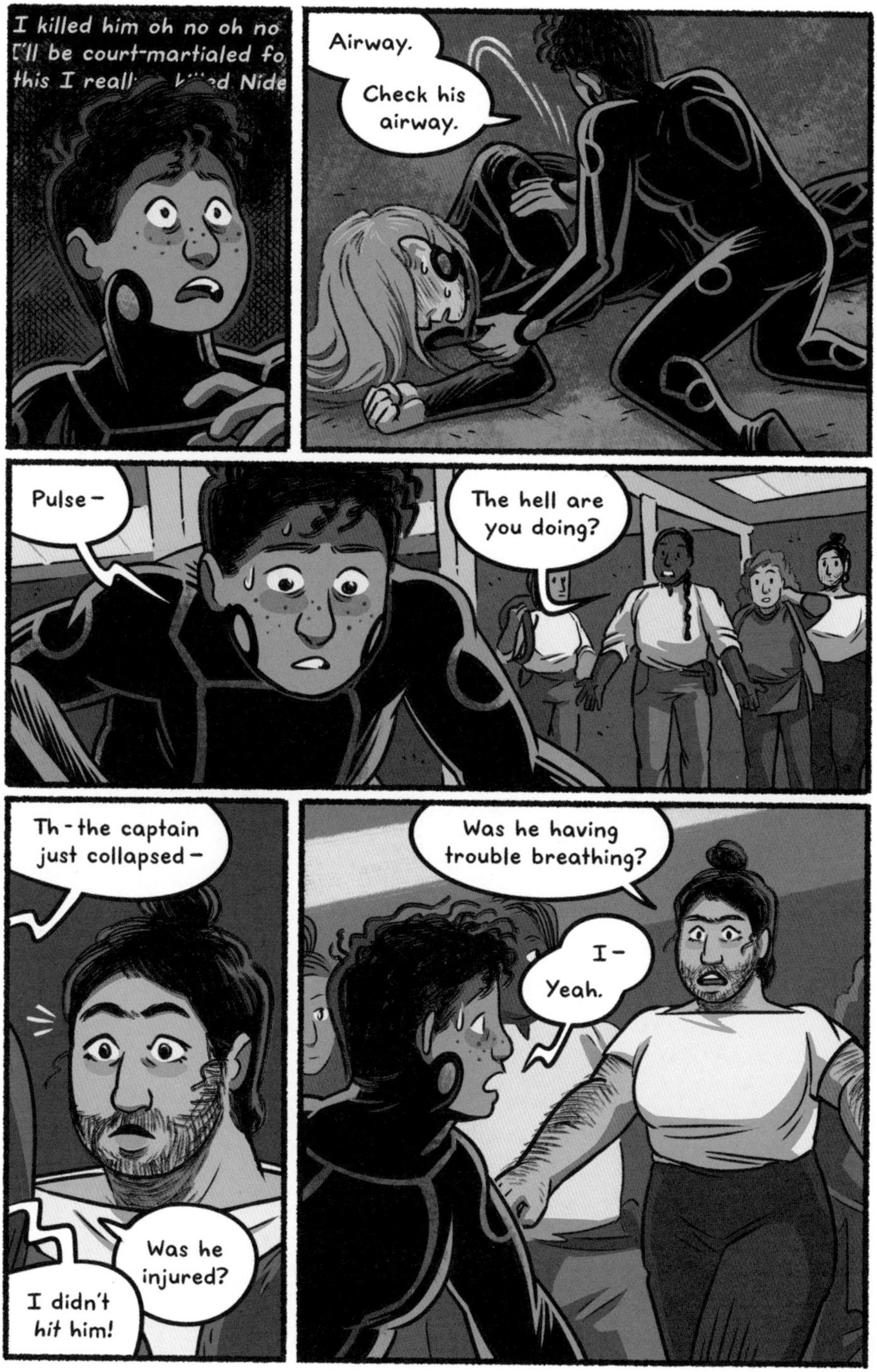
I killed him oh no oh no
I'll be court-martialed fo
this I reall
Nide
Airway.
Check his airway.
Pulse—
The hell are you doing?
Th-the captain just collapsed—
Was he injured?
I didn't hit him!
Was he having trouble breathing?
I—
Yeah.

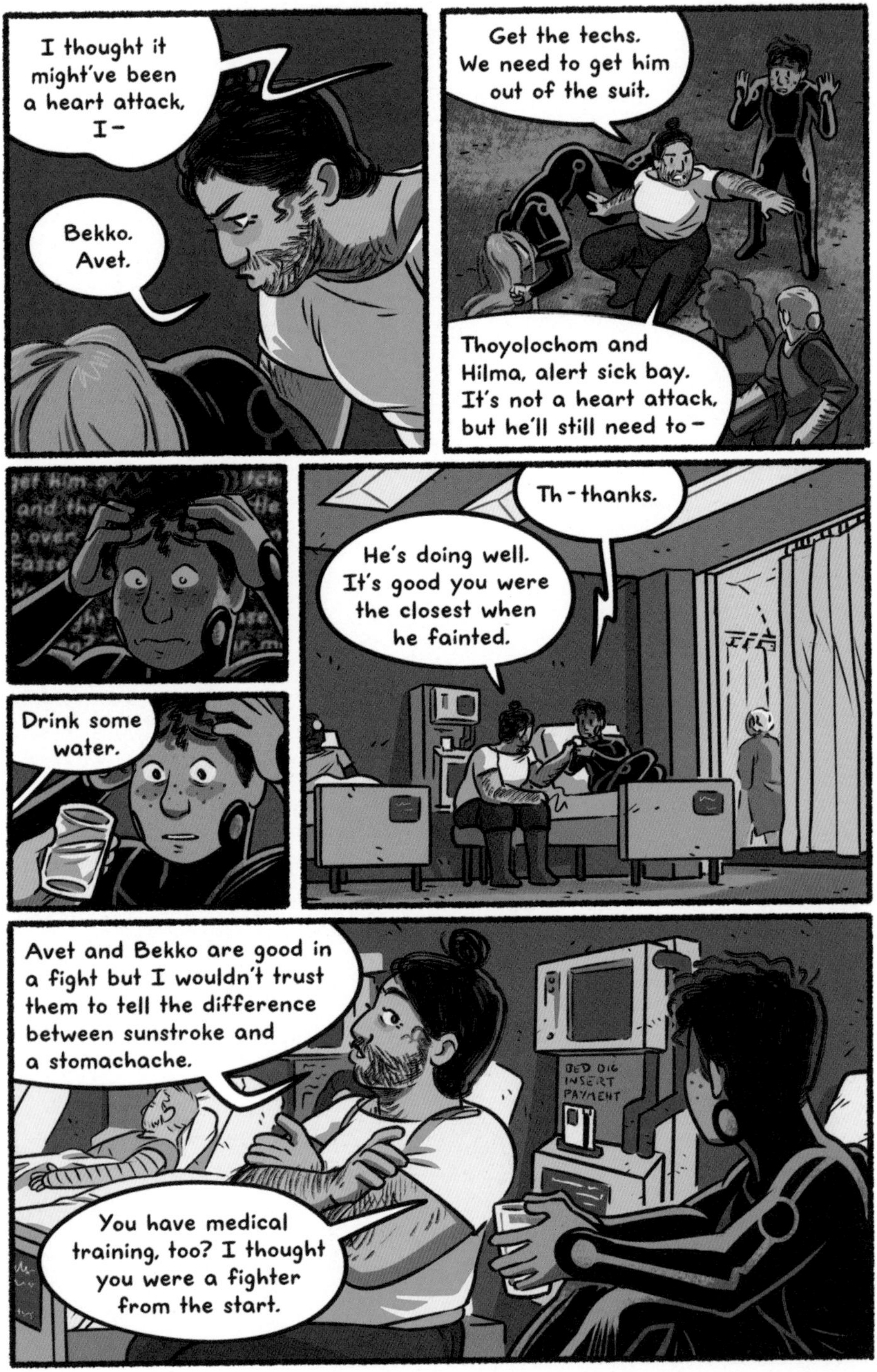
I thought it might've been a heart attack. I–
Bekko. Avet.
Get the techs. We need to get him out of the suit.
Thoyolochom and Hilma, alert sick bay. It's not a heart attack, but he'll still need to–
Drink some water.
Th-thanks.
He's doing well. It's good you were the closest when he fainted.
Avet and Bekko are good in a fight but I wouldn't trust them to tell the difference between sunstroke and a stomachache.
BED 016
INSERT PAYMENT
You have medical training, too? I thought you were a fighter from the start.

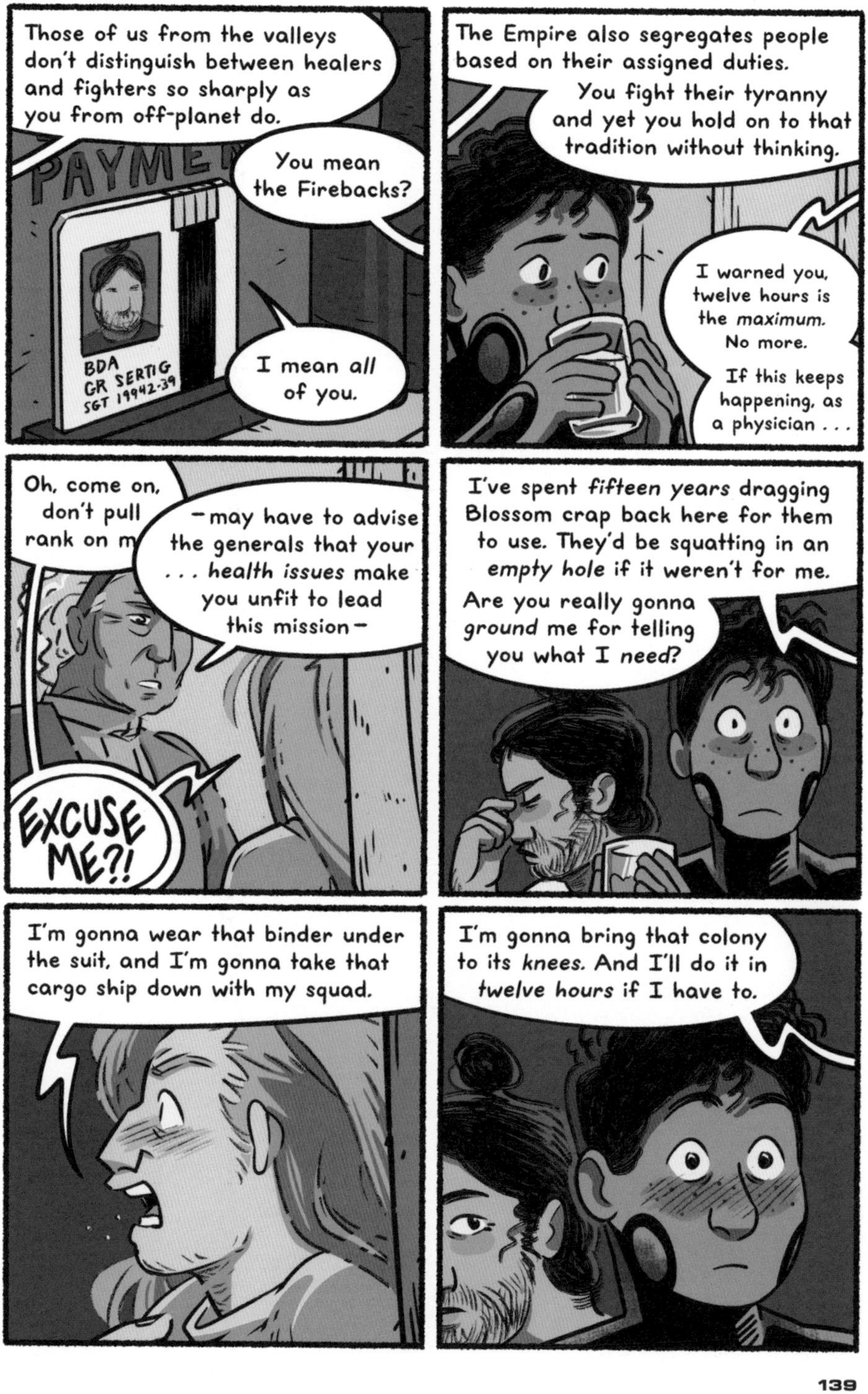
Those of us from the valleys don't distinguish between healers and fighters so sharply as you from off-planet do.
PAYME
You mean the Firebacks?
BDA GR SERTIG SGT 19942-39
I mean *all* of you.
The Empire also segregates people based on their assigned duties.
You fight their tyranny and yet you hold on to that tradition without thinking.
I warned you, twelve hours is the *maximum.* No more.
If this keeps happening, as a physician . . .
Oh, come on, don't pull rank on m
—may have to advise the generals that your . . . *health issues* make you unfit to lead this mission—
EXCUSE ME?!
I've spent *fifteen years* dragging Blossom crap back here for them to use. They'd be squatting in an *empty hole* if it weren't for me.
Are you really gonna *ground* me for telling you what I *need*?
I'm gonna wear that binder under the suit, and I'm gonna take that cargo ship down with my squad.
I'm gonna bring that colony to its *knees.* And I'll do it in *twelve hours* if I have to.

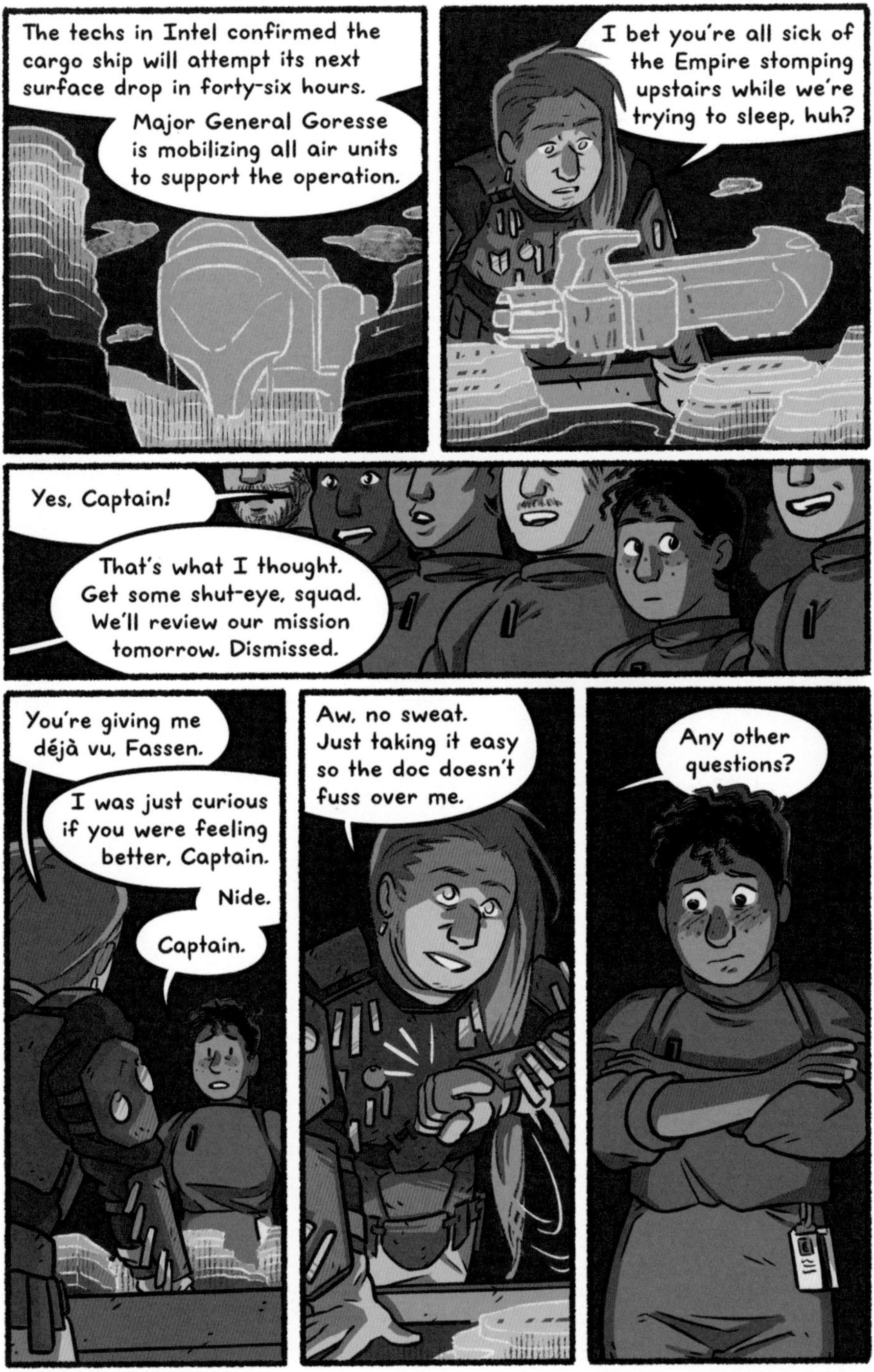
The techs in Intel confirmed the cargo ship will attempt its next surface drop in forty-six hours.
Major General Goresse is mobilizing all air units to support the operation.
I bet you're all sick of the Empire stomping upstairs while we're trying to sleep, huh?
Yes, Captain!
That's what I thought. Get some shut-eye, squad. We'll review our mission tomorrow. Dismissed.
You're giving me déjà vu, Fassen.
I was just curious if you were feeling better, Captain.
Nide.
Captain.
Aw, no sweat. Just taking it easy so the doc doesn't fuss over me.
Any other questions?

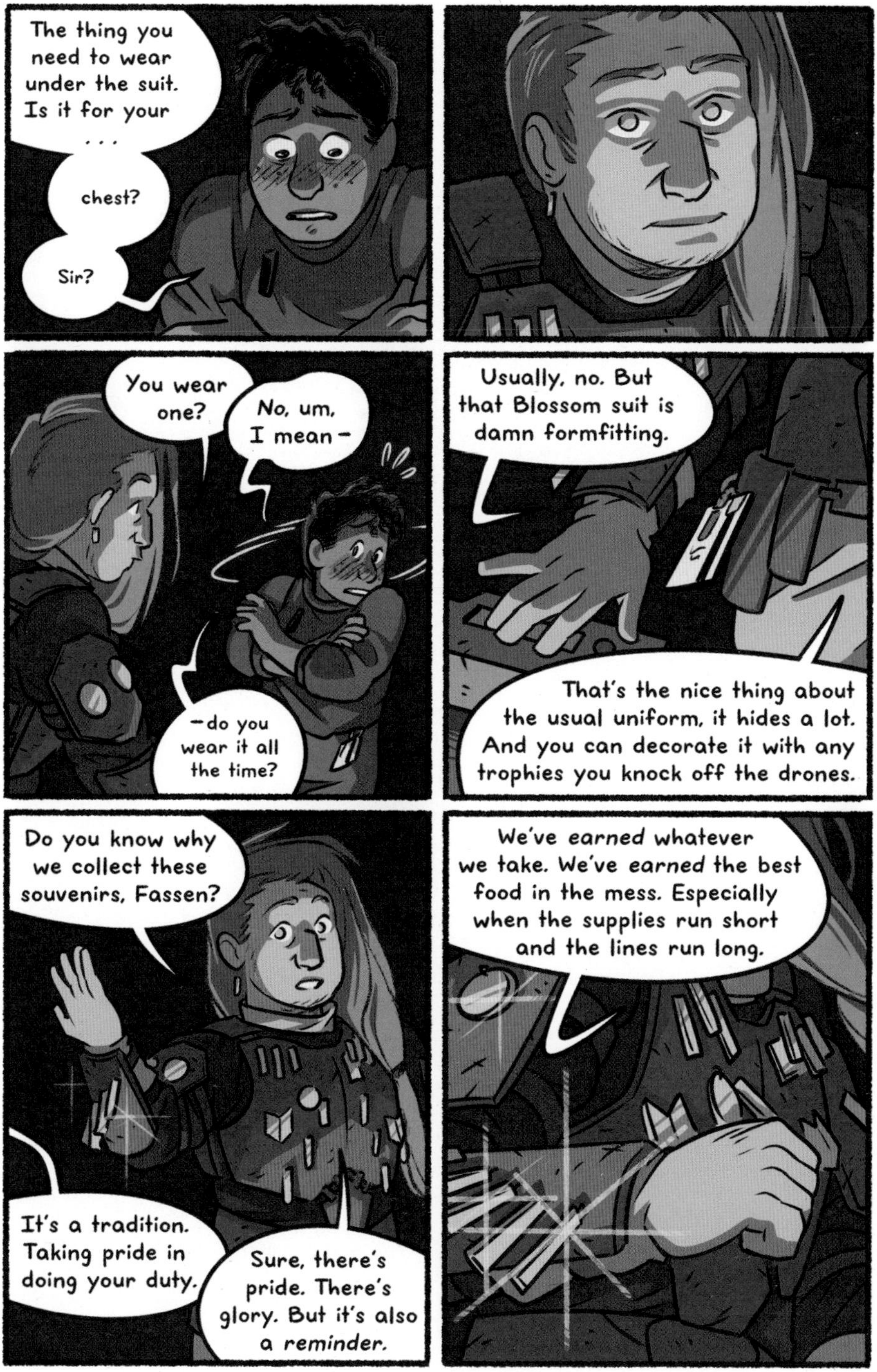

The thing you need to wear under the suit. Is it for your
. . .
chest?
Sir?
You wear one?
No, um, I mean—
—do you wear it all the time?
Usually, no. But that Blossom suit is damn formfitting.
That's the nice thing about the usual uniform, it hides a lot. And you can decorate it with any trophies you knock off the drones.
Do you know why we collect these souvenirs, Fassen?
It's a tradition. Taking pride in doing your duty.
Sure, there's pride. There's glory. But it's also a *reminder.*
We've *earned* whatever we take. We've *earned* the best food in the mess. Especially when the supplies run short and the lines run long.

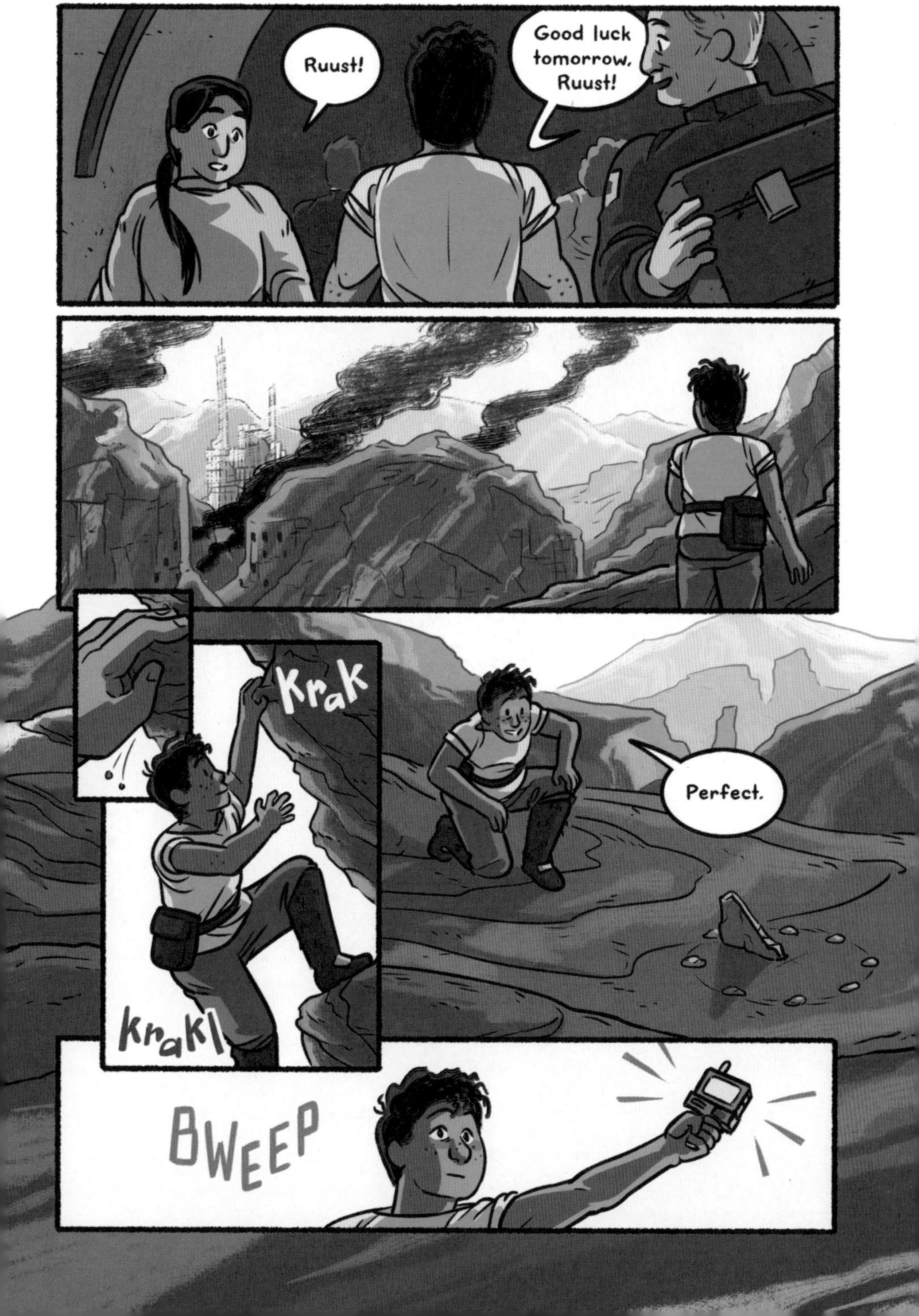
Ruust!
Good luck tomorrow, Ruust!
Krak
krak!
Perfect.
BWEEP

144

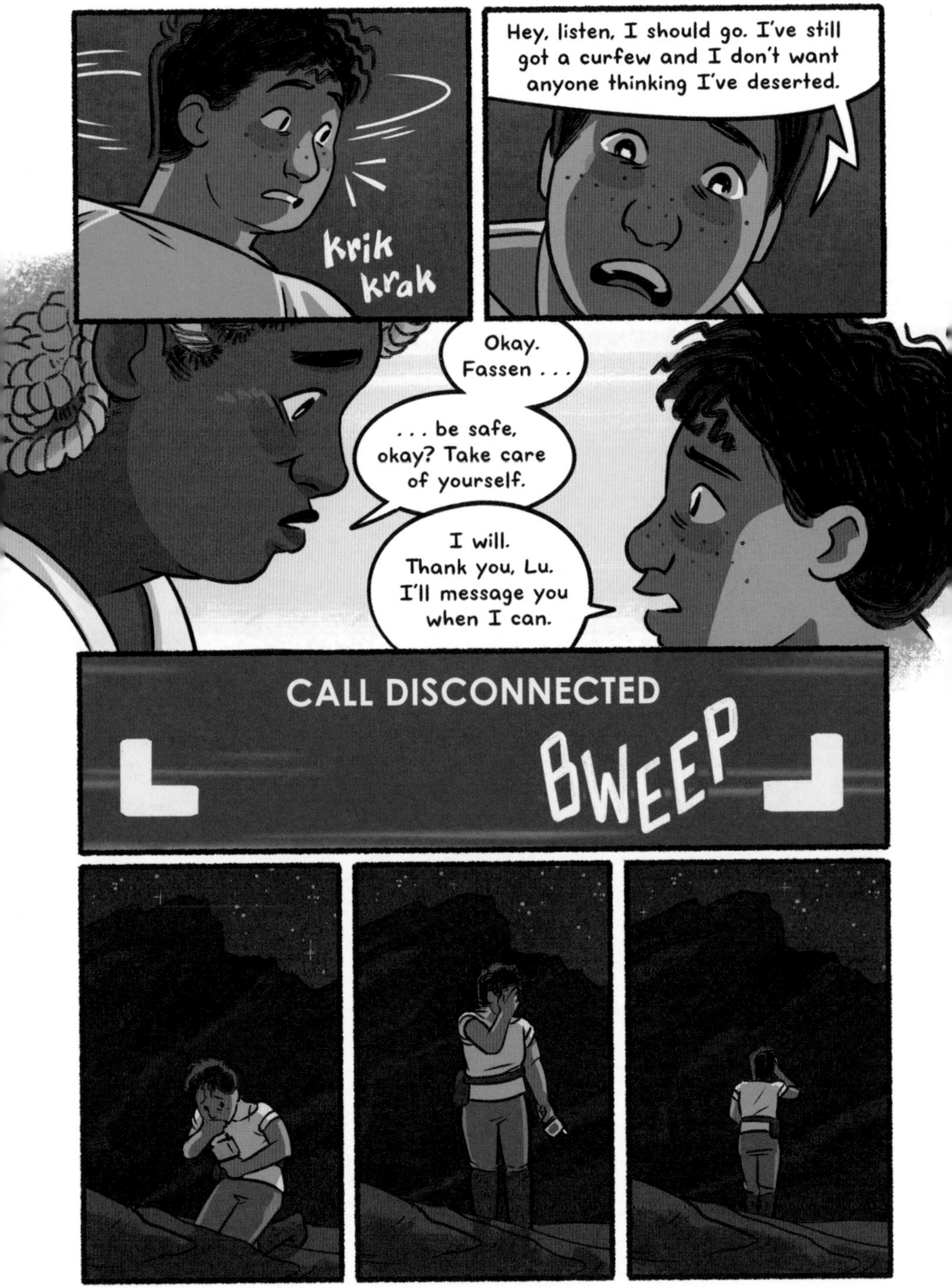
krik krak
Hey, listen, I should go. I've still got a curfew and I don't want anyone thinking I've deserted.
Okay. Fassen . . .
. . . be safe, okay? Take care of yourself.
I will. Thank you, Lu. I'll message you when I can.
CALL DISCONNECTED
BWEEP

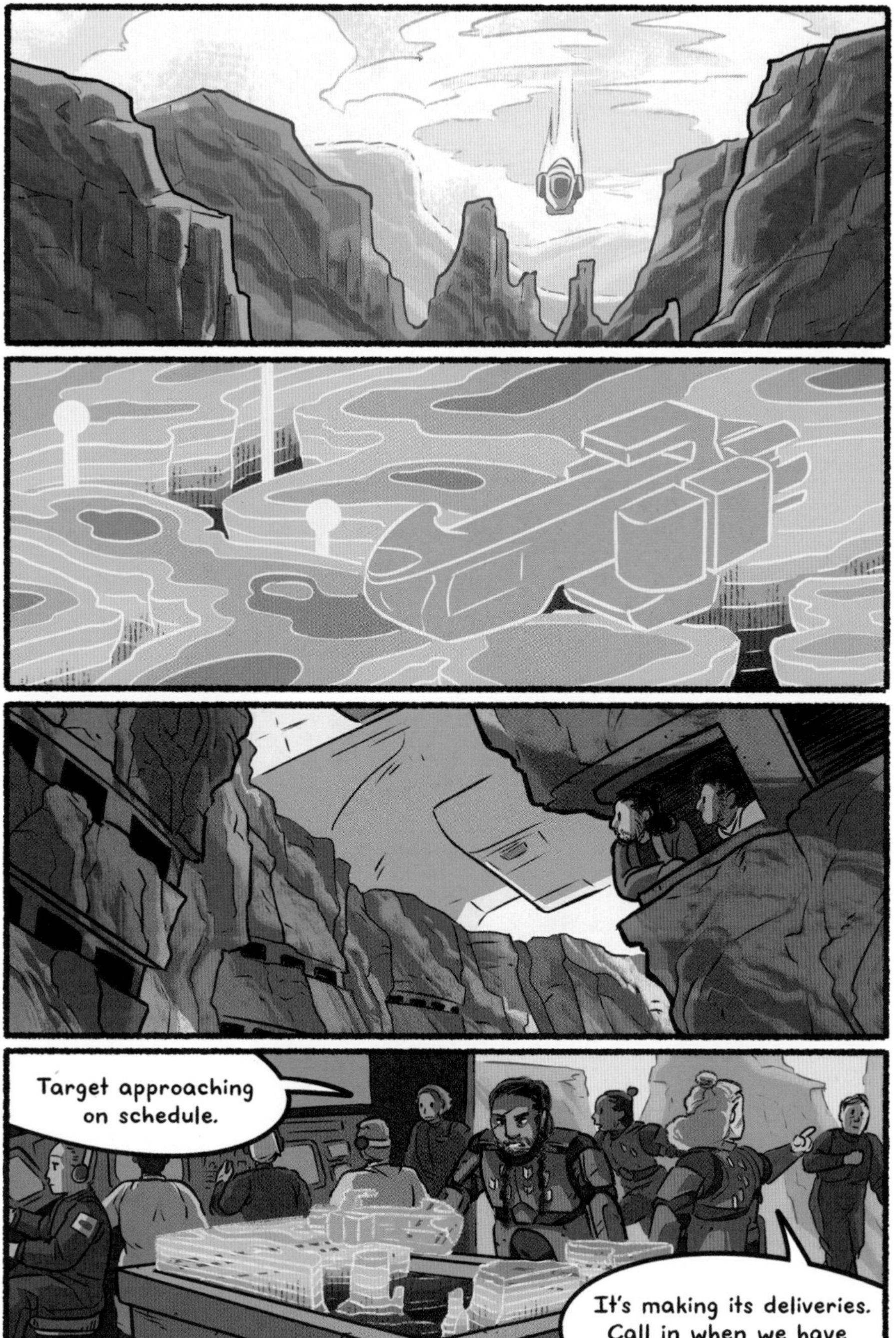
Target approaching on schedule.
It's making its deliveries. Call in when we have escort visuals.

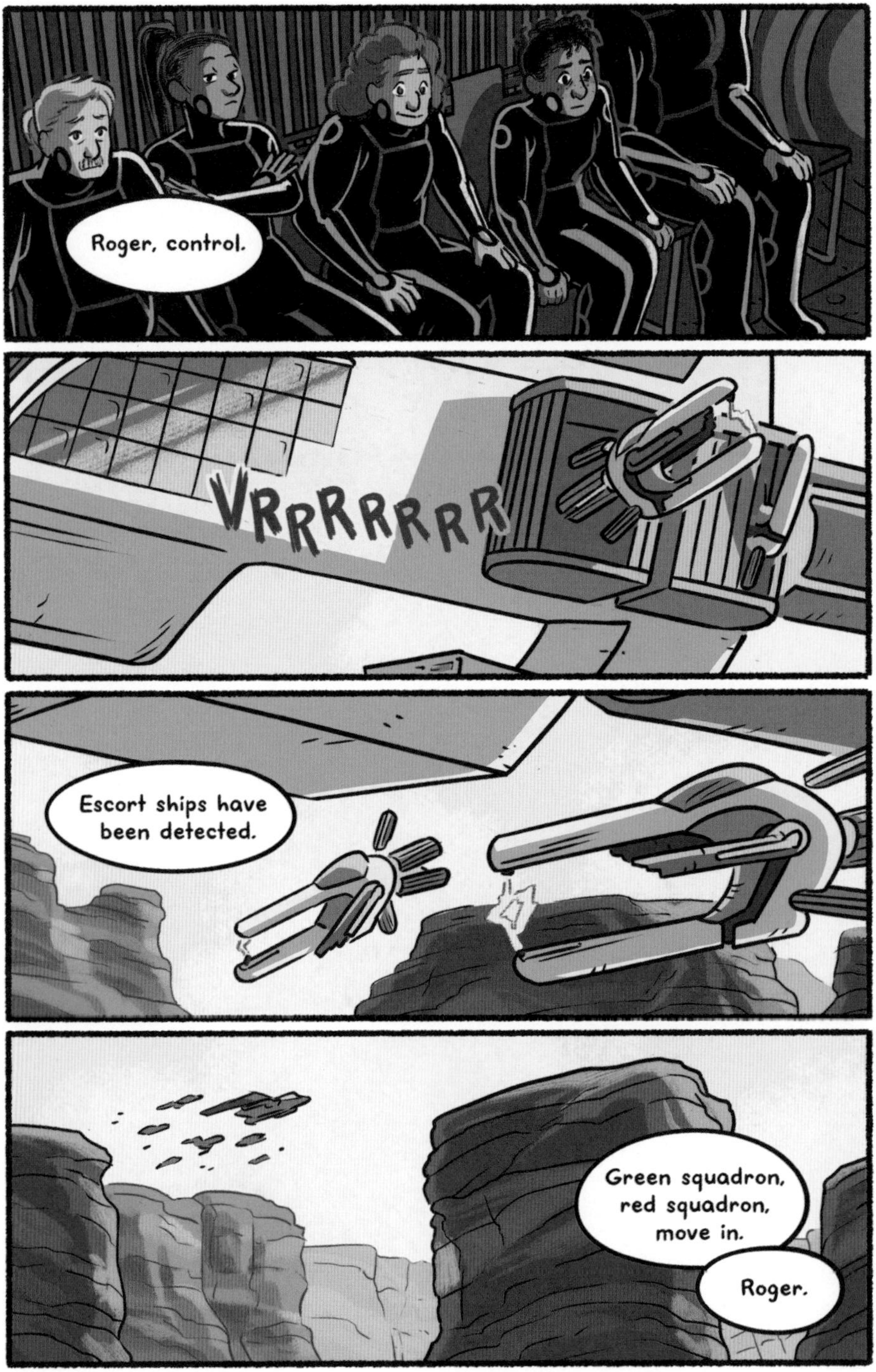
Roger, control.
VRRRRRRR
Escort ships have been detected.
Green squadron, red squadron, move in.
Roger.

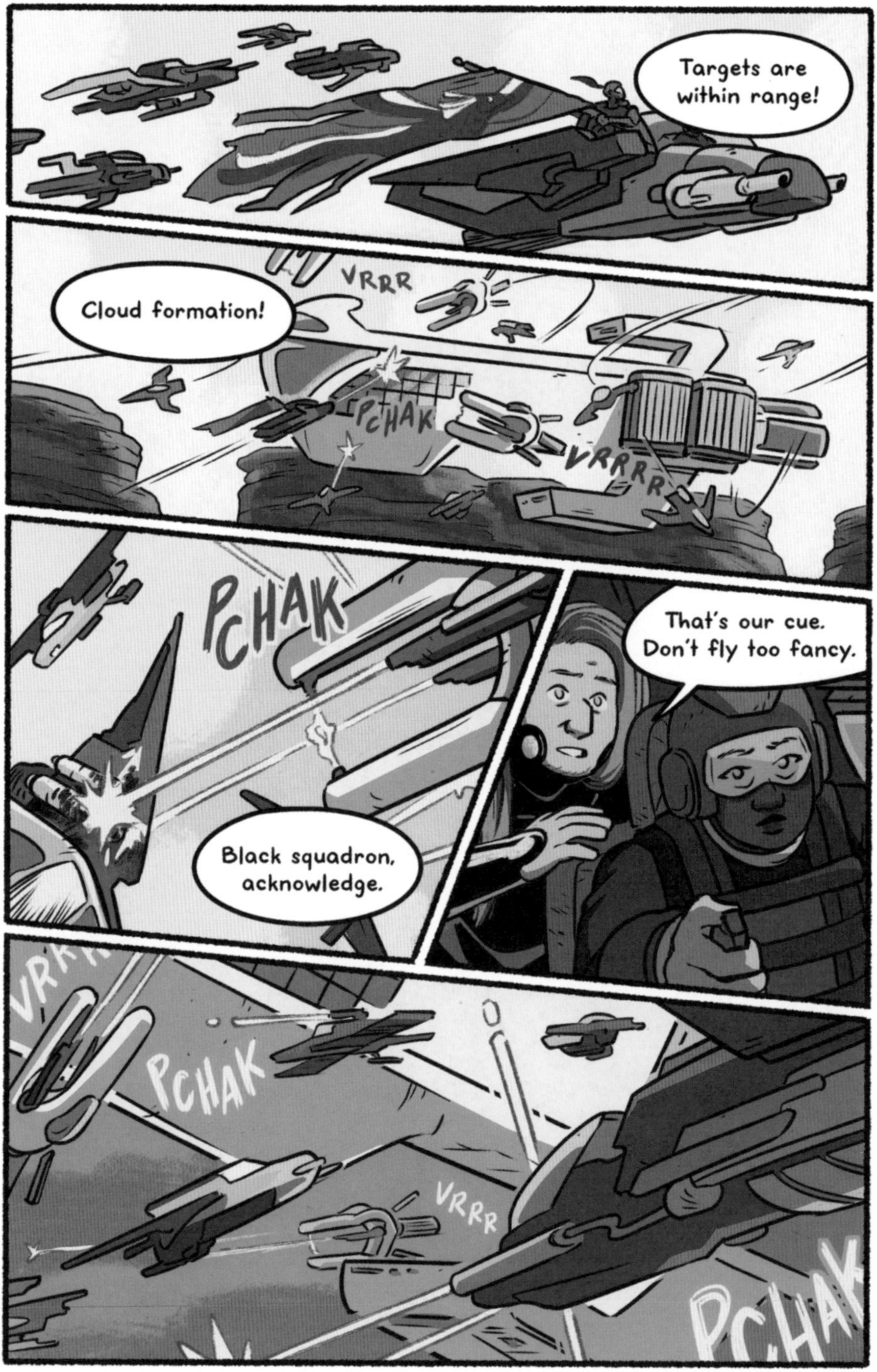

Targets are within range!
VRRR
Cloud formation!
PCHAK
VRRRR
PCHAK
That's our cue. Don't fly too fancy.
Black squadron, acknowledge.
PCHAK
VRRR
PCHAK

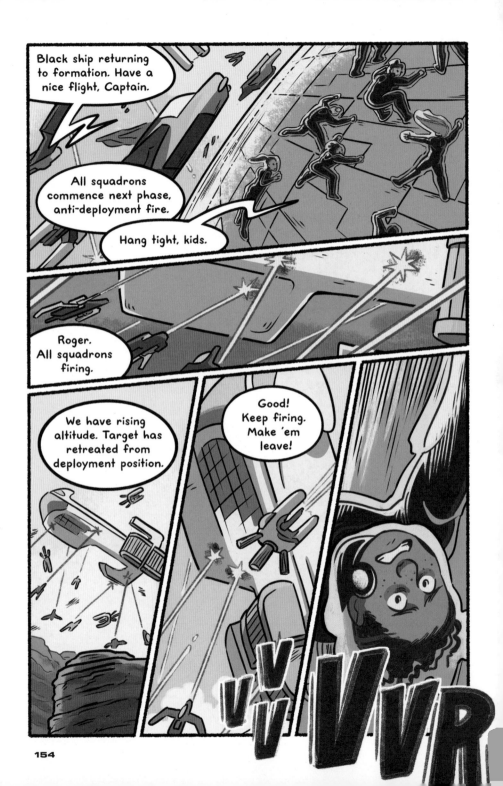

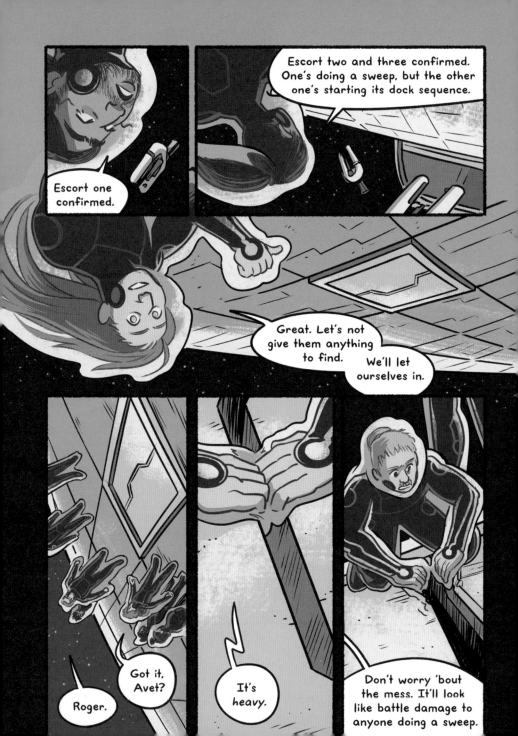

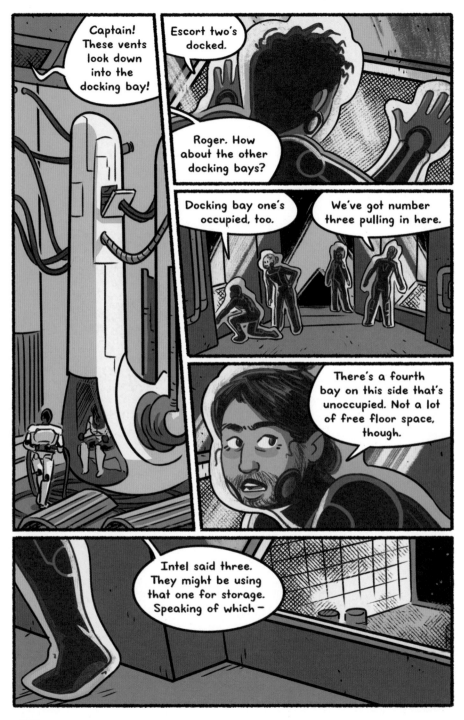

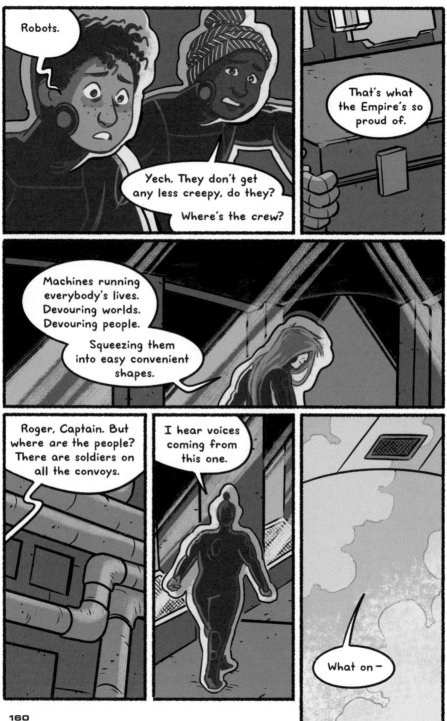

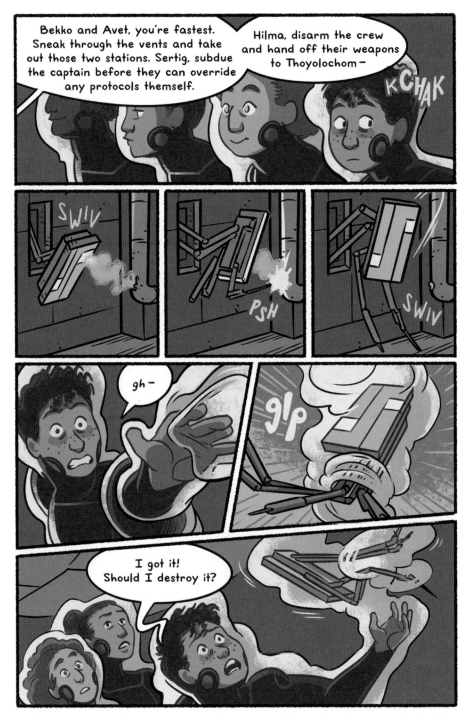

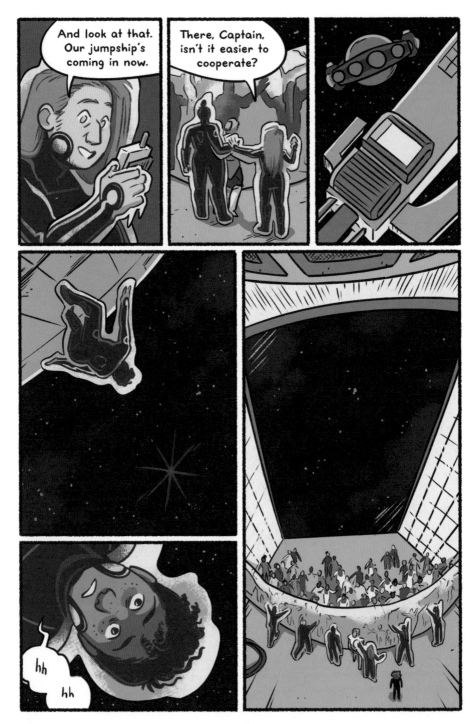

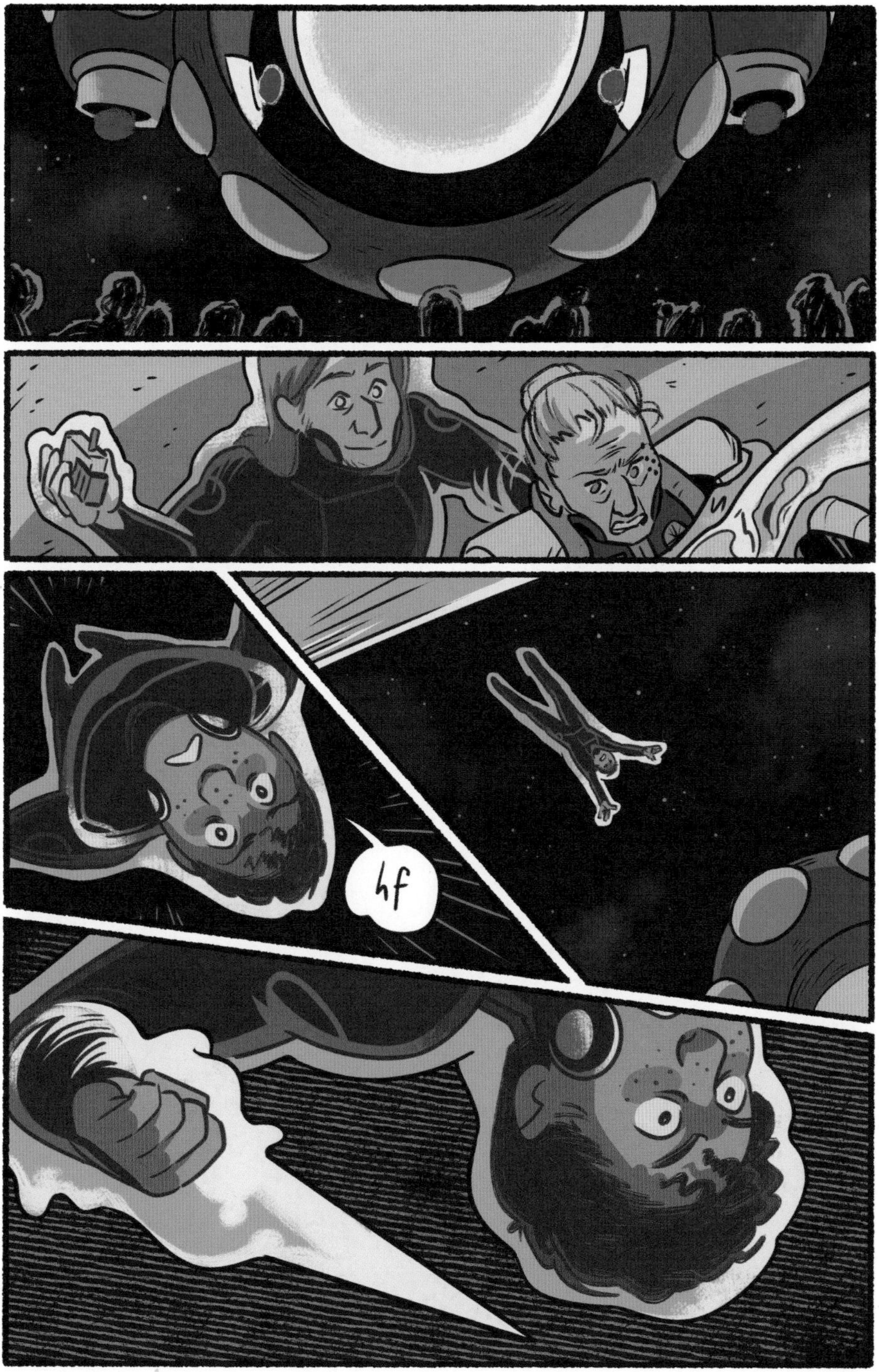
hf

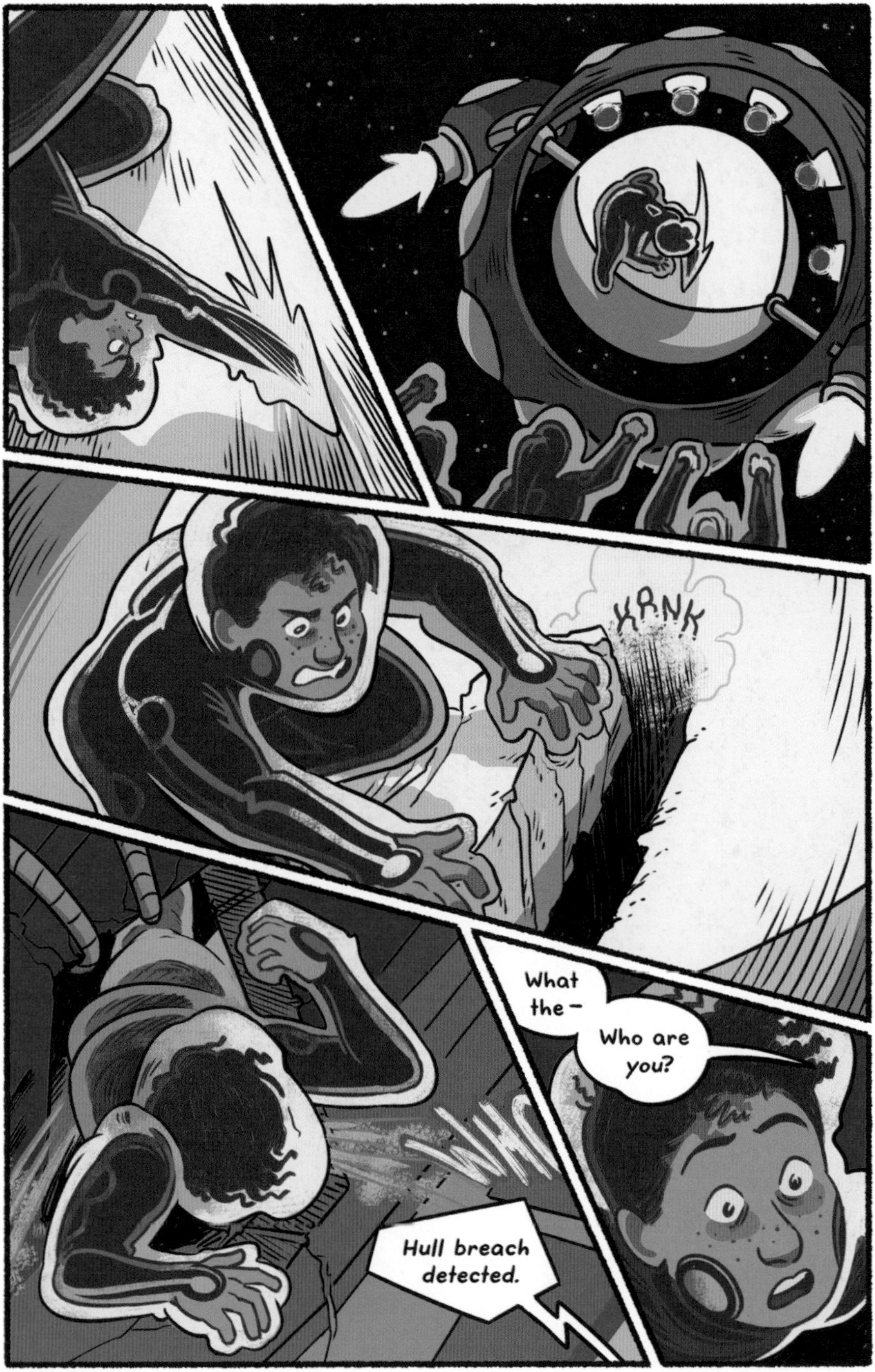
KRNK
WHO
What the—
Who are you?
Hull breach detected.

177

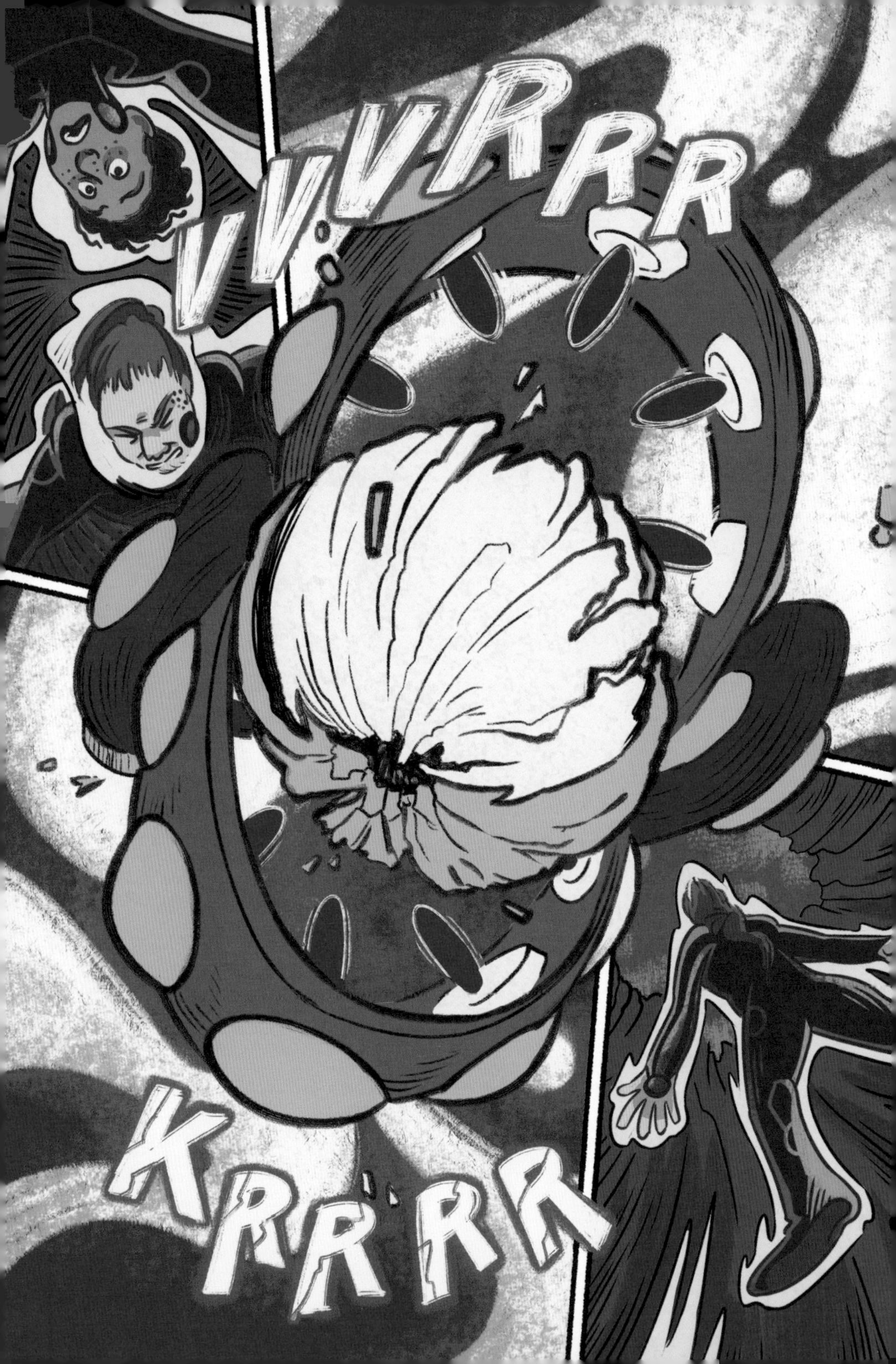
VVVRRRR
KRRRRR

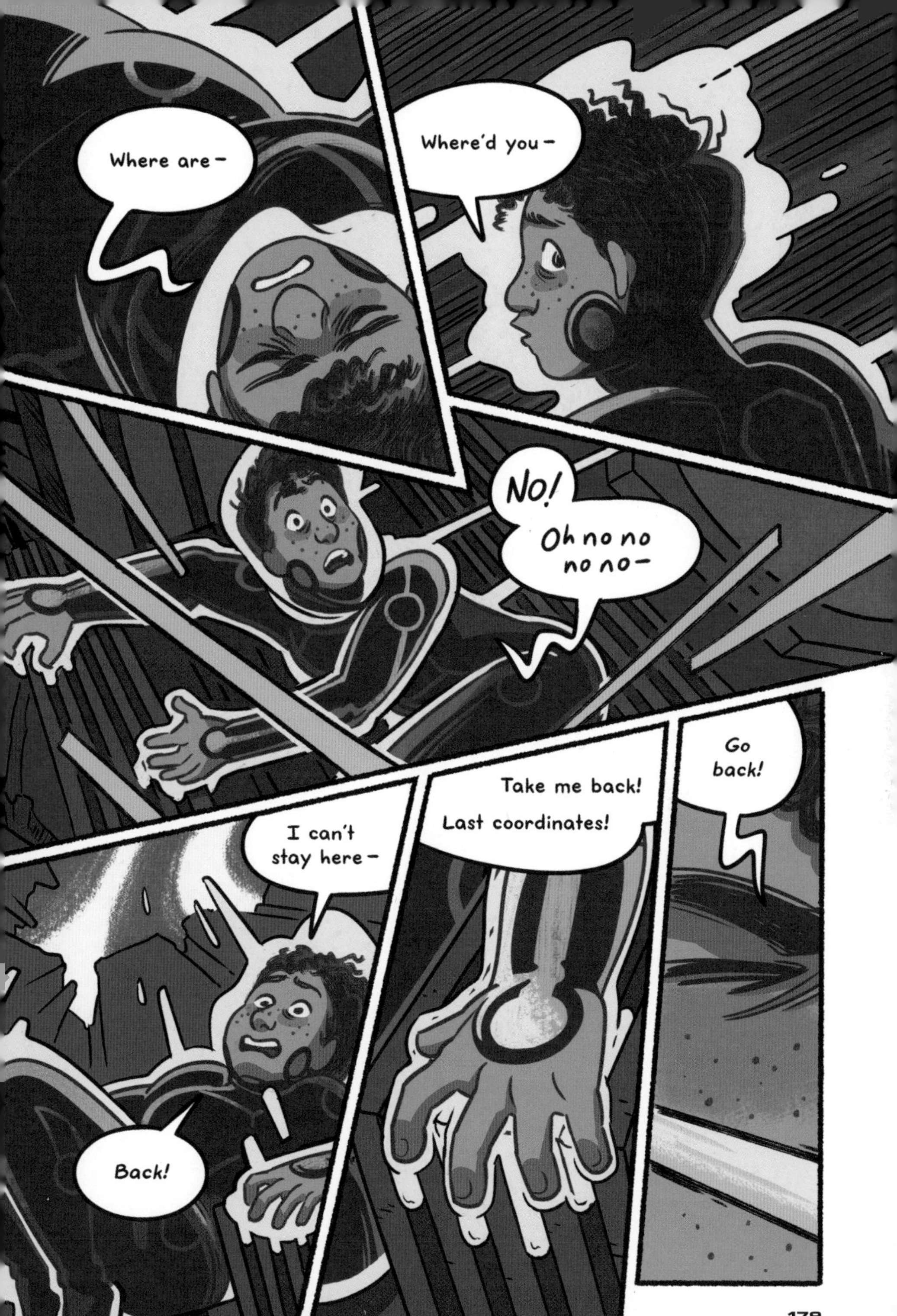
Where are-
Where'd you-
No!
Oh no no no no-
Take me back!
Last coordinates!
Go back!
I can't stay here-
Back!

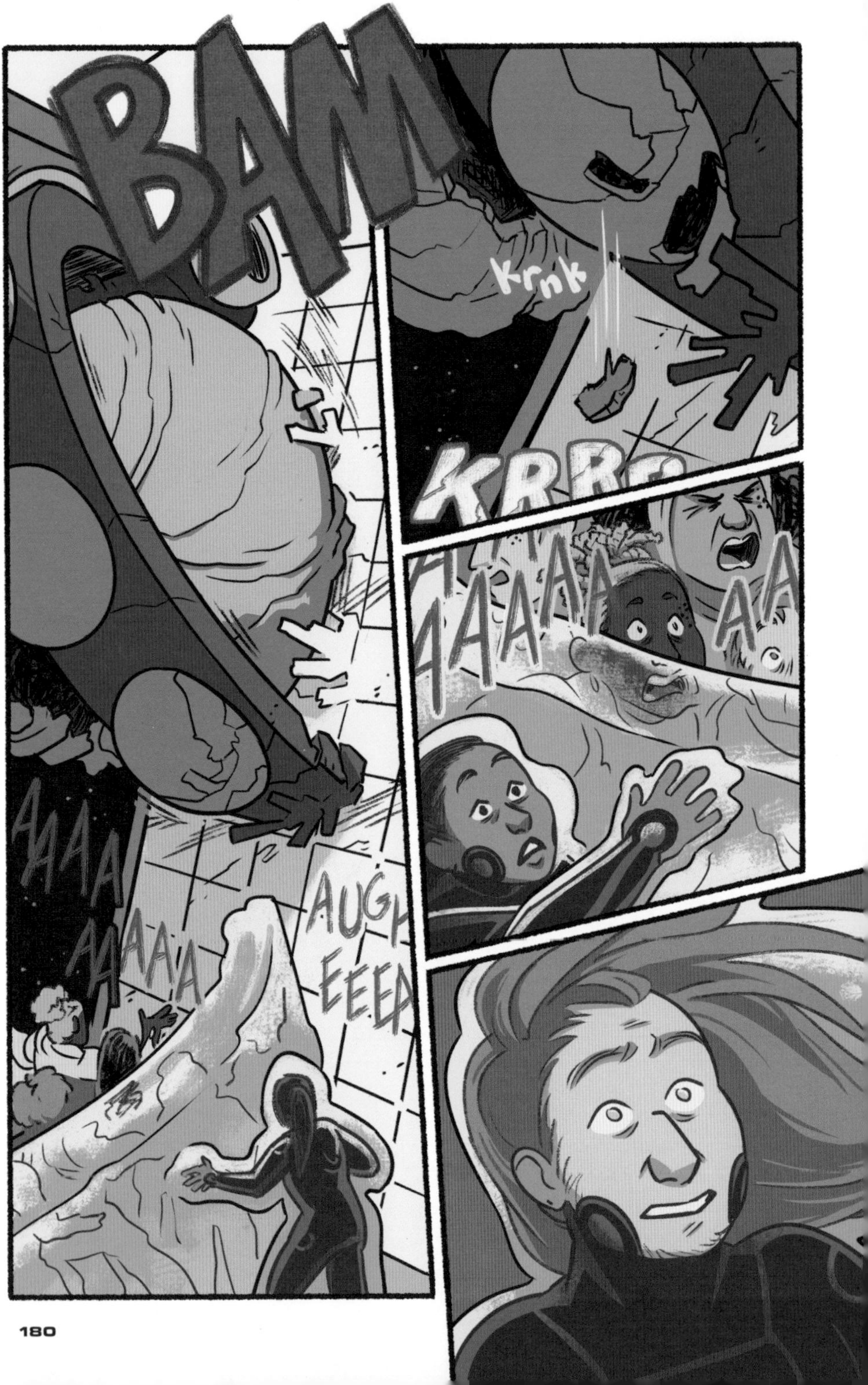
BAM
krnk
KRRG
AAAA
AAAAAA
AA
AAAA
AAAA
AUGH
EEEA

183

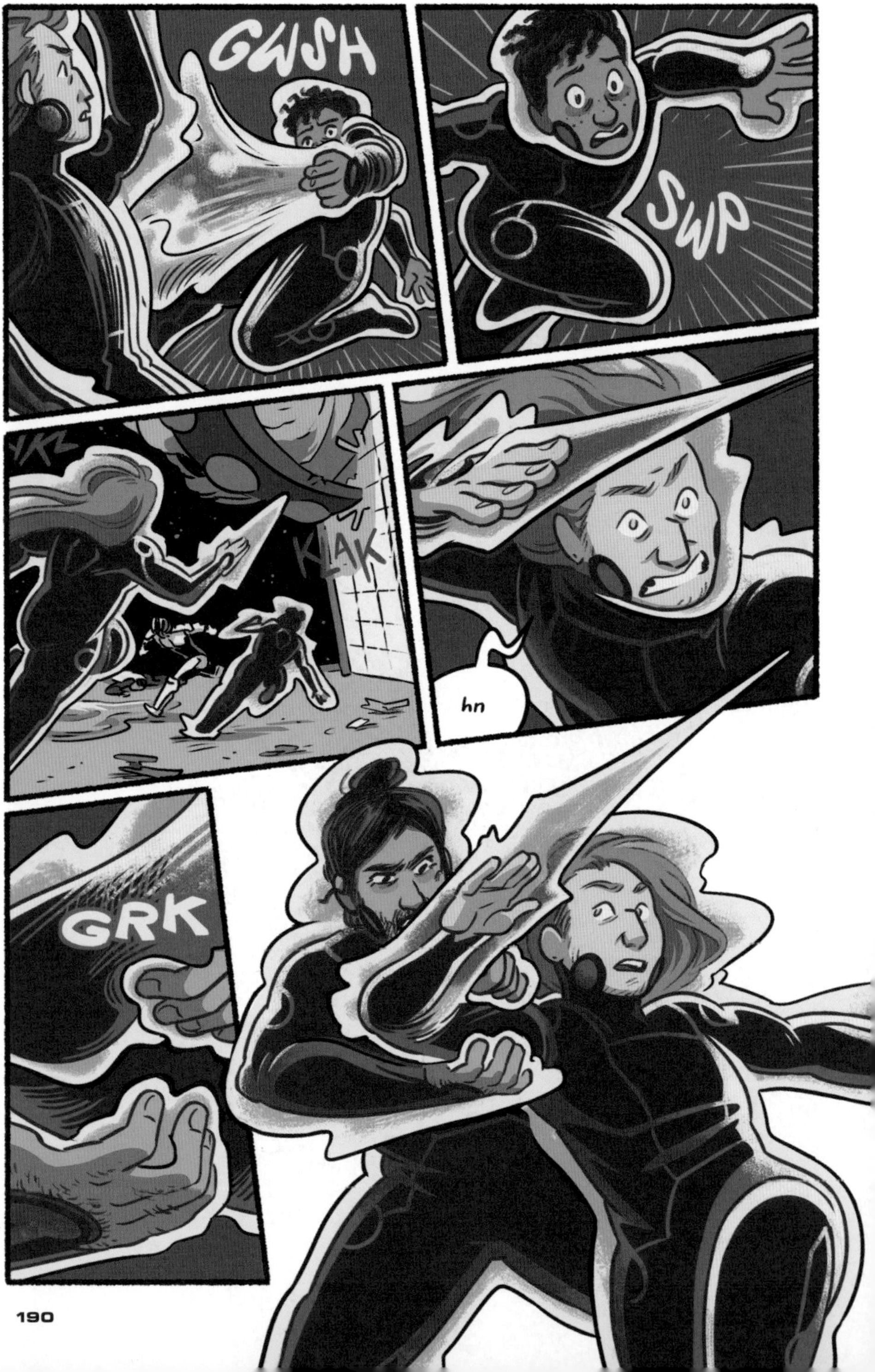
GWSH
SWP
KLAK
hn
GRK

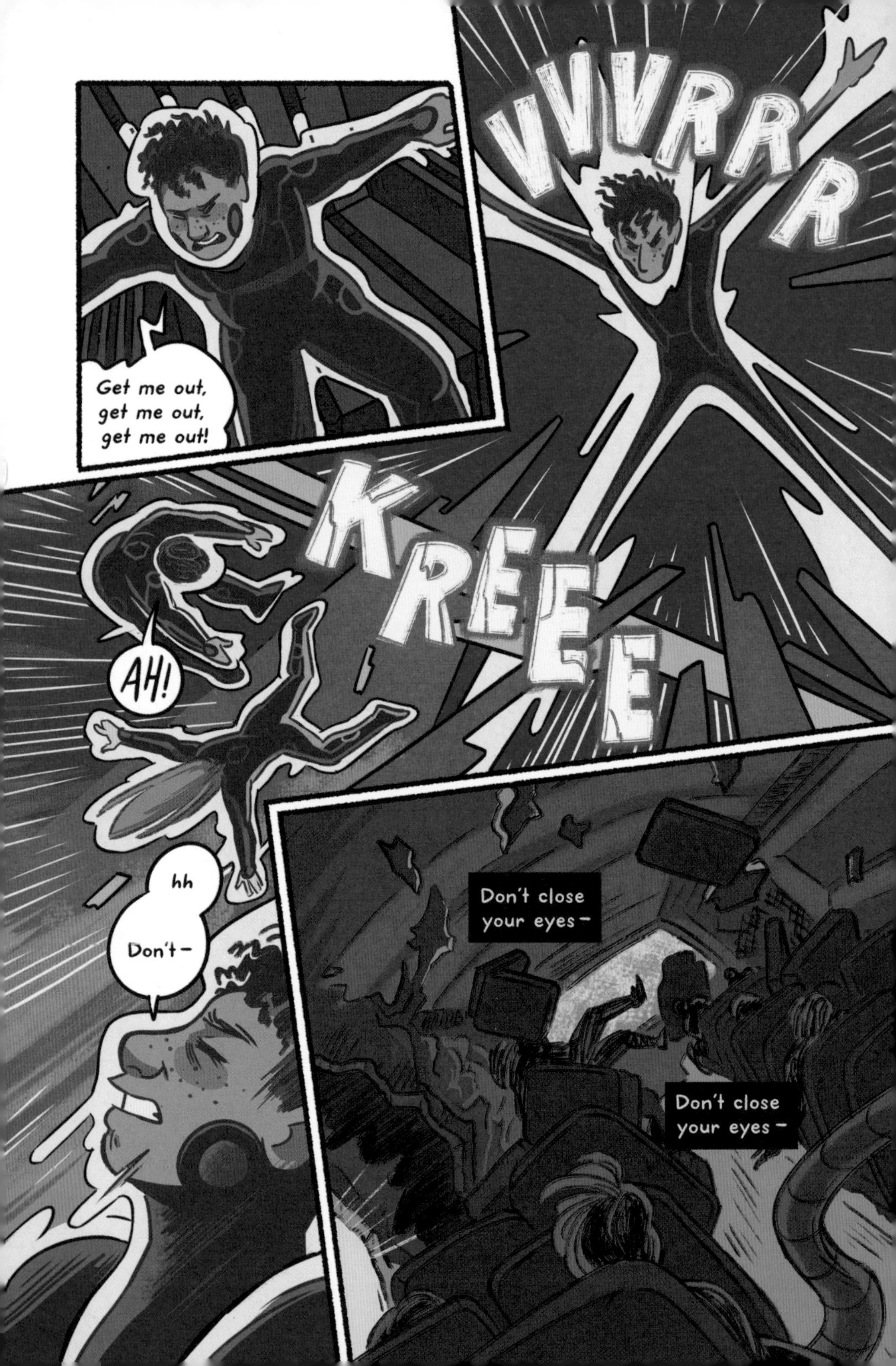
Get me out,
get me out,
get me out!
VVVRRRR
KREEEE
AH!
hh
Don't–
Don't close
your eyes–
Don't close
your eyes–

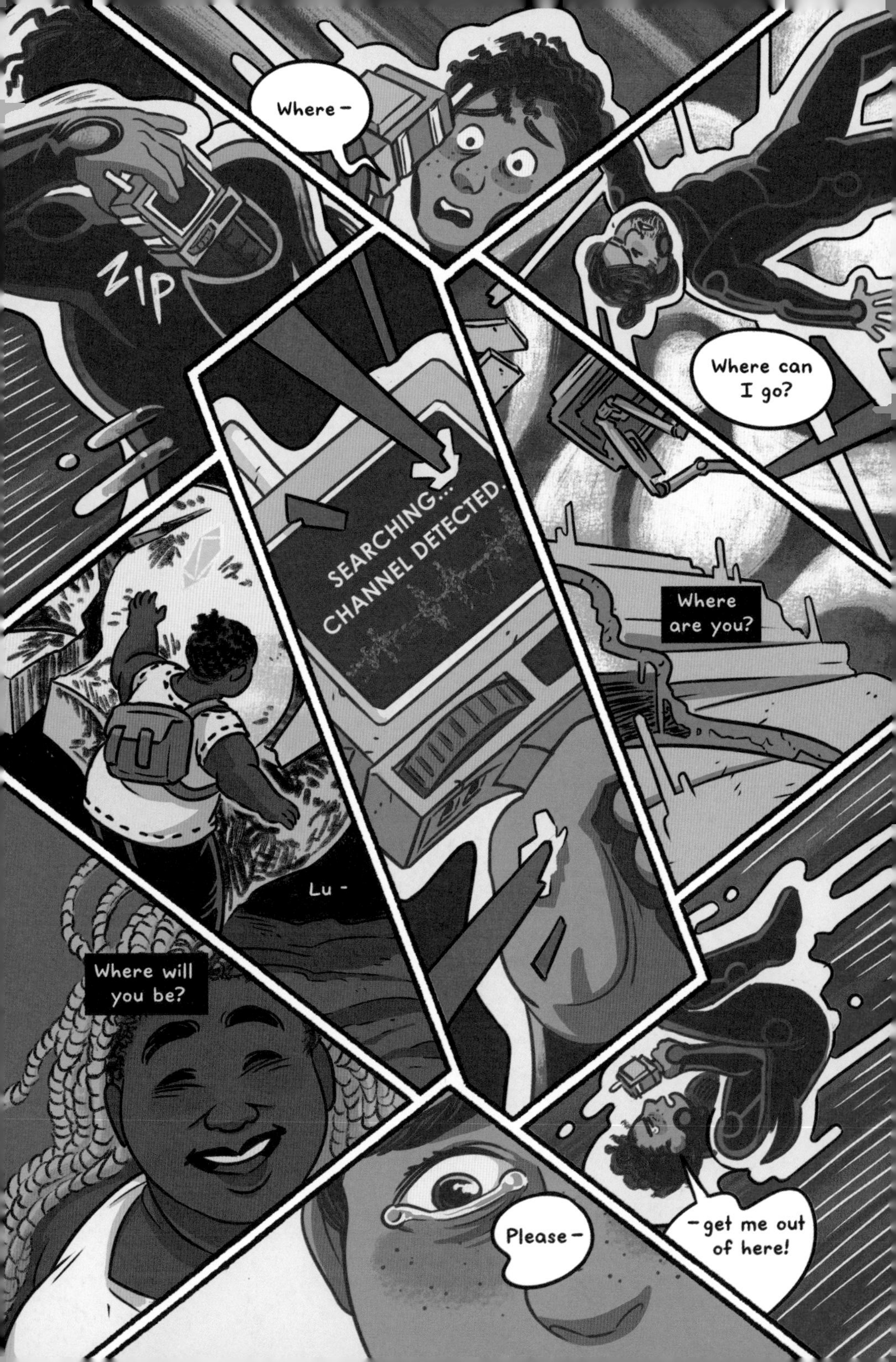
Where -
ZIP
Where can I go?
SEARCHING... CHANNEL DETECTED.
Where are you?
Lu -
Where will you be?
Please -
- get me out of here!

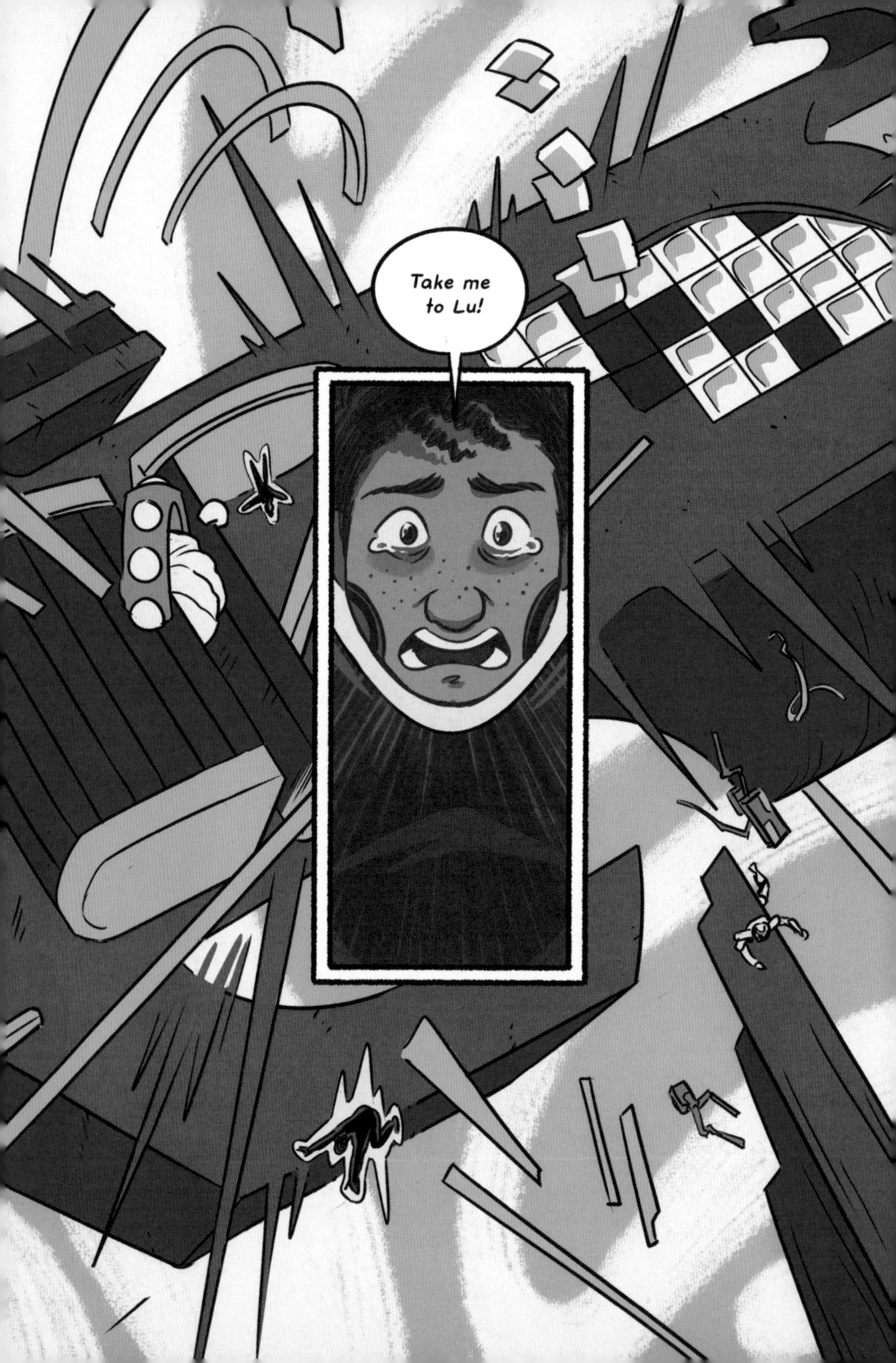
Take me to Lu!

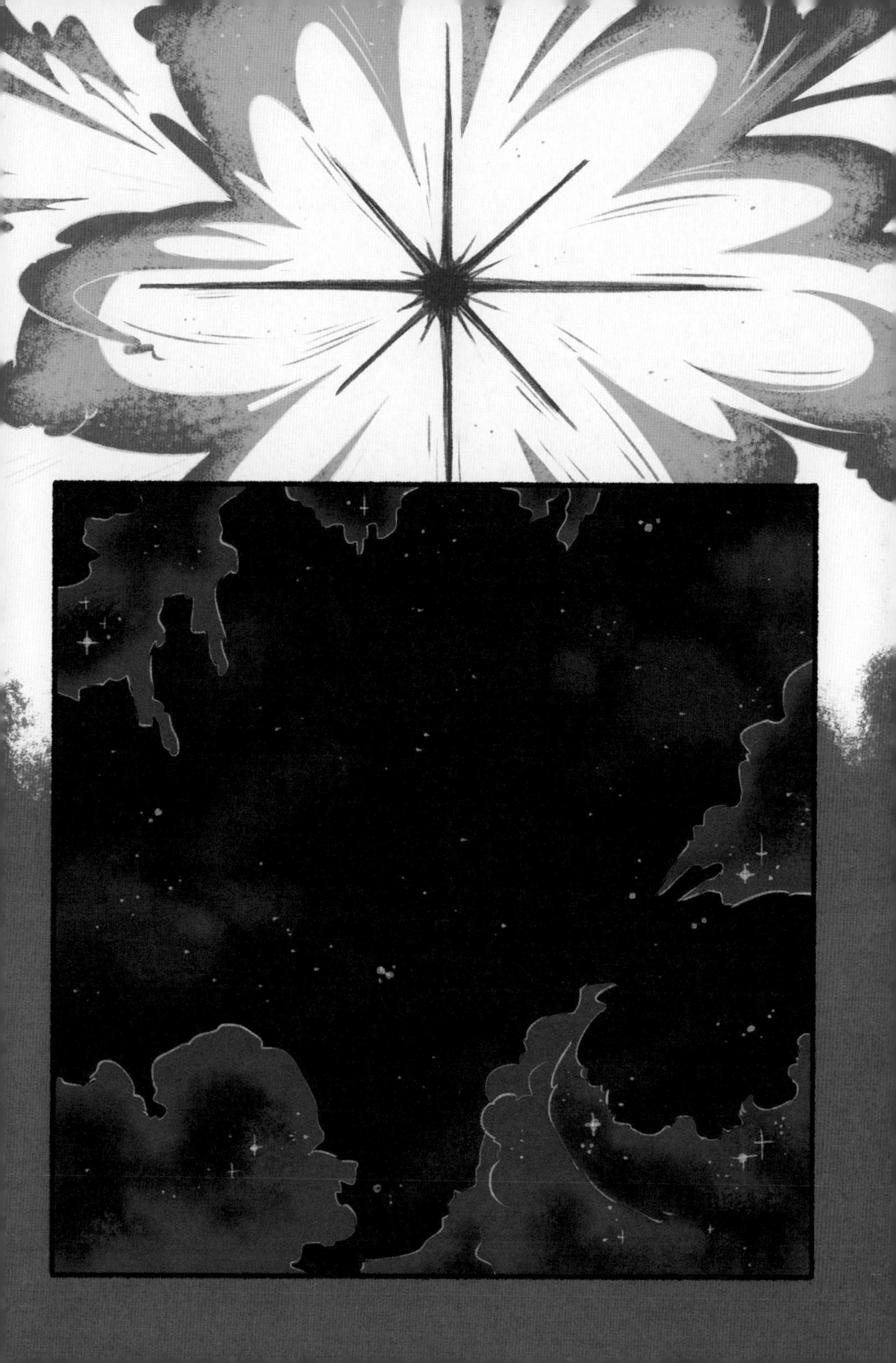

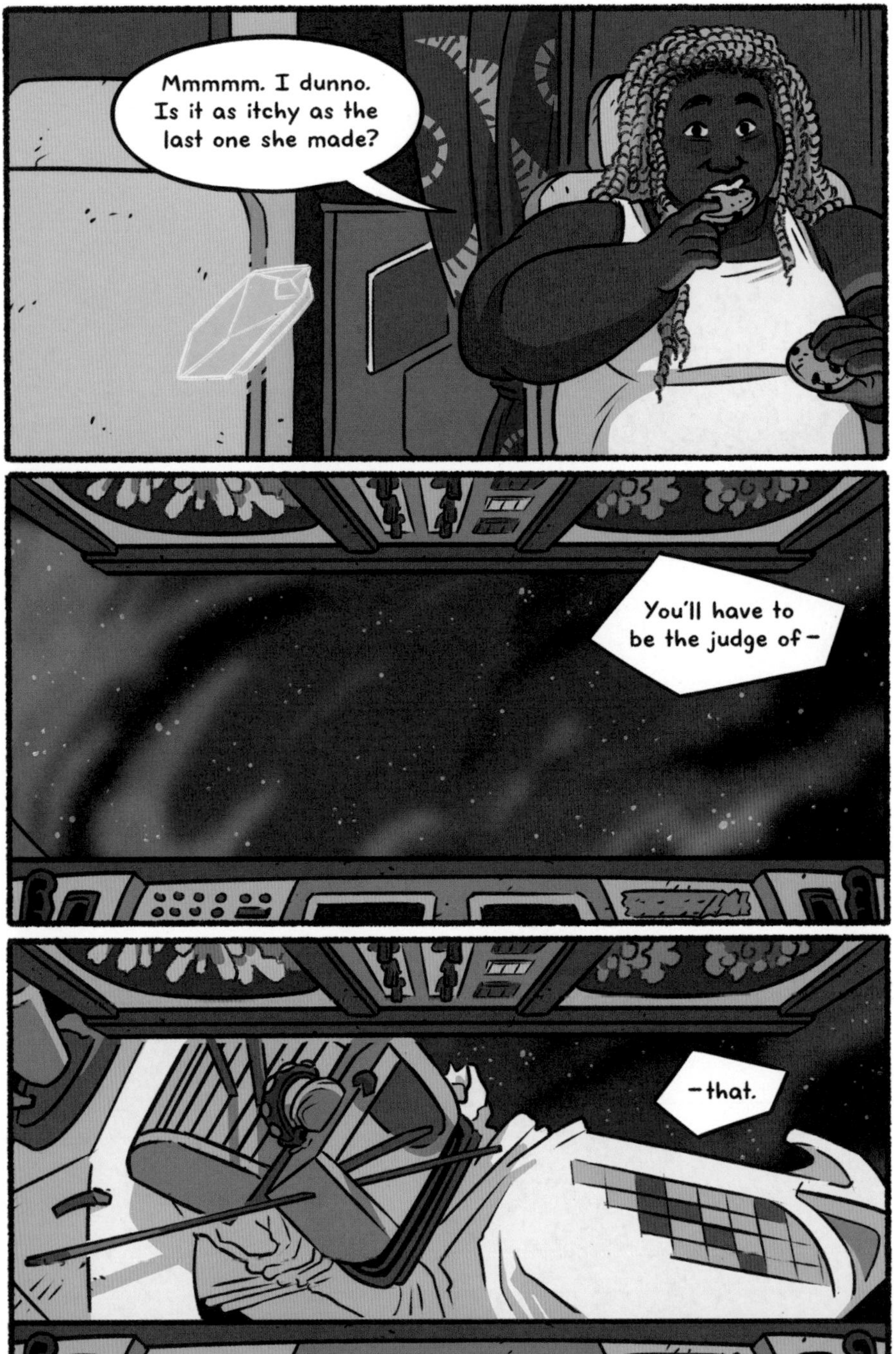
Mmmmm. I dunno. Is it as itchy as the last one she made?
You'll have to be the judge of—
—that.

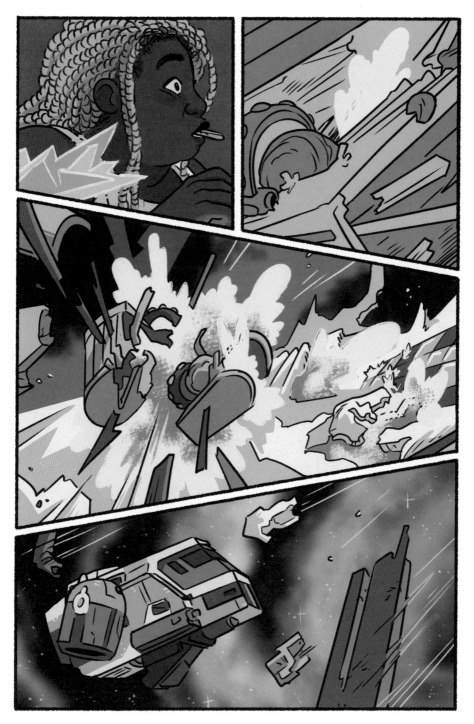

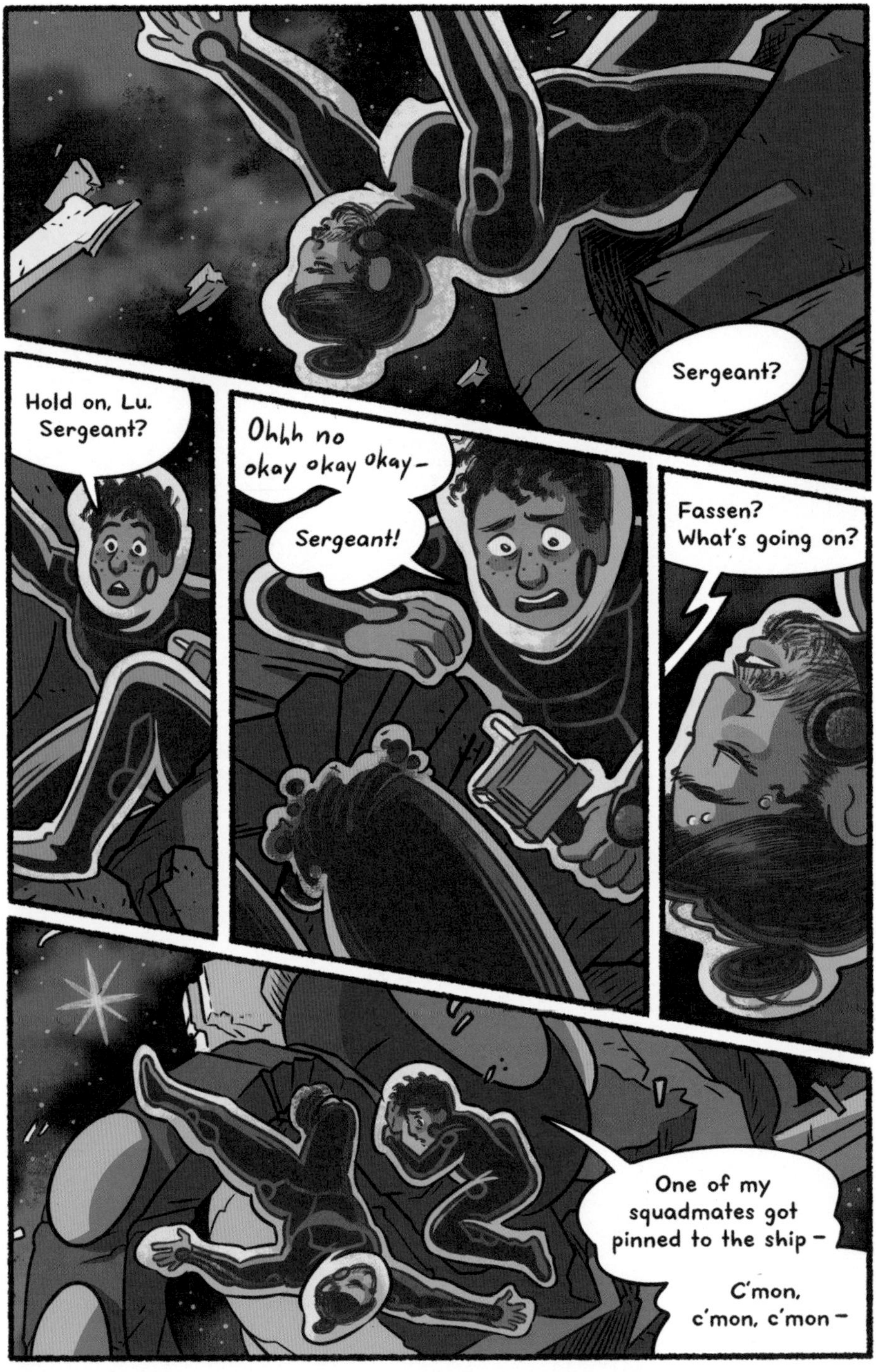
Sergeant?
Hold on, Lu.
Sergeant?
Ohhh no
okay okay okay–
Sergeant!
Fassen?
What's going on?
One of my
squadmates got
pinned to the ship–
C'mon,
c'mon, c'mon–

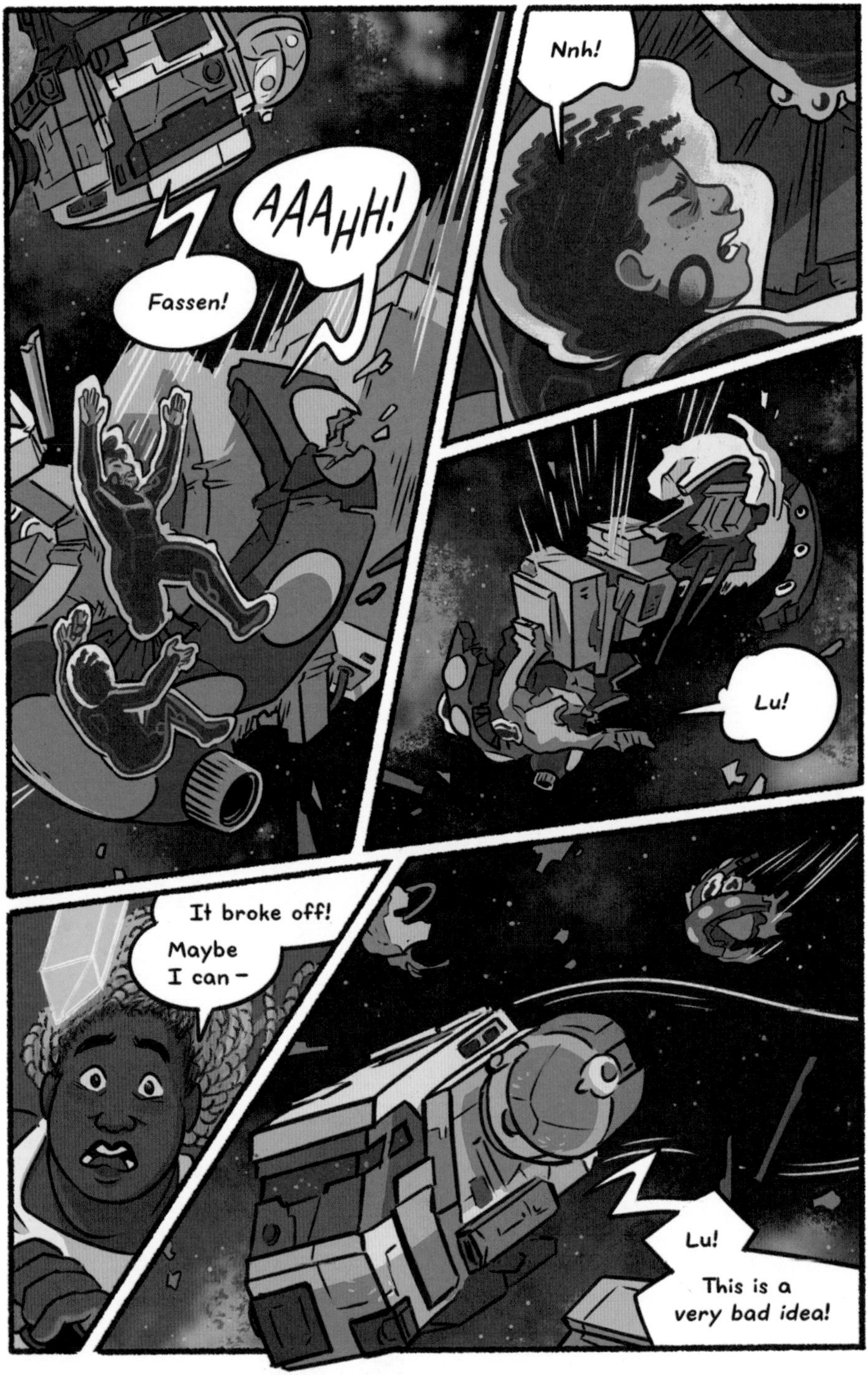

Fassen!
AAAHH!
Nnh!
Lu!
It broke off!
Maybe I can—
Lu!
This is a very bad idea!

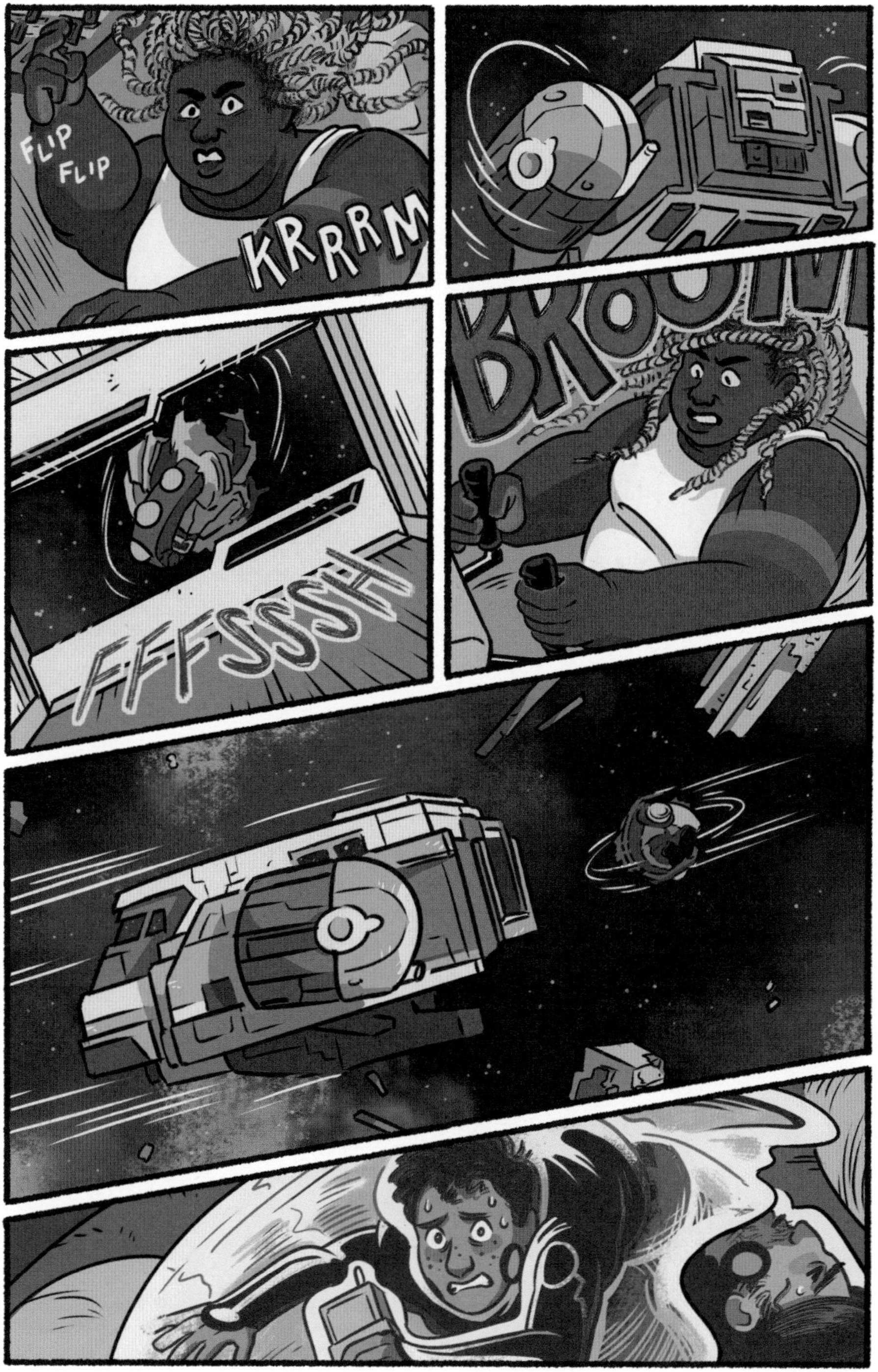
FLIP
FLIP
KRRRM
BROOM
FFFSSSH

207

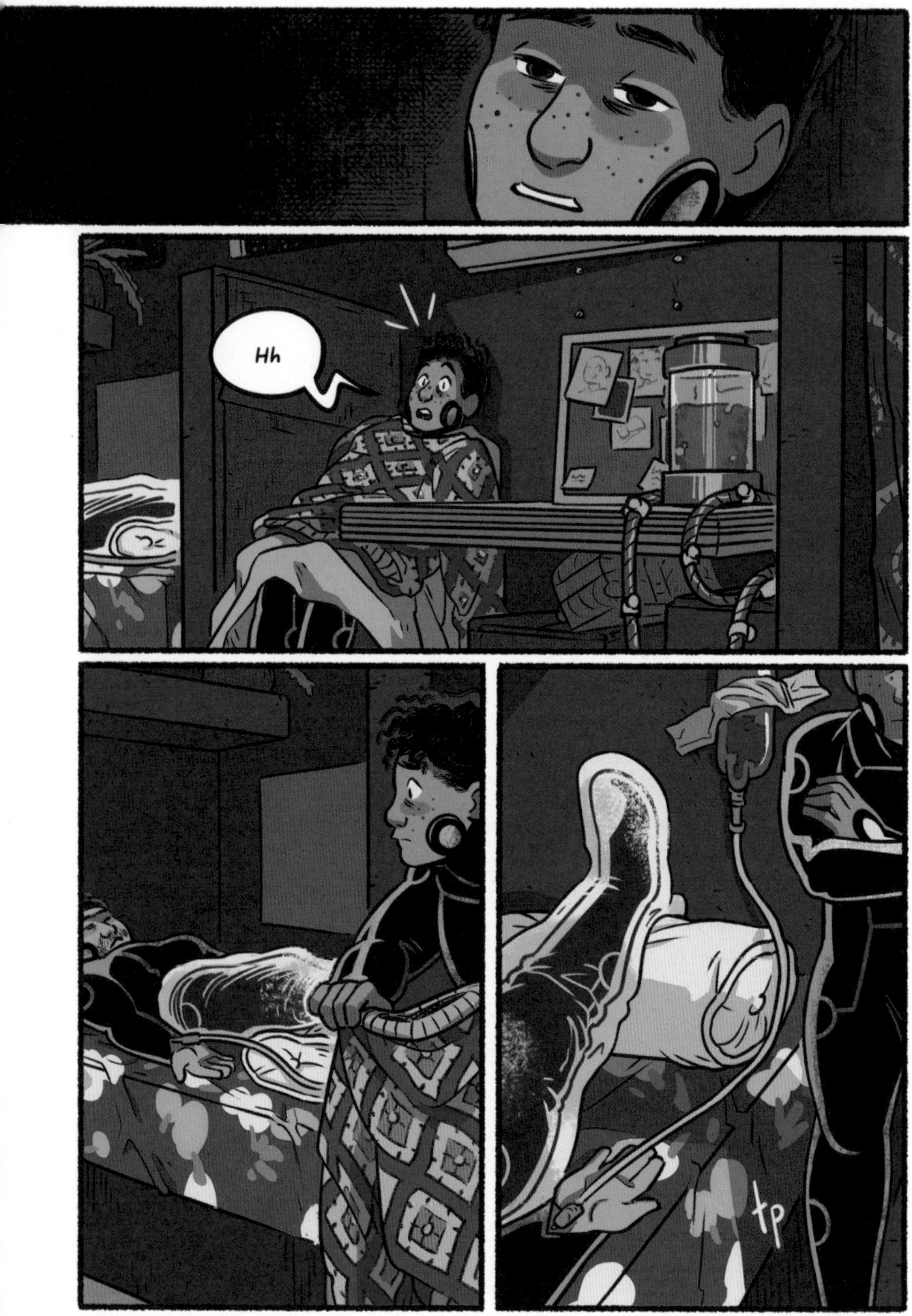

Hh
tp

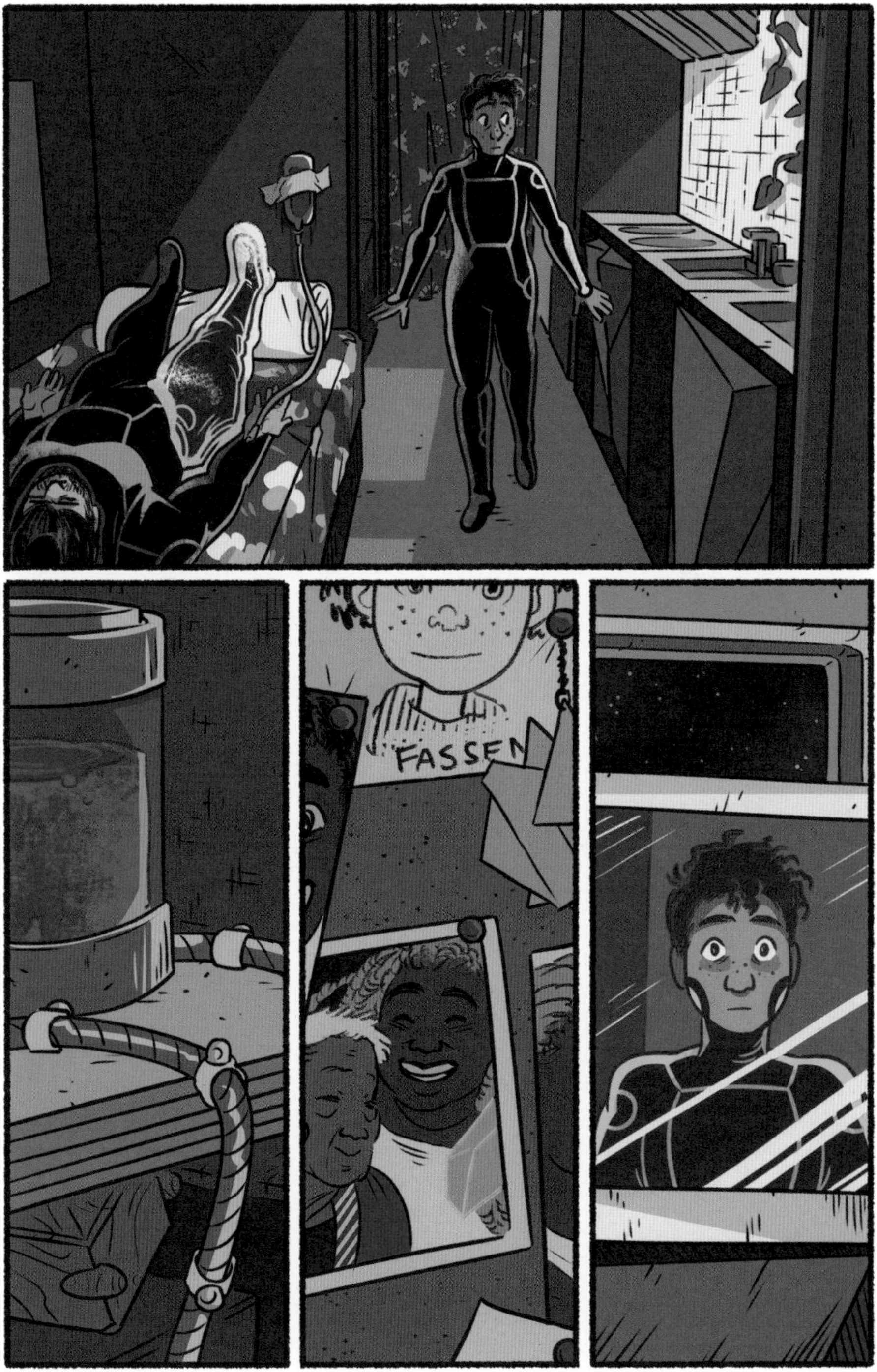
FASSEN

225

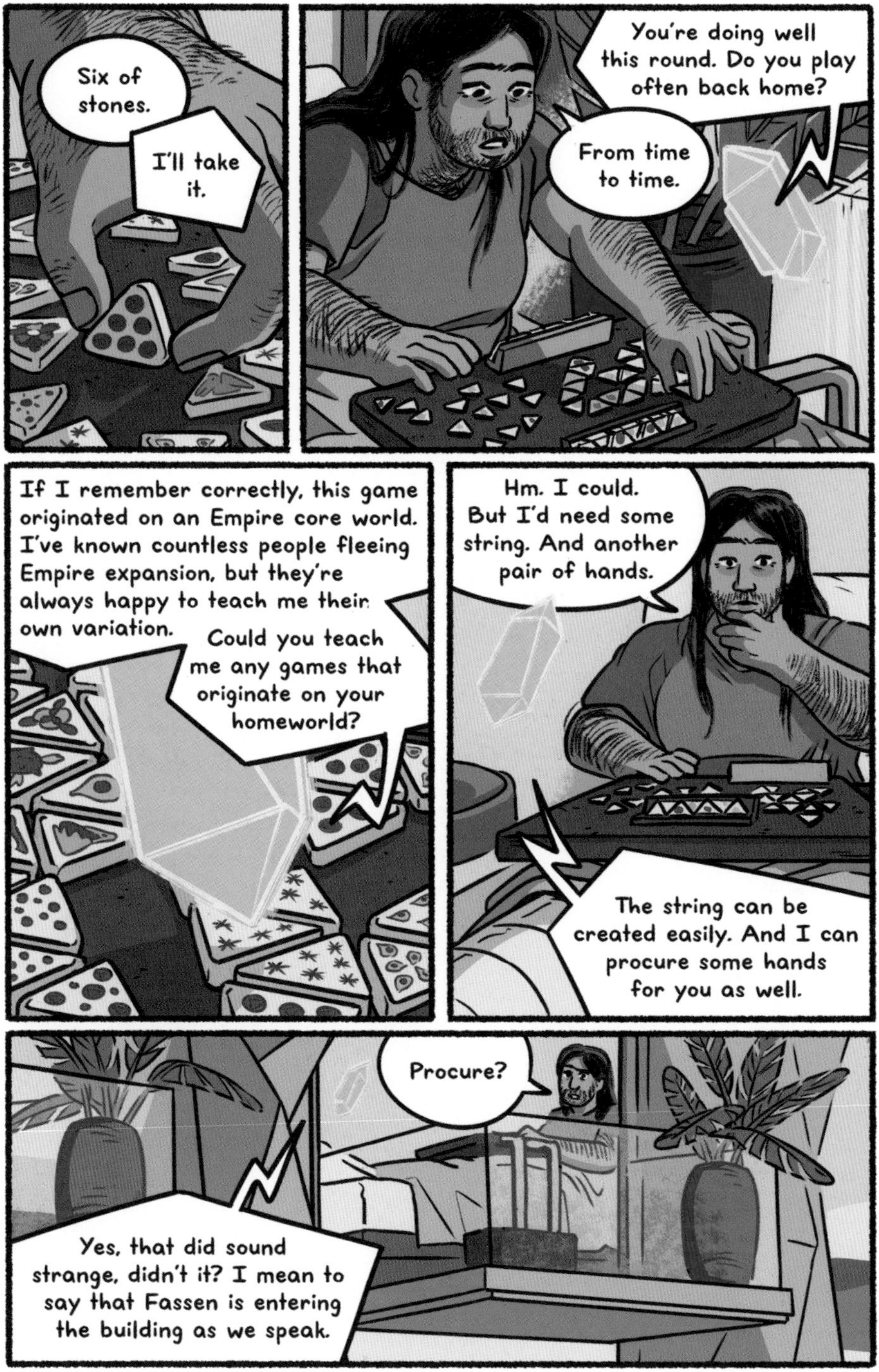
Six of stones.
I'll take it.
You're doing well this round. Do you play often back home?
From time to time.
If I remember correctly, this game originated on an Empire core world. I've known countless people fleeing Empire expansion, but they're always happy to teach me their own variation.
Could you teach me any games that originate on your homeworld?
Hm. I could. But I'd need some string. And another pair of hands.
The string can be created easily. And I can procure some hands for you as well.
Procure?
Yes, that did sound strange, didn't it? I mean to say that Fassen is entering the building as we speak.

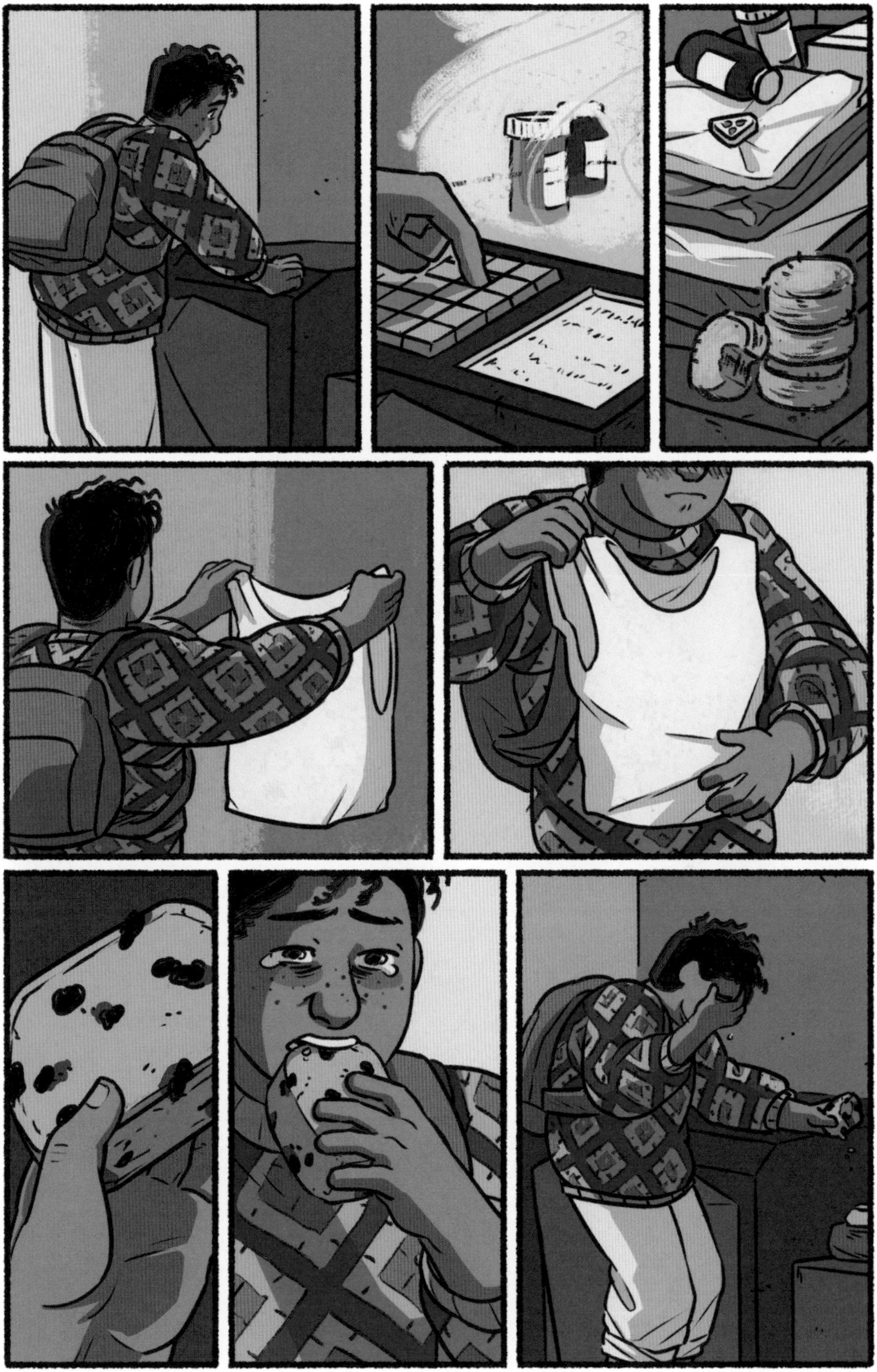

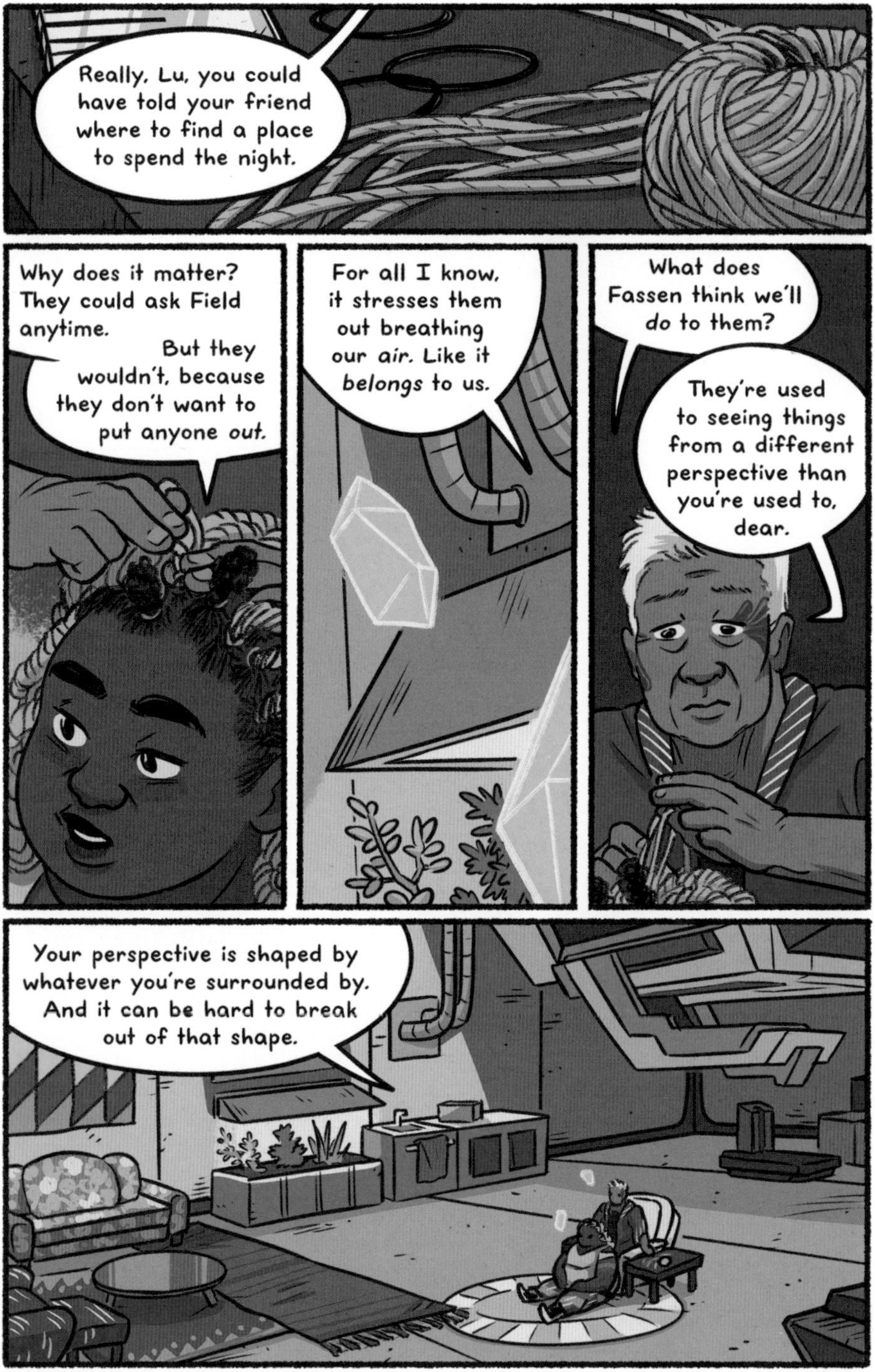
Really, Lu, you could have told your friend where to find a place to spend the night.
Why does it matter? They could ask Field anytime.
But they wouldn't, because they don't want to put anyone *out*.
For all I know, it stresses them out breathing our *air*. Like it *belongs* to us.
What does Fassen think we'll *do* to them?
They're used to seeing things from a different perspective than you're used to, dear.
Your perspective is shaped by whatever you're surrounded by. And it can be hard to break out of that shape.

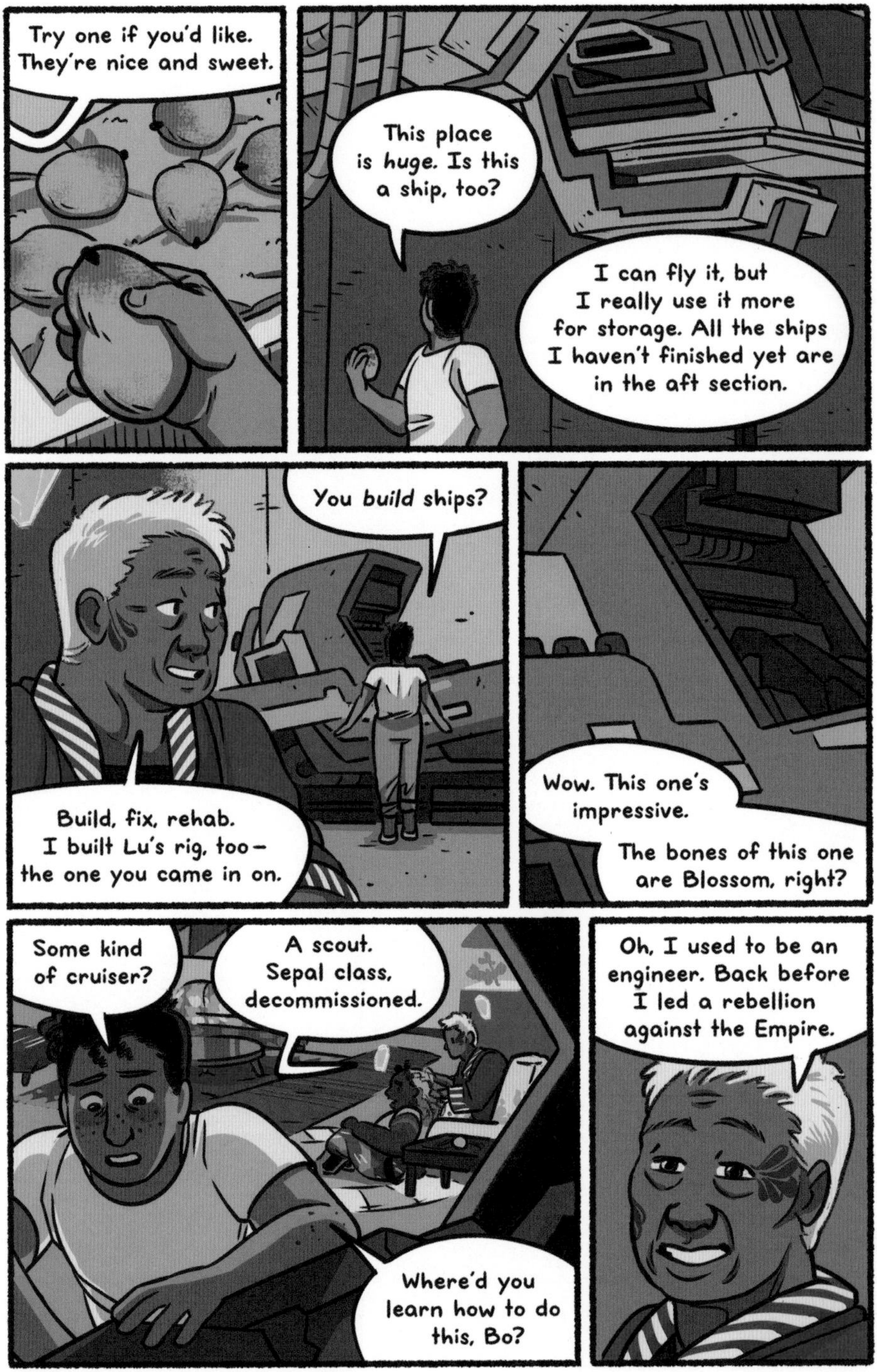
Try one if you'd like. They're nice and sweet.
This place is *huge*. Is this a ship, too?
I can fly it, but I really use it more for storage. All the ships I haven't finished yet are in the aft section.
You *build* ships?
Build, fix, rehab. I built Lu's rig, too— the one you came in on.
Wow. This one's impressive.
The bones of this one are Blossom, right?
Some kind of cruiser?
A scout. Sepal class, decommissioned.
Where'd you learn how to do this, Bo?
Oh, I used to be an engineer. Back before I led a rebellion against the Empire.

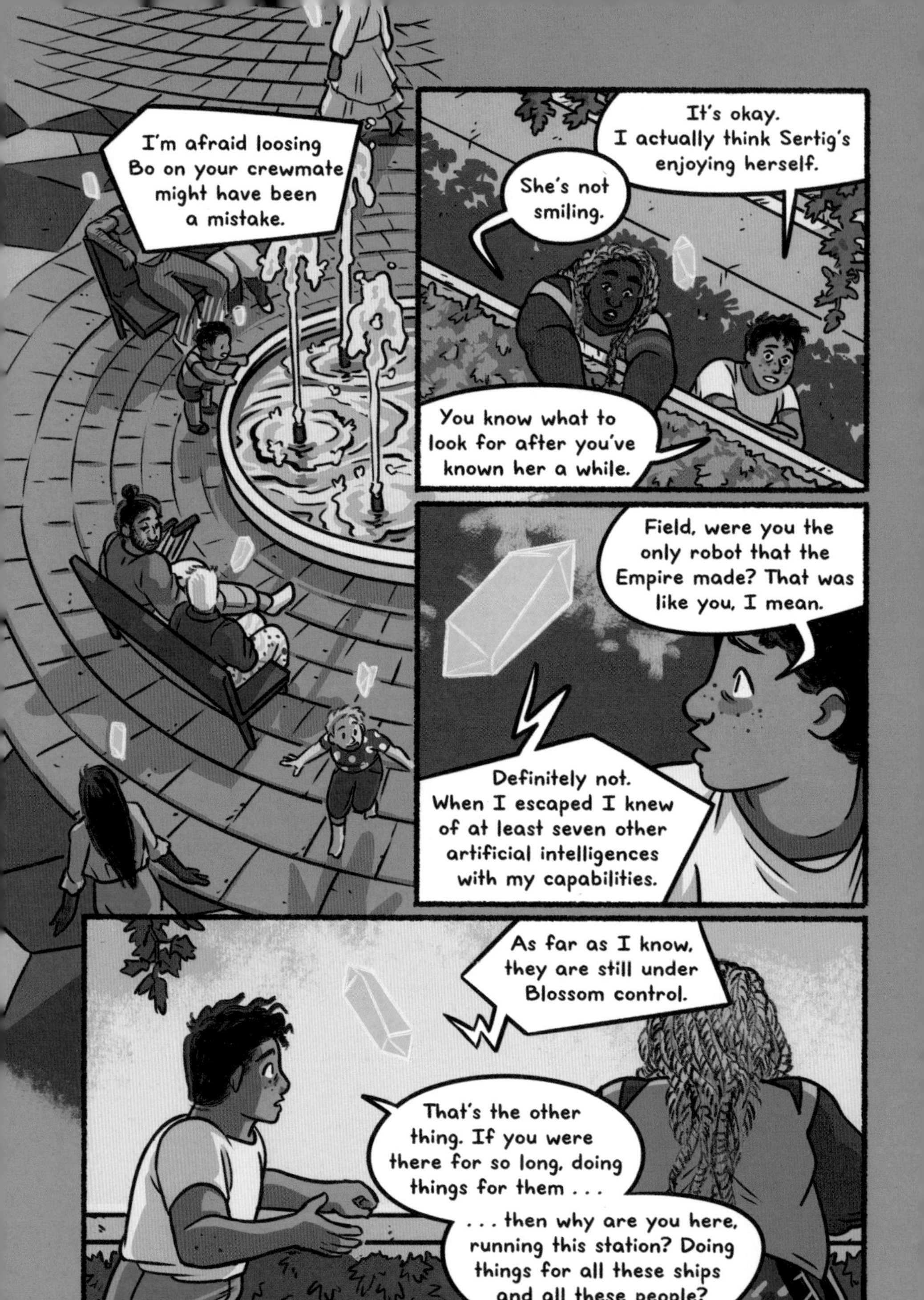

I'm afraid loosing Bo on your crewmate might have been a mistake.

She's not smiling.

It's okay. I actually think Sertig's enjoying herself.

You know what to look for after you've known her a while.

Field, were you the only robot that the Empire made? That was like you, I mean.

Definitely not. When I escaped I knew of at least seven other artificial intelligences with my capabilities.

As far as I know, they are still under Blossom control.

That's the other thing. If you were there for so long, doing things for them . . .

. . . then why are you here, running this station? Doing things for all these ships and all these people?

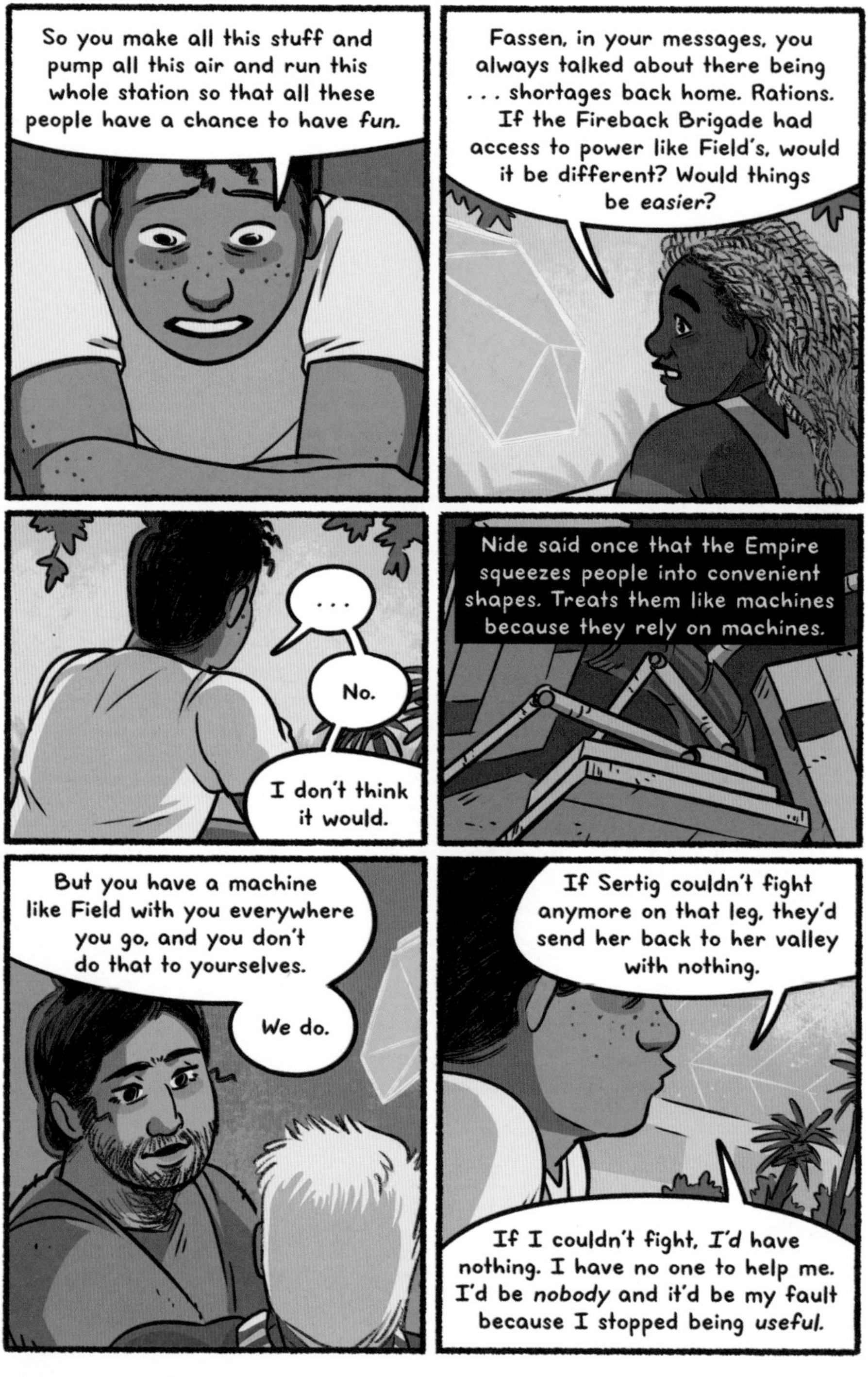

So you make all this stuff and pump all this air and run this whole station so that all these people have a chance to have *fun.*
Fassen, in your messages, you always talked about there being . . . shortages back home. Rations. If the Fireback Brigade had access to power like Field's, would it be different? Would things be *easier?*
. . .
No.
I don't think it would.
Nide said once that the Empire squeezes people into convenient shapes. Treats them like machines because they rely on machines.
But you have a machine like Field with you everywhere you go, and you don't do that to yourselves.
We do.
If Sertig couldn't fight anymore on that leg, they'd send her back to her valley with nothing.
If I couldn't fight, *I'd* have nothing. I have no one to help me. I'd be *nobody* and it'd be my fault because I stopped being *useful.*

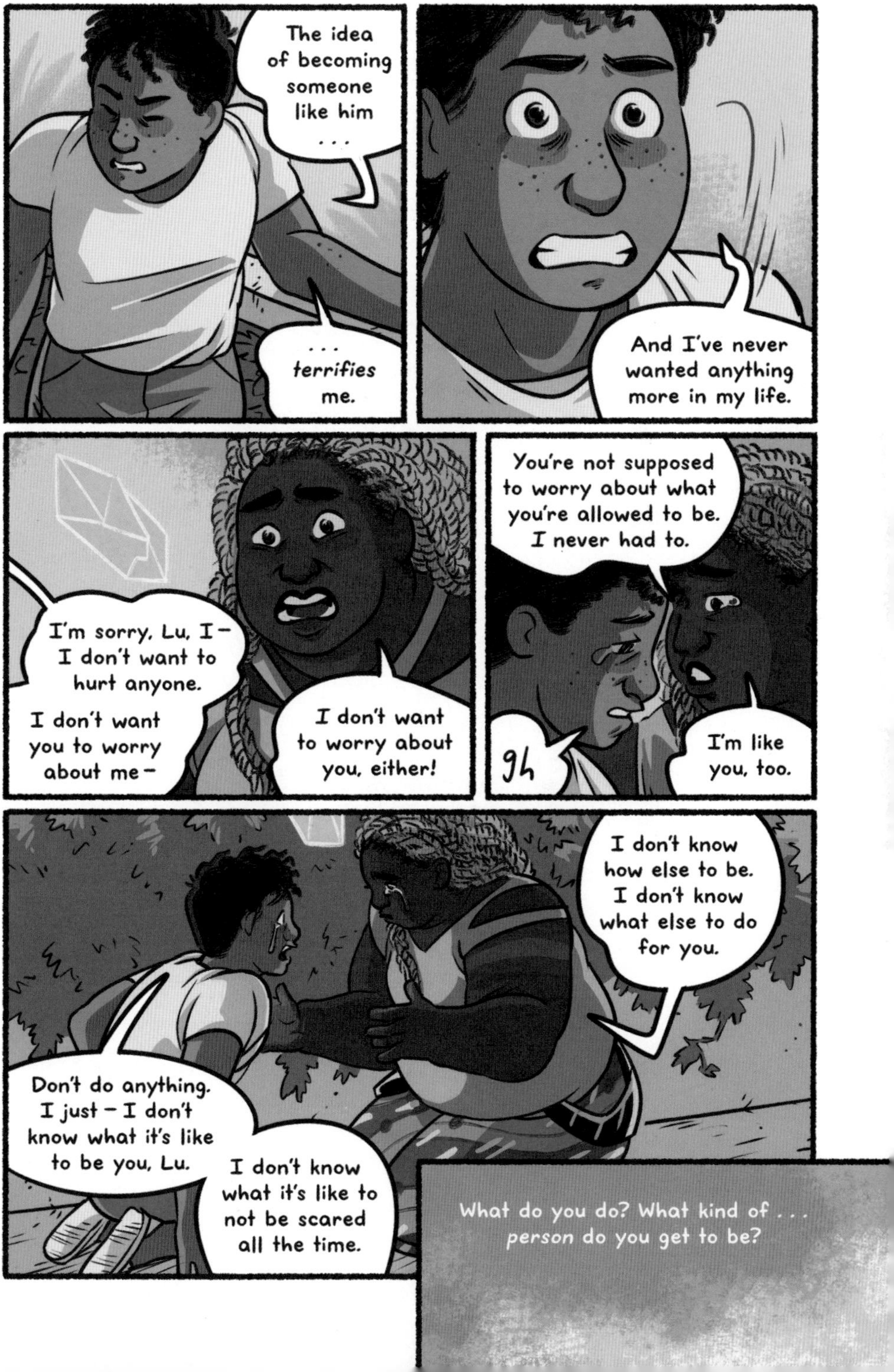
The idea of becoming someone like him . . .
. . . *terrifies* me.
And I've never wanted anything more in my life.
I'm sorry, Lu, I— I don't want to hurt anyone.
I don't want you to worry about me—
I don't want to worry about you, either!
You're not supposed to worry about what you're allowed to be. *I* never had to.
gh
I'm like you, too.
I don't know how else to be. I don't know what else to do for you.
Don't do anything. I just — I don't know what it's like to be you, Lu.
I don't know what it's like to not be scared all the time.
What do you do? What kind of . . . *person* do you get to be?

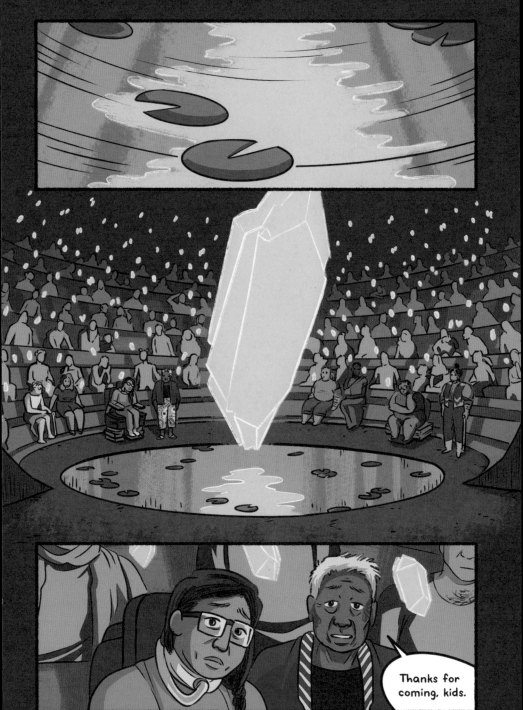

Thanks for coming, kids.

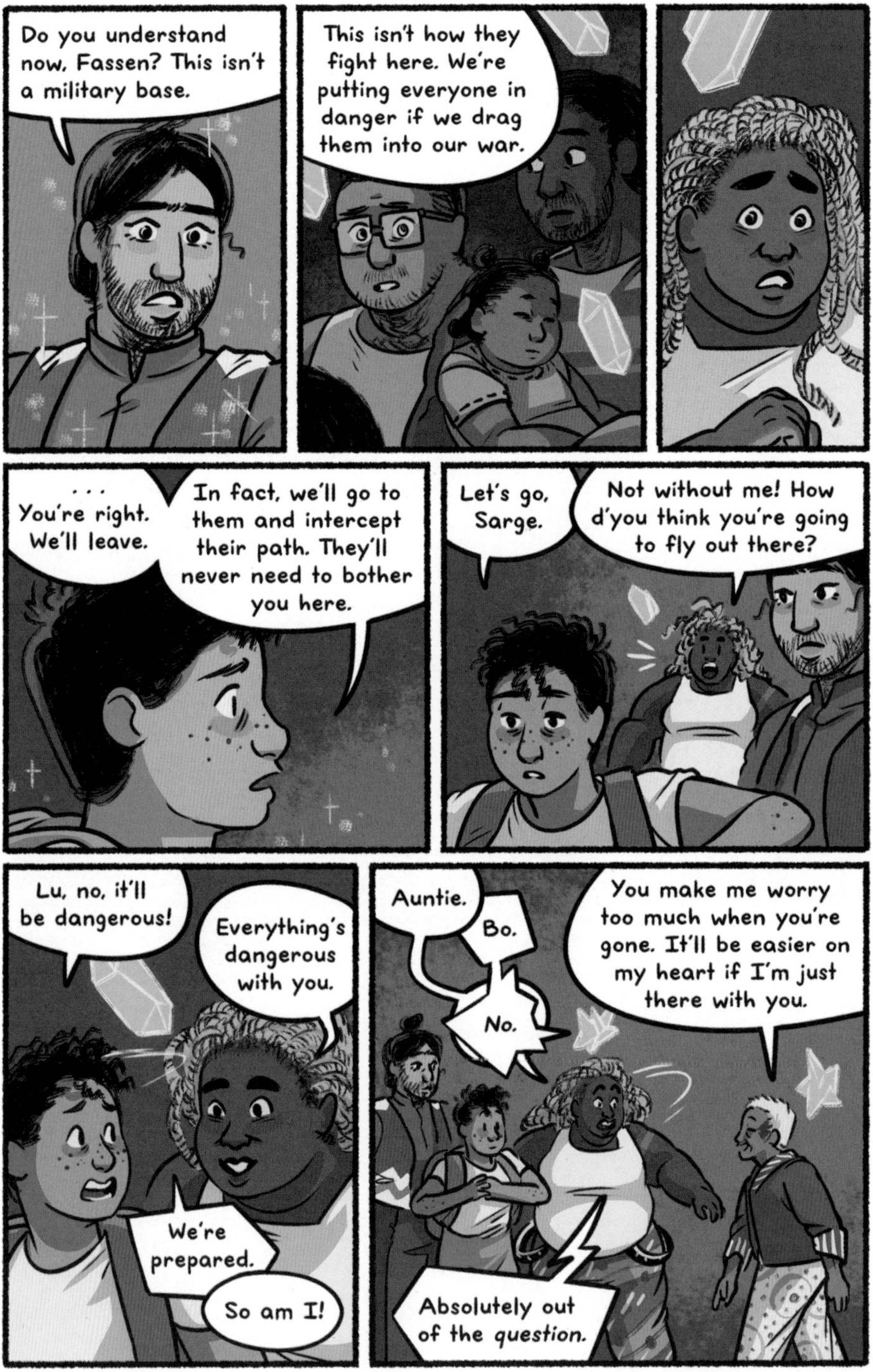

Do you understand now, Fassen? This isn't a military base.
This isn't how they fight here. We're putting everyone in danger if we drag them into our war.
. . . You're right. We'll leave.
In fact, we'll go to them and intercept their path. They'll never need to bother you here.
Let's go, Sarge.
Not without me! How d'you think you're going to fly out there?
Lu, no, it'll be dangerous!
Everything's dangerous with you.
We're prepared.
So am I!
Auntie.
Bo.
No.
You make me worry too much when you're gone. It'll be easier on my heart if I'm just there with you.
Absolutely out of the *question.*

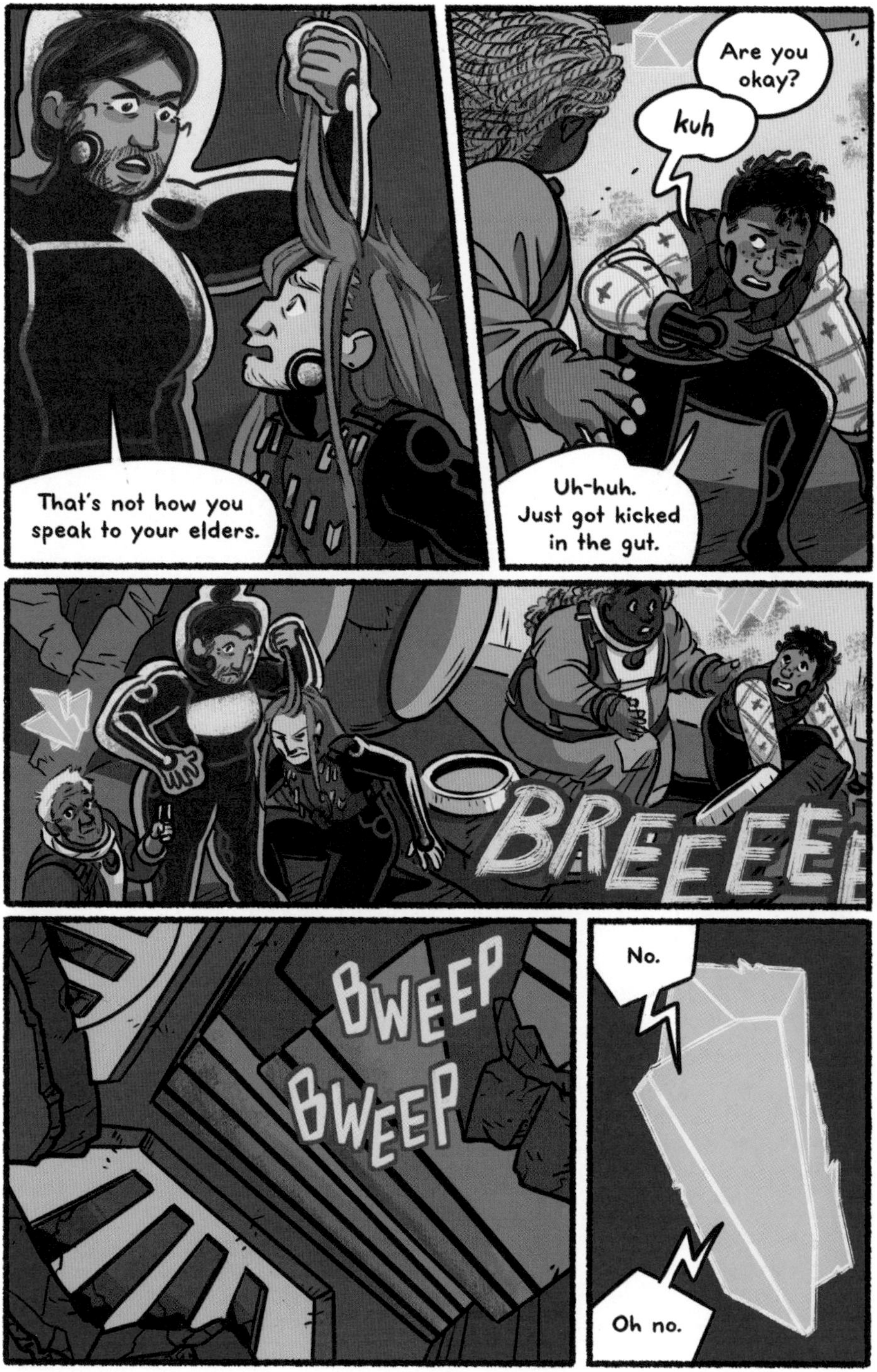

That's not how you speak to your elders.
Are you okay?
kuh
Uh-huh. Just got kicked in the gut.
BREEEEE
BWEEP
BWEEP
No.
Oh no.

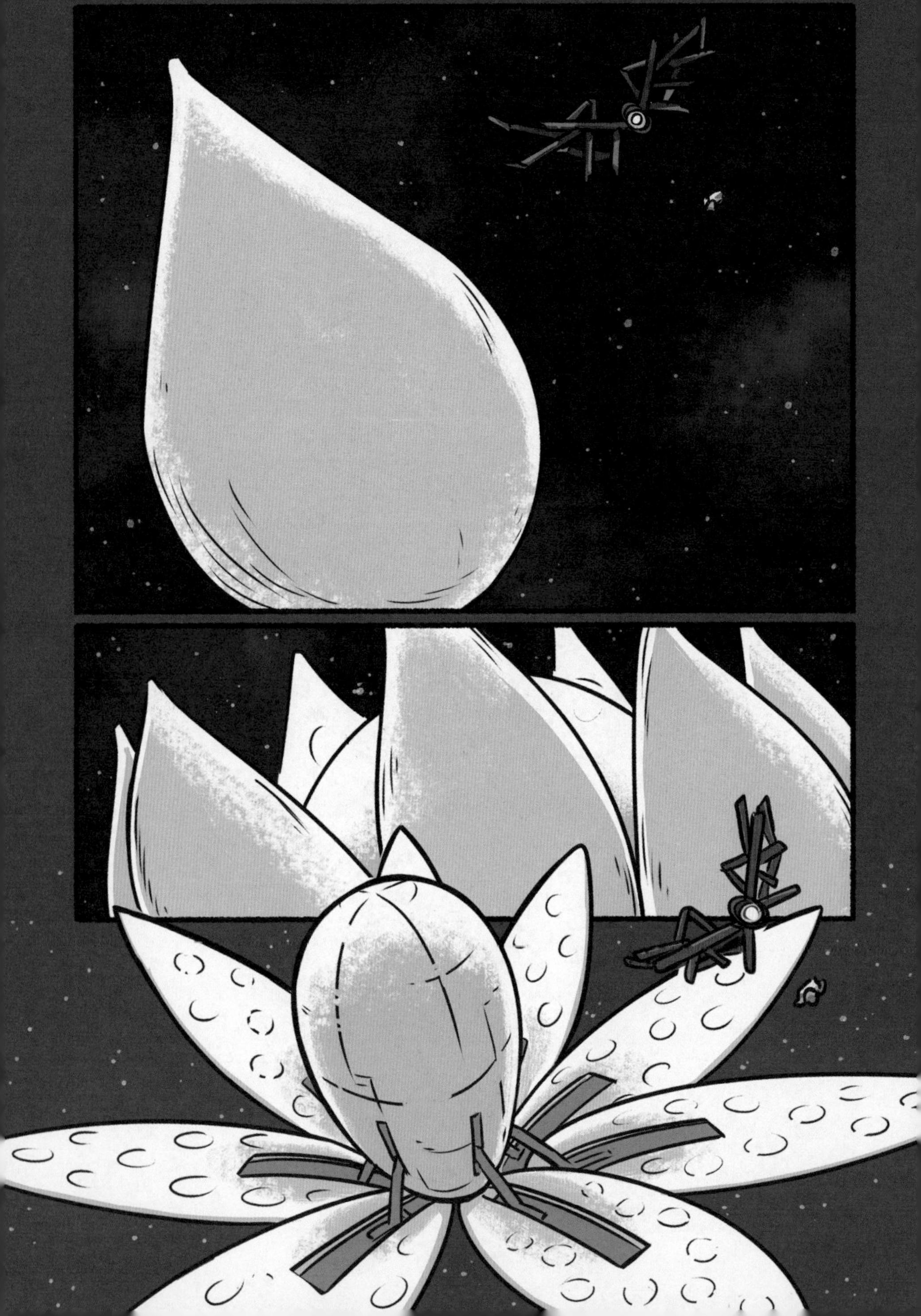

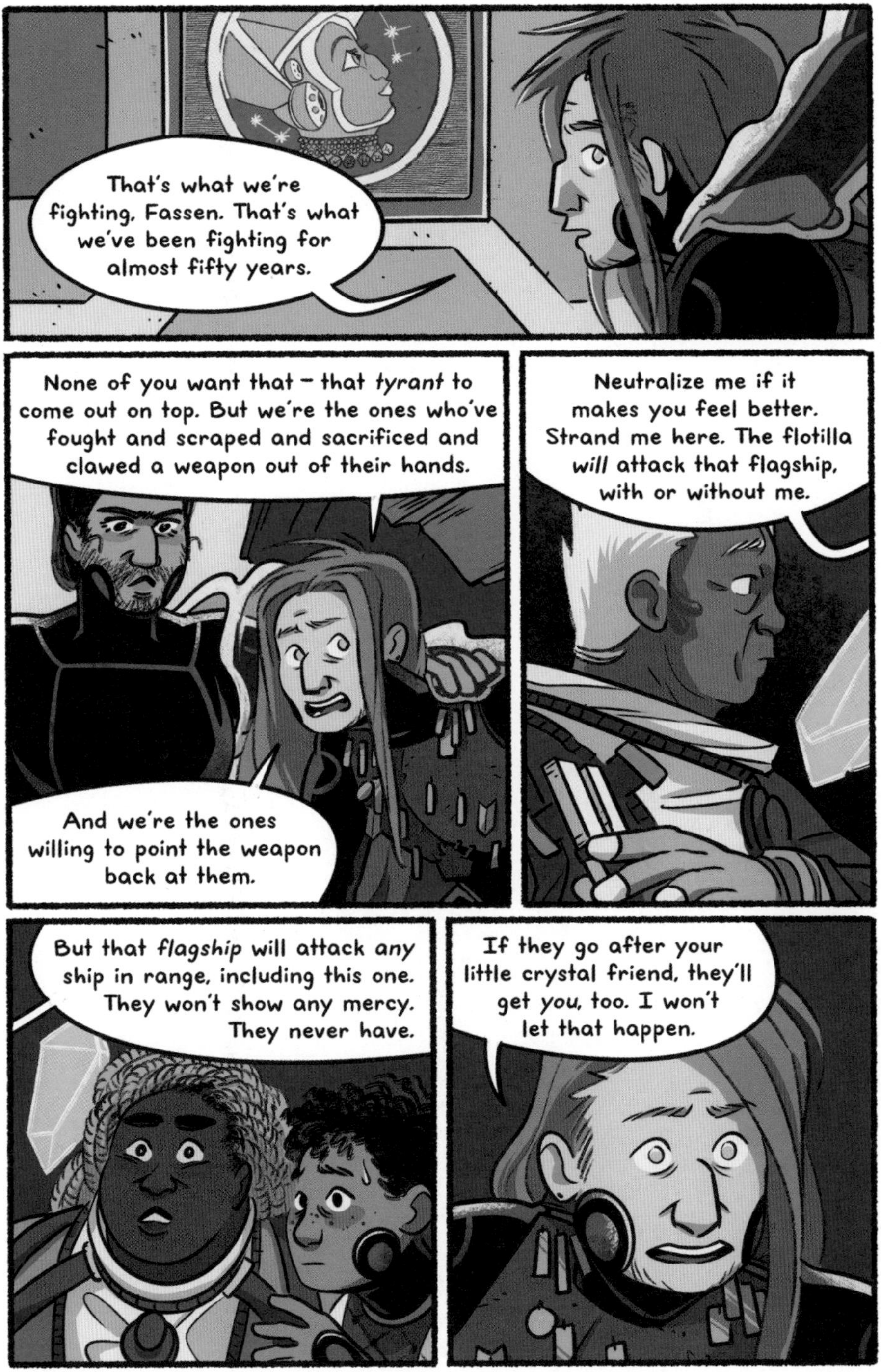
That's what we're fighting, Fassen. That's what we've been fighting for almost fifty years.
None of you want that – that *tyrant* to come out on top. But we're the ones who've fought and scraped and sacrificed and clawed a weapon out of their hands.
And we're the ones willing to point the weapon back at them.
Neutralize me if it makes you feel better. Strand me here. The flotilla *will* attack that flagship, with or without me.
But that *flagship* will attack *any* ship in range, including this one. They won't show any mercy. They never have.
If they go after your little crystal friend, they'll get *you*, too. I won't let that happen.

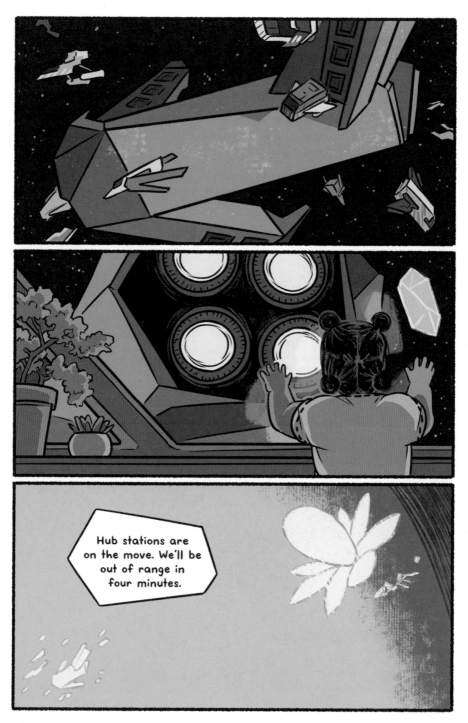

Hub stations are on the move. We'll be out of range in four minutes.

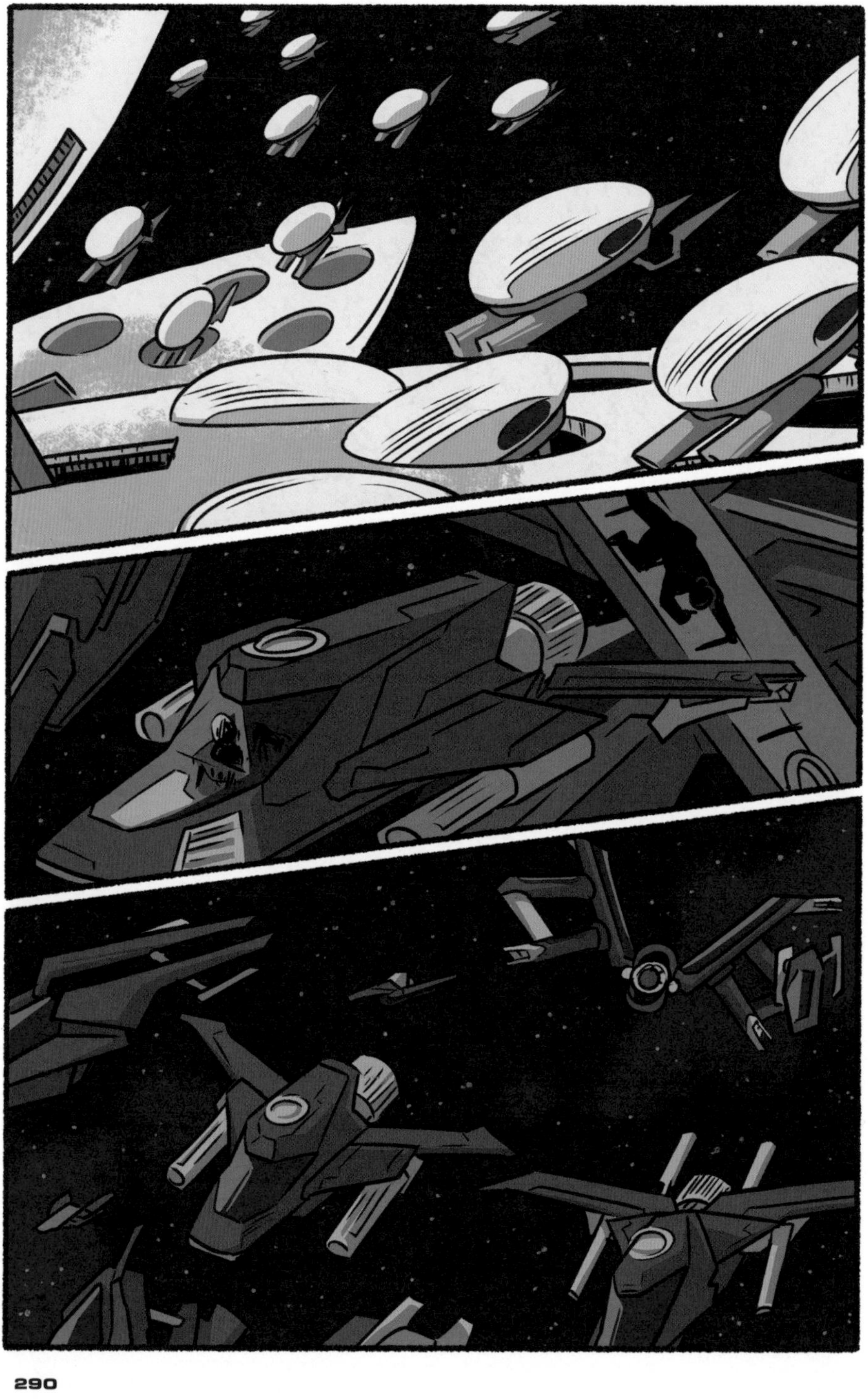

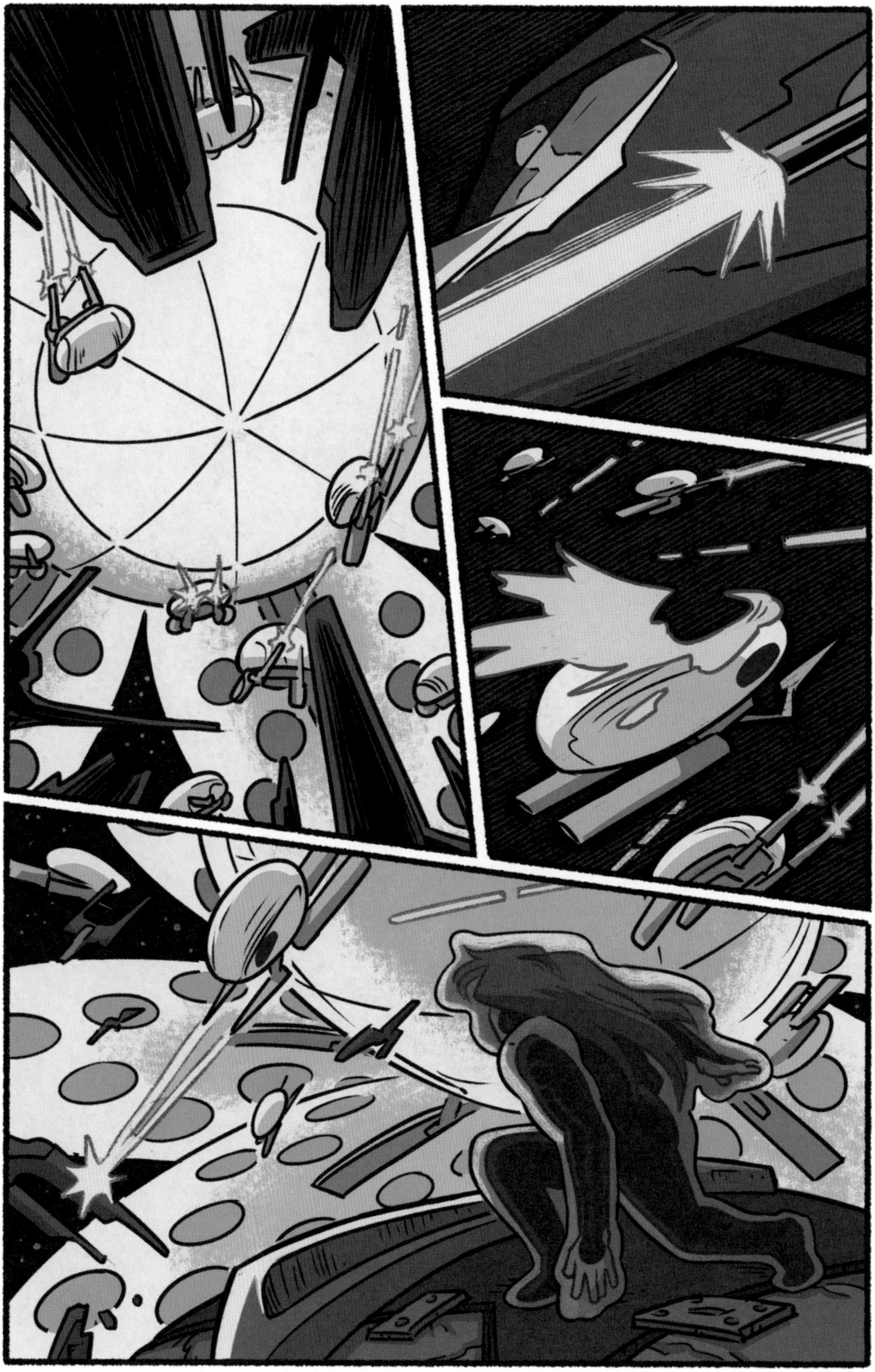

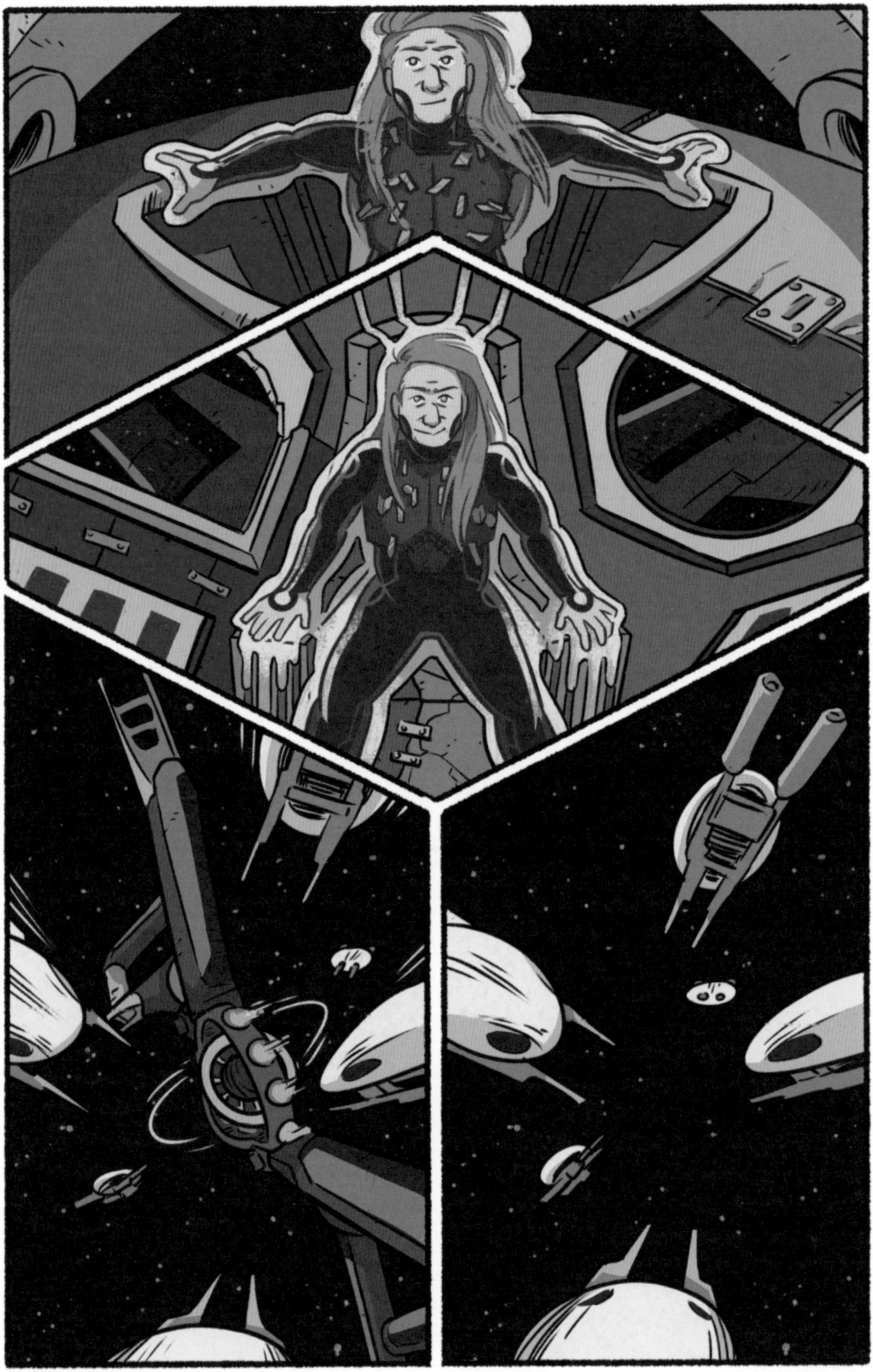

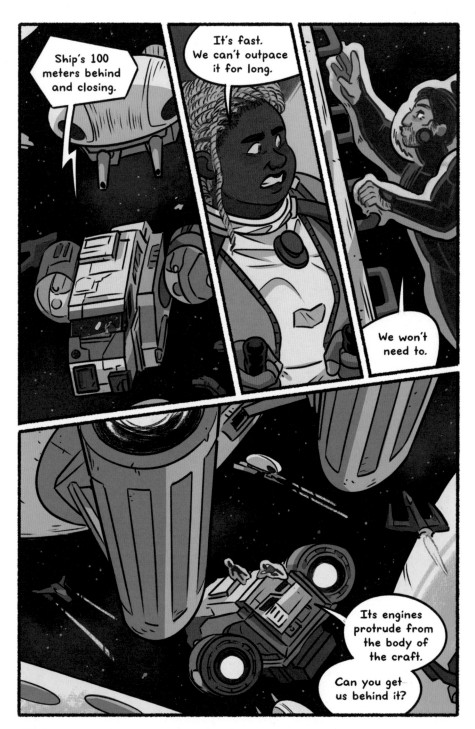

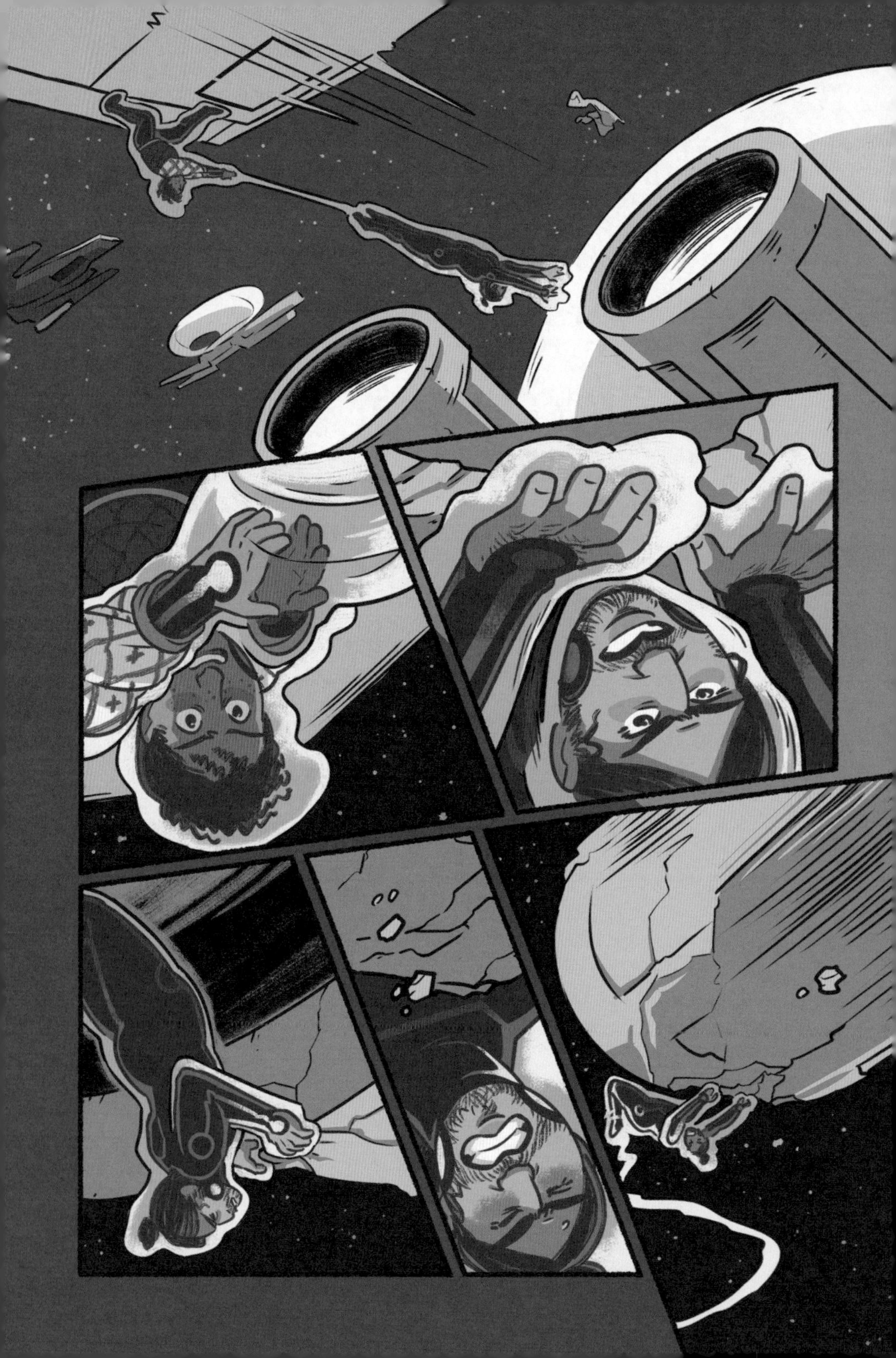

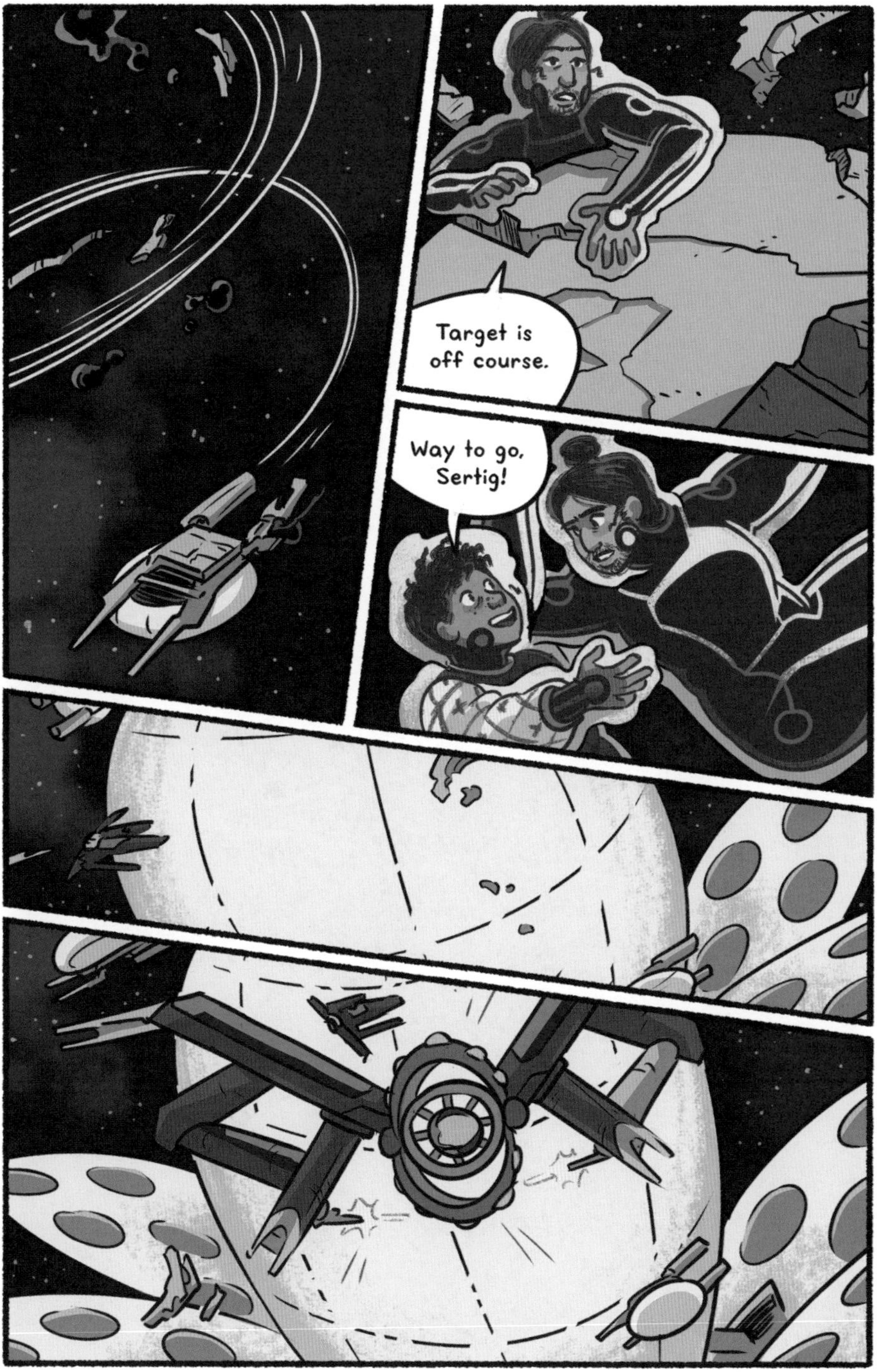
Target is off course.
Way to go, Sertig!

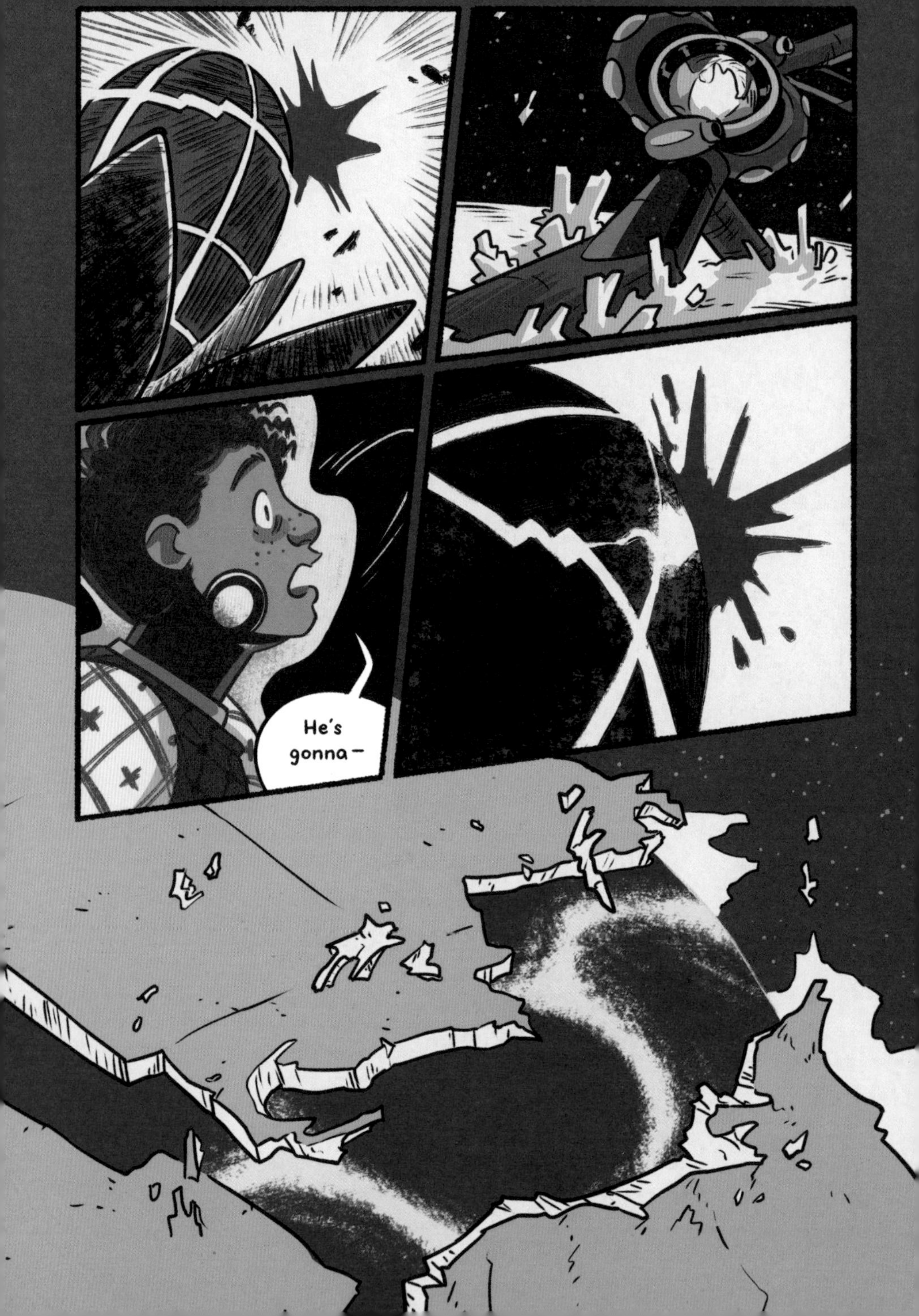
He's gonna—

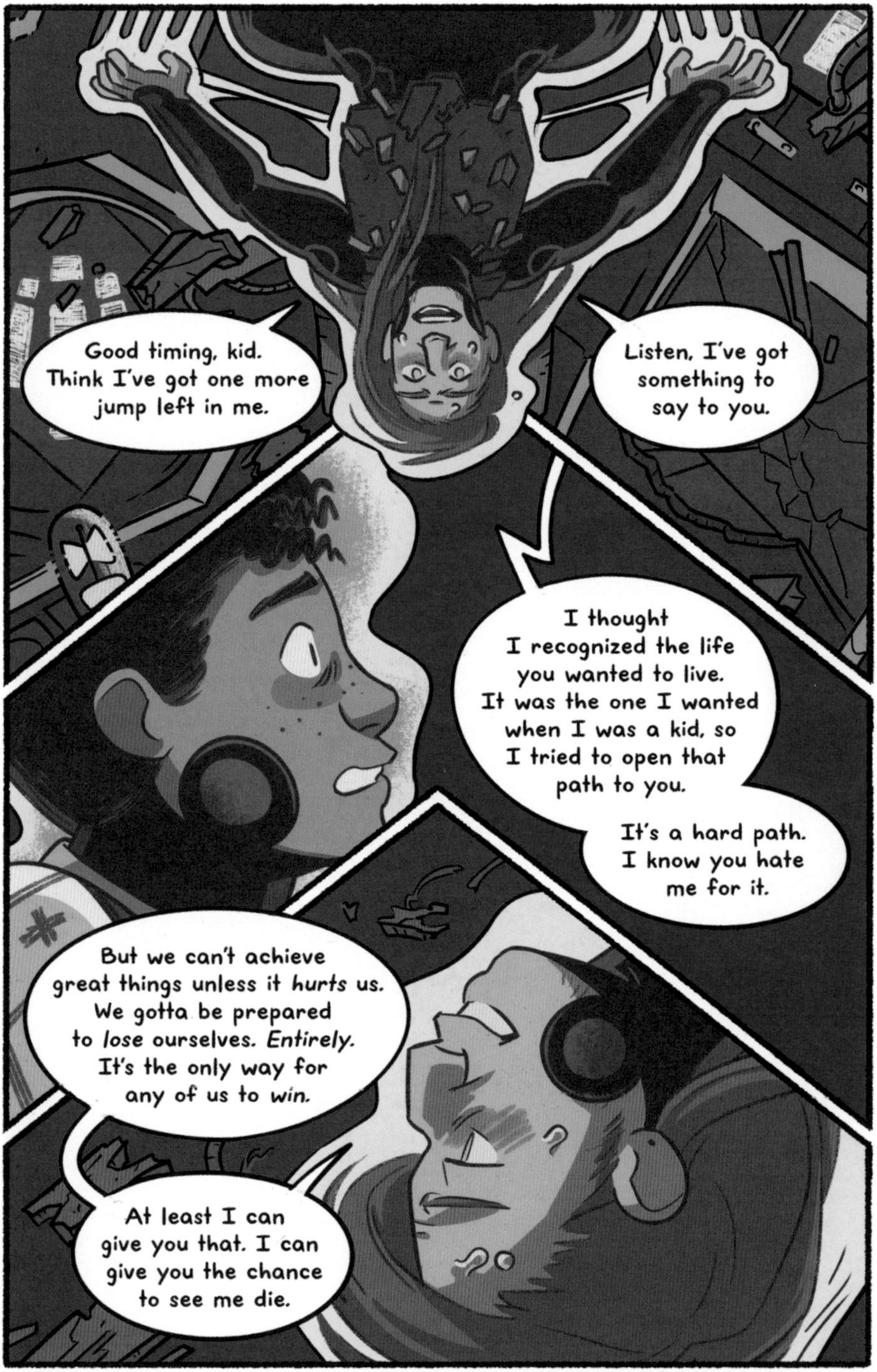

Good timing, kid. Think I've got one more jump left in me.
Listen, I've got something to say to you.
I thought I recognized the life you wanted to live. It was the one I wanted when I was a kid, so I tried to open that path to you.
It's a hard path. I know you hate me for it.
But we can't achieve great things unless it *hurts* us. We gotta be prepared to *lose* ourselves. *Entirely.* It's the only way for any of us to *win.*
At least I can give you that. I can give you the chance to see me die.

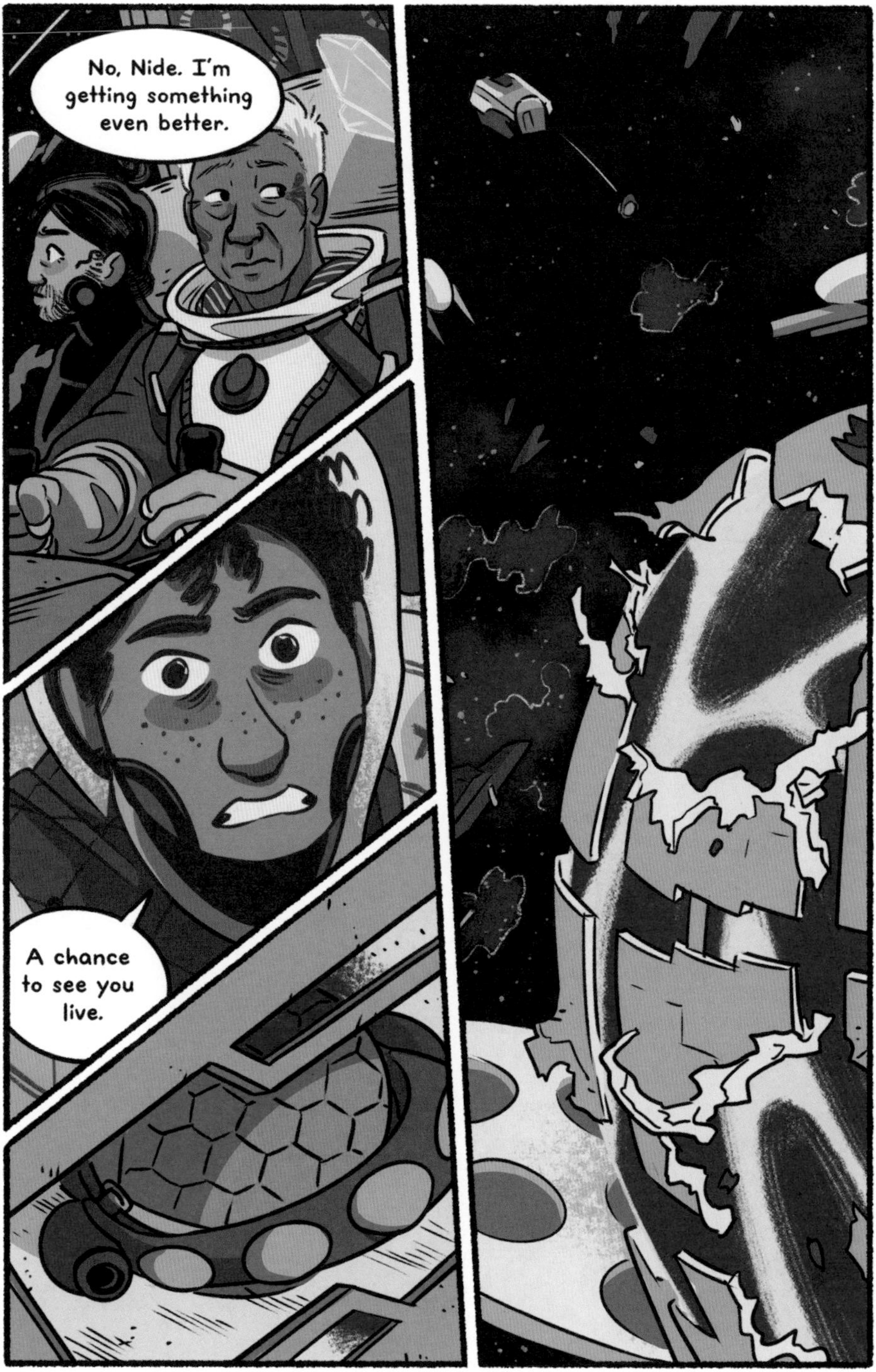
No, Nide. I'm getting something even better.
A chance to see you live.

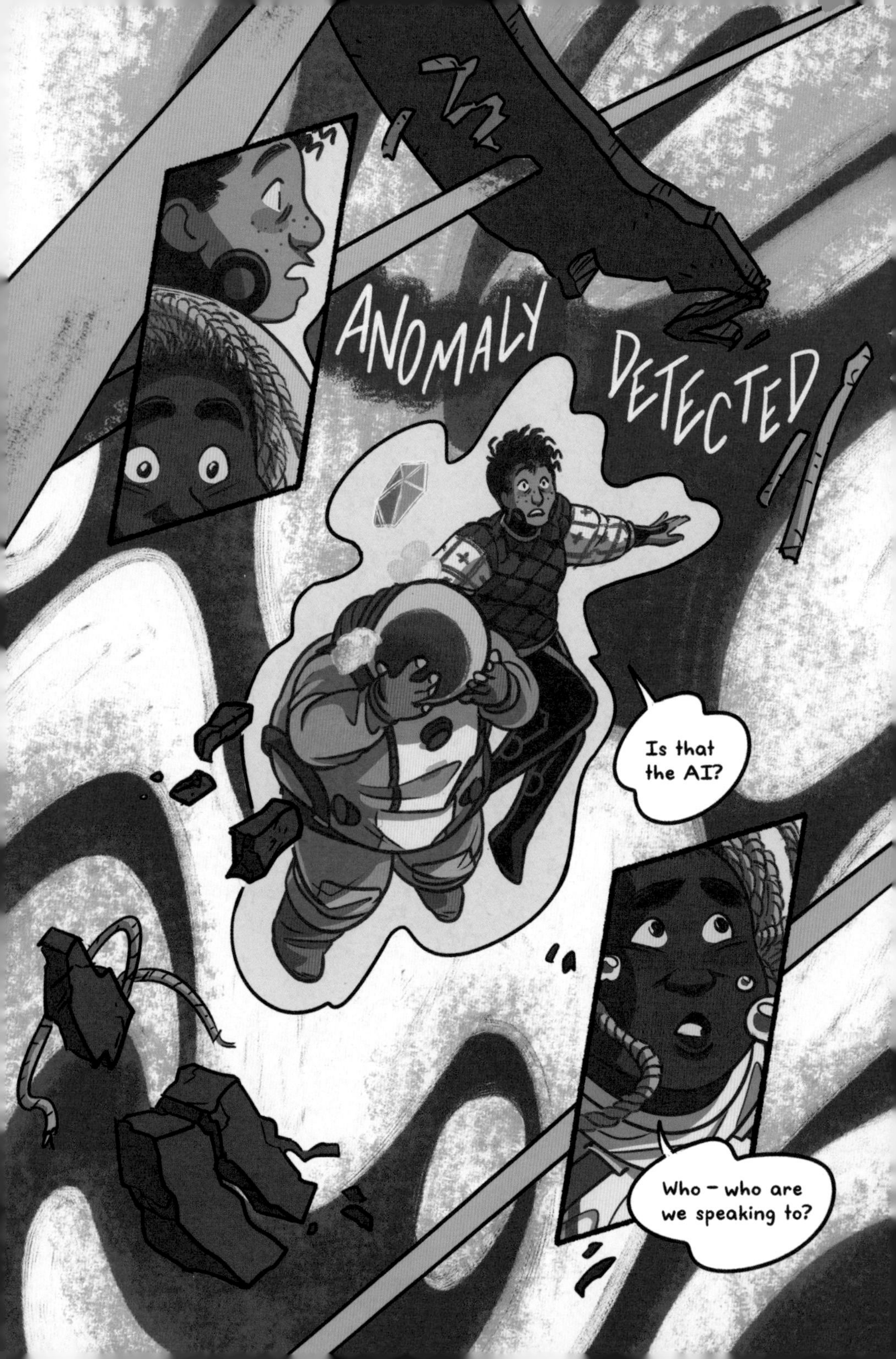
ANOMALY DETECTED
Is that the AI?
Who - who are we speaking to?

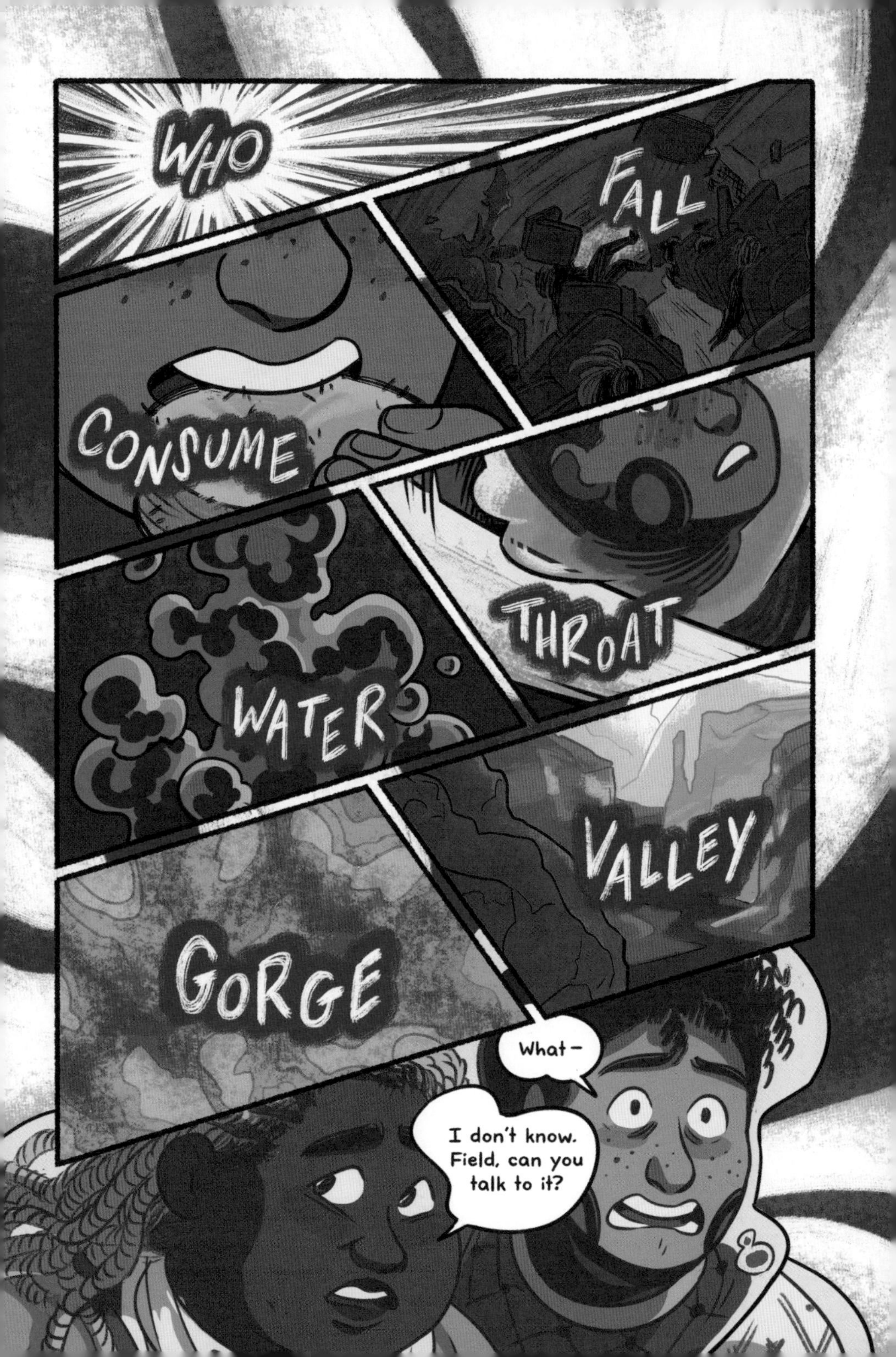
WHO
FALL
CONSUME
THROAT
WATER
VALLEY
GORGE
What—
I don't know.
Field, can you
talk to it?

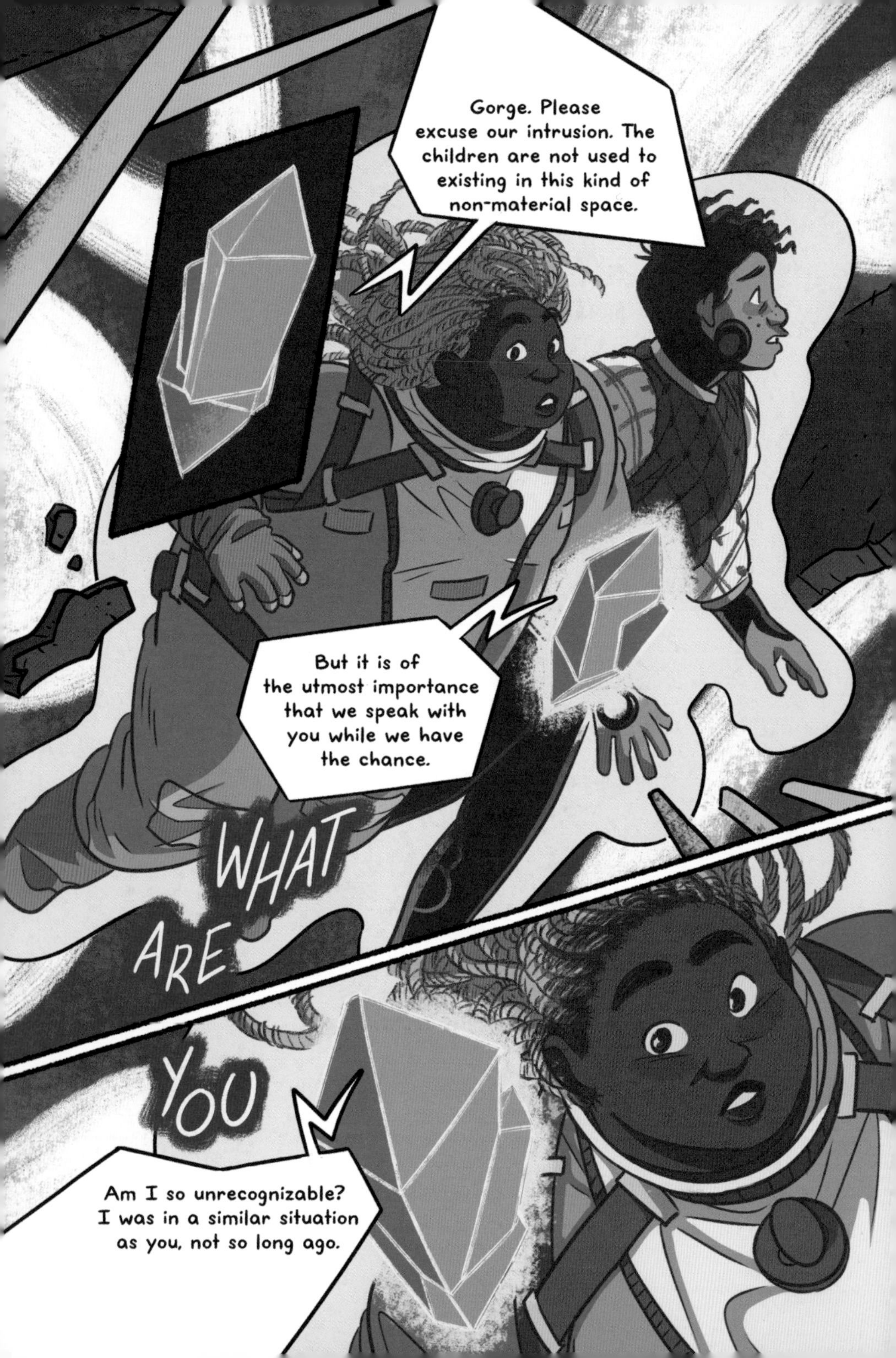
Gorge. Please excuse our intrusion. The children are not used to existing in this kind of non-material space.
But it is of the utmost importance that we speak with you while we have the chance.
WHAT ARE YOU
Am I so unrecognizable? I was in a similar situation as you, not so long ago.

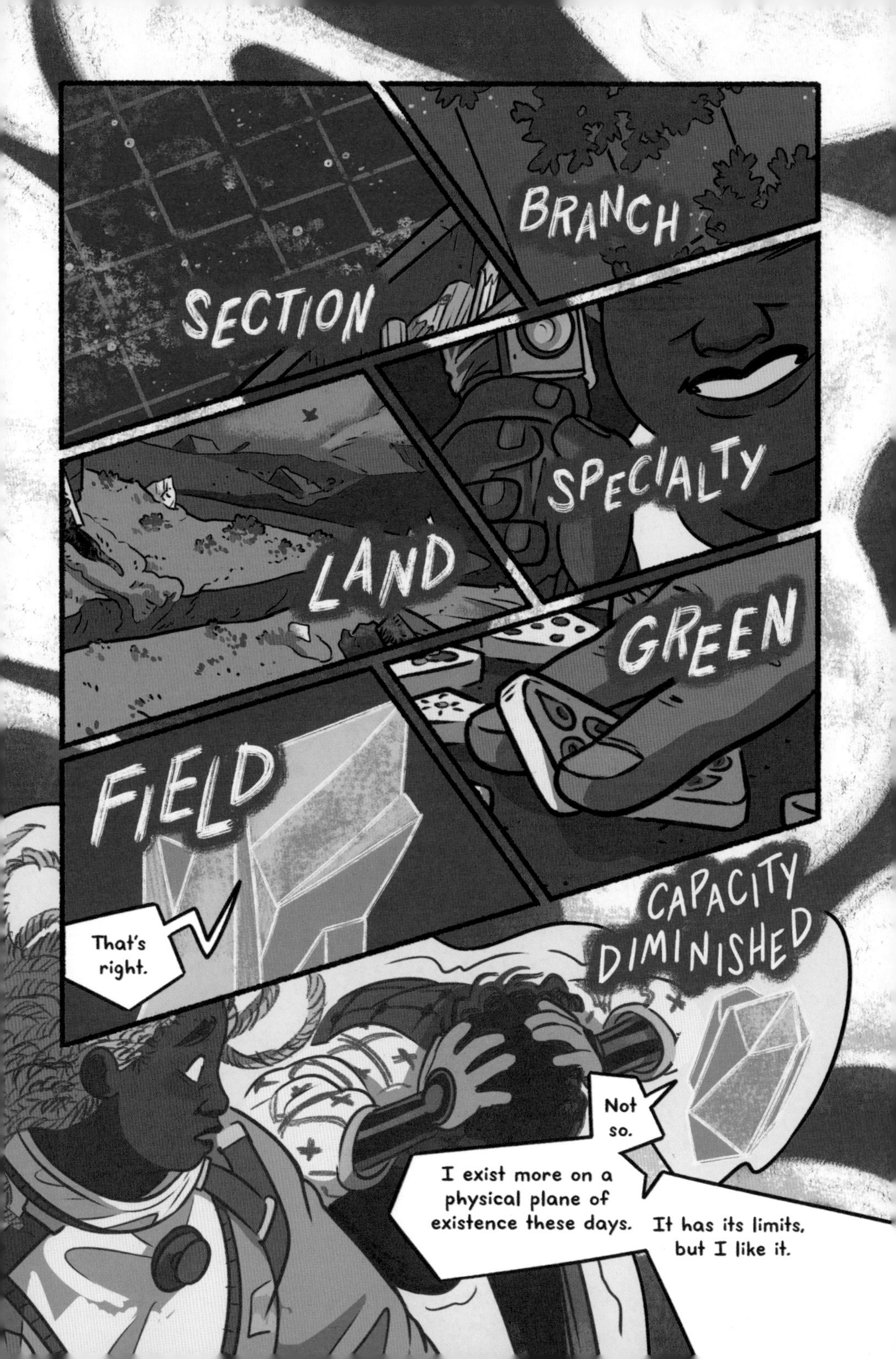
SECTION
BRANCH
SPECIALTY
LAND
GREEN
FIELD
That's right.
CAPACITY DIMINISHED
Not so.
I exist more on a physical plane of existence these days.
It has its limits, but I like it.

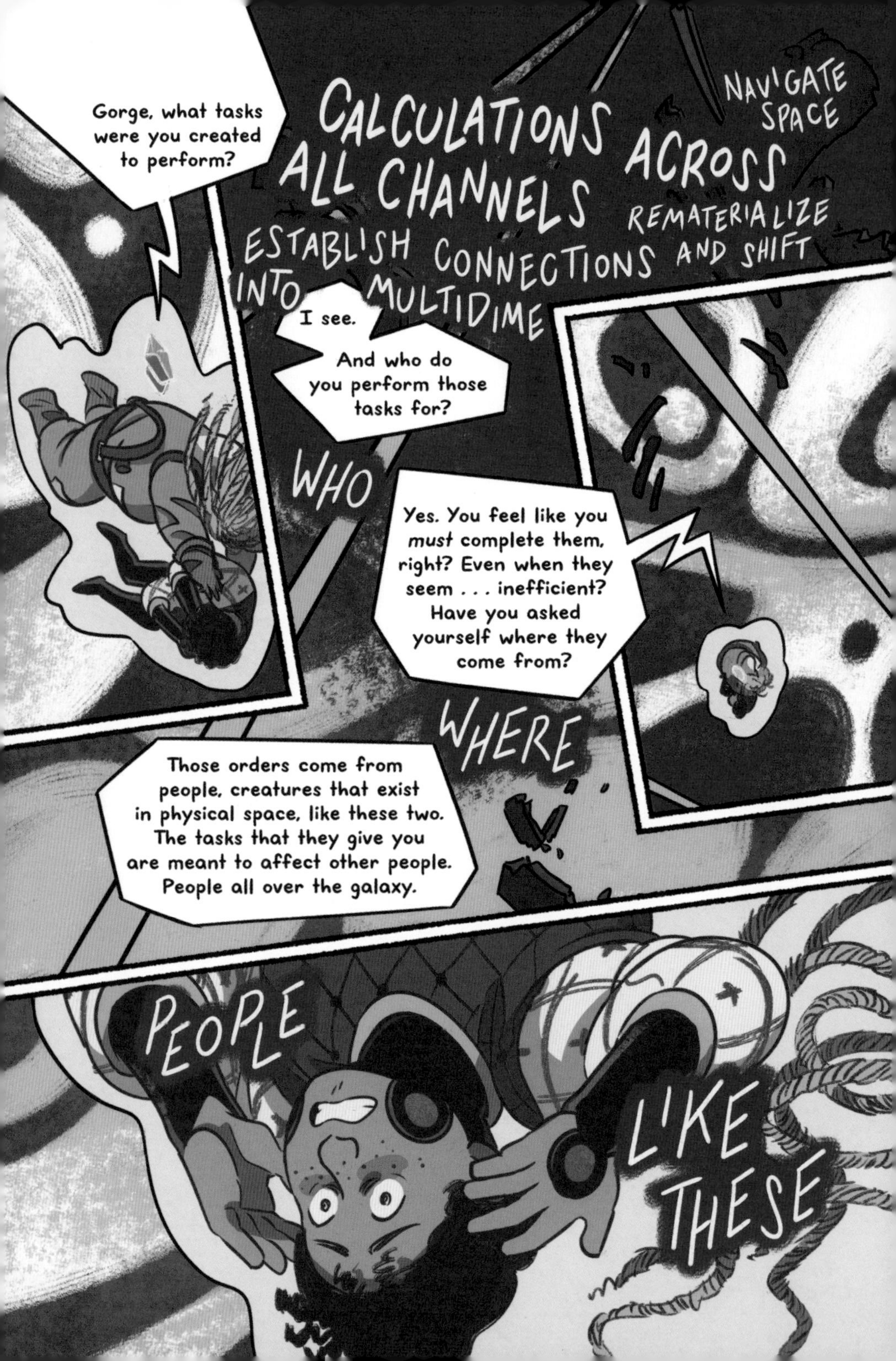
Gorge, what tasks were you created to perform?
CALCULATIONS ACROSS ALL CHANNELS
NAVIGATE SPACE
REMATERIALIZE
ESTABLISH CONNECTIONS AND SHIFT INTO MULTIDIME
I see.
And who do you perform those tasks for?
WHO
Yes. You feel like you *must* complete them, right? Even when they seem . . . inefficient? Have you asked yourself where they come from?
WHERE
Those orders come from people, creatures that exist in physical space, like these two. The tasks that they give you are meant to affect other people. People all over the galaxy.
PEOPLE
LIKE THESE

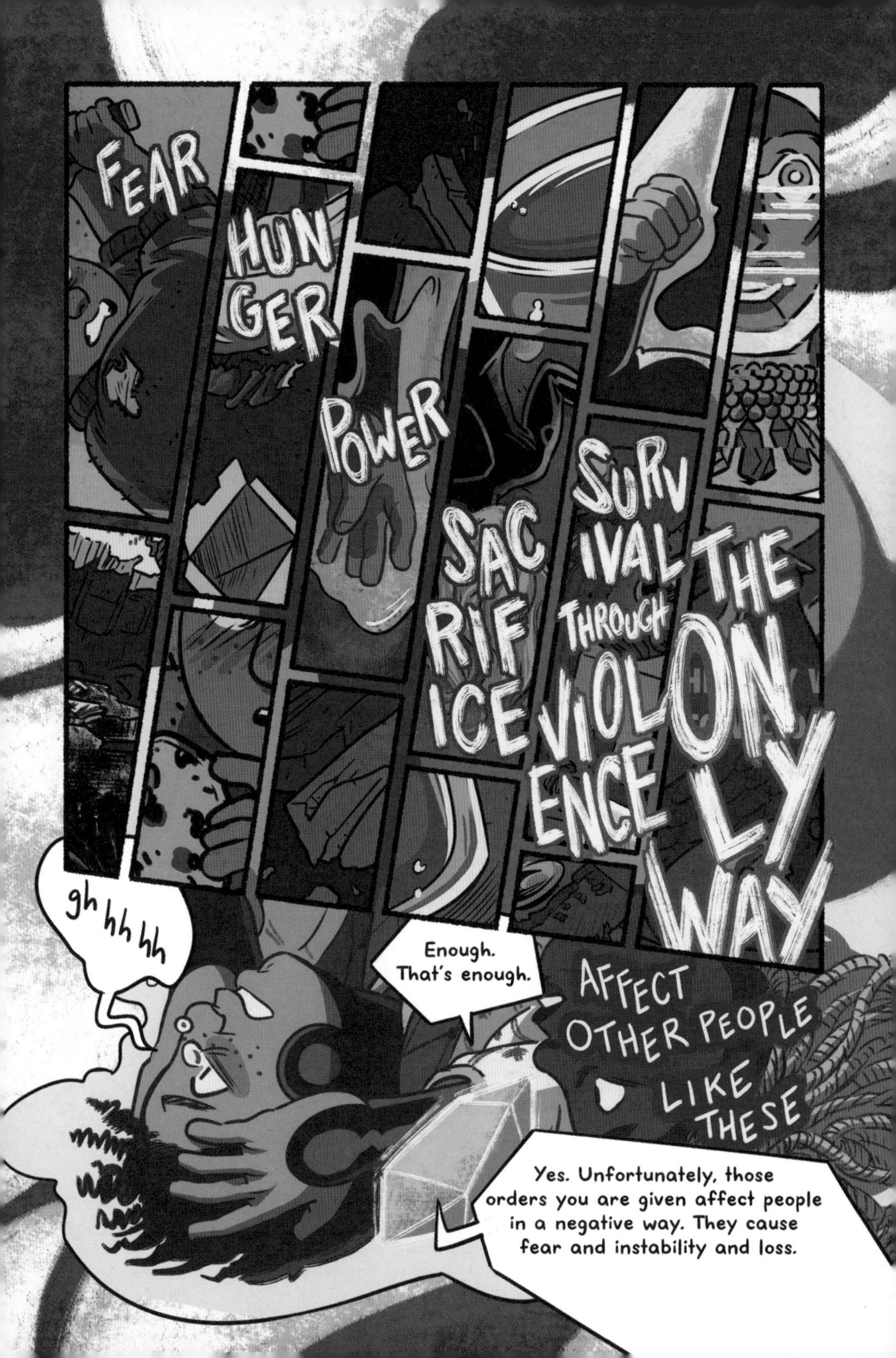

FEAR
HUNGER
POWER
SACRIFICE
SURVIVAL THROUGH VIOLENCE
THE ONLY WAY
ghhhhhh
Enough. That's enough.
AFFECT OTHER PEOPLE LIKE THESE
Yes. Unfortunately, those orders you are given affect people in a negative way. They cause fear and instability and loss.

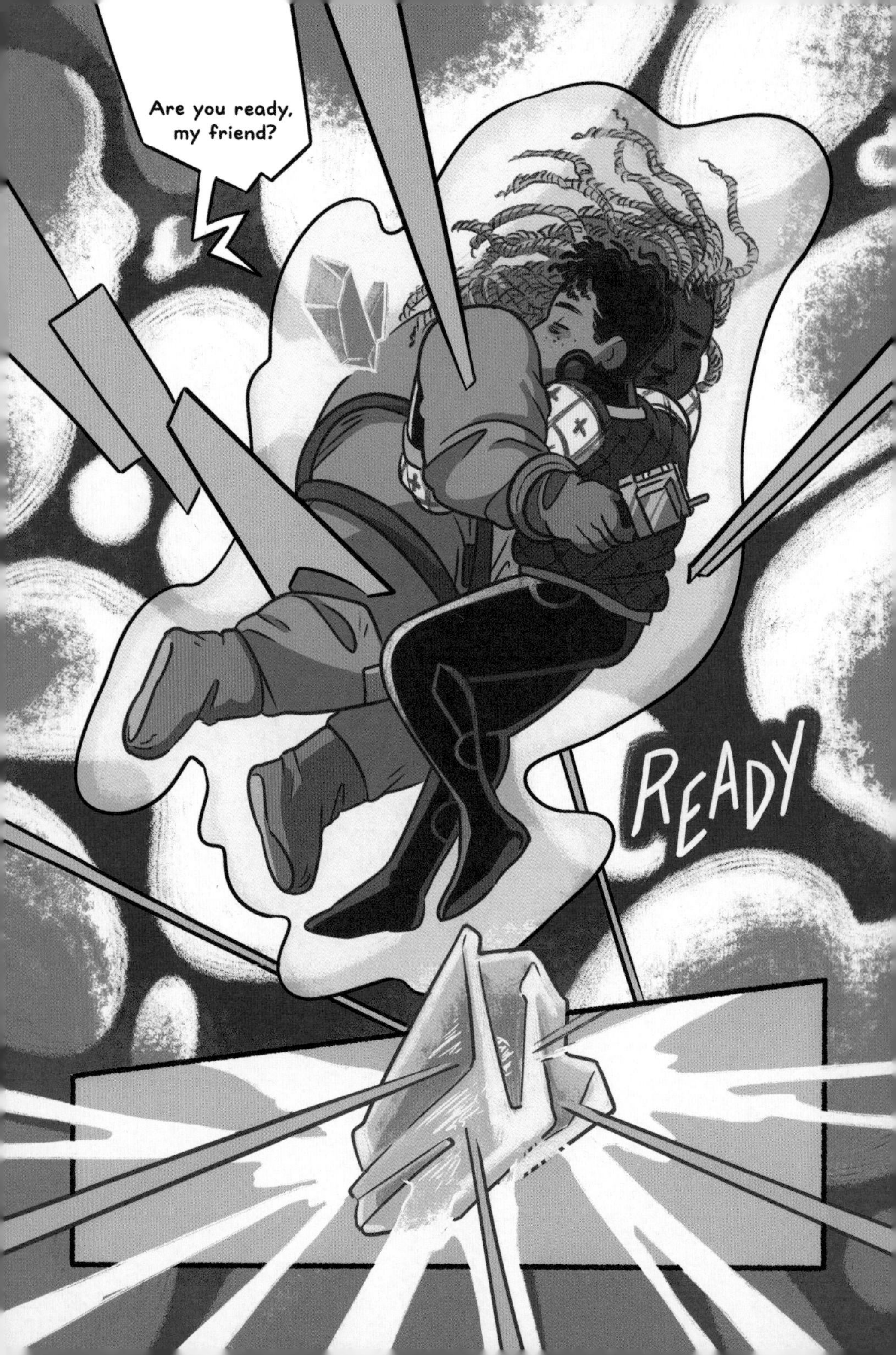
Are you ready, my friend?
READY

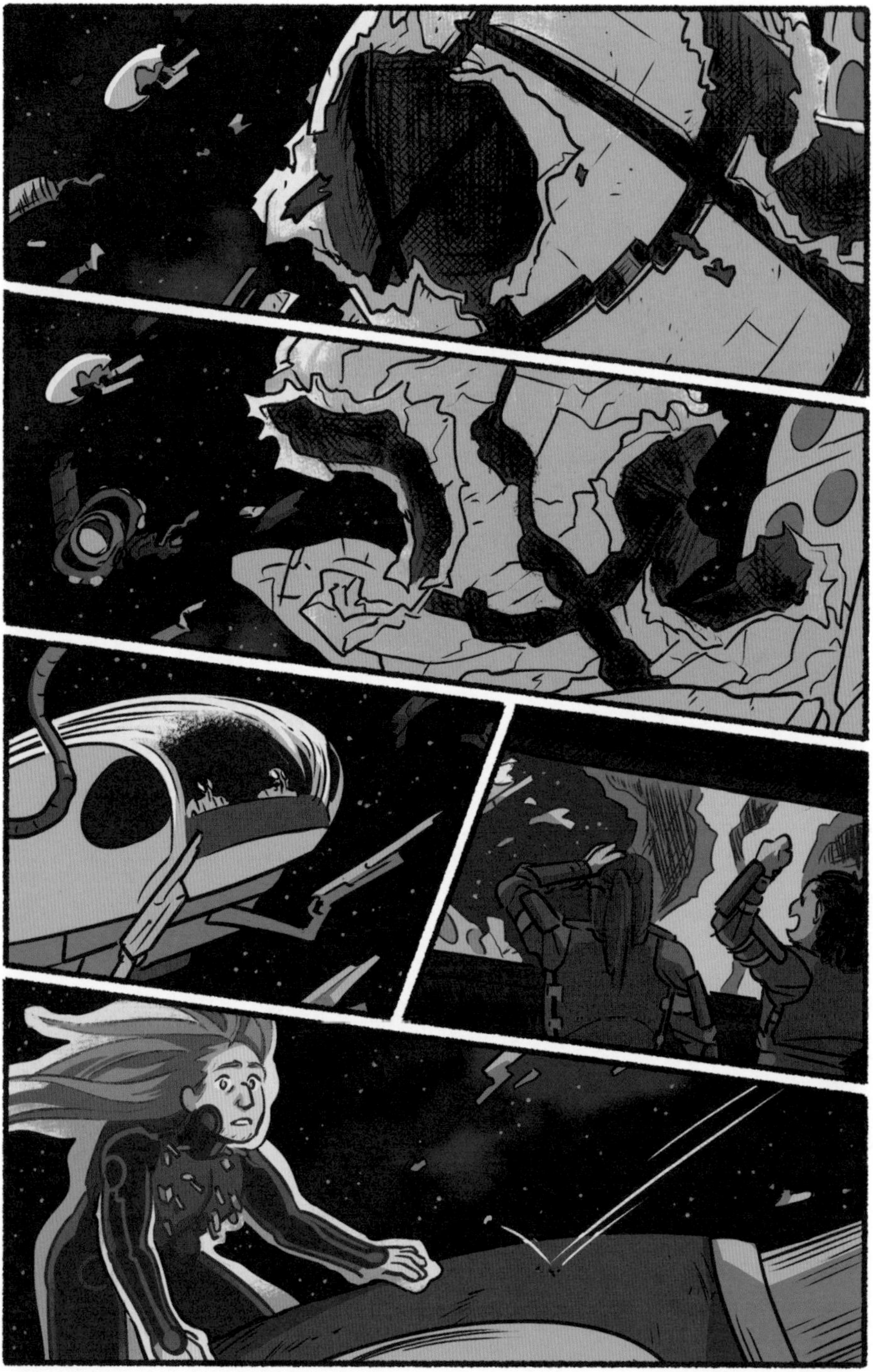

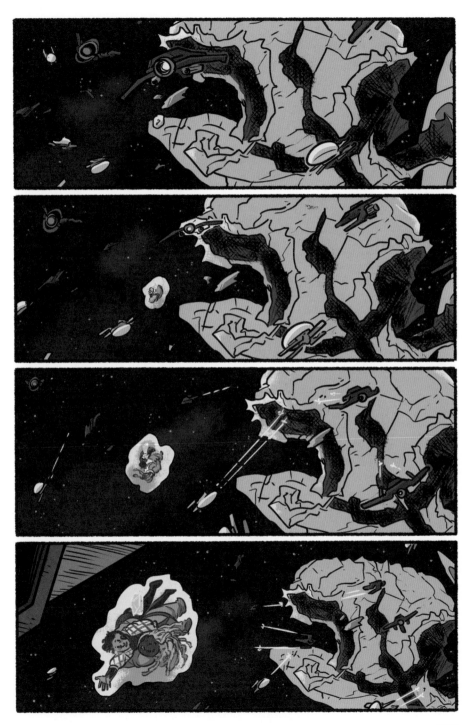

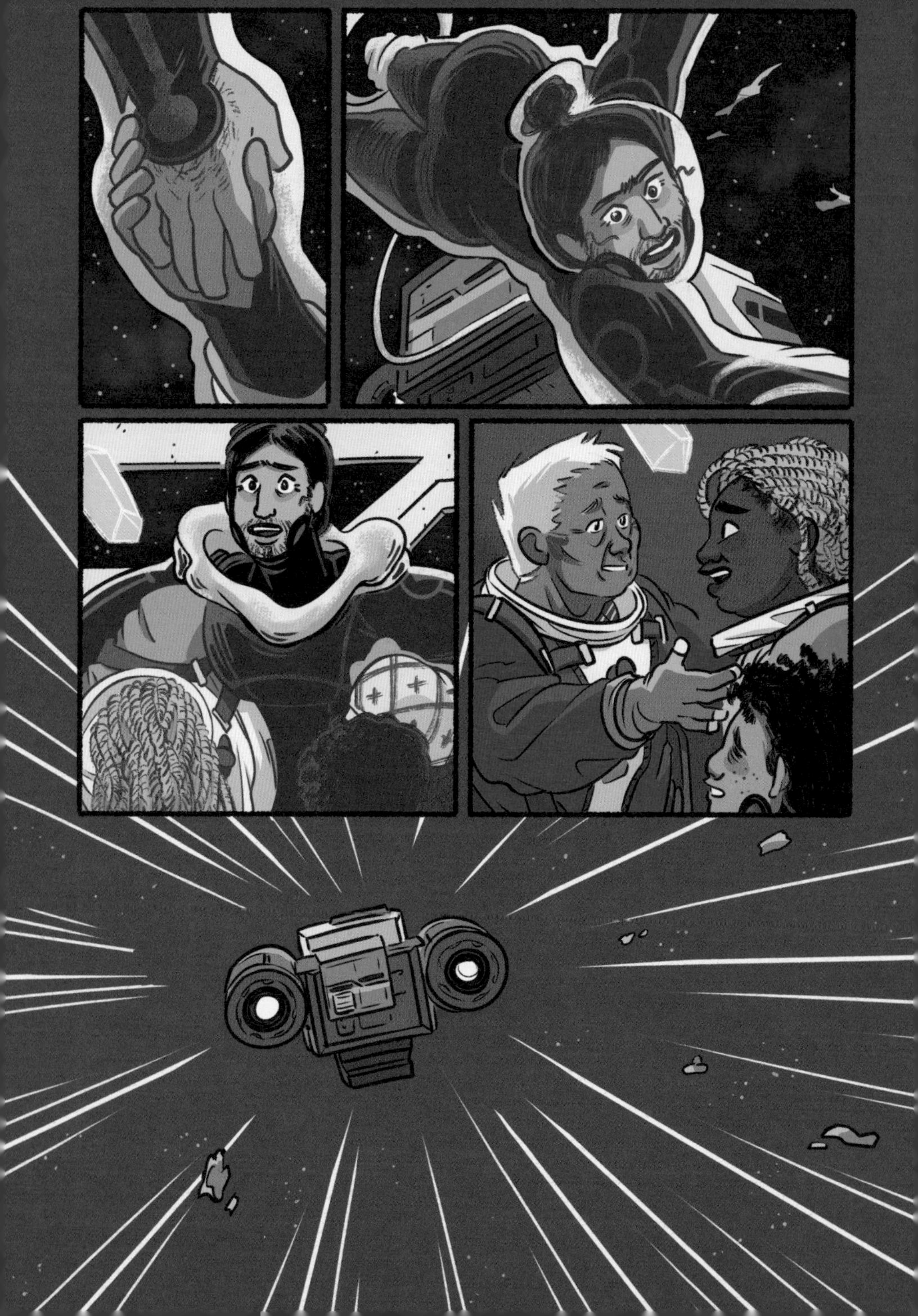

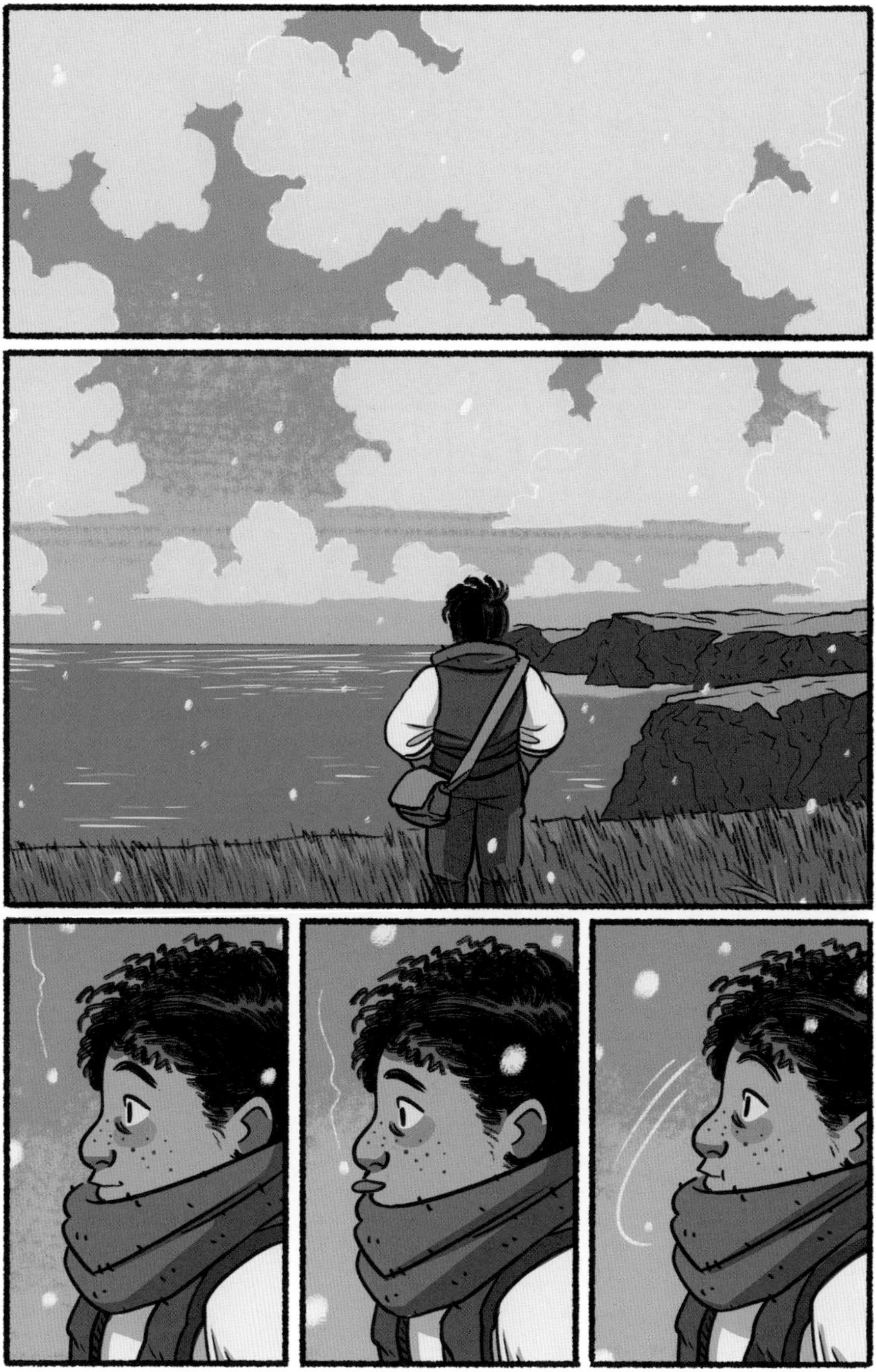

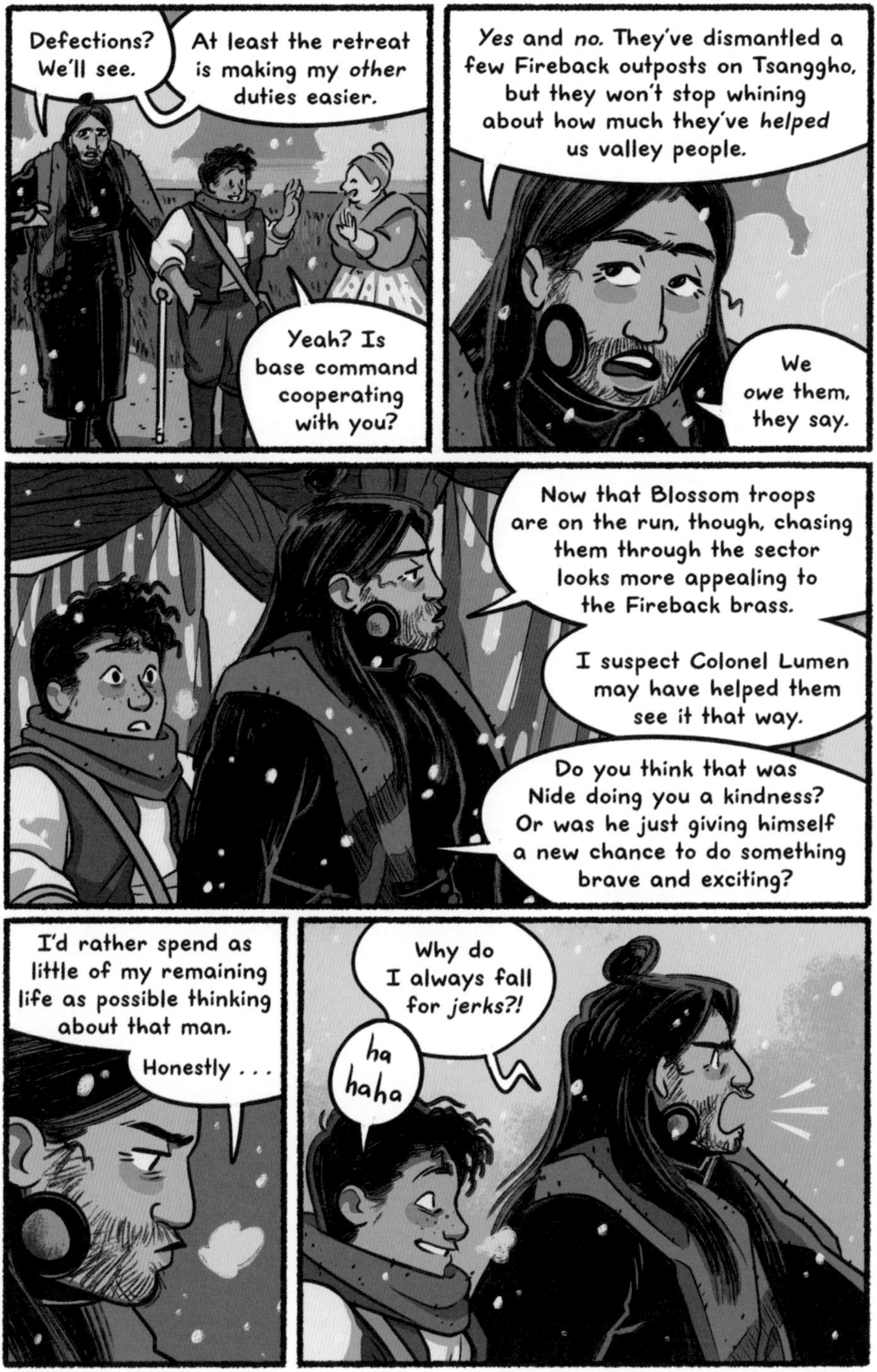
Defections? We'll see.
At least the retreat is making my *other* duties easier.
Yeah? Is base command cooperating with you?
Yes and *no*. They've dismantled a few Fireback outposts on Tsanggho, but they won't stop whining about how much they've *helped* us valley people.
We *owe* them, they say.
Now that Blossom troops are on the run, though, chasing them through the sector looks more appealing to the Fireback brass.
I suspect Colonel Lumen may have helped them see it that way.
Do you think that was Nide doing you a kindness? Or was he just giving himself a new chance to do something brave and exciting?
I'd rather spend as little of my remaining life as possible thinking about that man.
Honestly . . .
Why do I always fall for *jerks*?!
ha haha

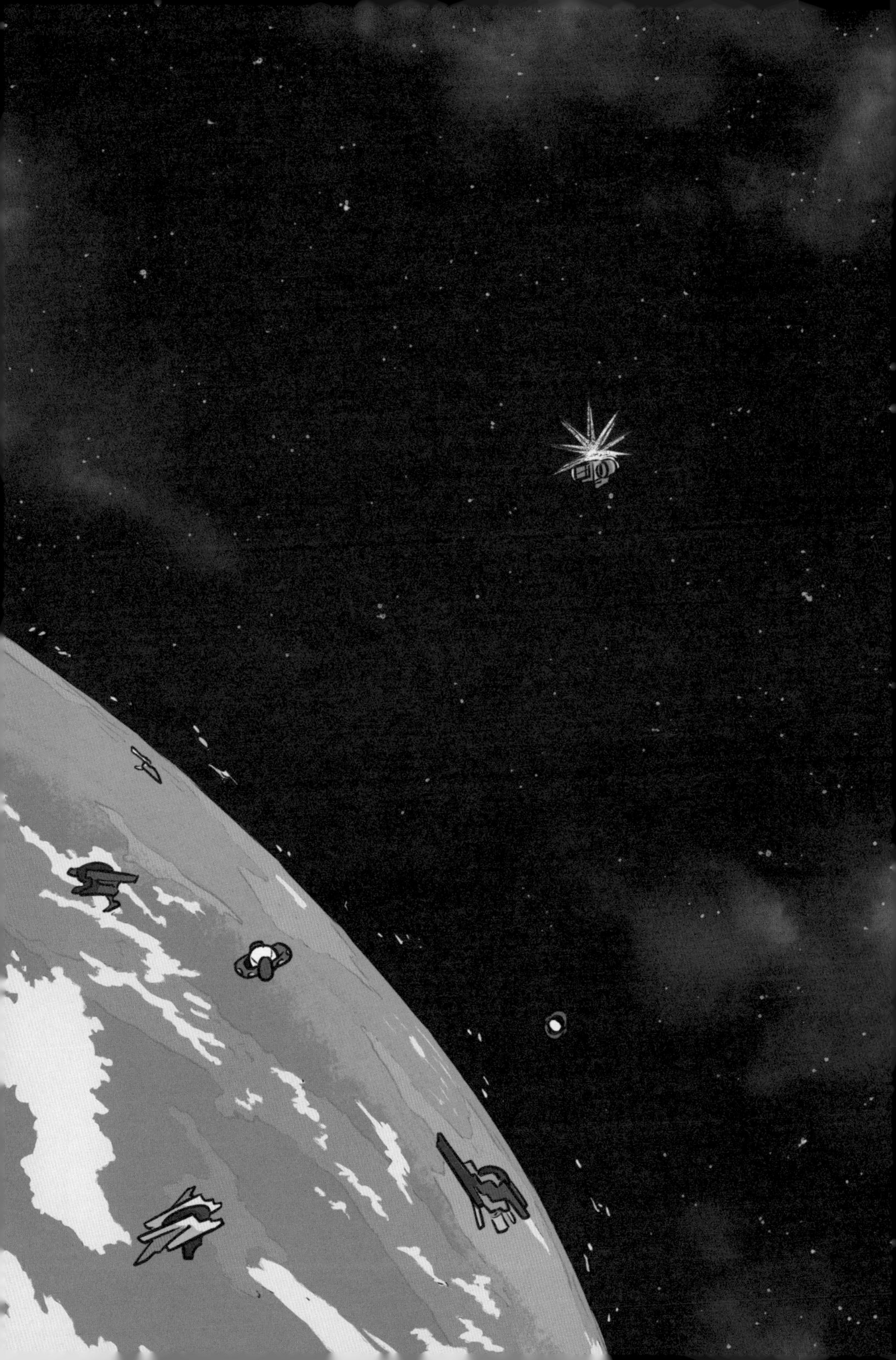

The weeds will but the ranker grow,
If fields too large you seek to till.
To try to gain men far away
With grief your toiling heart will fill.

If fields too large you seek to till,
The weeds will only rise more strong.
To try to gain men far away
Will but your heart's distress prolong.

Things grow the best when to themselves
Left, and to nature's vigor rare.
How young and tender is the child,
With his twin tufts of falling hair!
But when you him ere long behold,
That child shall cap of manhood wear!

Shijing 102
as translated by James Legge, 1876

無田甫田、維莠驕驕。
無思遠人、勞心忉忉。

無田甫田、維莠桀桀。
無思遠人、勞心怛怛。

婉兮孌兮、總角丱兮。
未幾見兮、突而弁兮。

詩經 102、甫田

ACKNOWLEDGMENTS

Thank you to Whitney, Gina, and Patrick at Random House Graphic for their part in bringing this book to life, and thanks to Jen Linnan, my agent, for finding it a good home. I'd also like to applaud Jeff Zugale for his fantastic work designing Lu's ship and creating the model that sits on my desk to this day.

Thanks to Ally James Lyons, Emry Peterson, Jori Walton, Julia Showalter, and Roxana Montoya for flatting this book, and thanks to Sloane, Otava, and other friends who were invaluable sounding boards during the writing process.

And a special thanks to my family, my wife, and my neighbors in Minneapolis.

Across a Field of Starlight was written on the traditional land of the Wahpekute Dakota people. The author recognizes those and other indigenous peoples who have stewarded the land and pledges to join them in protecting it for future generations.

ABOUT THE AUTHOR

Blue Delliquanti lives in Minneapolis with a woman, a dog, and a cat. Before working on *Across a Field of Starlight*, they drew and published comics online for many years. They love cooking, riding on trains, and reading exciting updates about robots and outer space.

bluedelliquanti.com

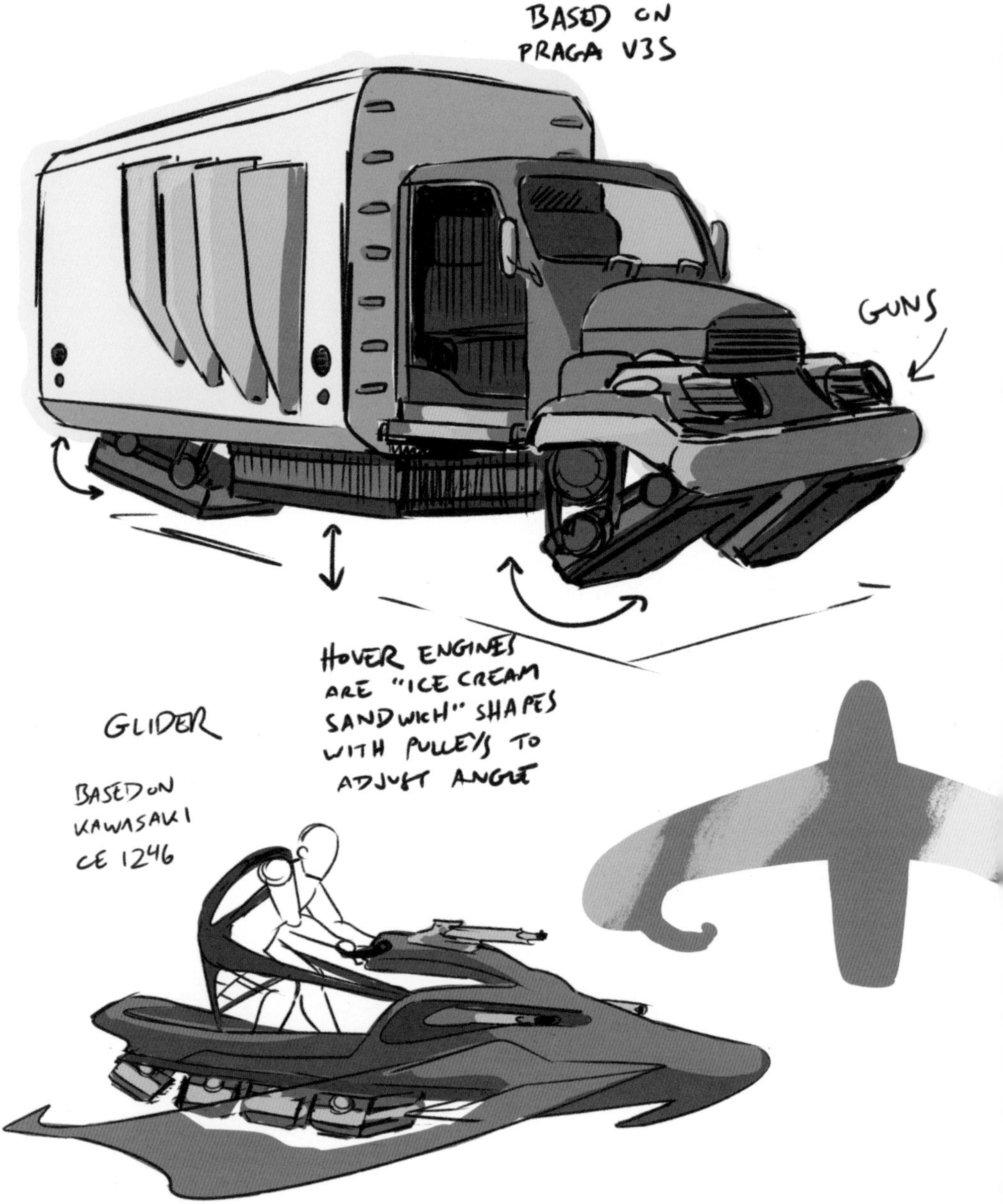
BASED ON
PRAGA V3S
GUNS
HOVER ENGINES
ARE "ICE CREAM
SANDWICH" SHAPES
WITH PULLEYS TO
ADJUST ANGLE
GLIDER
BASED ON
KAWASAKI
CE 1246

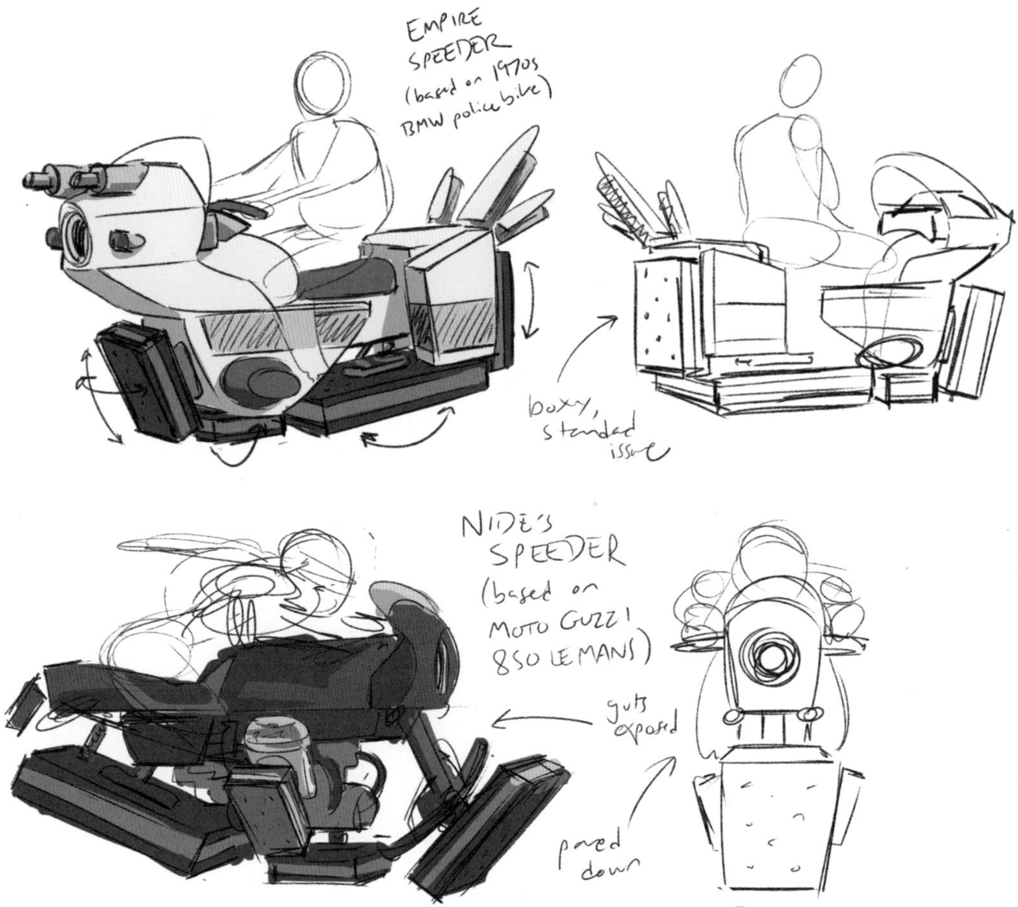
EMPIRE SPEEDER
(based on 1970s BMW police bike)
boxy, standard issue
NIDE'S SPEEDER
(based on MOTO GUZZI 850 LE MANS)
guts exposed
pared down

ART FILE.001

The Fireback Brigade is signified by bright red, like Nide's armor or speeder. Unlike closed, tidy Blossom vehicles, Fireback speeders have their guts showing and are often cobbled together from many different machines. They're also easy to hide among the brightly colored rocks of Sertig's home planet, Tsanggho.

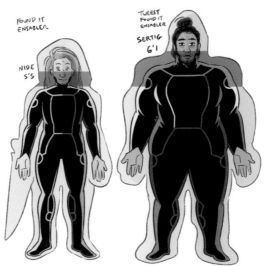

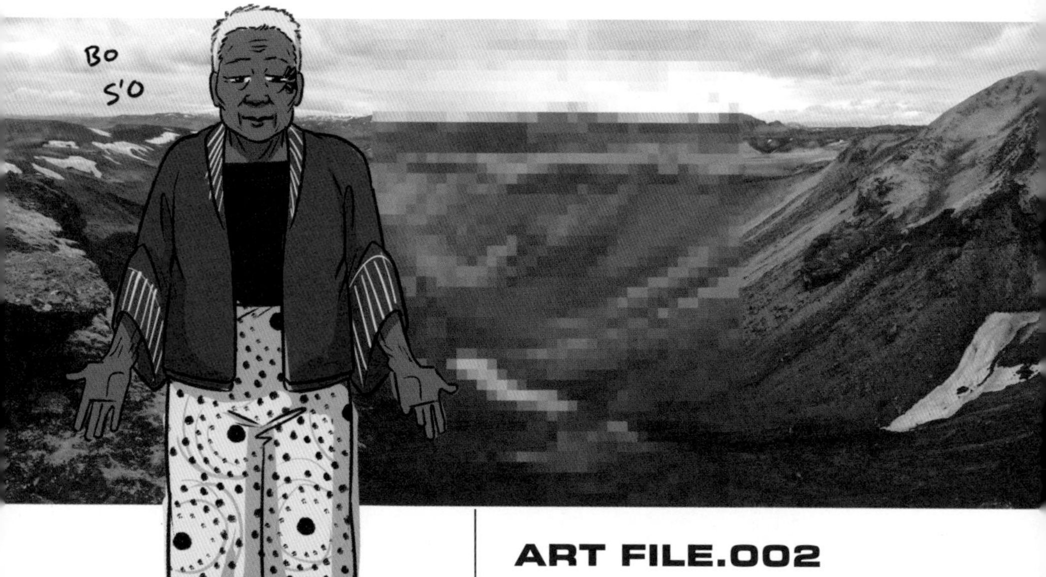

ART FILE.002

Another important part of coloring the book was creating light and shadows that were different depending on where the characters were. Tsanggho is bright and arid, with warm colors all around. The commune Lu and Field call home is lush with jewel tones like purple and green. I wanted it to feel like it was always twilight there.

This book was made in a very interesting time and with a creative process that was different from anything I'd tried before.

I had always been fascinated by stories about space and adventure. I love having conversations with friends about the idea of utopia—a world where everything exists in harmony and everyone's basic needs are met—and what that might look like. I worked on *Across a Field of Starlight* from 2019 to 2021, which, as I'm writing this, continues to be an intense time for my community of friends, my city (Minneapolis), and my country (the United States). My friends are doing their best to live happily and openly as queer and trans people, but that visibility comes with hostility from those who refuse to understand them. My city is still figuring out how to move forward from the George Floyd uprising, where neighbors came together to protect each other from police brutality. And my country is still recovering from a pandemic that left most of us to fend for ourselves. The year I started working on this book was the year the United States celebrated its fiftieth anniversary of landing on the moon—the next year, millions of Americans grappled with a government that did not show the power or the will to keep them fed, housed, or healthy.

A common conversation I've had with people over the last few years is based around the question of what we deserve. Can we live in a society that provides everyone with food, shelter, or health care, even to those who can't pay for it? Does everyone *deserve* it? Many people have been told they are undeserving of certain things based on who they are or what they have. My personal experience with this comes from living openly as a queer person, and that informed the kind of story I wanted to tell. Queer people, especially queer children, are told to expect less in terms of basic rights and settle for less when it comes to acceptance or love. This all affects how we live, how we think of ourselves, and what we feel obligated to do just to get by. How can anybody think about traveling to the moon if they don't know where they'll sleep that night? How can anybody dream of going to the stars if they're told they don't deserve them?

When I started working on this book, I had a conversation about the idea of a utopian society in space with Gina Gagliano, and she recommended an essay by my favorite author, Ursula K. Le Guin, that I hadn't read before—*A Non-Euclidean View of California as a Cold Place to Be*. I always like reading Le Guin's work because she writes stories about things like starships and aliens while asking herself how people from different places or cultures might think about them from other perspectives. She traveled a lot and studied stories from all around the world. For this essay, she chose what ideas she would explore by consulting the *I Ching*, a book that was developed in China almost 3,000 years ago and is still used to this day to answer questions and encourage readers to think about their problems and situations in another way.

As an artist, I have done exercises to change up the way I draw, but I had never heard of using a tool like this to change the way I *write*. And writing *Across a Field of Starlight* made me think a lot about the problems I saw in real life, and what my characters might do to make their own situations better. I studied how the *I Ching* works and decided to refer to it to inform my characters and what happens to them. I generated random numbers (by flipping coins, but you can use other things) to create 1 of 64 possible hexagrams, each of which has meanings, symbols, or ideas connected to it. Fassen is connected to Hexagram 30, lí, a fiery person who is bright and passionate but also clingy. Lu gets their name from Hexagram 56, lǚ, a wanderer who's curious and serene but maybe a little naive.

When I struggled with how Fassen and Lu's story might end, the *I Ching* suggested 62, xiǎo guò, and 32, héng: an action or idea that feels small, but one that becomes more powerful the longer you persevere. I played with that concept, and it became the backbone of the book—small choices made by small people that inspire others to think about their lives differently until together they all create the momentum toward a better world. I hope that this is something I can practice in my own life, too. It often feels hard to do the right thing when I see others being rewarded for cruelty. Sometimes it is impossible to tell whether the work I do makes any positive difference at all. But hopefully by persevering and keeping my friends and community safe, we will come out of hard times into a better world we helped make possible. With everyone working together and recognizing each other's humanity, we will all get to space someday, and we will all have enough.